I0576830

John Wesley

Wesley

The man, his teaching, and his work

John Wesley

Wesley
The man, his teaching, and his work

ISBN/EAN: 9783337104801

Printed in Europe, USA, Canada, Australia, Japan

Cover: Foto ©Raphael Reischuk / pixelio.de

More available books at **www.hansebooks.com**

Wesley:

The Man, his Teaching, and his Work.

MORRISON AND GIBB, PRINTERS, EDINBURGH.

John Wesley M.A.
Fellow of Lincoln Colledge Oxford

WESLEY:

THE MAN, HIS TEACHING, AND

HIS WORK.

*BEING SERMONS AND ADDRESSES
DELIVERED IN CITY ROAD CHAPEL AT THE
CENTENARY COMMEMORATION OF
JOHN WESLEY'S DEATH.*

REVISED BY THE AUTHORS.

LONDON:

CHARLES H. KELLY, 2, CASTLE STREET, CITY ROAD, E.C.;
AND 66, PATERNOSTER ROW, E.C.

1891.

Preface.

—·—o—·—

THE Sermons and Addresses in this volume were delivered (with one exception) in City Road Chapel, at the CENTENARY COMMEMORATION of the DEATH of JOHN WESLEY. They are reprinted for the most part from the reports published in the *Methodist Recorder*. In every case the preacher or speaker has revised the "copy," and re-revised the proof sheets. The volume, therefore, is issued with some degree of confidence that it presents the best thoughts of the respective authors in the best attainable form. It is only fair, however, to say that the necessity for rapidity of publication has compelled the writers to revise more quickly—not to say hurriedly—than is consistent with finished literary work. Although the interest excited by the Centenary Services was profound and widespread, it was feared lest the evanescence inseparable from every passing event of the day might prove too real to warrant the risk of delay.

To Dr. Cairns we are specially indebted. In response to the request of the final meeting, he has committed to writing the thoughts he would have spoken had not indisposition prevented his journey to London.

The President of the Conference, in common with many others, was anxious that, if possible, a selection from the many Centenary Sermons and Addresses, other than those delivered at City Road, might be included in this volume. It was found, however, that to step outside the central Commemoration circle would necessitate a much larger and consequently more costly volume than was desirable. Possibly, a second volume may be published, consisting of contributions from Scotland, Ireland, Wales, and a few English provincial centres.

Limitations of space, and other obvious considerations, have led to the omission of such public meeting accessories as are usually found in newspaper reports. In an Appendix, however, will be found extracts from a Centenary Diary, which preserve in some measure the local colour and give an idea—it must be confessed but faintly—of the enthusiasm and sustained interest of perhaps the most remarkable religious celebration modern Methodism has known.

To the gentlemen who so promptly, and often with minute care, have revised the proof sheets, grateful acknowledgments are due, as also to the President of the Conference and the Secretaries of the Committee, without whose courteous co-operation much of the material for this volume could not have been so perfectly prepared.

All the Centenary Services, not only in London but equally throughout the country, were most of all remarkable for spiritual fervour and devout gratitude. The God of our fathers was present with His people. That His name may be glorified, and that His work may be done with ever increasing faithfulness and zeal, is the earnest prayer of all who have contributed to this memorial of a great and solemn event.

> " The Lord hath been mindful of us : He will bless us.
>
>   .   .   .   .
>
> He will bless them that fear the Lord,
> Both small and great.
> The Lord increase you more and more,
> You and your children."

Contents.

—o—

Part 1.

SERMONS.

ix

Part 2.

ADDRESSES.

𝔓art 3.

The Wesley Centenary.

PART I.

Sermons Preached in City Road Chapel.

A

Rev. CHARLES HENRY KELLY,
Ex-President of the Conference.

Rev. CHARLES GARRETT,
Of the Liverpool Riverside Mission.

Rev. DAVID J. WALLER, D.D..
Secretary of the Conference.

Rev. W. F. MOULTON, M.A., D.D.,
President of the Conference.

Rev. R. W. DALE, LL.D.,
Minister of Carr's Lane Congregational Church, Birmingham.

Rev. PRINCIPAL RAINY, D.D.,
Of the Free Church College, Edinburgh.

Rev. JOHN CLIFFORD, M.A., D.D.,
Minister of Westbourne Park Baptist Church.

Rev. PROFESSOR F. W. MACDONALD,
Wesleyan College, Handsworth, Birmingham.

Rev. FREDERICK J. MURRELL,
Minister Resident in Mr. Wesley's House, 47 City Road.

SAMUEL D. WADDY, Esq., Q.C.. M.P.

The Man: His Teaching and Work.

By the Rev. CHARLES H. KELLY,

EX-PRESIDENT OF THE CONFERENCE.

—o—

> "*Not unto us, O Lord, not unto us,*
> *But unto Thy name give glory,*
> *For Thy mercy, and for Thy truth's sake.*"
> —PSALM CXV. I.

ONE hundred years ago to-day, John Wesley lay in "age and feebleness extreme" on his death-bed.

A hundred years ago to-morrow he said:

> "The best of all is, God is with us."

And in the house a few yards from the place in which we are assembled this morning, the greatest of modern apostles died.

The Methodists of to-day stand in a great court, in which the verdict is given of a trial that has lasted for a century. Men, principles, methods, work, and results have been sifted. Witnesses—good, bad, learned, illiterate, wise men and foolish, Wesley's own countrymen, and the sons and daughters of many climes—have given evidence, and with the verdict and judgment of the community and the nations we need not be dissatisfied; but in this great court the satisfaction of Wesley's followers in 1891 is not with man's opinion, it is in the continuance of the fact of old, and in their power to repeat the words of their dying patriarch,—as true to-day as on the 2nd March 1791,—

> " The best of all is, God is with us."

And for this they say :

> " Not unto us, O Lord, not unto us,
> But unto Thy name give glory."

We celebrate the Centenary of Wesley's death with mingled feelings. We are too far removed from the event to feel as they did who watched and wept on this estate in 1791. They mourned as for a father ; they wondered if Methodism could survive the loss ; and they felt the anguish of a great personal bereavement. . . . We can think of him as our " father in God ;" as one who, though we never saw him, left us a rich legacy, a blessed literature ; a system of theology ; a revived religion ; a Church established in the heart of the people, that can defy disestablishment by imperial power ; a world-wide parish ; a definite aim in work,—to spread scriptural holiness through the world ; an organisation for Christian teaching and Christian fellowship, and Christian extension ; —wonderful when he died—more wonderful when he has lain for a hundred busy years in his grave.

What, then, is our predominant feeling to-day ? Certainly not one of mourning ; as little one of vain-glory. We should be blind if we could not see the marvellous results of Wesley's life and work ; we should be fools if we did not recognise the influence and growth of Methodism at home, in the Colonies, in America, and in other foreign lands. We should be sinful if we did not consider earnestly our duty in the present and the immediate future, and also our vast possibilities ; but our deepest, strongest feeling at this hour is one of supreme thankfulness to Almighty God, and the cry that goes up from the heart of Methodism, as it stands by Wesley's tomb, at this celebration of the Centenary of his death, is,

> " Not unto us, O Lord, not unto us,
> But unto Thy name give glory."

There was great need for such a man, and for such a work as his, when Wesley appeared. Morals and religion were in a dark and murky state. English life was debased ; men swore and talked obscenely even in the presence of women ; every sixth house in London was one in which ardent spirits were sold; hundreds of the clergy made no profession of personal godliness ; few of them knew, and fewer of them preached the saving truths of the gospel ; many of them were vile, base, and debauched. The masses of the people were ignorant of spiritual religion, sunk deep in degradation, and utterly indifferent to the claims of God or the needs of their own souls. Surely a loud cry went up to the Lord of the Church for help and salvation. The moral and religious state of the English life, mind, literature, people, and clergy was such as to make itself heard in the ears of the Almighty.

God heard and answered. In His answer He worked according to His own old laws : " Man's extremity was God's opportunity."

Great renewals of religious life and knowledge have nearly always taken place in times of marked spiritual declension and decay. It was so in the ancient Church, as told in Old Testament history : it was so when in the fulness of time the Lord Jesus came; it was so when Martin Luther rose, and the Reformation did its wonderful work ; it was so in the eighteenth century, when John Wesley was sent of God.

In the Methodist revival, as in so many other great revivals, there was one great leader, there was a movement in harmony with the existing dispensation, there was a mighty movement brought about by one who was in the pale of the then dominant Church. Such a movement cannot be banked up in narrow channels, or confined within a sect. It was not in Luther's case : it was not in Wesley's. So that now Methodism, so called, cannot represent anything like the results of the Methodist revival, and John Wesley cannot be claimed as a mere Wesleyan, or the mere founder of a system : he belongs

not to Methodism, very much less to Anglicanism; not
to a sect or a party, but to the Church catholic, the Church
wider than any "ism," greater than any Establishment, and
to the parish whose boundaries extend beyond earth.

I. WE GIVE THE LORD THE GLORY FOR THE MAN, JOHN WESLEY.

A great man—a good man—is a great gift of God
to any nation or community.   The best products of
a country are not material; not in corn, cotton, coal,
or iron: the best products of a country are good men
and good women.   These make a nation rich.   When
Britain was in so sad a state religiously; when Voltaire
and his associates were poisoning France with a poison
whose virus curses her yet; when the Rationalists in
Germany were attacking the faith in the land where
Luther lived, and prayed, and toiled,—God in His providence, who reared and trained Samuel and Moses in the
earlier Church, was preparing a man to stand before Him
in England who should be the leader of many true men
and women, and of a great religious movement intended
to rescue His Church, and bless the world with a new
evangelism.   This is in accordance with God's plan.   All
along the ages God has raised up men whose lives and
labours have made history.   "The Lord built Him a
Solomon, that Solomon might build Him a house," and
Solomon's genius was seen in every part of the Temple.
The various great Churches show the work of those master-
builders who under God shaped their polity, formulated
their creeds, and illustrated their spirit.   No history of
Methodism could be given without the biography of Wesley.
Others were with him—Charles Wesley, the sweet singer;
what sweeter singer did the world ever know?   John
Fletcher, the saint; who more saintly?   Thomas Coke,
the missionary; what missionary more devoted?   George
Whitefield, the preacher; who more eloquent? and many
besides;—but to John Wesley belongs the pre-eminence.

It has been well said that "as Mount Everest lifts its tall head, not only above every other peak of the Himalayas, but above the tallest peak of every other mountain range in the wide world, so does John Wesley, as a revivalist and reformer, tower not only above the other great men of early Methodism, but above the greatest in all the other Churches in Christendom." England has produced many noble and worthy sons in her Churches, but only one John Wesley.

Good blood flowed in his veins. Men often owe much to such a blessing. There is very much in breed. He came of a good, strong Dissenting set ; he inherited sturdy virtues and strong resolves. He was the son of father and mother who were Church of England folk, and by whom he was trained to a strait, bigoted sort of Anglicanism. The poor country parson of Epworth, who was deep in learning, deep in piety, was also often deep in debt, and yet he managed, notwithstanding, to get his sons well educated. John was sent to the Charter-house School in the year Queen Anne died, and afterwards went to Oxford. Let us not forget that Methodism owes a debt to endowed scholarships, fellowships, and great schools of learning. Without them the Epworth family could never have had the educational training needed to fit them for the great work of life. Think of John Wesley, Charles Wesley, and George Whitefield. What could Methodism have done without them ? What could they have done without education ? How could they have got it without the help of the great endowments of learning in schools and university? It was needful that, as the Founder of the great movement, John Wesley should be a good scholar. For rough and ready work, other agents were needed and found, men of many trades and hard hands ; but an educated man was required to begin the work. And God sent him. Wesley was a thorough scholar, a profound logician, and deeply versed in the classics.

He was not only an educated man ; he was also an educationalist. Do not let his sons forget that in 1891.

He knew that ignorance was no helpmeet for religion. He wrote or edited numbers of books of useful knowledge, when literature was not widely diffused. He opened Kingswood School, and encouraged other schools. He established Sunday schools in Methodism in 1784, and had one in Georgia in 1736, forty-four years before Raikes began his work. He was a pioneer in tract distribution, for he had a Tract Society in 1747. A far-seeing man was he !

He was a man who grew. Some men never grow. Never! They never will ; and they cannot understand those who do. When Wesley went from cheerless Epworth to the Charter-house and Oxford, he found London was greater than his father's parish, and the world to be greater than London. When he started life he was a shrivelled sectarian ; when he got into the greater world outside mere Anglican boundaries, he found that churches and parishes were too small. His followers have learnt more on that subject than he did. He doubtless would have been glad if the Church of England had been expansive enough to contain Methodism, but it was not ; and notwithstanding his early prejudices and some of his earlier writings and sayings, he saw that Methodism could not become a Society in the Church of England. It never had been ; it never has been ; it never will be.

At Oxford, and for a good while after he left, Wesley was a Church of England ritualist. Studious, devout, self-denying, charitable ; he partook of the Lord's Supper once a week—often that, in those days ; persuaded men to attend prayers, sermons, sacraments ; observed the discipline of the Church in minute details ; tasted no food on Wednesdays and Fridays till 3 p.m. "Though perhaps he and the first Methodists never held the doctrine of the human nature of the Divine Redeemer being present in the elements of the Holy Sacrament, they held something approaching it, and spoke of 'an outward sacrifice offered therein.'" He religiously observed saint days, holydays, and Saturdays. He maintained the doctrine of Apostolical Succession, and believed no one had authority to administer the sacraments who was not episcopally ordained. In Georgia he excluded Dissenters from the Holy Communion, on the ground that they had not been properly baptized. He enforced confession, penance, and mortification. How he grew out of all this! How much more scriptural he became in belief and teaching! If any one doubts that, the answer is very practical, in the fact that he himself ordained men to the work of the ministry; and that he accepted and enforced the more scriptural teaching as to the constitution, discipline, unity, and worship of the Primitive Church. The Ritualists of to-day have gone further than Wesley did in his early life. He laid aside his popish follies and proud pretensions, and embraced the truth as it is in Jesus Christ; and then the Church, the nation, the world, were blessed by his energy, earnestness, diligence, self-denial, devotion, and mighty power as an evangelist.

No one can understand John Wesley and his career who knows nothing of conversion and of his conversion. He had been a stern religionist. He was a strict Churchman. He was a conscientious clergyman. He was a seeker after God and truth. But he had need of much more. He had no such spiritual experience as he heard of among the Moravians. He had no such personal saving faith in Jesus Christ as Peter Böhler told him of. But after much doubt and much delay he found that which he sought. He had rendered and sung a version of a German Moravian hymn:

> "My soul before Thee prostrate lies,
> To Thee, her source, my spirit flies:
> My wants I mourn, my chains I see,
> O let Thy presence set me free."

Charles Wesley had found peace with God on Whitsunday, 21st May 1738; but John Wesley was still a seeker, a mourner. He was burdened, heavy in heart. He felt there was no good in him; and that all his works, his righteousness, and his prayer, so far from having merit, needed an atonement themselves.   On 24th May, at five o'clock in the morning, he opened his Testament on these words :

> "There are given unto us exceeding great and precious promises, that by these ye might be partakers of the Divine nature."

On leaving home he opened again at the words :

> "Thou art not far from the kingdom of God."

In the afternoon he went to St. Paul's Cathedral, where the anthem was full of comfort.   It was :

> "Out of the deep have I called unto Thee, O Lord :
> Lord, hear my voice."

At night he went to a religious meeting in Aldersgate Street, where a layman was reading Luther's preface to the Epistle to the Romans, describing saving faith.   He heard that, possessed of this faith,—

> "The heart is cheered, elevated, and transported with sweet affections toward God."

Receiving the Holy Ghost, he was taught that the man " is renewed and made spiritual," and that he is impelled to " fulfil the law by the vital energy in himself."

While this preface was being read, Wesley experienced a great change.   He writes :

> "I felt my heart strangely warmed.   I felt I did trust in Christ, Christ alone for salvation ; and an assurance was given me, that He had taken away my sins, even mine, and saved me from ' the law of sin and death ; ' and I then testified openly to all there what I now first felt in my heart."

This experience was very joyous to Wesley.   It was the great event of his life.   He had the liberty of a son of God.   He had the key to all sound religious experience. He preached with mighty power.   The doctrine of a present, free, full salvation from sin, by faith in the Lord Jesus, was like fire in his bones.   His heart burned with love to his Saviour, and yearned over the souls of men. Eighteen days after his conversion, on 11th June, he preached his famous sermon, before the University of Oxford, on " By grace are ye saved through faith." That was his favourite theme. That was the keynote of his ministry. That sermon is Number One in the Standard Edition of his sermons. That great doctrine he began to preach in 1738, as soon as he experienced the blessing. It was the preaching of it that gave birth to the revival of religion—the religious movement of the eighteenth century—called Methodism. And the preaching of that doctrine, and the personal apprehension and application of the truth of it, will secure continuous revivals and conversions, and the conservation and perpetuity of Methodism, and of Christian life.

May we not say with Dr. Punshon?

> " Praise we then our God alone,
> Who made His servant thus complete !
> And pour we, in libation sweet,
> Our wealth of spikenard—each his own—
> In tribute at the Master's feet."

II. WE GIVE GLORY TO GOD FOR WESLEY'S TEACHING.

It was profoundly scriptural, comprehensive, distinct, definite, systematic, experimental, and intensely practical. It was such as only a highly-trained and very able man could have given. As a teacher, Wesley was prepared of God. He had both been taught, and had learned. He was both a scholar and a man of genius. Mere eloquence would not have sufficed, even when accompanied by earnestness in aim, sound piety, and converting power. This is seen in the contrast between Wesley and White-field. Whitefield was a great orator, a wonderfully eloquent man, of dramatic power, and able to sway the crowds ; but he had not the educational breed of the Wesleys: he was no scholar, and no scholar's son, and he was a poor theologian. He had fervour, passion, tears, magnetic influence, a strong personality, and sanctified boldness ; but he has not left his mark on the nation as

Wesley did, and although his work was very effective at the time, he was not destined of the Master to be the great teacher.

God raised up Wesley as a teacher in an hour of need. Controversy raged bitterly. There was terrible religious indifference. There were strong sacerdotal, popish claims on the part of many of the clergy, and there was a rampant Calvinism.

The teaching of Wesley went in direct opposition against all this. His preaching of the need of the new birth, of conversion, of the indwelling of the Holy Spirit, of the absolute necessity for the Christian believer to be a Christian worker, aroused the careless and indifferent.

Whatever High Church sacramentarian views Wesley had held, before his eyes were fully open, there can be no doubt that his ecclesiastical exclusiveness yielded long before his death.

He taught that sin was not a mistake, not a trifle,—not merely a misfortune, but a black, guilty, and damning fact. He taught that salvation was not a proposal of help made to a few people, to be conferred at some time and somehow, no man could tell when or how ; but to every guilty penitent it was a proclamation that he might now be saved—fully saved—saved to the uttermost, and have the witness of the Holy Ghost to the fact of this salvation.

No wonder the people listened, for at that time these truths came with the force of a new revelation to the masses of men.

.   .   .   .

The doctrines which Wesley taught were no discoveries or inventions of his own. They were old. They were Christ's. They were apostolic. They were Pauline. But he and his preachers, with their fervid declaration, so brought the old truths before the people, that they were new, fresh, vivid, and powerful. Yet they were the doctrines of the Scriptures, old as the Bible. Wesley's teaching was simply a revival of primitive doctrine, primitive fellowship, primitive discipline. Because of this we say

deliberately, that Methodism does not date from Wesley—
it is nearly 1900 years old. It began when Christ began
His life here—that Saviour whom it worships and serves,
and whose work in the world it perpetuates.

One of the chief characteristics of Wesley's teaching is,
that it is not merely theological, doctrinal, dogmatic ; it
was all that, but it was experimental. From the days
when the Holy Club met in Lincoln College, Oxford,
through the whole of his long ministry, all turned upon
the question of personal and experimental religion. It is
so yet in Methodism. Let men go into any Methodist
Church that is worthy the name, in Europe, Asia, Africa,
America, or any island in any sea,—and there are tens of
thousands of such churches,—and let them listen to the
hymns sung, the prayers offered, the sermons preached,
and the experiences narrated, and they will see that,
according to the idea of John Wesley and his followers,
religion is no mere set of rules or laws, no mere display of
ceremonies, no mere pietism, but a real, blessed, and
triumphant spiritual life.

We give all the glory to God for this great human
teacher. We thank Him that he took him, the studious
boy, the diligent student, the brilliant young tutor of
Oxford, and led him, as he groped along, to the full light
of the gospel day. We give all the honour to the Lord ;
we recognise that the light itself came from Him. We
rejoice that that light was sent by God into "one of the
clearest and strongest of intellects," and also into one of
the most marvellous hearts which ever the hand of the
Creator fashioned or the spirit of the Redeemer warmed.
That masterful intellect was hungrily striving after more
and more knowledge of God, from the days of the home
in Epworth Rectory, till the day when, at eighty-eight,
the eternal sun-burst flashed upon it. But no such mere
intellectual seeking, however successful, no mere theological study, could have produced the immense result
called "Methodism ;" and so, at the age of thirty-five, that
great soul saw God, changed doctrine into life ; and then

followed the extraordinary teaching and preaching which created modern Methodism, and blessed other branches of the Church; for all the Christian Churches to-day are fuller, deeper, wider, and richer because of the great outburst of Methodism.

But Wesley's teaching was not confined to theological doctrine. It greatly affected ecclesiastical practice. Under popish domination, and in the Church of England even, after the Reformation, the lay element had been drilled into silence. No hymn, no prayer, no exhortation was heard save such as was uttered by priests or under their direction. The Reformation had brought only partial freedom—freedom from Rome, but not freedom to work; freedom for the ministry, but not freedom for the laymen: these were kept under the thraldom of custom, the slavery of precedent. Women, too, were gagged in the Church, and consigned to the limbo of nonentities, so far as church-work was concerned.

Wesley changed that. He had first to be changed himself in opinion on the subject; but he *was* changed. His bigotry yielded. When Methodism arose and got fairly to work, the Pauline Churches were reproduced in history. Every man's mouth was opened, the membership found their voice, and praise and prayer sounded once more in the assembly of the saints. The Pauline liberty was practised, and the Phœbes and Dorcases were permitted to have an ecclesiastical existence and mention. They had liberty to speak and work as the Spirit of God moved them. This is the age of lay effort, the day of spiritual liberty; and we stand bathed in the light of it. Let us recall the early dawn; let us not forget the men who secured us the blessing; let us remember the obloquy those men endured, by whose prayers and labours the liberty and light came.

When men—outsiders—study the secret of the growth and success of Methodism, let them be pointed to the teaching of Wesley on this subject of lay effort and work. This great success can be traced, under the blessing of

God, largely to the fact that it has reproduced the Pauline energy in the organisation of the Churches. It has had, as one of its great aims, the utilisation of all spiritual forces. A man has been allowed to exercise his own special gift. A woman has not had her mouth shut by a perverted text of Scripture. Each has been allowed to serve the Master as God by nature and grace has qualified them. Much of the philosophy of the success of Methodism is in this,—it has found a place for every man, and generally a man for every place. It has been courageous. It has not been afraid of new methods. It has been conservative as well,—retaining the old if good, and not being terrified by innovations. It has not been afraid of respectability, nor ashamed of poverty. It has not run away either from beautiful sanctuaries or from ducking in horse-ponds. It has utilised as far as possible all appliances and varied conditions. It has its theology,—the landmarks are notable ;—but it has never made the mistake of carrying too much theology and too little active piety to live.

Surely we do well to praise God for Wesley as a theologian and teacher.

We recognise the Divine appointment and endowment. It is impossible to overestimate the influence of Wesley's theology. It is powerful in the schools, a great gift to the Church ; and it gives promise of becoming the theology yet more fully of the myriads of the future. " It asserts the liberty of the moral agent, and vindicates the spiritual nature and essential royalty of man. It is very clear as to the atoning work of Christ, and the office and work of the Spirit. It insists on the necessity of personal holiness, and holds out the possibility of a victory over the apostate nature, by asserting a sanctification which is entire, and a perfection in love which is not ultimate and final, but progressive in its development for ever. It looks on man as utterly lost on account of sin. But warm and generous as the sunlight of God, it looks every man in the face, and says, 'Christ died for you.' It preaches the glad news, that to every believer in Christ the invited Spirit will come and enthrone Himself in the heart as a witness of sonship and the living Comforter. It preaches the dreadful truth of eternal punishment, and warns men to flee from the wrath to come ; and it makes known the everlasting blessedness of those who fight the good fight and obtain the crown of righteousness."

It is pre-eminently the theology of the evangelist who seeks to revive and extend spiritual religion. The character of Wesley's teaching and theology is written on every page of the history of the mightiest revival the Church has ever known :

"Not unto us, O Lord, not unto us, but unto Thy name give glory, for Thy mercy and for Thy truth's sake."

III. WE GIVE THE LORD GLORY FOR WESLEY'S WORK.

God sent Luther to reform a corrupted Christianity : He sent Wesley to revive a dying Christianity.

Wesley's preaching was not of strange or new doctrines, but it exhorted to new life, and it was effective.

He was the leader of a Church for preaching to the poor, and for carrying the gospel to the masses. That was his work ; and it has been the hard work of his followers through the generations.

Unconsciously he worked out a Divine purpose. He no more contemplated at first, nor for long, the establishment of a separate branch of the Church,—of Methodism as a system,—than Luther did of leaving Rome and establishing Lutheranism ; but the Lord thrust them both forth, and led them whither they did not expect. Wesley, in the providence of God, was led, driven, inspired to start a great evangelistic and missionary organisation. The question for the living Methodists of to-day is not, "What did John Wesley wish for himself or his followers in relation to the Church of England ?" This is the question : "What did John Wesley and our God intend ?"

And on this subject we ask no man's dictum, but must be guided by providential indications.

He welded the members of his Societies into a compact body; gave them rules; established classes; promoted Christian fellowship; and insisted on and exercised godly discipline.

He was neither schismatic nor heresiarch, but he had a passion for saving souls, and was eminently a preacher.

His work was oratorical, diplomatic, administrative, constructive, and legislative. He did it all well; as only a man of genius, culture, intellectual force, extraordinary power of physical endurance, and true godliness could do it. For all this we give God the glory.

On New Year's Day 1740, — fifty-one years before Wesley's death,—there were not fifty Methodists in the world: on 2nd March 1791, when he died, he left behind him 80,000 members in the Societies he had founded: 1000 local preachers, and a pastorate of 300 itinerant preachers. And when his spirit took its flight, he entered into no City of Strangers, for troops of his friends and converts had preceded him to paradise, and doubtless gave him welcome there. One hundred years after his death, the work has so extended, that Wesley's followers living on earth at this hour number at least twenty-five millions.

Properly to judge of the work of Mr. Wesley, we need to read his Journals. What a record of travel! of toil! of holy joy! of persecutions! What an insight they give of the England and Ireland of 100 years ago! How they put to shame the indolent Christians, in the ministry and out of it, of other days! Let us urge every Methodist, and especially every young Methodist, diligently to read those fascinating Journals of Mr. Wesley, and devoutly to study his sermons and other works. He preached his last sermon at Leatherhead on 24th February 1791, from "Seek ye the Lord while He may be found; call ye upon Him while He is near." That was the last of more than forty - two thousand sermons.   He died a week after,—

> " His body with his charge lay down,
> And ceased at once to work and live."

Such was the man, such was his teaching, such was his work ; now what as to

THE PRESENT AND THE FUTURE OF METHODISM ?
FOR THIS, TOO, WE GIVE GOD GLORY.

It will be well if, in the spirit of our text, the Methodists of to-day will resolve henceforth to shout no more pæans on mere Wesleyanism, to cease from self-glorification, but to go directly, distinctly, and earnestly to the work that requires to be done in the world.   It is high time that now, a century after Wesley's death, Wesley's sons in the faith, and successors in toil and the service of God, should seek to become, more and more, leaders in religious thought, as well as leaders in religious life and work. They will do well to think much of Methodism and Methodist topics, and study them deeply.   They will love their Church in proportion to their knowledge of Method- ism.   The Methodists well read in our literature will be the most industrious, enthusiastic, and earnest workers and Wesleyans ; but they must remember that the world is greater than any "ism ; " and they must launch out into the deep, and cast their nets on the other side of the ship for greater draughts of fish than they have ever yet caught —and for greater and other sort of fish.

We give glory to God for the past, but we give glory to Him also because there is abundant proof that the course of Methodism is not yet run.   The causes of its past pro- gress are permanent and perpetual.   Like the trade-winds, or the flow of the Gulf Stream, the way of Methodism is onward.   In England—this little isle—we cannot see what God has done by it.   In the great West it is the mightiest

Church ; and there still the promise of the future is bright
—brighter than ever before.

Let the past teach and stimulate for the future. Men
differ when they account for the marvellous growth of
Methodism. They speak of its doctrines, polity, itinerancy,
elasticity, as to forms of worship, hymnology, sayings,
revivals, fellowship, ecclesiastical freemasonry,—all these
have been dwelt upon.

But no one of these things, nor all of them put together,
is sufficient to account for the result. God must be taken
into the reckoning. The glory—and all of it—must be
given to Him. His "mighty working" in all of them, by
men and women "full of faith and the Holy Ghost," is the
secret. The doctrines, however good, would have been
powerless if they had not been preached ; the preaching
would have been in vain without the energy of the Spirit ;
the economy would have been cumbrous despite the
wisdom that invented it, if the living power had not been
in the machinery ; the inspiring songs had to be sung by
inspired singers. It is because men and women have
preached, lived, sung, toiled under the constraint of the
love of Christ, and under a weight of responsibility that
never lost sight of the judgment-day, that Methodism has
won its greatest victories.

The secret of success has been in downright consecration
to God. Earnest, plodding, unconquerable hard work,
—work prepared by the Lord, and then energised by His
Spirit.

Surely the lesson to the Methodists of to-day is clear
enough. Let us cherish the memory of our forefathers ;
let us emulate their spirit ; let us cling to their God-given
doctrines ; let us cultivate, as they did, communion with
the Master, and fellowship with each other ; let us aim each
one to do his own duty ; let us strive to make our Church
a greater power for evangelism among the people of the
earth than ever; let us look to the Holy Spirit for a richer
baptism of grace. And Methodism, so blessed of the Lord
in the past, will yet be blessed. Her mission is not accom-

plished. Her work is not done. Long may she live and prosper! Peace be within her walls; prosperity within her palaces. For my brethren and companions' sakes,— the faithful living and the sainted dead,—I will now say, "Peace be within her!"

A Hundred Years Ago.

Hymn written for the Centenary of Methodism, 1839.

BY JAMES MONTGOMERY.

Used at the Ex-President's Service, 1st March 1891.

ONE song of praise, one voice of prayer,
  Around, above, below;
Ye winds and waves, the burden bear,
  "A hundred years ago!"

"A hundred years ago!"—What then?
  There rose the world to bless
A little band of faithful men,
  A cloud of witnesses.

It look'd but like a human hand:
  Few welcom'd it, none fear'd;
Yet, as it open'd o'er the land,
  The Hand of God appear'd.

The Lord made bare His holy Arm,
  In sight of earth and hell:
Fiends fled before it with alarm,
  And alien armies fell.

God gave the word, and great hath been
  The preacher's company:
What wonders have our fathers seen!
  What signs their children see!

One song of praise for mercies past,
  Through all our courts resound;
One voice of prayer, that to the last
  Grace may much more abound.

All hail "a hundred years ago!"
  And when our lips are dumb,
Be millions heard rejoicing so,
  A hundred years to come!

Sermon to the Young People

By the Rev. CHARLES GARRETT.

—o—

> "*Therefore, my beloved brethren, be ye stedfast,*
> *unmoveable, always abounding in the work of the*
> *Lord, forasmuch as ye know that your labour is not*
> *in vain in the Lord.*"—I COR. xv. 58.

THIS is the conclusion of one of the most eloquent and
impressive parts of God's Word, and, though eminently
practical, it is in perfect harmony with that which has preceded it.   Paul had been demonstrating the certain truth
of Christianity, and he then endeavours to bring his
reasoning to bear upon the daily life of the Corinthians.
He seems to say, seeing that Christianity is true, and that
the resurrection is sure ; seeing that Christ has made a full
atonement for the sins of the world, and thus has made
it possible that every child of man may be a child of God ;
seeing that your destiny is in your own hands, and that
your position hereafter will depend upon your conduct
here : "Be ye stedfast, unmoveable, always abounding in
the work of the Lord."

After much anxious thought, I can find no passage more
suitable than this to guide our thoughts in this important
service.   It is a Divine picture of the Methodists of the
past.   I know of none more striking, and the prayer of my
heart is that it may be an equally correct description of
the Methodists to come.

The text puts before us our work and our encouragement.

I. *Our Work.*   Work is the law of the universe ; man

21

is the only idler, and idleness is sin. Work is also the law of the Church. Christ did His work that we might do ours. If we neglect that, then, as far as we are concerned, we "receive the grace of God in vain." The text teaches that we must begin with ourselves. It is much easier to recommend religion to others than to receive and carry it out ourselves. It is far more easy to be a Sunday school teacher, a tract distributor, a teetotaller, a social reformer, than it is to be a Christian. I want you to see this, for whatever you may do for the promotion of the spread of Christianity, if you are not right yourselves, you will at last join in the sad, sad cry, "They made me a keeper of vineyards, but my own vineyard I have not kept." Let me then urge you, as you value your present and eternal welfare, to listen to the apostle's words.

First, "*Be stedfast*," *settled, decided.* Till this is done nothing is done. Indecision in religious matters is the ruin of multitudes. They don't openly reject Christ, but they don't loyally and lovingly receive Him. They halt between two opinions, and forget that indecision is really decision : that not to receive Christ is to reject Him. This, I fear, is the state of many of you. You have come from Methodist homes, you attend Methodist chapels, you defend Methodism if it is attacked in your shops and warehouses ; but you have not decided for Christ. Let me beseech you to end this hesitancy, and decide to-day. Remember, if you ever get to heaven, you will have decided. Why, then, not decide to-day? Can you imagine a more favourable time for decision? Here in this glorious old chapel, every place in which is holy ground, with all the memories of the past crowding in upon you, with thousands of God's people on their knees praying that the service may be blessed ; with many a mother away in the country village, who knew that you were coming to this service, pleading with God that to-day her many prayers for your salvation may be answered : can there ever be a more favourable time for decision? Remember you must decide for yourself. No one on

earth or in heaven can decide for you. Christ has put
away sin, and opened a way to the mercy-seat ; God urges
you to come, and promises to receive you. But the
decision rests with you. You must act, or perish for ever.
God help you here and now to take the great step in life,
and say, "This people shall be my people, and their God
my God." You will no longer be tossed about ; you will
be on the Rock of Ages. This day will be to you the
beginning of days ; the light of seven days will be in it; and
long as life shall last, and may be, even in heaven itself,
you will sing,

> " O happy day, that *fixed* my choice
> On Thee, my Saviour and my God."

Now, having got right, remain right. The text urges
you to be "unmoveable." Remember that entering the
Church is not entering heaven. True, you have become a
Christian, but it is a Christian in the battlefield, and you
will need Divine help or your song of triumph will end in
the wail of despair. Whoever else may believe in the
doctrine that if a man is once in grace he is always in
grace, it is clear the devil doesn't. If he did, he wouldn't
torment some of us as much as he does. No ; he knows
your value ; " he goeth about like a roaring lion, seeking
whom he may devour," and he will use the world and the
flesh for your destruction. Be therefore on your guard.
Put on the whole armour of God :

> " Leave no unguarded place,
> No weakness of the soul ;
> Take every virtue. every grace
> And fortify the whole.'

Then build yourselves up in your most holy faith.
" Add to your faith virtue, and to virtue knowledge, and
to knowledge temperance, and to temperance patience,
and to patience godliness, and to godliness brotherly
kindness, and to brotherly kindness charity." " If ye do
these things, ye shall never fall," but the winds and waves

of life and time shall sweep around you in vain. Lastly, see that you grow in grace. In order to this, *treasure up God's promises.* They are the food of the soul; you will have no permanent strength or peace without them. You may have your dreams and visions and joyous feelings, but if you have not a "Thus saith the Lord," your faith will be mere enthusiasm, and when the days of darkness come, you will be hopeless and helpless. Treasure up the promises, and you will feel as safe in the dark as in the light. Darkness doesn't affect the value of banknotes, the solidity of the promises, nor our relationship to God, and hence, grasping the promises, we shall be able to say, "Though He slay me, yet will I trust in Him." To this end, commit the promises to memory. You can easily learn one each week, and with fifty-two hid in your heart you will be prepared for any emergency. Remember, however, that no promise in the Bible will be of any use to you unless you know it. God will never perform a miracle to compensate you for your idleness. Next, *read the records of God's dealings with His people.* It is our privilege to "sing a performing God." Read His wonderful works and rejoice, remembering that what He has done for others He can do again. Don't read books that are calculated to chill your love and weaken your faith. What can be more unwise than for Christians to spend their money in buying doubts. If you and the devil cannot manufacture more doubts than you can solve, it is strange to me. Buy doubts! No; if you have money to spend, buy books that will feed your faith, and brighten your hope. Read the lives of your Methodist forefathers, such as John Nelson, John Haime, and John Smith; or of Samuel Pearce the Baptist, and R. M. M'Cheyne the Presbyterian, or Bishop Hannington the Episcopalian; and before you have finished them you will be in Beulah-land, where the sun shines all the day long.

Next, *Keep up close communion with God.* Nothing helps the soul like this. It strengthens our faith, increases our love, and gives us a foretaste of heaven. " O taste and see that the Lord is good." Experimental religion cannot be affected by the sneers of the infidel. If a man has once tasted honey, all the scientific men in the world couldn't persuade him that it wasn't sweet. So it is with the soul. Let a man's fellowship be with the Father, and with His Son Jesus Christ, and the pratings of the infidel will produce no more effect upon him than the baying of the dogs upon the moon. To all their arguments he will joyously reply, "I know whom I have believed, and I am persuaded that He is able to keep what I have committed to Him against that day." He will be " stedfast " and " unmoveable."

Right yourselves, now set to work to make other people right, be " always abounding in the work of God." The Christian religion is the determined enemy of idleness and selfishness. As soon as God says, " Thy sins which are many are all forgiven," He says, " Go work to-day in My vineyard." God does not make us Christians merely to get us to heaven, He makes us Christians that we may be co-workers with Him in bringing heaven here. This is the work of the Church, and God holds us each responsible for doing all in our power for its accomplishment. We are to do " the work of the Lord." What is this? We are not left in ignorance. The Lord has been here and " left us an example that we should tread in His steps." What then did He do? Here also the answer is clear: " He went about doing good." He taught the ignorant, He fed the hungry, He comforted the sorrowful, He sought and saved the lost. This is " the work of the Lord" that we are to do. We are His representatives, and we should seek to live " as Jesus lived below." As Dr. Arnold said, " Our work is to make earth like heaven, and every man like God." Beware of the idea that some work is religious and some secular. Christ's life teaches us the opposite. Every act that benefits man or glorifies God is Christlike work, and this work every one of us is called to do.

We are to do this work *heartily*, not grudgingly or of necessity, but "abounding." We are not hirelings, but sons and daughters; we are not Jews, but Christians. We are not under the dominion of law, but of love. And love does not want commands, it only wants opportunities. Love never thinks of an eight-hours Bill, for it can never do enough for its object. We must also do this work *continuously*. We are to be "always" abounding in it, in youth and age, in sunshine and in storm. Some professors of Christianity are spasmodic in their service. They are a kind of ecclesiastical rockets. They go up with a great deal of noise at revivals, and then we hear no more of them. See to it that you are not like that : be stars, not rockets ; let your light shine more and more unto the perfect day.

II. *Our Encouragement.* "Forasmuch as ye know that your labour is not in vain in the Lord." What cheering news. Most of us have been so dissatisfied with our work, that we only thought of asking for mercy. Here, however, is the promise of reward. Yes, "our labour is not in vain " *here*, for it will increase both our strength and our happiness. It is the best possible remedy for weakness and gloom.

"It will not be in vain" *hereafter*, for it will be acknowledged and rewarded by God. When we think of our many failures, it seems impossible that this should be, but remember love soon forgets a wrong, but never forgets a kindness. See the mother. Her son was not one of the best of boys, but one day when she was ill he got up and lighted the fire for her, and now that he has gone to America, if you go and talk to her she will tell you he was a good lad, and that when she was ill, he used to get up and light the fire for her. So it will be with our infinitely loving Father. Our sins shall be blotted out—be behind His back—be forgotten ; but no act of kindness to men or service to God shall ever be forgotten; and even if we make the attempt and fail, He will say, " Thou did'st well that it was in thine heart." So at the day of judgment

there is not to be a word about our failures, but a proclamation of our service, and many a man will find himself
to be a millionaire who thought himself a bankrupt. "Then
will the King say to those on His right hand, Come, ye
blessed of My Father, inherit the kindgom prepared for
you from the foundation of the world: *for* I was hungry,
and ye fed me. Then will the righteous answer Him and
say, Lord, when saw we Thee hungry and fed Thee?"
And the Lord will say, "Don't you remember when you
were sitting at your dinner one day, you said, There is a
poor woman down the court yonder that rarely gets a bit
of hot dinner, let us send her some ; and you cut it off and
sent it down to her?" You will say, "Lord, I had forgotten
that I ever did this." "Ah," Christ will say, "I have not
forgotten it ; I was there, and I whispered to you, Well
done, good and faithful servant, thou hast done it unto Me."
"I was naked, and you clothed Me." And you will say,
"Lord, when?" And the Lord will reply, "Don't you
remember when the snow was falling, and the keen east
wind was smiting the strongest, that you saw a little
orphan boy hurrying by and trying to shelter himself from
the biting blast, and you said, Our little Willie is grown
out of his clothes, and they would just fit that little fellow,
let us call him in; and you clothed him and sent him away
rejoicing?" "Lord, I had forgotten that I ever did it." "Oh,"
Christ will say, "I have not forgotten ; I was there, and I
whispered, Thou hast done it unto Me." "I was sick, and
you visited Me." And you will say "When?" And He will
say, "Don't you remember when the young man in your
warehouse was sick unto death, and was far from home and
friends, that you proposed to the other young men that
you should sit up with him in turn?" And you will say,
"Lord, I had forgotten it." He will say, "I have not forgotten it ; I was there all night breathing blessings upon
you, and no service you ever rendered was so pleasing to
Me as that." Young men, this is not a dream, but the
teaching of God's Word ; and if the Church believed it
there would not be a want unmet, or a sorrowing one

uncomforted, or a sinner unsaved. There would be a holy rivalry who should be the first in the sick-room and the first to minister to the wants of the needy, and first to seek the wanderer. See that you believe and act upon it, and so lay up for yourselves treasures in heaven.

"Therefore, my beloved brethren, be ye stedfast, unmoveable, always abounding in the work of the Lord, forasmuch as ye know that your labour is not in vain in the Lord."

The Chosen Vessel.

BY THE REV. DAVID J. WALLER, D.D.,

SECRETARY OF THE CONFERENCE.

——o——

" Go thy way: for he is a chosen vessel unto Me, to bear My name before the Gentiles."—ACTS ix. 15.

THERE is nothing more remarkable than the way in which the Divine Head of the Church has raised up specially gifted and qualified instruments to do His work. This is strikingly illustrated in the conversion of Saul of Tarsus. Who so unlikely to become a Christian and apostle of the Cross as the zealous and persecuting Pharisee who held the clothes of the men who stoned the first martyr Stephen? And yet Saul was a "chosen vessel" to fulfil the Divine purpose. By the revelation of the glorified Christ, he became a changed man, and the persecutor "straightway preached Jesus." In subsequent periods of the Church's history, Christ has raised up men who, like St. Paul, were "chosen vessels" for the Master's use. If their conversion has not been marked by heavenly vision, or the manifestation of the glorified Redeemer, there has been the operation of the same gracious providence, the revelation of the same Divine Saviour, and the gift of the same Holy Spirit. Such a man was Martin Luther, who became the Apostle of the Protestant Reformation. And such a man was John Wesley. He, too, was a "chosen vessel," selected and qualified for a special work, who, "after he had served his own generation by the will of God, fell on sleep," a century ago.

" A chosen vessel " implies selection and fitness for a special work.

I. IN THE DIVINE SELECTION THERE WAS AN ANTECEDENT PREPARATORY FITNESS.

There is frequently an " ancestral fitness " in connection with the Divine choice. This was so in reference to John the Baptist. He was " a man sent from God," to " go before the face of the Lord to prepare His ways, to give knowledge of salvation unto His people by the remission of their sins." But Zacharias and Elizabeth were specially chosen of God, and to them were committed the childhood and training of the Prophet of the Highest. First in the Hebron home of the pious priest, and afterwards in the wilds of the Judean desert, the Baptist was fitted for the great work of preparing the way of the world's Redeemer.

No angelic visitant was sent to announce the birth of Saul ; and there were no indications of the Divine choice apparent during the period of his youth or early manhood. But as we listen to the announcement made by the heavenly Saviour to Ananias, and then glance along the pathway of his previous history, it is not difficult to see how—though unconsciously to himself and others—there had been a remarkable preparation for his subsequent career as an Apostle to the Gentiles.

Saul was born in a Hebrew home, and he was carefully educated in the Jewish faith. He was taught to receive the Scriptures as the sacred oracles of God ; and was *brought up* in " the straitest sect " of the Jews' religion. He " was a Pharisee and the son of a Pharisee ;" and he " served God from his forefathers." When he wrote these words, probably he had before his mind the example of his father, " praying and walking with broad phylacteries, scrupulous and exact in his legal observances."

But, educated in a Hebrew home, he was surrounded by Gentile influences. Tarsus was a Roman city, and the schools of Gentile teaching, of a high order, were at his very door. He had abundant opportunities of becoming acquainted with Greek literature, and there are sufficient evidences that he availed himself of them.

May we not see the wisdom and providence of God in selecting one to " bear Christ's name before the Gentiles," who had spent his early youth in contact with the vital forces of the Gentile world ? Though his was a Hebrew home, it was not in Palestine, where neither the language nor the special influences would have fitted him for his great work ; but in Cilicia, where he was subject to Greek and Roman influences, and where he became familiar with the languages and ideas of the Gentile world.

At the same time, Saul was *so effectually guarded against the Gentile* influences by which he was surrounded, that neither the philosophic schools nor the sensual idolatries of Tarsus quenched in any degree his devotion to the Jewish faith. His formal education was completed, not at Tarsus, but at Jerusalem, at the feet of the famous Gamaliel, from whom he learnt, in its best form, the tradition of the elders. He was one of the foremost champions of the Hebrew faith, and one of the most zealous members of the Jewish propaganda. " It was," said they, " no longer possible to fortify Jerusalem against the heathen ; but the law could be fortified like an impregnable city. The place of the brave is on the walls and in the front of the battle ; and the hopes of the nation rested on those who defended the sacred outworks, and made successful inroads on the territories of the Gentiles."[1] Saul was one of those brave defenders ! When he heard, therefore, of the spread of the Nazarene sect among his own nation, his indignation was extreme. His anger was only equalled by his determination to exterminate the hated society. And yet this man, consenting to Stephen's death, " breathing out threatenings and slaughter against the disciples of the Lord," is himself a " chosen vessel " unto Christ to bear His name before the Gentiles. The strict religious training, the careful education, the know-

[1] *Conybeare and Howson*, vol. i. 40.

ledge of the oracles of God, the familiarity with the range
of ancient philosophy, were acquirements which fitted
him for his high vocation. Then the intensity of his
nature, his passionate zeal, his unflinching courage, his
strength of will, his superior mental endowments, were
qualities which, when purified by the fire of the Holy
Spirit, and sanctified by the grace of Christ, all fitted him
to bear His name before the Gentiles.

John Wesley was in a lesser degree "a chosen vessel"
to bear Christ's name before the people ; and in his case
there was an antecedent preparatory fitness for the work.

If we transfer our thoughts from the Hebrew home in
Tarsus to the more familiar rectory at Epworth, we may
observe influences which in no small degree fitted John
Wesley for the great part he was designed to take in the
Revival of the Eighteenth Century. There was an
ancestry which had been ennobled by sacrifice and the
endurance of persecution, and family traditions of no
small value. The example of a devout father was before
the children, and the still more valuable and potent
influence of the mother. The world is principally indebted
to Susannah Wesley for the early religious training by
which the foundation of the eminent characters of her
children was laid. It has been truly said that "the mother
makes us most," [1] and no son was more indebted to his
mother than was John Wesley.

If we trace the history of the child in the Epworth
home,—with its careful moral and religious training,—of
the boy at public school, or of the undergraduate at the
Oxford University, it is easy to see how all this prepared
him for his life's great work. The thorough education,
the superior scholarship, the highly-trained intellect, the
extensive knowledge, all fitted him for the work to which,
by a gracious Providence, he was designated.

---

[1] "Mind is from the mother," says Isaac Taylor, when speaking of John
Wesley's mother. With this agrees Tennyson's line,

"The mother makes us most."

—Bishop M'Tyeire's Sermons, pp. 109, 110.

Then mark his reverent devotion. As a student in preparation for Holy Orders he was most exemplary. He prayed and fasted, he attended the sacraments, and strictly conformed to all outward acts of piety. This was in no formal spirit, for he was intensely in earnest, and thoroughly aroused to the importance of vital religion. He was convinced, moreover, that outward conformity, however strict, and good works, however manifold, do not constitute true religion, but that it consists in a right state of the heart ; and so by reading, meditation, and prayer, he sought for the Divine image in the soul. It was at this period that an Oxford student satirically applied the term "Methodist" to Wesley and his associates, little thinking that in process of time millions would be designated by that name.

All this was part of the preparation, but it did not constitute his *essential fitness* for the work Christ had chosen him to fulfil. His thorough education, his knowledge of languages, his intellectual culture, his moral elevation, and his intense religious earnestness, constituted an antecedent fitness for his calling. But the "chosen vessel" received a higher and Divine qualification.

II. THE "CHOSEN VESSEL" WAS SPECIALLY PREPARED BY THE PERSONAL MANIFESTATION OF CHRIST.

Saul was on his way to Damascus that he might bring the disciples bound to Jerusalem, when the Lord whom he persecuted appeared to him. St. Paul never doubted as to the reality of Christ's appearance. It was no dream or vision of the night, but an actual appearance at noon-day, and with a splendour which outshone the brilliancy of a Syrian sun. Years afterwards he asked, "Am I not an apostle ? Have I not seen Jesus Christ ?"

It was by the personal manifestations of the glorified Christ that the marvellous transformation was effected which made the persecuting Saul the chosen vessel to bear Christ's name before the Gentiles.

C

The first effect of the manifestation of the risen Saviour to Saul was to produce in him great distress and anguish of soul. He fell to the ground blinded by the intense glory of the vision, and overwhelmed with terror and astonishment. Then, after three days, Ananias was sent to him. He put his hands on him, and the humble penitent received his sight; "there fell from his eyes as it had been scales." At the same time, by the touch of the Divine Healer, his spiritual eyes were opened, and he saw by faith that same Jesus who had appeared unto him in the way. He passed from "darkness to light;" he knew whom he had believed, and he was filled with the Holy Ghost. We are told that "straightway he preached Christ in the synagogues, that He is the Son of God."

Thus was the "chosen vessel" prepared to bear Christ's name before the Gentiles and kings, and the children of Israel. Afterwards, when standing before kings, he declared how Jesus, whom he persecuted, had appeared to him "for this purpose" to make him "a minister and a witness," both of the things which he had seen, and of the things in the which Christ would appear unto him. It was this heavenly Saviour who had sent him to the Gentiles, "to open their eyes, and to turn them from darkness to light, and from the power of Satan unto God, that they might receive the forgiveness of sins, and inheritance among them which are sanctified."

The conversion of St. Paul *was brought about by personal bitterness and suffering.* Is not this part of the Divine plan of salvation? "God wills to save sinners, but to save them as sinners." The salvation of a sinner is by way of repentance toward God, as well as faith in our Lord Jesus Christ.

But the manner of God's approach to the human soul is wonderfully varied; and the motions of the Divine Spirit are beyond human comprehension. Some are startled, and flee from "the wrath to come;" whilst others are secretly drawn into the vale of contrite sorrow and of humble trust and love.

It will be found, however, that some of the most distinguished of Christ's "chosen vessels" have experienced deep penitence and clearly marked conversion. Martin Luther, after taking his university degree at Wittenberg, was making his way to his Saxon home. He was at the same time the subject of great internal conflict. He thought of the assassin's knife that went to the heart of his comrade; and then asked himself if it had gone to his own heart, how he would have appeared before God. Just then a tempest burst over him, and the thunderbolt fell at his side. He thought his hour was come. "Death, judgment, and eternity surrounded him," and, wrapped in agony; he fell upon his knees, and vowed to abandon the world, and give himself to God. He entered an Augustine monastery, but in vain by prayer and penance did he seek for peace with God. At last a pious monk pointed him to "the Son of God who came thither for the pardon of our sins." It was not in vain that he believed the "acceptable saying, that Jesus Christ came into the world to save sinners."[1] He was a "chosen vessel" unto Christ, and by that experience he was fitted for his work. "The day then broke on Luther's soul, and the Reformation dawned on Christendom."[2]

It was so in the case of Whitefield, whose clarion voice was heard more distinctly than that of any other herald of the great Revival of the Eighteenth Century. Whitefield's conviction of sin was attended with the deepest distress. Of the anguish which he endured when an undergraduate at Oxford, he says : " God only knows how many nights I have lain groaning. Whole days and weeks have I spent prostrate on the ground in silent or vocal prayer." The day of redemption came, when he laid hold of the Cross by faith, and "the spirit of adoption sealed him unto the day of everlasting redemption." This "chosen vessel" unto Christ then went forth on his gloriously successful career. The effects which he wit-

---

[1] *D'Aubigné*, vol. i, p. 116.
[2] *Life of Dr. Coke*, Etheridge, pp. 25, 26.

nessed have probably not been equalled since the day
of Pentecost.   In one week he received a thousand letters
from those who had received spiritual benefit under his
ministry.

John Wesley was led to conscious salvation in a less
tempestuous way, but the deepest conviction of sin was
wrought in his heart by the Holy Spirit of God.   This
he experienced when by prayer, fasting, and the sacraments he sought for the image of God in his heart.   When,
on the voyage to Georgia, he witnessed the meekness and
patience and the calmness in the midst of peril which the
Moravians, who were fleeing from persecution, manifested,
he saw that they possessed a peace which passed his
understanding.   His mission to Georgia was a failure, but
it was fruitful in its effect upon his religious experience.
On his return to London, he learned the way of salvation
more perfectly from Peter Böhler.

At this time his conviction of sin was clearly marked.
He tells of an inward sense of sin, of sorrow and heavi-
ness of heart, and of a despair of saving himself by any
works of righteousness.   Here are his words :—" How am
I fallen from God. . . . All my works, my righteousness,
my prayers, need an atonement for themselves."   " God
is holy.   I am unholy, and altogether a sinner meet to be
consumed."   " Yet I hear a voice (and is it not the voice
of God ?), saying, ' Believe, and thou shalt be saved.'   ' He
that believeth is passed from death unto life.'   ' God so
loved the world, that He gave His only-begotten Son,' etc."
His prayer was heard.   The day of redemption came.
These are the words in which he records the blessed fact:—

" I think it was about five this morning that I opened
my Testament on those words : ' There are given unto us
exceeding great and precious promises, even that ye
should be partakers of the Divine nature' (2 Pet. i. 4).   Just
as I went out, I opened again on those words : ' Thou art
not far from the kingdom of God.'

" In the afternoon I was asked to go to St. Paul's.   The
anthem was, ' Out of the depth have I called unto Thee,

O Lord : Lord, hear my voice. O let Thine ears consider well the voice of my complaint. If Thou, Lord, wilt be extreme to mark what is done amiss, O Lord, who may abide it ? For there is mercy with Thee ; therefore shalt Thou be feared. O Israel, trust in the Lord, for with the Lord there is mercy, and with Him is plenteous redemption. And He shall redeem Israel from all his sins.' "

How suitable these words to the devout seeker who, out of the depths of his contrite spirit, called unto the Lord ! How full of comfort the assurance of mercy, as the swelling anthem filled that grand Christian temple ! He was to taste the sweetness of that mercy by the personal manifestation of Christ to him as his Saviour, ere the light of that day's sun had died out of the western sky.

" In the evening I went very unwillingly to a Society in Aldersgate Street, where one was reading Luther's preface to the Epistle to the Romans. About a quarter to nine, while he was describing the change which God works in the heart through faith in Christ, I felt my heart strangely warmed. I felt I did trust in Christ, Christ alone, for salvation ; and an assurance was given *me*, that He had taken away *my* sins, *even mine*, and saved *me* from the law of sin and death."

John Wesley was thus specially fitted for his work by the revelation of Christ as his personal Saviour.

When Christ chose Saul to make him a minister to the Gentiles, and sent him " to open their eyes and turn them from darkness to light," the heavenly Lord began the work by opening Saul's eyes, and by bringing him into the true light. So it was by opening the eyes of John Wesley to the way of salvation by faith which is in Christ Jesus, and by the revelation of Christ to his soul as his own personal Saviour, that he obtained his spiritual fitness for the work which God called him to fulfil. He tells us that when he went to convert the Indians, he needed himself to be converted. He startled his friends by declaring that before he experienced this change he was not a Christian. "When," said he, " we renounce everything but faith, and get into Christ, then, and not till then, have we any reason to believe that we are Christians." This was the great essential change in order to his fitness for the work to which God had chosen him. Charles Wesley did not accept the doctrine of salvation by faith until after his brother, but he found acceptance before him. These two brothers, both of them accepted in the Beloved, could now go forth and joyously proclaim,—

> " What we have felt and seen,
>   With confidence we tell,
> And publish to the sons of men
>   The signs infallible."

Without this revelation of Christ to him as his personal Saviour, and the transforming change which it wrought within him, John Wesley could never have become the apostle of Christ to the eighteenth century.

III. THUS SPECIALLY FITTED, THE CHOSEN VESSEL BEGAN HIS DIVINELY APPOINTED AND SUCCESSFUL EVANGELISTIC CAREER.

From the time of John Wesley's conversion, he bore Christ's name before the people—" he preached Jesus."

As soon as he was convinced that salvation is by faith, he declared it. " He preached faith *till* he had it, and then he preached it because he had it." The first person to whom he offered salvation was a prisoner under the sentence of death. Whilst in prayer with the criminal,— first using the collects, and then praying in language suggested to his mind,—the man sprang upon his feet, and exclaimed, " I am now ready to die. I know Christ has taken away my sins ; and there is no more condemnation for me."

A remarkable career now opened before him. He believed it to be the glory of the gospel that in Christ Jesus there is a personal Saviour for every one ; that salvation is alone by faith in Christ ; and that the knowledge of the forgiveness of sin is the common privilege of believers by the witness of the Holy Spirit. All this he most stedfastly believed and fearlessly proclaimed. Because of this strange doctrine, the churches soon closed against him, but the providence of God opened a wider door; the voice of the Risen Saviour said within him, " Behold I have set before thee an open door, and no man can shut it." Shut out of the churches, he took his stand under the dome of heaven ; and when parochial barriers would have circumscribed him, he said, "The world is my parish."

Whitefield had set him the example of open-air preaching, and advised him to take to the fields. And now Wesley, who had been " so tenacious of every point relating to decency and order," that he tells us " he should have thought the saving of souls almost a sin if it had not been done in a church," began his career as a field preacher. First at Bristol, then at Bath, next to the colliers at Kingswood, afterwards in London, and then all over the kingdom. He laid aside his manuscript, and used the simplest language. The common people heard him gladly, whilst all classes were attracted by his preaching. Thousands found salvation by faith in Christ Jesus, and entered into the glorious liberty of the children of God.

As might have been expected, he was censured for his disorderly proceedings. He was the subject of slander and opposition. " They were forbidden," says Wesley, " from Newgate lest they should make men wicked, and from Bedlam lest they should drive men mad." When the hostile spirit gathered in still fiercer persecution, his answer was : " It were better for me to die than not to preach the gospel ; yea, in the fields, when I may not preach in the church, or when the church will not contain the congregation."

Mobs of infuriated men—not unfrequently stirred up by the clergy, and sometimes led on by them—assaulted him. But few men could command a crowd as Wesley could.

Violent men were awed by his calm courage. And, as in the case of St. Paul, opposition and persecution helped in no small degree the cause which God had raised him up to promote. The persecutions of St. Paul enabled the apostle to bear Christ's name before kings, and his imprisonment tended to the furtherance of the gospel, "so that his bonds were manifest in the palace, and in all other places ; and many of the brethren in the Lord, waxing confident by his bonds, were much more bold to speak the word without fear." So in the early days of Methodism. The opponents guaranteed the masses of eager listeners, and the word of Christ's servant, attended by the Holy Spirit, subdued the crowds. The speaker's high courage charmed and attracted other Christians into devoted sympathy ; and the preacher's voice was multiplied as they also boldly testified for Jesus.

God raised up an army of evangelistic helpers. Wesley was led to take another step, by which "the system we call Methodism became possible." I refer to the fact that laymen were permitted to preach. Wesley was a High Churchman, and he considered that this function belonged exclusively to the clergy. When he learnt that during his absence from London, Thomas Maxfield, a layman, had taken this office upon himself, he was both shocked and angry. It was his mother, as wise as she was beautiful, who said to him, "Thomas Maxfield is as much called to preach the gospel as you are. Examine what have been the fruits of his preaching, and hear him yourself." He did so, and was convinced that the stamp of God's approval was on the work. "It is the will of the Lord," said he ; "let Him do what seemeth Him good." Lay agency then became a recognised part of the movement, and was essential to rural Methodism. It grew so that in due time lonely villages and distant moorland hamlets heard the glad tidings of salvation. The agency has continued ever since, and there are now in England 16,000 Wesleyan lay preachers, and to-day from seven to ten thousand villages have heard the gospel from the lips of Methodist laymen.

There is no fact more patent than that Methodism was not originated in either a political or ecclesiastical movement, but that it began in the revival of religion, and was the outcome of spiritual life. Wesley himself found "salvation by faith." He preached it, and others had the same blessed experience. With remarkable wisdom and foresight, he gathered the graciously awakened sinners and the penitent and rejoicing believers into the "United Societies." Thus he sought to build up the believers, not only in *doctrine*, but also in *fellowship;* and by this means he established permanent churches, which are still increasing with the passing years.

It then became necessary that these infant churches should have meeting-places. Like the early Christians, these churches met in the houses of some Christian brother or sister. Another step is taken; and property is acquired, and places of worship established. The erection of chapels and the opening of places of worship was not merely because the churches were closed against Wesley, his helpers and evangelists. These chapels were needed in order to carry on the varied and interesting services of Methodism.

The first Methodist place of worship was the Old Foundery, which stood to the north of what is now Finsbury Square.[1] This provided a large preaching-house, where crowds heard the word of life. Often in early morning, whilst it was yet dark, they made their way with lanterns across the open field to the preaching. But a visit to the Old Foundery must have left an impression as to the variety of Methodist work. There were preaching services, and meetings for fellowship and prayer. John Wesley was a lover of children, and one room was set apart for a day school. He established orphanages for poor children. A Children's Home is as old as Methodism! Another room is set apart for the suffering poor, where they may obtain medical relief; and thus Wesley showed himself a disciple

[1] It had been in the use of Government as an arsenal for casting brass cannon.

of the humane and the human Christ. Another room is for the distribution of religious books. He was the pioneer of cheap and useful literature. The opinion has been expressed, that no single man ever placed a larger mass of useful reading within the reach of the common people. Probably his collection of hymns, composed largely by his brother Charles, did more for the promotion of evangelical and spiritual religion than any book he ever issued. Witness how those hymns entered into the experience of the early Methodists, and how they lingered on their dying lips! The mere announcement of some of these hymns is a glorious proclamation of the gospel.

The "United Societies" had become churches in reality if not in name. The erection of City Road Chapel in 1777, with the ministers' houses and with the provision for the pastorate and the administration of the Lord's Supper, marked another period in the development of Methodism. In Mr. Wesley's sermon preached at the opening, he reviewed the progress. "May we not ask," said he, "what hath God wrought? For such a work, if we consider the extensiveness of it, the swiftness with which it has spread, the depth of the religion so swiftly diffused, and its purity from all corrupt mixture, we must acknowledge cannot easily be paralleled in all these concurrent circumstances by anything that is found in the English annals since Christianity was first planted in this island."

But Methodism had spread far beyond the British Isles and Ireland. It had been planted in the West Indies, and had struck its roots deeply into the American soil.

After the declaration of the American Independence, the spiritual needs of the American people presented a wonderful opportunity for Methodism; and John Wesley, in 1784, was led to do an extraordinary thing. He ordained Dr. Coke a bishop, and sent him to America to ordain Asbury elder and bishop, so that elders might be ordained to administer the sacraments.

We are being constantly reminded from certain quarters that John Wesley was a Churchman, and that Wesleyan ministers who administer the sacraments are not only so many Korahs, Dathans, and Abirams, but that we are faithless to our Founder. It is stated that Wesley's *Korah* sermon ought to convince Wesleyans not only of their sin, but of their gross inconsistency, in allowing their so-called ministers to take upon themselves "the *priesthood* of the new law."

What is the priesthood of the new law? Under the gospel dispensation, Jesus Christ is the one and only High Priest, to the exclusion of all other priests. He has offered one sacrifice for sin for ever; He ever liveth to make intercession. There are no priests under the "new dispensation," for there are no sacrifices to offer. In the only sense in which any one can be a priest, all believers are priests,—priests to offer spiritual sacrifices; priests with right and privilege to draw near to God. The sin of Korah is surely committed when a human priesthood is interposed betwixt the sinner and the Divine Priest upon His throne. Bishop Lightfoot truly says, "The kingdom of Christ interposes no sacrificial tribe or class between God and man, by whose intervention alone God is reconciled and man forgiven. Each individual member holds personal communication with the Divine Head. To Him immediately he is responsible, and from Him directly he obtains pardon and draws strength."[1] "So it was also with the Christian priesthood. . . . The priestly functions and privileges of the Christian people are never regarded as transferred or even delegated to these officers. They are called stewards or messengers of God, servants or ministers of the Church, and the like: but the sacerdotal title is never once conferred upon them. The only priests under the gospel, designated as such in the New Testament, are the saints, the members of the Christian brotherhood. As individuals, all Christians are priests alike."[2]

It is beyond question that John Wesley was a Church-

---

[1] *Commentary on the Philippians*, p. 179.
[2] *Ibid.*, pp. 182, 183.

man—a High Churchman (but a High Churchman of that day was something very different from the ritualistic sacerdotalist of to-day),—and that at one time he intended that the revival should be kept in its organisation within the pale of the Church. But the movement was directed by a higher power than that of Wesley ; and it was often with no small reluctance that Wesley followed the indication of providence. The bishops of the Church of England refused to ordain certain of his preachers, and then Wesley ordained them himself. He tells us that he was convinced " that bishops and presbyters are the same order, and consequently have the same right to ordain." His brother Charles expressed an opinion that, having come to the conclusion that " he had a right to ordain his preachers, he would soon be led to exercise it." Charles Wesley was right, and John Wesley did ordain some of his preachers to give the sacraments. He advised them to follow his example, and continue united to the Established Church, *" so far as the blessed work in which they were engaged would permit."* [1] Wesley found that the blessed work did not permit them to remain within the Church; and before his death he executed a legal instrument, by which the Conference was constituted, and Methodism received its present organic form ; and it is beyond the power of the Conference to alter the main features of Methodism as John Wesley left it.

But the end was drawing nigh. He had been in labours more abundant, and in journeyings oft. He had travelled five thousand miles a-year, and preached at the rate of fifteen sermons a-week. The high courage which had borne him up did not give way, his intellectual eye was not dim, nor had his foresight forsaken him, but his constitution of steel was worn out.

The movement, of which he was the inspiration and the instrument, had been carried to a remarkably successful issue. There were about eighty thousand members in the " United Societies " in this country, and in Canada and the

[1] Smith's *History of Methodism*, i. 580.

United States from forty to fifty thousand. Thousands born for God had preceded him to glory. He had recorded with thankfulness, "Our people die well."

The Church of England does well to celebrate this Centenary, for no Church owes to Wesley a larger debt of gratitude. Isaac Taylor says of the Established Church at that period : "The Anglican Church was a system under which men had lapsed into heathenism." Green, in his *History of the English People*, says: "The Methodists themselves were the least result of the Methodist revival. Its action on the Church broke the lethargy of the clergy. . . . But the noblest result of the religious revival was the steady attempt, which has never ceased from that day to this, to remedy the guilt, the ignorance, the physical suffering, the social degradation, of the profligate and the poor."

From the first, clergymen like John Fletcher, the Perronets, and others gathered around him ; but towards the end of his life he was esteemed and honoured by large numbers, including bishops. The Bishop of London (Dr. Lowth) refused to sit above him, and said : " Mr. Wesley, may I be found at your feet in another world."

When contemplating the churches which under God he had been largely instrumental in gathering, there was no boasting, but he ascribed all the praise to God. This was the language of thanksgiving :—

> " Oh, the fathomless love, that hath deigned to approve,
>   And prosper the work of my hands !
> With my pastoral crook I went over the brook,
>   And, behold, I am spread into bands !
>
> Who, I ask in amaze, hath gotten me these?
>   And inquire from what quarter they came :
> My full heart it replies, they are born from the skies,
>   And gives glory to God and the Lamb."

The end has come ! Being asked the ground of his hope, he replies :

> " I the chief of sinners am,
>   But Jesus died for me."

He then burst forth in the noble strain :

> "I'll praise my Maker while I've breath,
> And, when my voice is lost in death,
>   Praise shall employ my nobler powers ;
> My days of praise shall ne'er be past
> While life and thought and being last,
>   Or immortality endures."

His last words were :

> "The best of all is, God is with us."

At ten A.M., March 2nd, 1791, he entered into rest.

"God buries His workmen, but carries on His work."
That is the sentence inscribed on Charles Wesley's tablet,
and it was strikingly illustrated in the history of Methodism after John Wesley had passed away. When the
Conference assembled, it was a time of great solemnity :
but instead of vain regrets, "they sought to give proofs of
their veneration for the memory of their father and friend,
by endeavouring, with great humility and diffidence, to
follow and imitate him in doctrine, discipline, and life."
They gave themselves afresh to God. The whole country
was divided into districts, and they carried on the work
God had committed unto them. They proved in an
abundant manner that "Jesus Christ is the same yesterday,
to-day, and for ever."

The Centenary of Methodism as an organised Society
was celebrated fifty years after the death of Wesley. It
was then found that the 80,000 members in England at
the time of Wesley's death had increased to more than
296,000 ; there were 3000 chapels, and a large number of
other preaching-places ; the 312 ministers had increased
to 1019, and the number of local preachers was estimated
at 4000 : 3300 Sunday schools had been formed, with
341,000 scholars. The Foreign Missions which had been
established had proved most successful, in Ceylon, South
Africa, and especially in the South Seas, where nations
had been born in a day. In the meantime, Methodism in
America had far outgrown the parent stock. "With an

instinctive prescient of the future," the pioneers "had struck for the country." Our fathers of that day could only take up the language of John Wesley when he opened this chapel, "What hath God wrought!"

Fifty years more have elapsed, and it is now the Centenary of the death of Wesley. It is right that we should look back across the intervening years, and mark the progress we have made. There has been success which demands our gratitude ; but what abundant room for humility, when we think how much larger it might have been!

The number of church members in **Great** Britain, including those on trial, is 512,000; there are more than 2000 ministers, and nearly a million scholars in our schools. There are not less than two million members and adherents of our Church ; and, with the other branches, not less than three millions who profess and call themselves Methodists. There are about 10,000 chapels and other preaching-places, with accommodation for more than two millions.

In thirty years we have raised and expended on chapels, schools, and other Connexional property more than *eight millions of pounds ;* and yet the total debt does not exceed £800,000, which is less than the yearly income of the chapels with the sum raised annually for new schemes.[1] Then there are our Mission Churches, —the Irish Conference, — the Affiliated Conferences of Australasia, South Africa, and the West Indies. In addition, there are the great Methodist Churches in the United States and Canada. Methodism is the most numerous Church in America. In the various branches there are about five million church members, and with the adherents, probably twenty millions. There are 55,000 churches, and 32,000 ministers. For two years past they

---

[1] The annual income, including the maintenance of the ministry, the various circuit organisation, the Connexional Funds, Foreign and Home Mission, and special efforts for extension, is not known, but it probably exceeds a million and a-half of pounds sterling.

have added 500 a day to the Church roll. If we take into account the various Methodist Churches throughout the world,—and there is a close kinship and a strong family likeness amongst them all,—then the century of progress since the death of Wesley has made Methodism one of the largest forms of Protestant Christianity.

It is a small matter whether our Churchmanship is acknowledged. The Apostle St. Paul wrote to the Corinthians, and said: "Am I not an apostle? am I not free? have I not seen Jesus Christ? are not ye my work in the Lord? If I be not an apostle unto others, yet doubtless I am to you, for the seal of mine apostleship are ye in the Lord" (1 Cor. ix. 1, 2). Are we not a Church? are we not free? have we not seen the Lord? The vast and growing Methodist Churches throughout the world are the seal of our Churchmanship in Christ Jesus.

Let us not glory in the past, but rather let us think of our responsibilities for the future. We rejoice in the activity and successes of other Churches, but we have yet our own future mission to fulfil.

(1) *There must be the same evangelical utterance.* In the changed conditions of the times,—with the great social and moral problems to solve, — we must "show forth Christ's name." Those who understand the signs of the times will see the need there is for the proclamation of Gospel truth. It is impossible to listen to certain priestly pretensions, or to consider the ultimate effect of the extreme sacerdotal teaching, without apprehension for the future of religion and of the nation. There are abundant indications clearly showing that Methodism is likely to be more needed in the next century than it has been in the past.

(2) *We must be true to our traditions.* "Go not only to those who want you, but to those who want you most." We cannot afford to forsake the poor! Better far that we should lose the rich, than that we should lose touch with the masses of the poor.

In many of our places of worship there must be more ample and suitable accommodation of free sittings. The pew system has sadly encroached upon the provision formerly made. When this chapel was built, there was provision for many hundreds of poor people. The pews in the larger part of the chapel above and below are a subsequent innovation. We need "to repent and do our first works," if we would have our early successes. We must adopt various social measures, and see that Methodism is sufficiently elastic to adapt itself to the conditions of modern life.

(3) Let it be our constant aim *to bring sinners to Christ, and to build them up in the faith and fellowship of the gospel.* When we succeed in this, then we answer our calling. Less than this is failure.

The best monument we can raise to John Wesley is, not one in marble or in bronze, but the successful carrying on—in this time-honoured sanctuary—of that "work of God," which he was raised up by the great Head of the Church to begin. May the spirit of the Founder of Methodism animate the millions of his followers; and may the abundant blessing of the eternal Godhead be outpoured on the Universal Church. Amen.

The Centenary Service.

By the Rev. W. F. MOULTON, M.A., D.D.

PRESIDENT OF THE CONFERENCE.

——o——

> "*Brethren, I count not myself to have appre-*
> *hended: but this one thing I do, forgetting those*
> *things which are behind, and reaching forth unto*
> *those things which are before, I press toward the*
> *mark for the prize of the high calling of God in*
> *Christ Jesus.*"—Phil. iii. 13, 14.

WITH these words St. Paul closes a memorable passage
in the Epistle which he addressed to the best-loved of all
his Churches. The pretensions of false teachers, who
sought to undermine his authority, that they might sub-
vert his doctrine, have led him for a moment to speak
of claims which he too might have advanced had his
principles been akin to theirs. But, with characteristic
self-abnegation, the fruit at once of genuine humility and
of loyalty to truth, he enumerates possessions only to
renounce them, claims pre-eminence only to confess how
utterly he had been constrained to cast it all aside.
There is no trace of the vanity which displays the sacrifices made for the cause espoused. Nay rather, every
ground of boasting, every "gain" is compelled by the
touch of an Ithuriel's spear to reveal itself in its proper
form: the "gain" shows itself as "loss," the prized

inheritance is very refuse. As long as Paul was rich, he was poor. When he left all, and not till then, could he find the Christ.

But his present attitude is such as may well amaze us as we read.

When the twelve were called by Christ, they too left all, and followed Him. They renounced what would have kept them back from Him; but they found Him. They lived in His presence, by His words were they trained, His spirit was their life. St. Paul has lost, but has he found? No word asserts a possession gained, every sentence proclaims that he is seeking still. He has not been baffled in his quest, but he has learned that *to be a seeker* is the object he sought. He found—only to discover how much remains for him to find. He gains— the lifelong resolve to gain. The horizon flies before him as he seeks its bound. The Christ, the knowledge of Christ, seem most completely out of reach when most truly attained, as the informing influence of daily life. "This is life eternal," the Lord Himself has taught us, "that they may know" (and the word implies "may be ever gaining knowledge," "come more and more to know") "Thee, the only true God, and Jesus Christ whom Thou hast sent." St. Paul and St. John are at one. The stedfast purpose ever realising itself, and never completely realised, is the essence of the Christian life. No sacred teaching sanctions a thankful com- placency of spirit, the sigh of glad relief when the lofty height is gained. The whole passage now before us suggests—is full of—breathless, pauseless haste. Now and again, when the future issue comes before us, it is spoken of as if in language of doubt. It is not the doubt of the dispirited and enfeebled man, who toils along the weary road and fears his strength will fail; it is the doubt, if doubt it can be called, with which the eager athlete presses on in the race, overcoming each difficulty as he descries its presence, thinking only of the space that remains untraversed, striving whether possibly he may attain the goal. "That I may know Christ, and the power of His resurrection, and the fellowship of His sufferings, becoming conformed to His death, (seeking) whether I may possibly attain unto the resurrection from the dead." "Not that I have already received possession, or am already one made perfect; but I haste along, (seeking) whether I may indeed take hold," may grasp the object which I strive to gain. You are carried along with the writer in his fervid career. You feel the influence of his breathless speed. The same thought comes before us later, but for a moment it is interrupted by a conception altogether different. Paul is first the racer who speeds along in eager hope to grasp what he seeks, and then the man whom Christ Himself has grasped. Consistency of figure gives place to truth of Christian experience. The man on whom Christ has laid hold, and only he, is the man who is fitted for the life-long struggle. The first possession gained is—to be grasped by Christ. The beginning of the Christian life is passive, not active—receiving, not giving—yielding, not victory—trust, not mastery. Fresh from the touch of Christ, he girds himself for the race to which he has been called, as by a voice from heaven. "Brethren," he cries,—as if he said, "This is not an apostle's experience, an apostle's duty: if for one, it is for all,"—"I do not yet reckon myself to have taken hold; seeking, not attaining, is the picture of my life. But one thing I do, forgetting the space that is behind, and stretching forward over that which lies before me, I press forward to the mark for the prize of the high calling of God in Christ Jesus."

Nowhere, perhaps, does this servant of Christ more completely reveal himself. Other Epistles depict his human life, if I may so speak, his natural affections, discouragements, temptations, sorrows, joys, sympathies. But in what we may speak of as his Christian experience, this passage stands alone in its fervency and power. And yet I am earnestly solicitous that we should understand that St. Paul never made the severance, which so often seems natural to us, between Christian experience and allotted duty.

I will not deny that the distinction may often appear both wise and necessary. The allotted tasks of life often seem to have very little in common with the life of faith and hope and love. The student of ancient records, for example, or the artisan whose hourly labour taxes all his faculties, may well look on life as compound and not single, and may sharply distinguish the sapless wood from the living tree. Yet even here we know what the words of our Lord teach, and what His Spirit can effect.

But I am thinking chiefly of those whose work is like St. Paul's—not, indeed, in its maturity and splendid power, but in its character and aim. My brethren in the Christian ministry will understand the object I have now in view. We have had the temptation before us, even if we have not yielded to its power. Conscious that no external service or ministration can bind the soul to Christ, it may be that we have unwittingly allowed ourselves to draw too sharp a line of division between our inner life, as Christ's own servants, and the sacred duties to which we have been set apart by His call and in His presence. It is but too easy thus to put asunder what God has joined together. Let St. Paul be our teacher here. Look at the records of his life in the Acts and in the letters which he wrote, and listen to his burning words : " Though I preach the gospel, I have nothing to glory of : for necessity is laid upon me ; yea, woe is unto me, if I preach not the gospel ! For if I do this thing willingly, I have a reward ; but if against my will, a dispensation is committed unto me. . . . I am made all things to all men, that I might by all means save some. And this I do for the gospel's sake, that I may be partaker thereof with you. . . . They (they which run, they which strive) do it to obtain a corruptible crown : but we an incorruptible. I therefore so run not as uncertainly ; so fight I, not as one that beateth the air. But I keep under my body, and bring it into subjection : lest that by any means, when I have preached to others, I myself should be a castaway." Again, after describing his position while in captivity at Rome, with brethren on the one hand taking up in love his testimony for Christ, with others actuated by unfriendly purpose, he adds : "What then? notwithstanding, every way, whether in pretence, or in truth, Christ is preached ; and I therein do rejoice, yea, and shall rejoice. For I know that this shall turn to my salvation through your prayer, and the supply of the Spirit of Jesus Christ." Would we see how inseparable are his life and his work, let us read his pathetic address to the elders of Ephesus ; or the confession of his "great sorrow and unceasing pain" of heart, when he even said, "I could wish that I myself were anathema from Christ for my brethren's sake ;" or the expression of his readiness either to bear affliction or to receive comfort for the comfort and salvation of his converts, to be "offered upon the sacrifice and service" of their faith, constrained by the love of Christ.

It is hard to say where the thought of personal loyalty to Christ passes over into the thought of apostolic duty. What more personal than "To me to live is Christ, and to die is gain"? And yet the immediate context, as we have seen, is entirely occupied with the diffusion of the gospel message, with Christ preached in Rome. The elements of St. Paul's spiritual life were those of his spiritual work. Faith was the means of his life ; faith the power through which he spoke. The love of God had been shed abroad in his heart ; love impelled him to spend and be spent for the sake of men. The consecration of heart and soul to Christ was a consecration to Christ's work. By prayer he lived ; by prayer utterance was given to him to make known the mystery of the gospel.

Here is the blessed privilege of the Christian minister, if he is a follower of the apostle in intensity of life. Here is his peril if his energies grow slack. All the day long the same food sustains his highest life and his habitual work. He reads the Holy Word to his flock ; he is their guide in prayer; he teaches, warns, points out the way of truth. As he does this in official duty, he may take as he gives, feed himself as he offers food, receive help of unutterable value in the very act of helping. Here is his present rich reward. And yet there is no certainty that so it will be with him, for the outward habit may remain when the life of it is gone; and the almoner of God, in the very ministration of His bounty, may starve his own soul.

Here minister and people in some measure stand apart. Both have hours of directly sacred labour, both are more or less involved in the cares of secular toil. But the minister of Christ has, or ought to have, but little of these worldly cares; and those to whom he ministers must have many. Yet amidst these many lower but still necessary toils, all must find room for the higher efforts to do work like that of Christ. Leave no work unsanctified; make the whole life Christian! But be not satisfied till some portion of the precious time God lends can be devoted to Christ's saving work. In that you will find your own spiritual sustenance. Whatever has been said to ministers of Christ's Church applies to all workers, in so far as they can minister Christ. Life and work must co-exist, each throwing light upon the other, each fostering the other, till the day when the earthly yields place to the heavenly, and there exists no longer any care or toil which can be called secular, or can absorb a thought away from Christ.

The subject of our thoughts this afternoon has been St. Paul: the occasion which has suggested the subject has been the life and labours of the servant of Christ, the follower of the apostles, whom we commemorate to-day. To fulfil my appointed task, I came anew to the study of John Wesley's wonderful career. I came without expectation that I could add to the rich store of knowledge we possess. On every hand we meet with students of the history. Friends, dissentients, and (in trifling number) foes have given to us their varied impressions of the character and achievements of the foremost Evangelist of the Eighteenth Century. On such a theme one cannot hope to speak with freshness or the attractiveness of novelty.

That is not my aim. I have sought to imbue myself with the spirit of the man we all revere, to follow his life till I could feel the hidden spring of all his activity and influence. And the spring is here. Underlying and including all he planned, and all he accomplished, during half a century, is this one principle of St. Paul. Looked at from any other point of view than one, John Wesley's life was manifold, inconsistent, heterogeneous. This simple clue leads through what some have regarded as a labyrinth, this light shows harmony amongst actions apparently discordant. No other principle than St. Paul's own can make it possible for successors to continue his work ; and hence the words we have been considering most fitly suit the day which ends a hundred years of Methodist toil in the absence of its Founder, and which begins a new era for our Church.

The picture of the Oxford scholar is familiar to us all. Not less well known is the strict High Churchman, overwhelmed by strong convictions as to sin and holiness, in labours more abundant, living in complete devotedness to the service of man for Christ's sake ; in all this—yet never by means of all this—striving to save his soul. Through the power of the same impulse he went to preach among the Indians of Georgia. " Our end in leaving our native country was singly this, to save our souls, to live wholly to the glory of God." He is a man "who has but one business, to exercise himself unto godliness." Painful experience, faithful help, with the guidance which never fails the man of prayer, led him into the liberty of the gospel, and into conscious union with the Lord he loved. Church order was dear to him : to the Church of his fathers he would not willingly be disobedient in a single point of discipline. " Woe is unto me if I preach not the gospel," was the cry of his heart ; and wherever churches

were opened, he proclaimed the message God had given
him. But so great was the shock which the doctrine of
conversion, *necessary* conversion, justification by faith
alone, man's ruin unless saved by grace, gave to the easy
decorous orthodoxy of the age, that church after church
was closed against the evangelist, now brought face to
face with a choice terrible to him. By preaching still in
parishes forbidden him, he will incur the charge of schism;
by holding his peace, he will set at nought the command
of God. "God in Scripture commands me to instruct the
ignorant, reform the wicked, confirm the virtuous. Man
forbids me to do this in another's parish—that is, in effect,
to do it at all. Whom, then, shall I hear, God or man?
Suffer me now to tell you my principles in this matter.
I look upon all the world as my parish; thus far, I mean
that in whatever part of it I am, I judge it meet, righᵗ
and my bounden duty to declare unto all that are willing
to hear, the glad tidings of salvation." "Catholic principles," if by this men meant "any other than scriptural,"
weighed nothing with him. Preaching in the open air
was at first a thing abhorrent to his taste and convictions.
" I could scarce reconcile myself to this strange way of
preaching in the fields, of which Mr. Whitefield set me
an example, having been all my life (till very lately) so
tenacious of every point relating to decency and order,
that I should have thought the saving of souls almost a
sin if it had not been done in a church." Yet at a later
day he wrote: "It is field preaching which does the
execution still; for usefulness there is none comparable
to it." All his work he looked on as work compatible
with faithfulness to his Church. Nothing that he raised
up was designed by him to stand in its place or undermine
its influence; he wished to extend, to supplement, to increase the true strength of the Church by his disregard of
human limitations which were dangerous and hurtful. All
that he regarded as essential in the Church of England
commanded his reverent love. The Church prayers he
found "full of life." Usages which, though not claiming

vital importance, his Church had inherited from primitive times, were altogether to his taste ; though, as his time and thoughts became absorbed in practical labour, we hear little about most of these from him.   Church seasons were times of especial enjoyment to this loyal son.   All Saints' Day lifted his rapt soul into the joys of the communion of saints.   To such a man, thus bound by ancestral ties, attached to the Church in all the tastes and habits of his life, one with the Church in the strongest convictions of his mature thought, the very idea of desertion was intolerable ; and with all his power, with words of the greatest vehemence, with reiterated appeal, he cried out against separation.   He was in his own belief to the very last a true member of the Church of England.   And yet, with an inconsistency which he acknowledged, though he seems never to have deeply felt its force, he broke through the most binding laws of the Church he so much loved. Three years before his death he reviewed his action in this regard.   He specifies the points of discipline in which he and his followers had taken a separate course.   They had preached in the fields.   They had used extemporary prayer.   They had employed lay-preachers, had formed and regulated Societies, had held yearly Conferences. But they were not conscious of varying from the Church in any point of doctrine ; nor had they premeditatedly or willingly varied even in a single article of discipline. What variations there had been he declares had been forced on them.   "We did none of these things till we were convinced we could no longer omit them, but at the peril of our souls."   The one chief transgression of Church order Mr. Wesley does not in this passage directly specify. Though only a presbyter, he had presumed to *ordain*. Most unwillingly, after long hesitation, did he come to this point, the crowning point of disunion.   The work of God required that men should be set apart to help.   Lay evangelists could accomplish very much, but they could not furnish to the souls whom God had given him all they needed.   The Lord who had saved these souls in myriads,

and had prescribed the needed ministries of grace, could
not design that these ministries should be wanting. John
Wesley sought earnestly that the want might be supplied
according to the established usage of his Church; but he
sought in vain. Still he was fain to struggle on with the
small band of clergymen who lent their aid. But wider
claims pressed upon him, followers in distant lands had no
such provision as his flock at home possessed, and—lest
God's work should suffer—this loyal-hearted Churchman
at last passed the Rubicon, assumed what hitherto he had
held to be a bishop's right, and ordained pastors and
superintendents of the Church. The action brought him
obloquy, but there was no misgiving in his mind. He
felt himself linked with primitive times, but in such actions
he offered in sacrifice the instincts and habits of his life.
To a man so constituted the wrench was terrible. All
these actions of his were consistent in their inconsistency:
"This one thing I do." To spread scriptural holiness
throughout the land was the one object of his life; whatever conflicted with this must be thrust aside, whatever
this entailed must be accepted as ordained by God. A
man so single in his aim could be turned aside by no
opposition from friend or enemy. Raging mobs assailed
his people, and laid hands on himself. With calm courage
he faced his foes, and daunted them by his simple stedfastness. "He who fears God," says Leighton, "knows no
other fear;" and this righteous man was "bold as a lion."
His reputation was from time to time threatened by
slanderers; he could not pause to defend his good name,
for his record was on high, and to God he committed his
cause. His keen logical mind delighted in definitions
and in points of dogma carefully laid down, and yet he is
never weary of proclaiming the worthlessness of mere
orthodoxy and right opinion. The very man who effectually secured the adherence of his workers after him to the
general body of teaching which he received as truth,
glories in the possibility of combining the love and service
of God with most diverse convictions as to points of

doctrine. " Is a man a believer in Jesus Christ ? and is his life suitable to his profession ? are not only the *main* but the *sole* inquiries I make in order to his admission into our Society." Vehement in maintaining essential truth, stringent, even to apparent intolerance, in correcting practical error, whether promulgated by friends or by foes, he was just as ready to accept correction : he went through life seeking to learn, accepting new light with eagerness. He took up the burden of responsibility, when Providence assigned it to him, with a readiness that smaller and less single-hearted men have wholly failed to understand. " Ambition was his ruling passion," says one ; " He was an autocrat who clung to power with tenacious grip, as for very life," is the opinion of others. But patient study of his life has vindicated as well the ruler as the preacher of Methodism. Only a firm rule could keep together the hosts of converts which God had brought together, the helpers whom he had called to work at his side. But here also were the certain signs of the single aim—nothing for himself, everything for the work of God ! Unwearied, unfaltering, thinking nothing done if only something remained to be done, strong in the consciousness that the cause was God's, upheld by the habitual reference of all difficulty, perplexity, misadventure, persecution, to the same Almighty and All-Wise Guide, he patiently and calmly, but at full stretch and without a thought of faltering, went through his amazing course of toil, leaving to all his followers the spectacle of labours that perhaps no man ever surpassed. When more than sixty years of age, he preached fifteen or sixteen times a week ; at particular periods, as often as eighty or ninety times a month. Even beyond the age of eighty-seven he still pursued his unresting toil ; and his last sermon was preached only a week before his death.

The lesson of this wonderful life is not impaired when we listen to the imperious demand which critics make, that we should acknowledge the presence of faults and weaknesses of intellect or character. We set up no object of worship in the man we one and all revere. True, we say but little in the critic's peculiar vein ; for what reverent and loving child will keenly scrutinise a parent's features that he may find a wrinkle or a scar? We whose calling it is to imitate the grand life-purpose, feel our littleness too deeply to be willing to dwell long on this or that alleged error of judgment or mistake in action. But this we fearlessly declare, that the inconsistencies and shortcomings to which some point with scorn or ridicule, do but make the lesson of the life more manifest and enhance its greatness.

Let us come back to his own words in description of the consistent attitude of his whole career. They are well-known words; but in their solemnity, their vividness, their transparent truthfulness, they are ever fresh, ever fraught with energy and power. "To candid, reasonable men," he says, in the preface to his sermons, written in the year 1747, "I am not afraid to lay open what have been the inmost thoughts of my heart. I have thought I am a creature of a day, passing through life as an arrow through the air. I am a spirit come from God, and returning to God—just hovering over the great gulf, till, a few moments hence, I am no more seen ; I drop into an unchangeable eternity ! I want to know one thing—the way to heaven ; how to land safe on that happy shore. God Himself has condescended to teach the way. For this very end He came from heaven. He hath written it down in a book. Oh, give me that book ! At any price, give me the book of God ! I have it ; here is knowledge enough for me. Let me be a man of one book. Here, then, I am, far from the busy ways of men. I sit down alone ; only God is here. In His presence I open, I read His book ; for this end, to find the way to heaven. Is there a doubt concerning the meaning of what I read? Does anything appear dark or intricate? I lift up my heart to the Father of Lights : 'Lord, is it not Thy word, "If any man lack wisdom, let him ask of God"? Thou "givest liberally, and upbraidest not." Thou hast said, "If any be willing to do

Thy will, he shall know." I am willing to do; let me
know Thy will.' I then search after and consider parallel
passages of Scripture, 'comparing spiritual things with
spiritual.' I meditate thereon with all the attention and
earnestness of which my mind is capable. If any doubt
still remains, I consult those who are experienced in the
things of God, and then the writings whereby, being dead,
they yet speak. And what I thus learn, that I teach. I
have accordingly set down in the following sermons what
I find in the Bible concerning the way to heaven; with a
view to distinguish this way of God from all those which
are the inventions of men. I have endeavoured to describe the true, the scriptural, experimental religion, so as
to omit nothing which is a real part thereof, and to add
nothing thereto which is not. And herein it is more
especially my desire, first, to guard those who are just
setting their faces toward heaven (and who, having little
acquaintance with the things of God, are the more liable
to be turned out of the way), from formality, from mere
outside religion, which has almost driven heart religion
out of the world; and, secondly, to warn those who know
the religion of the heart, the faith which worketh by love,
lest at any time they make void the law through faith, and
so fall back into the snare of the devil."

These memorable words show that Wesley was "ambitious" and an "enthusiast." His enthusiasm was to save
the perishing, and to raise up for God a holy people; his
ambition was to be a father to those whom by God's grace
he had gathered from the world. In the simplicity of his
purpose, in the single-heartedness of his toil, he, were he
present with us now, would rebuke the expression of our
filial reverence and love, if we rested content with admiration of a life-service long since fulfilled. The justification
of our study of the past is in the teaching which it affords
for the present age and ages yet to come.

The Divine method of training is through the power of
example. One perfect model has been granted to man.

" How sayest thou, Show us the Father? Believest thou not that I am in the Father, and the Father in Me? He that hath seen Me hath seen the Father." " He," therefore, " who saith he abideth in Christ, ought himself so to walk even as He walked." The life of Christ, like the words of Christ, is ever in advance of man. As successive ages bring stores of added knowledge, and develop new powers, and bring to light new wants, they at the same time and by consequence prepare men for discovering the wider scope and deeper meaning of the words that have grown familiar, and the well-known features of the perfect life. But lower examples possess a power of their own. " Be ye imitators of me," says the Apostle Paul, " even as I am of Christ." With limited range, with conditioned application, the example of an apostle, because nearer to our level, may be fraught with special blessing. Descending lower still, but still high above us, the consecrated lives of the great and good are powerful to raise us towards the higher region in which they served their Lord. But if their example is easier for our study and contemplation, the principles displayed can less certainly be taken *as they are* for the shaping of our life. Each man is moulded by his age, even though his stamp impress itself again upon that age. In our study of the heroes of the past, we must learn to distinguish between what is fleeting and what is permanent in the characteristics of their life. The action of a past year may be out of place to-day, though its living spirit may be the very guide we this moment need.

It would be a task of deepest interest and lasting importance, to inquire how John Wesley's life from first to last stood related to the spirit of the eighteenth century. This is a subject I cannot touch to-day. We have a harder task before us—a problem not to be solved in this brief hour, but to be worked out by us all ; for even if it be in spite of ourselves, we must be *makers of history.* How may the lessons of John Wesley's life be adapted to the conditions

of the age in which we live? It is idle to exclaim that
they may be adopted without change, that we may imitate
as a faithful copyist reproduces the manuscript before him.
We live in an age whose novel characteristics have hardly
yet lost their power to cause surprise.   The world of
thought has been revolutionised by the spirit of historical
study, and by the wonderful scientific discoveries of our
time.   A deeper and truer study of events in their mutual
relations, a more exact investigation of the witness that
describes the past, have now given firm compactness to
our knowledge of that which was in earlier days.   We
may have lost by the tendency to rest content with
second causes; but the light of an ever-present Providence
will soon illumine all the scene.   There has been a deeper
study of men, and complex human nature is felt to possess
true unity.   There is a more real and profound sympathy
between man and man.   We rejoice in a growing spirit of
toleration, though we see with troubled hearts how easily
our growing respect for the convictions of others may
pass into an enervating influence, so that we feebly grasp
our own.   The amazing revelations of physical science
have reorganised our modes of life.   Separate communities
have developed into a single, ever-moving mass of human
life; and, as many have gone to and fro, knowledge has
been increased and experience widened.   Alas! life has
well-nigh lost its quietness: the impetuous torrent rushes
past, and we look on with bewilderment.   The hurry of life
has led to a longing for compensating ease and comfort,
and a spirit of indulgence hovers about us, threatening
many of us with the curse of indolence and sloth.   The
keen scientific method claims admission everywhere, and
will bring all things to the test.   Creeds and dogmas that
have stood the scrutiny of centuries, are fearlessly put to
the question.   There is distrust of established formulas:
veneration retires ; respect for authority, as authority, grows
ever less.   Thankfully, however, do we recognise a growth
in sincerity, a hatred of hollow profession, an impatience

when the life belies the creed uttered by the lips. Man's
life is developed on many sides, and a broader culture (we
may well believe) is preparing the way for more perfect
and deeper knowledge. The Church of Christ has felt
both the stimulating influence and the testing power of the
new spirit that breathes around us. In the midst there
has been the ever-present Spirit of God. His blessed
influence has at one time been brought to clearer manifestation by the influences we have traced, but at another
it has been disguised and trammelled by the adverse
forces which have been permitted for a while to exert
their power.

In the Church of England we recognise a marvellous revival of religious earnestness and personal devotion. We
mourn, as a child for a parent, when we see the noble
organism animated by a spirit of priestliness, which often
prevents true fellowship of the sinner with his Saviour.
By the side of the Church of England, other noble and
powerful Churches are rising into new life and vigour.
The blessed message of God's love was never more widely
diffused ; but, on the other hand, doctrines which seem to
us the true criterion of a standing or a falling Church, are
not always proclaimed with a clear and certain sound.
Most of all is our gratitude kindled by the abounding
zeal with which the holy Word of God is studied, the
loving care with which every line of Sacred Writ is
scanned. The strong light which has been concentrated
on the written revelation, has disclosed new problems and
new difficulties ; but difficulties have from the beginning
been the alluring charm by which God has drawn us on
from stage to stage in our pursuit of truth. The Church
has recognised its full responsibility for the life of men to
whom it proclaims the call of God's Spirit ; and if the new
be so guided as not to eclipse the old, if the spirit of
evangelistic work move side by side with that of social
amelioration and tender beneficence, we may look forward with exultant hope to the triumph of love over a
selfish world.

E

Hurry and turmoil invade us even in these sacred courts. Terribly has the Church suffered from the frequent sacrifice of quiet hours, of privacy in working, of meditative study amid the atmosphere of fervent and continued prayer. But great has been the gain by the wide diffusion of sacred knowledge, by the influence which has been seized for good by many who have understood that light is power, and have dragged the deeds of darkness from the secret places in which they had lingered from age to age. The influences throughout have been of mingled character : evil and good have been at war. But the evil tendencies may be resisted, and the good are leading on to victory. But, whether for evil or for good, these are the moulding forces of our age. We may look back on a former age, and say, How easy would it then have been to live. But this is a word of cowardice, not of faith. The present *must* bring difficulty, because the Christian life is a life of faith. We may fear when we " enter into the cloud ; " but it is only through the cloud that we can win our way to the light.

What shall our future be ? The Methodism of to-day has already felt the influence of those very forces which we have passed under review. I have not attempted to trace the difference between Methodism as it is to-day, and as it was when its Founder passed from earth's conflict to heaven's rest. This is a matter of historical inquiry, most attractive and most beneficial if thoroughly pursued. But we are not historians : we are men of action, women of action. The future waits for us who are the living Methodists of to-day,—depends upon us, must be moulded by us. In so far as we apprehend and make our own the living influences around us and within us, shall we be a source of living power for the years that are not yet born.

Oh that we may now catch the inspiration of the words with which we began our meditation this afternoon ! We have seen the comment on them furnished by John Wesley's life. He was wide in his sympathies, open to all the teaching of God's providence, a man ever learning, broad in his culture, one who sought by every means and appliance to attract men and to train every power and faculty into the obedience of Christ. But the great doctrines of salvation stood first with him, and a profound Christian experience was the life of his life. Oh, Methodists of to-day, hold fast the doctrines of our fathers with a firm and steady grip; but let them never be divorced from the Christian experience which reveals the life and soul of the doctrines themselves! May our conversion be clear, our conviction of sin intense, our joy in the Lord exultant, our consecration to Him complete! And when we pass from the thought of the common possession of all Christ's servants, and have to choose each one for himself what special gifts we shall seek, what special course we shall follow, then may we be saved from distraction by the simplicity of our aim! If we have St. Paul's singleness of purpose, St. Paul's breathless effort and energy of life, we shall be free to choose, we shall see our appointed work, we shall serve the Lord without distracting thought. Every element of life belongs to Christ, but in the absence of the one mighty and constraining force it is possible that we may cultivate the lesser faculty and neglect the higher. Learning and art and science, citizenship, business, trade, recreation, literature, travel, the quiet home, the busy market, the toil of solitude, the excitement of thronged assemblies,— whatever may be the calling of each man, each woman, —we shall be fitted for all our work, if the principle that guided Paul and Wesley alike is our unfailing guide. Temptations to sloth will not touch the man thus armed, wider culture will not mean a looser hold of truth, zeal for the aggrandisement of a Church will not take the place of devotion to the Lord Himself. We shall live in the world, move in the world, but our life will be animated by the faith which overcomes the world, and our movement will be ceaselessly to press forward to the mark

for the prize of our high calling of God in Christ
Jesus.

> " O God, to whom the faithful dead
> Still live, united to their Head,
>   Their Lord, and ours the same,
> For all Thy saints, to memory dear.
> Departed in Thy faith and fear,
>   We bless Thy holy Name !
>
> " By the same grace upheld, may we
> So follow those who followed Thee,
>   As with them to partake
> The full reward of heavenly bliss :
> Merciful Father ! grant us this
>   For our Redeemer's sake ! "   Amen.

The
Theology of John Wesley.

By THE REV. R. W. DALE, LL.D.

———o———

> " When it was the good pleasure of God, who
> separated me, even from my mother's womb, and
> called me through His grace, to reveal His Son in
> me, that I might preach Him among the Gentiles :
> immediately I conferred not with flesh and blood :
> neither went I up to Jerusalem to them which were
> apostles before me."—GAL. i. 15-17.

THE faith of the Galatian Churches was being corrupted
by Judaizing teachers, who assailed that large and spiritual
interpretation of the gospel of Christ which was given by
Paul ; and they sustained their assault by insisting that
he was not one of the original apostles who had received
their authority from our Lord, and that the original
apostles had given him no commission. He does not
attempt to qualify his independence of the first preachers
of the Christian gospel, the divinely-authorised founders
of the Christian Church. He shows a certain eagerness
and exultation in asserting it. He asserts it in the very
first sentence of his letter : he is *not* an apostle "from
men," his commission was from Heaven ; and his commission had not come to him "through men," he had
not received it through the intervention of any Church

rulers to whom Christ had delegated any part of His authority, but direct from "Jesus Christ" Himself, and "God the Father who raised Him from the dead."

He will stand in no succession. This, for which his enemies reproached him, is the secret of his power ; in this he glories. In the text he expands the declaration with which the letter begins. It was the "good pleasure" of God—God's free, spontaneous, unsought, unmerited grace—that had made him an apostle ; and this grace had been manifested in several ways.

GOD'S GRACE MANIFESTED TO PAUL.

(1) First, he says, "From my very birth God 'separated' me to this work." As Paul looked back upon his life, he could see that the Divine purpose had been controlling his personal history from the very first, and preparing him for a service of which he had no thought, and which, if it had been proposed to him, he would have regarded with horror. His birth, by which he inherited the rights of Roman citizenship,—though he was also "of the stock of Benjamin, a Hebrew of the Hebrews:" his early years in Tarsus, a great Greek city, famous for its wealth, its commerce, and its schools of learning and philosophy ; his life as a student in Jerusalem ; his zeal in mastering the doctrines and methods of the Rabbis ; the earnestness and fidelity with which he had submitted to the discipline of the most austere of Jewish sects, so that "touching the righteousness which is in the law" he was "blameless ;"—all these had contributed in various ways to his fitness for the work to which God had destined him.

(2) God Himself—without the intervention of apostles, without human intervention of any kind—had spoken to him the strong and gracious word which had broken his heart to penitence, and which had drawn him to Christ. There had been no movement towards Christ on his own part. He was on his way to Damascus, vehement, passionate in his hatred of the new sect ; resolved to suppress it :

it was God's "grace"—what else?—that "called" him to receive the Christian redemption and to preach the Christian gospel. At that point, indeed, his own free response to the grace of God came in. Till now all that God had done to prepare him for his apostleship was done without any free concurrence of his in God's great purpose ; he had known nothing of it. But now he might have thwarted and defeated the Divine love ; but, as he says elsewhere, he "was not disobedient to the heavenly vision."

And (3) he adds, "It was the good pleasure of God . . . to reveal His Son in me that I might preach Him among the Gentiles." The revelation came, not for his own sake merely, but for the sake of the heathen men to whom he was to preach it ; and it, therefore, came to him in a form which was determined by their condition as well as his own.

GOD'S GRACE MANIFESTED TO JOHN WESLEY.

These three manifestations of God's free, spontaneous grace to Paul have their parallel in the history of John Wesley, whose great and venerable name has drawn us together this morning.

(1) He too might have said that from his very birth God had "separated," set him apart, for the work of recovering large masses of the English people from irreligion and vice, and founding a religious Society which would extend to all lands. There was an heroic strain in his blood : his parents, on both sides, were the descendants of Puritan ministers, who had endured cruel persecution for their fidelity to what they believed to be the will of God. But he was saved from the peril which comes upon men who are the heirs of great religious movements which have spent their strength ; he was not to attempt to rekindle the glorious fires of Puritanism, and so he was born in a country rectory. In the discipline of his childhood and youth, a reverence for authority, and a care for the external institutions and aids of the religious life characteristic of

the great Anglicans, were blended with the traditions of Puritanism. His father, a High Churchman, was a man of courage and zeal ; he was deeply moved by the condition of heathen countries, proposed a scheme for carrying the gospel of Christ to the remotest shores that had been reached by English trade, and offered to go out among the first missionaries. For his mother John Wesley had always the profoundest reverence. She was a woman of remarkable natural sagacity, and he had almost unmeasured confidence in her judgment. She had a vigorous and cultivated mind, and there was great depth and strength in her religious life.

As he was passing from youth to manhood, the best elements in the Oxford of those days and the worst, the zeal for righteousness of the small group of young men of whom he became the leader, the scorn, the mockery, the insult which their zeal provoked,—all these were part of the discipline by which he was prepared for his work. His experience in Georgia was part of it. By God's grace he had been separated to it from his birth.

(2) By God's "grace" he was "called," if not with the accompaniment of visible miracle, as Paul was called on the road to Damascus, yet by a movement of the Divine love, not less free and not less supernatural. For John Wesley would have said with an earnestness as deep and passionate as that of the most faithful disciple of John Calvin, " I sought God because God sought me. I found God because God found me." The saints are divided by their theologies, but they are one in their faith, and they all confess, " We love Him because He first loved us."

(3) It is, however, to the third illustration of God's grace in Wesley's history that I propose to direct your special consideration. He too could have said with Paul, " It was the good pleasure of God to *reveal His Son* in me, that I might preach Him." You will understand at once that I refer to the experience through which he passed on the evening of Wednesday, the 24th of May 1738, when he was thirty-five years of age, an experience so

remarkable that for many years he was accustomed to speak of it as his real conversion, the time when his sins were forgiven, the beginning of his life in God through Christ. That wonderful experience, that revelation of Christ, had, as I think, a direct and vital relation to all that has given the name of John Wesley an enduring place in the history of Christendom. But for *that*, there would have been no Methodist revival ; but for *that*, the great sisterhood of Methodist Societies represented at this commemoration, belonging to many races, speaking many tongues, and which might be described, with pardonable rhetorical exaggeration, as gathered out of every country under heaven,—but for that great experience, that revelation of Christ in John Wesley, these Societies would have had no existence. The "good pleasure" of God, the purposes of His grace in relation to England and the world, might have been fulfilled in other ways, but not by you.

THE METHODIST REVIVAL AND THE NONCONFORMIST CHURCHES.

Nor is it the Methodist Societies alone that have reason to look back with deep and devout interest to that memorable hour. As you have done me the great and unmerited honour of permitting me to be here this morning, I desire to acknowledge with devout gratitude the grace of God which through you has reached many Churches having an earlier origin than yours, and a polity different from your own ; Churches which for more than two generations were widely separated from yours by mutual distrust—distrust created in part by serious theological differences, in part by differences in relation to evangelistic methods and the discipline of the spiritual life.

The obligations which, under God, the older Nonconformist Churches of England owe to Methodism cannot be measured. When John Wesley began his work, their strength had been seriously diminished. There were complaints that congregations were wasting away; that the sons and the daughters of the wealthier Nonconformists were passing over to the Episcopal Church. It was said that between the accession of George I., in 1714, and the year 1731, more than fifty Dissenting ministers took Orders in the Establishment. Those who contested the accuracy of the stronger statements concerning the decay of the Dissenting interest, and who insisted that if in some parts of the country Dissenting Churches were declining, in others their numbers were growing, acknowledged that the Dissenters were discouraged; that they were suffering from a want of buoyancy and energy in their religious life; that the stricter manners and the severer morals of an earlier generation were disappearing; and that the movement of theological opinion gave occasion to great anxiety. To you for a long time our fathers did not look for deliverance. Wesley's Arminianism filled them with alarm. Nor was their alarm without reason. There had been a great drifting among the Nonconformist Churches during the first thirty or forty years of the eighteenth century from the central articles of the Christian faith, and this was one of the principal causes of their weakness. The Divinity of our Lord had been denied, and the atonement which He achieved for men by His death; and these grave and ruinous errors had almost always begun with a surrender of the characteristic doctrines of Calvinism. Even where Arminianism had not come to these disastrous issues, it had paralysed the strength of Christian faith, and quenched the fire of spiritual earnestness.

But creeds which coincide in some of their principal articles may cover wholly different systems of religious thought, and wholly different conditions of the spiritual life. The Arminianism of many of the Nonconformists, at the beginning of the eighteenth century, appears to have come in part from that cold and powerless conception of God which is given by Deism, a conception which removes Him to an infinite distance from all His creatures.

It was the result of a decaying sense of the energy and freedom of the life of the Eternal, and of God's immanent presence and activity in the material universe and in man. It affirmed that man was free, partly because it conceived of God as remote.

Wesley's Arminianism had a wholly different root. For him the universe was not a wonderful mechanism which had been projected into being by a succession of creative acts, and then left to work according to the laws of its structure; for him God did not live apart from the creation, reigning in heights of inaccessible majesty. He believed that in God we live and move and have our being. And yet in the strength of his own moral life he had a most vivid consciousness that he was morally free—free to receive or reject the infinite grace which the living God was pressing upon him; and therefore he was an Arminian. For a time the more serious Nonconformists did not discover the immense moral and spiritual difference between the old Arminianism and the new. The walls of mutual distrust which separated your fathers and mine stood firm and without a breach till long after George III. was king.

But while the separating walls were still standing, the fires which were kindled on your side were burning so fiercely that the heat came through. The flames rose high, and sparks fell over. You made the very atmosphere so hot that dry timber took fire, we knew not how. We listened—at first reluctantly—to Whitefield and the leaders of the Calvinistic revival, and discovered that God was doing a wonderful work before our very eyes, though it was not being done according to our traditions. Then we began to listen to you; it was not far from the Tabernacle to the Foundery. A little later we drew closer to each other. I could give you a considerable list of eminent Congregational ministers who, towards the close of the last century and the beginning of this, brought to the service of the Congregational churches the religious life which had been originated, the religious zeal which had

been kindled, among Methodists. William Jay of Bath
discovered the glory and grace of the Christian redemption
at a Methodist service. My colleague and predecessor,
John Angell James, did not attribute his religious decision
to Methodist preaching ; but he says in his Autobiography,
that when he was a boy at Blandford, the only religious
fire in the town was among the Methodists; he was taken
by his mother to Methodist meetings on Sunday nights,
and there was a touch of Methodism in him to the very
last. He always smelt of that fire. Thomas Raffles of
Liverpool in his early life was a member of the Wesleyan
Society. John Leifchild of Craven was originally one of
your preachers. The great revival which originated
Methodism restored life, vigour, courage, fervour to the
Congregational churches of England.

JOHN WESLEY'S GREAT EXPERIENCE.

And, as I have said, Methodism owes its existence,
under God, to that great experience through which John
Wesley passed in a little room within a mile of this place
on the evening of May 24, 1738. You all know the story.
I am conscious of presumption in venturing to speak
about it in such an assembly as this ; but I ask you to
bear with me,—I care to speak of nothing else.

Wesley became a Fellow of Lincoln in 1726, and from
that time his great concern was to live a religious life.
During the following twelve years, the earnestness with
which he endeavoured to carry out his purpose was constantly becoming more intense. He began by setting
apart an hour or two a day for prayer and religious
meditation. He received the Lord's Supper every week.
He fasted on Wednesday and Friday. His method of life
was severe. He visited the prisoners in Oxford gaol ; he
went from house to house among the poor and the sick of
the city, and denied himself not only the "superfluities"
— to use his own words — but "many that are called
necessaries of life," that he might do what good he

could by his presence or his little fortune to the bodies and souls of all men. He diligently strove against all sin. He pursued "inward holiness,"—the "union of the soul with God." He became the leader of a number of devout young men who were of the same mind as himself; he was their counsellor and their strong support. He had a passion for the conversion of the heathen, and went out to Georgia with the hope of being able to preach the gospel to the Indians in that part of America. The attention of the whole University was drawn to his extraordinary zeal.

But when he returned from America he was in an agony of distress about his own salvation. He had gone to Georgia to convert the heathen; and he had learnt—so he thought—that he himself was not converted. In his later years he modified his opinion concerning the true nature of the experiences through which he passed in May 1738. He came to the conclusion that he was not, as he supposed, "alienated from the life of God" till then, "a child of wrath," "an heir of hell;" and I think that most thoughtful readers of his Journals will be of the same judgment. But he always retained the belief that that great experience was of transcendent importance. In this he was wholly right. If not critical for Wesley himself, in the way he had once supposed, it was critical for Methodism.

Immediately after he had passed through it, he wrote this explanation of what he believed to have been the fatal defect of his previous religious life :—

"In my return to England, January 1738, being in imminent danger of death, and very uneasy on that account, I was strongly convinced that the cause of that uneasiness was unbelief, and that the gaining of a true living faith was the 'one thing needful for me.' But still *I fixed not this faith on its right object. I meant only faith in God, not faith in or through Christ.* Again, I knew not that I was wholly void of this faith, but only thought I had not enough of it."

As the result of his conversations with Peter Böhler, he

came to see that he must renounce all dependence, in whole or in part, upon his own works or righteousness, and seek by continual prayer what he describes as "justifying, saving faith, a full reliance on the blood of Christ shed for *me*, a trust in Him, as *my* Christ, as my sole justification, sanctification, and redemption."

The faith came. Listen to his own account of what happened on that memorable evening.

"I went," he says, "very unwillingly to a Society in Aldersgate Street, where one was reading Luther's Preface to the Epistle to the Romans. About a quarter before nine, while he was describing the change which God works in the heart through faith in Christ, I felt my heart strangely warmed. I felt I did trust in Christ, Christ alone for salvation. And an assurance was given me that He had taken away *my* sins, even *mine*, and saved *me* from the law of sin and death."

Tell me whether he might not have described all this in Paul's words, "It was the good pleasure of God to reveal His Son in me"?

Is there any account to be given of the nature and sources of the change through which he passed on that evening? I will make the attempt.

It is apparent that at the very core of Wesley's nature there was an immoveable conviction that his will was morally free. This made him an Arminian. His acts were his own; they were not determined by blind fate or any Divine decree. It is also apparent that to him the Divine law was august, awful. He saw, as few men have ever seen, the infinite significance of the contrast between obedience and disobedience, sin and righteousness. He had sinned, and the sense of his guilt sometimes became intolerable. During his misery he felt that it was God's own hand that was heavy upon him; and that the condemnation of conscience revealed, but only partially revealed, the more appalling condemnation of God.

Further, it is apparent that he believed that our knowledge of God is real as far as it goes; and that what we

call His attributes are not mere subjective representations
of Him determined by the structure and laws of our own
minds, but answer to something real and objective in the
life of the Eternal; that as His will is not identical with
His knowledge, His justice is not identical with His
grace. In one of his sermons he speaks of men who
quiet their fears "by saying 'God is merciful;' confound-
ing and swallowing up all at once in *that unwieldy idea of
mercy*, all His holiness and essential hatred of sin; all
His justice, wisdom, and truth."

He knew that God was merciful. His mercy had been
revealed in Christ, who had come to seek and to save the
lost, and who had set forth the freedom of the Divine
grace in the parable of the Prodigal Son. Yes; but God
was just; and to Wesley the justice was as real as the
mercy, and as essential an element and force in God's
eternal, unchangeable, absolute life. Indeed, apart from
justice, mercy cannot even be thought; any more than
the finite can be thought apart from the infinite, the
relative apart from the absolute. There is no mercy where
there is no guilt. If sin is nothing more than a transient
though necessary incident of human development, or if it
is nothing more than a disease of the moral life, it needs
no forgiveness; there is nothing to forgive. If a disease
and nothing more, it appeals—not to the Divine mercy to
pardon — but to the Divine compassion and power to
cure. If a necessary incident in the development of the
moral life of man, then, again, as it cannot be the object
of Divine hostility and resentment, there is nothing in it
for the Divine mercy to forgive; it will gradually dis-
appear in the predetermined process of that Divine movement by which the race is advancing towards perfection.

But to Wesley his own sin was a violent and voluntary
disturbance of the ordered relations between man and
God. It was not a misfortune, but a crime. The responsibility for it was his; the guilt of it was his; and he
believed, and believed rightly, that his sense of guilt was
in truth his apprehension and sense of the righteousness

of God condemning him for his sin, and menacing him with awful punishment. It was because he was *justly* condemned, and because he was *justly* menaced with punishment, that he was in such sore need of mercy. He had heard, he had received, he had preached the gospel of the Divine grace, offering to all men the remission of sins; but his conscience demanded a gospel of which, during the twelve years preceding 1738, he had no real grasp, and this prevented him from finding peace. Justice condemned him, if mercy forgave him. In his conception of God he could not suppress the justice, even in the presence of the strongest assurances of the mercy. To him the two ideas, each necessary to the other, were irreconcilable contraries. He found, not their transcendent, but their actual and concrete synthesis in Christ — in Christ whose "blood was shed for him;" in Christ, who was his "sole justification, sanctification, and redemption." Till now, to use his own words, his faith had not been fixed on "its right object;" it had been "faith in God, not faith in or through Christ." Now his faith rested in Christ, and, as he says, "an assurance was given me that He had taken away *my* sins, even *mine*, and saved *me* from the law of sin and death."

It is no part of my duty this morning to offer any proofs of the fact that Christ died for the sins of men, or to attempt any illustration of the mystery. It is enough that I should remind you that in John Wesley's personal discovery of the reality of the atonement — the synthesis of justice and mercy in the death of Christ—he found the inspiration and the force which, under God, created Methodism. Methodism has its roots in a living faith in Christ as a real and objective atonement for the sin of the world. Surrender that faith, and the roots of your life are destroyed.

JOHN WESLEY'S DEFINITION OF FAITH.

Wesley proclaimed his new discovery with vehement energy. Within a month he was at Oxford, preaching before the University in the pulpit of St. Mary's on the text, " By grace are we saved through faith," and insisting that the death of Christ is "the only sufficient means of redeeming man from death eternal," and that His resurrection is "the restoration of us all to life and immortality." In a later sermon, also preached before the University, he gives his definition of faith, a definition drawn from two separate sentences in the third of the Homilies of the Church of England appointed to be read in churches in the time of Queen Elizabeth. Wesley's definition reads thus :—

" The right and true Christian faith is not only to believe that Holy Scripture and the articles of our faith are true, but also to have a sure trust and confidence to be saved from everlasting damnation by Christ. It is a sure trust and confidence which a man hath in God, that, by the merits of Christ, his sins are forgiven, and he reconciled to the favour of God ; whereof doth follow a loving heart to obey the commandments."

He repeats the substance of this definition in several of his sermons. It is a formal statement of the nature of that faith which had made so immense a difference in his own religious life. I do not propose to criticise it. The dullest intellect in Christendom might see that it is apparently open to one very elementary objection : if saving faith is a condition precedent of the forgiveness of sins and restoration to the favour of God, saving faith can hardly be a belief that we are forgiven and restored to His favour already. But as this objection is so very obvious that it must occur to the dullest of men as soon as the definition is stated, modesty requires us to assume that it probably occurred to John Wesley himself, who was one of the acutest. Indeed, there is evidence that it did occur to him.

In his old age, as the result of a deeper knowledge of the ways of God and of the religious life of man—not for mere logical reasons—he modified his judgment concerning the nature and contents of what the theologians call "saving faith." "Nearly fifty years ago," he says, "when the preachers commonly called Methodists began to preach that grand scriptural doctrine of salvation by faith, they were not sufficiently apprised of the difference between a servant and a child of God;" and now, with a breadth of thought which is not commonly attributed to any of the men of the Evangelical Revival, he defines faith as "such a Divine conviction of God as, even in its infant state, enables every one that possesses it to 'fear God and work righteousness.' And whosoever, in every nation, believes thus far, the apostle declares, is accepted of Him. He actually is, at that very moment, in a state of acceptance. But he is at present only a *servant* of God, not properly a *son*. Meantime, let it be well observed, that ' the wrath of God' no longer ' abideth on him.'"

But Wesley still insisted on the power and blessedness of the nobler faith, which he describes as "a Divine conviction, whereby every child of God is enabled to testify, The life that I now live I live by faith on the Son of God, who loved me and gave Himself for me." He still presses upon those whose faith is of the lower kind, the obligation to seek the higher; and he confidently assures them that if they seek it they will sooner or later possess it.

In the earlier years of the movement he had refused to recognise the distinction implied by the terms, "faith of adherence" and "faith of assurance." He found no such terms in the Bible. There were not "two faiths in one Lord;" but "one faith in one Lord." He said that he had never known a man saved from outward and inward sin without what was called "the faith of assurance,"—"a sure confidence that by the merits of Christ he was reconciled to the mercy of God." If he allowed any distinction between "the faith of adherence" and "the faith of assurance," he insisted, to the astonishment and confusion of the theologians, that "the faith of assurance" came first.

There were good reasons, no doubt, for revising his

original definition. It was true, as he said, that the earlier teaching made " sad the hearts of those whom God had not made sad ; " and had led to the discouragement, perhaps the fatal discouragement, of many sincere penitents. And yet that paradoxical definition of saving faith, as " a sure trust and confidence which a man hath in God that by the merits of Christ his sins are forgiven, and he reconciled to the favour of God," is perhaps truer than it seems. It is a paradox ; for if faith is the condition precedent to salvation, how can it be a belief that we are saved already ? But the definition is the result of a violent effort, breaking through the forms of the logical understanding, to express transcendent spiritual realities.

For is it not true that God has already given us—has given to all men, believers and unbelievers alike—eternal redemption in Christ ? Is it not true that we can trust God for nothing, ask God for nothing, that lies beyond the wealth of blessing which in Christ is already ours ? Does not the gift of Christ, according to the Divine thought and purpose, include all gifts ? And when we find Christ, do we not discover that in Him we already possess—and had always possessed—all things ?

Yes, it may be answered, But until we have faith in Christ, Christ is not ours, nor are the infinite blessings of His salvation ours. Is that true ? You, surely of all men, are not going to say that Christ died for those only who, as God foresaw, would afterwards believe in Him ? You, surely, are not intending to introduce into the next edition of your Hymn-book the famous verse of the great Hymn-writer of Congregationalism ?—

> " My soul looks back to see
> The burdens Thou didst bear,
> When hanging on th' accursèd tree,
> And *hopes* her guilt was there."

You do not *hope*—you *know*; and what you know is true for yourselves you know is also true for every man, saint or sinner, heathen or Christian, in every country and in every age ; for Christ is " the Propitiation " for the sins "of the whole world." There is a relation between Christ and man antecedent to man's faith and independent of it. Faith does not create that relation—it merely accepts and consciously realises a relation which exists before faith, and apart from which faith would be impossible; a relation wonderfully and mysteriously modified by the death of Christ for our sins, but which is part of the Divine order of the universe. For in Christ "were all things created, in the heavens and upon the earth,"— sun and stars, mountains and seas, angels and men; and "in Him all things consist"—hold together and endure through all the millenniums of created existence. When I find Christ, I do not fine One who till now has been far from me. I find One who has always been the very ground of my being, the very root of my life. By faith I take up my citizenship in the kingdom of God, but the citizenship was already mine by God's gift and God's purpose. By faith I accept and realize my sonship in the Divine household; but I was created in Christ to be a son. By faith I receive and rejoice in the forgiveness of my sin; but the forgiveness was already mine in Christ Jesus my Lord.

Wesley's paradox, by the very revolt to which it provokes the logical understanding, compels us to confront the transcendent mystery of the real relation of God to the human race in Christ.

THE WITNESS OF THE SPIRIT.

Finally, his original definition of faith was organically connected with the great doctrine to which Methodism has given such magnificent emphasis, That the Spirit of God bears direct witness to the spirit of man, and assures him of the forgiveness of his sins, and his Divine sonship. Indeed, the faith which the definition demands is impossible, and was seen by Wesley to be impossible, apart from this "witness."

From the very first—from the time, I mean, that he

passed through his great experience, in May 1738—
Wesley saw that for the power as well as the joy of the
Christian life it was necessary that a man should have
the complete certainty that he was no longer a "child of
wrath," but a child of God. In this he was of one mind
with Luther. For in maintaining the doctrine of Justification by Faith, it had been Luther's aim to recover for
men that full assurance of their personal salvation which
had been discouraged, if not rendered impossible, by
Romish doctrines, and by the Romish discipline of the
spiritual life. To the nations of Northern Europe which
received the Lutheran gospel, there came a sudden burst
of glorious sunshine; the clouds were driven away to
distant horizons, and men rejoiced in the light of God; it
seemed as if the age of gold had begun. But it was not
possible for Christendom to break at once with its past.
The clouds gathered again too soon. The iron times
returned.

When Wesley began his work, the religious life of
England—its best religious life—was wanting in buoyancy,
courage, vigour, adventure; and even among devout men,
the joy of the Holy Ghost, which can never be known apart
from the certainty of personal salvation, was not general.
But he knew that he himself had received from God the
direct assurance of the forgiveness of his sins and of his
Divine sonship, and he refused to believe that this was an
exceptional privilege inaccessible to other men. What *he*
had received every man that believed in Christ might
receive; for the glorious blessings which God has given to
men in Christ are the common inheritance of all believers.
From the very first, therefore, he insisted that no man
should rest until the same divinely authenticated certainty
came to him.

By the testimony of the Spirit, he means "an inward
impression on the soul, whereby the Spirit of God immediately and directly witnesses to my spirit that I am a child
of God; that Jesus Christ hath loved me and given Himself for me; that all my sins are blotted out; and I, even

I, am reconciled to God." After twenty years' consideration, he sees no cause to retract any part of this statement.
This doctrine seems to him the "grand testimony" which
God has given to the Methodists to bear to all mankind.
He says that it is by God's "peculiar blessing upon them
in searching the Scriptures, confirmed by the experience of
His children, that this great evangelical truth has been
recovered, which had been for many years well-nigh lost
and forgotten."

Yes, *confirmed by the experience of His children.* That
was the strength of Wesley's position. In the religious
life of the early Methodists, there was exhilaration, vigour,
triumph. Their joy was irrepressible. It broke out in
shouts of Hallelujah! It sang exulting songs. The old
Dissenters were perplexed—sometimes scandalised. They
heard of irreligious men, vicious men, who were writhing
in an agony of repentance yesterday, and who were
rejoicing in the certainty of forgiveness and in the sure
hope of eternal glory to-day. It was not only the sudden-
ness of the transition that confounded them, but its completeness. A fulness of assurance had come to penitents,
which, as many of them had supposed, was hardly possible
to saints.

This "assurance" was a large part of your power. It
gave to Methodism its hosts of preachers—preachers of
many kinds, and bearing many names. Personal testimony
to the power of Christ to restore men to God, this can be
given by every man to whom the witness of the Spirit has
come. For this no protracted training at college is necessary; no Hebrew, no Greek, no mastery either of Arminius
or Calvin. The man who was drunk in the streets a week
ago, if he now knows Christ for himself, can stand under
a tree or against a wall to-day, and say to every one who
will listen to him, "Christ Jesus came into the world to
save sinners, of whom I am chief." He needs no leisure
to think over that text. He has no occasion to consult
commentators as to its meaning. The carpenter can put
aside his saw and his plane; the blacksmith can throw

down his apron and his hammer, and begin at once to expound the words; his own sin, his own salvation—these have revealed to him their wonderful contents. But for Wesley's doctrine of the Witness of the Spirit, Wesleyanism would never have had its great army of lay-preachers and class-leaders; if the power of the doctrine is ever lost, that army will gradually break up and melt away.

But the doctrine did something more than give you your preachers. If the new form of the religious life, illustrated by Methodism, perplexed the grave and thoughtful Christian men of the older Churches, the common people found in it an irresistible attractiveness. It seemed to them now that the gospel was true after all—a real discovery of some infinite good, that was within the reach of every man—the revelation of an actual redemption which had been wrought for the human race. The loud Amens which came from your people confirming the words of the preacher, the glad outcries of "Glory to God!" "Praise the Lord!"—these carried home the gospel to the hearts of men who might have been almost unmoved by the testimony of a solitary man.

Nor was it on Sunday only, or only when engaged in religious services, that the Methodists had this abounding joy: it remained with them all the week through; there was a light resting upon their common path; their hearts were filled with music when there was no song on their lips. And so weary men, and men who had been discouraged and broken down by trouble; and men who had come to despair of themselves because they had been defeated in every attempt to lead a better life; and men who were miserable because they hated and despised themselves for their vice, and knew that others hated and despised them too; and men who had become lethargic and dull because their horizons were narrow and their occupations and thoughts monotonous—men whose imaginations had never been kindled, whose hearts had never been stirred; and men who were happy as yet, but who had begun to see that the streams of earthly happiness soon run dry;—

all sorts of men were charmed, excited, by the discovery that people like themselves had found the springs of an immortal gladness and strength. There was mystery in it ; but mystery itself has an eternal power over the hearts of men. The Methodists said that they were filled with joy because they had found God ; and is there not a secret conviction in the heart of every man that to find God is man's supreme blessedness ?

It was largely in the strength of your testimony to the witness of the Spirit that you won your early triumphs. I have said that if your faith in this doctrine ever declines, you will lose your preachers. I say now that even if you kept your preachers, their great successes would be over ; for it is the common experience of the Methodist people, confirming every declaration of their preachers concerning the reality and greatness of the Christian redemption, that, under God, gives to the testimony of your preachers pathos and power.

CONCLUSION.

I have spoken with a freedom which, as a minister of another Church, I have no right to assume ; and yet it is not another Church, for we are all one in Christ. In your strength Evangelical Christendom is strong ; in your weakness Evangelical Christendom would be weak. If I have ventured to appeal to you with unbecoming and presumptuous urgency to be loyal to our common faith, it is because I am so deeply conscious that the fortunes of the Congregational churches of England cannot be separated from yours. You are the heirs of great traditions. You stand in a noble succession. But—

> "They who on glorious ancestry enlarge,
> Produce their debt instead of their discharge."

You have done so much, that you are under awful responsibilities to the nations in which your Societies are already planted, and to the nations to which you have still to make known the unsearchable riches of God's grace. Keep faith with your fathers, keep faith with Christ; keep faith with your children and your children's children, transmit to coming generations the gospel which has already won such splendid triumphs. That "Word of God" which Wesley preached, "liveth and abideth for ever." It is translated into new tongues; it is conceived in changing forms by the changing minds of men; every deeper discovery of the relations between God and man adds to its wealth and power; but it remains—that living Word of God—the same in its substance through all centuries, its strength unspent, its glory undimmed.

It is a great gospel, which you and your fathers have preached during the hundred and fifty years of your history, a gospel which declares the love of God for all men. Preach it still with the same confidence of faith and the same passion of joy. Tell men that, while they inherit by their birth the infirmities and sins of the race, they also inherit by their birth the salvation which Christ has achieved for all mankind. Tell them that they live— not in a lost world, but in a redeemed world; a world lost by its revolt against God, and its alienation from the life of God, but redeemed in the blood of Christ, and with powers in Christ and in the Spirit of Christ which render all righteousness possible. Tell men—all men— that they were created in Christ, and that when they discover and accept their true relation to Him, they will live under new heavens and in a new earth, and will know the greatness of the sons of God. Tell them that they are blessed with every spiritual blessing in Christ; that God chose them in Him before the foundation of the world, that they should be holy and without blemish before Him in love; charge them not to defeat the purposes of the Divine grace, but to work out their own salvation with fear and trembling, and so to make their calling and election sure. See to it that through God's grace you know for yourselves that, by the merits of Christ, your sins are forgiven, and that you are indeed and of a truth the children of God, that your testimony to the Christian redemption may not rest on tradition, but on your own personal experience.

Assembled for this sacred commemoration, the hearts of millions of men in many lands are drawn to you, and they trust that in these services a Divine flame will kindle that will spread over the whole world. I think I see descending upon this assembly the glorious forms of millions of men of other generations, who through the ministry of your fathers escaped from eternal destruction, and whose home is in the fair city of God above. We are encompassed by a great cloud of witnesses. In their presence, in God's presence, over the very ashes of your Founder, whose death we commemorate, but who lives for evermore in the light of the Eternal, I call upon you to resolve, with all the solemnities of an oath, that you will stand fast until you die, in your fidelity to the truths which have given to Methodism its power and glory, and that henceforth you will pray with a deeper earnestness and a firmer faith that the fires of Methodism may never be extinguished. I call upon you to invoke in this great hour the good help of God, that you may surrender yourselves to His will and to His grace with a consecration so complete and unreserved, that it shall be possible for you to receive the fulness of His Spirit; and let your hearts wait on Him, in confident hope, till the fulness of His Spirit shall be yours.

Characteristics of Wesley and his Teaching.

By the Rev. PRINCIPAL RAINY, D.D., of the Free Church College, Edinburgh.

—o—

> "The things which ye both learned and received and heard and saw in me, these things do : and the God of peace shall be with you."—Phil. iv. 9.

If it is right to commemorate the mighty works of the Lord, done through His more notable servants in days gone by, then it follows that you are doing exceeding well in calling up before this generation the record of him who one hundred years ago closed his remarkable life. And when you invite some of us from other lines of ecclesiastical descent to take part in your commemoration—a summons which we receive with gratitude and pride—one asks oneself with what view the friendly invitation is given. Partly, chiefly perhaps, that it may be seen that many more besides yourselves claim part in the benefits which Wesley conferred, and are forward to own, with you, how much we all owe him. But partly also, perhaps, because you desire to hear what it occurs to those to say who look at Wesley's goodness and greatness from other standpoints than those which are furnished by Wesleyanism. I feel, at all events, that it is as natural for me to act in this view as I suppose it may be for you to expect it of me. Leaving, therefore, others, to whom it more properly falls, to estimate the influence which Wesley has exerted in the world, and to pronounce the due panegyric on his life and work, I propose only to note one or two impressions and lessons which I think we may all lay to heart, especially in times like ours. I take the text as embodying this admonition, that men whom God has eminently blessed to us should be studied both in their teaching and in the manner of their life and work. Whatever their limits or their imperfections, it is likely that we shall find in this way suggestions as to following and serving Christ, which we cannot afford to want.

Wesley was the leading spirit in a great work of awakening. That awakening has been propagating its effects ever since. It proved to be God's way of redeeming the battle, in days when the battle went sore against truth and life both. It proved to be decisive in its influence on the whole religious history of England and America, not to speak now of influences in other fields. And if others shared with Wesley the honour of beginning this work of God, yet it was as controlled, organised, and sent on its way by Wesley that the movement became decisive, and made its great mark upon the religious history of the world. To him, under God, we mainly trace it that new thoughts, new aims, new hopes arose everywhere among the Churches, coming as spring after winter, with life and with hope.

It is natural to ask what it was in Wesley that led on to so great a success. For while we own the Divine grace which prepared him for his service and crowned his efforts, yet we suppose that God fitted the agent to the work. So far as one can see, stress might be laid on two undoubted facts—first, that Wesley had native power to move his fellows, and secondly, that he was sagacious in affairs. Influence in those two lines is conspicuous throughout his life ; but I do not think that in those quarters we shall find the eminence which made his work so exceptional in its extent and permanence. We are nearer to the true secret when we dwell on his singleness of purpose and of aim.

SINGLENESS OF AIM.

Wesley knew what he wanted. And in a remarkable degree it may be said of him, that he wanted nothing else but that. God had so prepared and disposed this man, that his eye rested steadily and always on the one thing. It was not taken off either by seductions, or by assaults, or by perplexities, or by the mere number and variety of objects appealing to him. He saw these things, but he saw them always in relation to his one object, which fixed and drew him. Now, "if thine eye be single, thy whole body shall be full of light." Because he gazed so steadily on the one object of attainment, his view of it became clear ; also the way to it revealed itself ; the manner in which his own powers, and the resources at his disposal, could be put in play, with a view to reach it, became plain. The whole situation fell in its place before him, and the way in which it could be influenced revealed itself. Wesley knew what he wanted. He had not a very quiet life, but he had in a wonderful degree the wisdom of a "quiet eye." He might be occupied with interminable activities, journeys to make, sermons to preach, books to write, business arrangements to plan and execute, people to talk to—reasonable and unreasonable—mobs might howl him down and pelt him, magistrates might bully him, Calvinists (like the present preacher) might rave at him. But all through there was a vision from which John Wesley's eye could not be turned away. It was not a vision of heaven, but, on the contrary, emphatically of the earth. It was a vision of English men and women—predominantly, not exclusively, of the lower classes—loving and serving God. Neither was it at all a fancy picture. He knew exactly what it meant out of his own experience. When was he disobedient to that vision ? It was this steady eye that enabled him to clear his way through influences that might have swayed him, and entanglements that might have fettered him and marred his work.

LOVE OF POWER.

It is a small thing to say of John Wesley, that his eye was not caught by money, or by ease, or by reputation; that no dread of hostility or of slander seemed to distract his attention or preoccupy his mind. But the same thing may be said of a matter that has been debated, and may seem to be debateable. Was not Wesley animated and drawn by love of power? Now to that I feel no great difficulty in replying. Every man who is working with his powers at full stretch must be conscious of them, more or less. And every man who is enabled to put forth exceptional powers must desire to have a field for them. Wesley did so in his own case. But it seems to me that Wesley is totally misunderstood, unless you realise that with him the governing question was, How his powers could be best expended to bring to pass, under God's blessing, the result on which his heart was set. In a given line and way of working, Wesley saw a road to his end, and his experience showed him how remarkable the results might be. His decision was that his powers should be expended on that line, and that he would not be turned away from it. Neither would he allow himself to expend much strength on negotiating and disputing about it. If other Christians did not like it, they could go and make a road for themselves. Now Wesley may have been right or wrong in coming to these conclusions as to his way of working, and certainly only a very strong and capable man could have justified them in the result. But whether right or wrong, he was not seeking power; he was settling the economy of his life—how it and the powers of it could be best spent to gain the end on which his heart was set. Very likely some love of power did cling to his exercise of it. Most men like what they can successfully achieve.

SINGLENESS, NOT NARROWNESS.

When I speak of the singleness of Wesley's eye, I ought to observe that this does not necessarily imply narrowness. One may remark in him an openness to take into his own life, and recommend to others, a great variety of forms of well-doing and of Christian activity. But one can also see that in his own case they all receive definite limits; the space allotted to them is determined by the main end to which his life was given. I am inclined to recognise this same controlling influence in connection with his controversial writing. Wesley judged it needful for him to engage in controversial writing in order to avert errors, and to keep his main movement on right lines. Personally I am not with him in all his contentions; and I do not know that anybody is concerned to maintain that he escaped all the temptations which beset controversialists. But controversy could not absorb him. He shut it up vigorously as soon as he judged it had done its work, and went on with his main business. He went on with it, very little ruffled, with little sign of having lost his breath or lost his temper.

DEVOTEDNESS.

I have dwelt on Wesley's singleness of purpose. It is not quite saying the same thing when I go on to speak of his unsparing devotion. It is possible to have a clear and steady eye for a great object, and yet through some lassitude or inertia to fail to respond to its attraction. But in Wesley one seems to see a devotedness that spares no effort and loses no opportunity. As his great object and the conditions of attaining it grew clear to him, he seemed to put himself in play, and those whom he could influence, to press on to it through every opening that was given. What a fine courage there was in the way he faced his great problem! As its greatness loomed out upon him, he set himself the more to subdue it to his

Master's will.   The common fault is that we see our
problem well enough, but we falter and flinch.   All that
Wesley was, and all that he had, was thrown into his
battle with a serene, intense persistency that never seemed
to flag.   Doubtless he owed much to his bodily and
mental health, and to the cheerful elasticity of spirit
which so wonderfully characterised him.   But those are
qualities far from being always or necessarily consecrated
to high aims or to self-denying life.   We must here own
the working of the faith which subdues kingdoms and
stops the mouths of lions.   As we follow him through his
life, really, the question rises, How could a man come
nearer to forsaking all that he had than Wesley did?
And he did it, not as one pondering and moralising over
so great an effort.   He did it cheerfully, in the way of
business, as it were, making investments for his Master.
If we too could better learn this lesson of forsaking
all, should not we too find life becoming significant
and victorious?   Should not *our* world also begin to
move?

WESLEY'S AIM.

We recognise these as dispositions and influences under
which Wesley became so singularly serviceable towards the
end he lived for.   This brings us to the question, What
that end was.   Many phrases could be used.   It was, let
us say, to bring God into the lives of men and women; to
awaken, sustain, and animate within them the blessed
consciousness of knowing, loving, and serving God.   At a
time when Christianity for multitudes had become a dead
form, and when those for whom it was more than a form
were perplexed and could not find their hands, this man
was sent on to take order that Christianity by the grace
of God should become real all over the country.   This is
a description in terms that are pretty general and wide,
and the generality may be vindicated from the circumstance that Wesley himself sometimes liked to speak of
true religion in the most general terms.   But if we do so,

we must take care that we do not miss what was essential
to the work before us.

God was to be known ; but He was to be known as the
God and Father of our Lord Jesus Christ, who has drawn
near in Christ to pardon and to save the undeserving and
the sinful.   And human hearts were to be awakened ;
but it was to be an awakening to the wonder of redemption, and an experience of God's holy mercy, making
salvation welcome and real to the awakening heart.

WHAT IS IMPLIED.

There are two things here.   The first is the supernatural
grace of the incarnation and the atonement.   There are
those who strive, as much as may be, to reduce Christianity
to a sublime ethic.   It appears to them that this is the
safest ground on which to put its claims.   They call it,
in fact, the Christianity of Christ.   I shall have something
to say presently as to John Wesley's relation to the
ethical aspect of things.   And for myself—and you probably—I may say that every fresh illustration of the
depth and height of the Christian conception of duty,
goodness, sacrifice, is good service done to a great cause,
and so far should be gladly accepted.   But then the very
meaning of Christianity is that behind all that, there is
the astonishing love of God coming into the very heart of
our need and shame, in the gift and in the sacrifice of His
Son.   That, too, is the source of the ethical peculiarity
and splendour of Christianity, as it is the source of
the gift of the Spirit, who translates Christian ethics
into Christian character.   Now, if that is renounced or
eliminated, you will not maintain Christianity.   You will
find in the end that you are unconsciously letting go the
Christian religion.   Moreover, after a brief glow of interest
and impression, you will find that you have lost the power
to move and bow the souls of men.

I am not saying this by way of invidious attack upon
those who feel themselves called—at present, for instance

G

—to dwell emphatically and much on duty and on character. I should hold that to be very unjust. They may have very good reasons for the course they take. And John Wesley himself has said very sharp things about the worthlessness of mere traditional harping on the doctrinal outlines of the scheme of grace. But no man can rightly appreciate Wesley's work, who does not apprehend the strength it drew from the intense conviction that God was in Christ reconciling the world unto Himself, not imputing unto us our trespasses. Wesley and his work simply vanish if you suppose him withheld from going forth as one who says, "Behold, we declare unto you glad tidings."

That is one point. The other point here to be noticed is, the necessity for men and women individually to be brought into this blessedness, which in Christ is set before us, and to become partakers of pardon and of life—the necessity, in short, of conversion. It is very true that the longer one lives and learns, the less one is inclined to lay down rules for God as to the way in which He brings men to Himself, and the steps by which He does it; or as to the measure of light and the form of thought and feeling under which His children may be holding communion with Him. Thank God, all our thoughts about this are nothing to the various and unsearchable grace of His ways. But yet we must be born again: there is such a thing as becoming conscious of the call of Christ as something for ourselves; there is such a thing as submitting to the righteousness of God; there is such a thing as a contrite heart being persuaded of the loving-kindness of the Lord; there is such a thing as receiving power to become a son of God. And Wesley's work challenged men upon the point whether Christ was in them. It held up actual pardon and power to serve God as benefits to be sought and found. Frank and unfettered as Wesley might be in recognising true godliness in forms far removed from those of his own ministration, surely his whole ministry drew its inspiration from that experience at a quarter to nine on a

May evening in 1738, when he became conscious of the meaning of Christianity, of the love of God in Christ, as a possession and inheritance for himself.

OUR AIM AND METHOD.

Perhaps there are reasons for dealing with many congregations in our day circumspectly rather than roughly. Perhaps it is right to keep before our minds the possibility that some good thing towards the Lord God of Israel may have been planted early in young hearts, though it is not yet conspicuous, and needs fostering rather than more radical treatment. Perhaps it is well to consider that, under the complex conditions of human souls, some may be more hopefully approached, more persuasively dealt with, by stealing in upon them with now this and now that of the various aspects of Christian life and service, suffusing their lives with influences that may gain them —that, one may hope, are gaining them by degrees. Perhaps so. But yet is not this true of many gospel hearers in our congregations, that they never have discovered with any application to themselves what Jesus Christ is for? It is all vague, uncertain, unpractical, unreal. And often they themselves feel, and we shall help them best when we feel, that they simply need to be converted.

WESLEY'S CONCEPTION OF CONVERSION.

As to the conception of conversion, the working idea of it which obtained among the early Methodists, and which guided much of their activity, I shall only say this, that we must have working conceptions to guide practice, and at the same time we must remember that these are commonly provisional and rough. Usually every extensive work of conversion or awakening has proceeded on some conception of conversion kept in view as that which was to be consciously realised; and this has been, generally, such a conception that when it is stated and defined, it is too narrow and imperfect to cover all cases, and yet is near enough to verify itself in many. In different religious movements these ruling ideas have varied a little ; and so the type and style of experience to which the good Spirit of God has condescended to adjust his working has varied also. On the other hand, no way of defining conversion that man can propose or enforce, will exclude the possibility of imitative and deceptive experiences.

ALLEGED WEAKNESS OF EVANGELISM.

This experience of conversion may be held liable to a certain weakness and danger. A very vital element of it is a revelation, or apprehension, of a wonderful kindness to myself, out of which blessedness, if it is vividly apprehended, there comes naturally, and most legitimately, a sense of great gladness. It may be said, then, that at this point self can rise fatally into ascendency ; the sentiment of immense gain for me—deliverance, security, and personal elevation for me—may usurp a most undue place ; self-complacency, self-congratulation, self-adulation, may break out in a great stream ; and the very process which was supposed to carry us towards God, and to dispose us to duty, may take a turn which supplants both in a great degree. It is in view of this that some critics of the Evangelical administration of Christianity have spoken with contempt of the anxiety of people about saving their souls—as if it were only a religious form of self-seeking.

WESLEY'S DEMAND FOR THE PRACTICAL.

This is not the place to argue out the question. What I have at present to say is this, that no Evangelical man could be less liable to the charge of concentrating attention exclusively on safety, on privilege, on the passive or

receiving side of things, than Wesley was. One does not
see that this was at any time even a danger or temptation
to him. He was in the first place a man of an intensely
ethical turn; duty appealed to him with great constitutional force. When he began to think seriously of
Christianity, he conceived a high ideal of a Christian's
character and attainments, and spent years in trying to
realise it. Then, when he found peace and liberty in
Christ, the very feature of the new experience which
stood out to his own mind was, that it included power to
overcome sin and to serve God. No doubt his conception
of practical Christianity changed at that time,—but only
in the sense of being deepened, widened, and glorified.
Instead of mere conscientious endeavour to conform
himself to an ideal of devout life, there came the great
inspiration of the love of God shed abroad in the heart
through the Holy Ghost given to him. But that only
sent him on his way with a new conception of the magni-
ficence of his calling, and a new assurance of success.
Every method he had proved before, as adapted to
promote practice, service, diligence, came into play at
once in the new career, with a new freedom and power.
And accordingly his work of awakening aimed at rousing
men to own the claims of holiness—that is to say, of consecration to God, and devoted service of men. He wanted
people awakened and converted; but part of the meaning
of that in his mind was that they should be set against
sin, emancipated from the world, and free and strong in
practical well-doing. He wanted Christians that should
believe in these things, aim at these things, and attain
them. And there are two features of his ministry which
impress an outsider as regards their relation to this great
and good ambition.

TWO FEATURES OF HIS MINISTRY.

First, there was the method of organising and training
the fruits of the ministry, by assembling the awakened into

classes. No doubt this came in at first as an expedient, wisely struck out in connection with the early conditions of Methodist itinerancy, which precluded continuous pastoral care. But it remained afterwards, as a permanent expression of the thought that Christians, whose hearts are in their profession, may be expected to join together to watch and help one another under approved leadership, in the endeavour to prove and to fulfil the good and acceptable and perfect will of God. Whether this was and is the best way of providing for the objects, I do not know. Many of us know about the work of the Methodist class chiefly through the example of one *Daniel Quorm*, and if he is an average specimen of Wesleyan class-leaders, there remains little room for discussion. What I have to own is, that this Wesleyan way contrasts with the great absence in most of our Churches of any *regulated* way of providing for the same end. And though pastoral care and Christian friendship do, of course, come largely in to meet the necessity, yet often there is among us serious want of helpful companionship and counsel in early and critical stages of the life of awakened persons. At all events, most of our Churches cannot but remark here in Wesley's system, a striking practical tribute to the truth that the business of Christians is to take pains and combine their efforts to be Christians indeed.

The other feature to which I referred, is nothing else than the Wesleyan doctrine of attainable perfection in holiness. Here, too, I am not to engage in discussion. It is well known that some of us conceive that matter somewhat differently. But I refer to it for the purpose of laying emphasis on this, that in the mind of Wesley, and of those who followed him, that doctrine stood connected with the noble desire to stir Christians to aim at the fulness of Christ. For this reason he desired to clear out of their way whatever seemed to him likely to weaken the sense of obligation, whatever might intercept the influence of the Master's call to follow Him.

For the rest, Wesley's conception of Christian holiness

was not narrow, and it was abundantly practical. It anticipated also a great deal that is put abroad to-day as newly discovered. For there is hardly a form of benevolence to men's bodies or souls, and hardly a line of action on the manifold problem of human sin and misery, that is not somewhere exemplified among the activities of that remarkable life—exemplified, and then commended and inculcated.

LESSON FOR THE FUTURE.

Well, it is not for me to say how far the Methodists have been enabled to keep up to the standard set for them by their great teacher. But I daresay that in your churches, as in ours, there is some room, not a little room, for progress; some ground, not a little, for lamenting our shortcoming and compromise in the field of practical Christianity. At least, however, it lies to you to take a forward and conspicuous place in rousing the Church afresh to this great interest. It is part of the work which John Wesley left to you. And this seems to be a present-day business. People are prepared to be interested in it. Ours is a time in which we find people realising fragments of Christianity with extraordinary vividness. And some parts of the teaching of Christ as to the sacrifices His followers should make, and the work they should do, have been flashed into men's minds with startling effect. The question is stirring, Are we doing justice—how are we to do justice to the teaching of Christ? We have to learn this that we may teach it.

Religious awakening and movement come from vivid apprehensions of the mind of God, in some aspect of it, flashing in on the Church and on the world, so as to possess men with a sense—unfelt before—of the reality and majesty of spiritual things. Perhaps the next great awakening may come, not in the wake of what our fathers called a law work—an intensifying of the witness of conscience—but by a strange and vivid sense of what Christ meant His followers to be, of what men are called to receive from Christ. That may be felt to be real, wonderful, credible, and near. If so, what an awakening that will be for the Church as well as for the world.

CONSECRATION OF COMMON-SENSE.

So far I have spoken of master principles of Wesley's activity. As to the means by which he worked out his object in detail, I will make one remark. They seem to me to consecrate this principle, viz. the right of common-sense to regulate Church methods in dealing with the exigencies presented by God's providence. Churches, dealing with sacred interests, and, as they trust, under some degree of Divine guidance, are apt to be very inflexible in their methods. What was right before must be right now; and what has been sacred till this moment it is sacrilege to alter. Now Wesley sets no example of flightiness, of sudden, inconsiderate change. He was conservative enough to have a good deal of inward difficulty about the changes he made; and what he did adopt after consideration, he adhered to with a fine tenacious consistency. But his visible conservatism only throws up into clearer prominence the dominant sagacity of the man. One expedient after another is considered, adopted, worked out, simply on the ground that it was the way by which, in fact, the necessary work could be done; so it was with open-air preaching, classes, lay-preachers, and all the rest of it. If Wesley had been a mere ecclesiastic, occupied with the play of the machinery, it might have been otherwise. But here again we feel what he had his eye upon— it was that vision of saved and holy men and women to be reached across the cruelly adverse circumstances of the time. Now, it is a great principle that if you want to go anywhere you must take the road to it that lies open. Really that is so, unwilling as we of the Churches have been to believe it. And there is nothing in the revealed will of Christ intended to hinder us, while we administer

His gospel for the ends of His glorious kingdom, from making use of those adaptations which have the simple consecration of common-sense.

That seems a fair inference from Wesley's practice; and I think the Churches need to lay it to heart. We need greater flexibility, and more of wise, considerate, yet courageous inventiveness. We are too slow in getting out of the ruts. I speak of what I know in the regions familiar to me, confessing my own share in it. I am not acquainted enough—to my own loss it is, I am sure—with the inner working of Wesleyanism to know how it is with you. But I should be surprised to learn that with you, as well as with us, the surprising principle did not hold, in some degree, that the innovations of one age become the traditional fetters of the next, and that the fact that our fathers looked at things with their own eyes, comes to be taken as binding us never to look at them with ours.

HIS SUSTAINED CONSECRATION IN ITS BEARING ON MINISTERIAL SUCCESS.

But in speaking of the detail of Wesley's work, the explanation of its daily strength, I must be allowed, in closing, to go back on the point with which I began. That which was the secret of his strength in dealing with his enterprise as one immense whole, was the secret of it also in its daily and detailed successes. I am thinking now of that without which all the rest would have been nothing—Wesley's success in getting into living contact with souls as God's messenger, and his kindling a fire that went on burning where his personal influence could not reach. Here we all own the wise and loving grace of the Spirit of God. But let us mark this quality in His agent —the sheer honesty and thoroughness of Wesley's life. Long before he found peace and liberty in Christ, these qualities are already apparent. And when Wesley had been enlightened and set free, they received a new con- secration and a new energy. It is not necessary to adopt

all the judgments which Wesley made with reference to
his own duty as necessarily binding on others. But the
decision, downrightness, resolute consistency that appear
in his conduct about money, in his systematic self-denial,
in his redeeming of time, in his almost incredible diligence,
—the unselfish consecration with which he gave himself
utterly to the one end,—all this backed his preaching with
a moral force, informed it with a cogency and reality
which made it the proper instrument of the great result.
It is not only that the people knew his devotedness,
though they did know it, and bowed to it; but the man
himself embodied it as an inspiration and a force. When
he spoke of the claims of God, he spoke what was for ever
echoing through his own life. Such men have full right
and power to speak. Whatever may be true of possible
effects from strong words spoken by spiritually weak men,
or even from the good words of bad men, there is given
to the words of a man whose life in its details has been
steadily consecrated and devoted, a force all their own.
No thought in connection with Wesley's life has impressed
my own mind more than this.

We that are ministers cannot afford to lose this lesson.
It is not difficult to believe of very many of us that we
are sincere men, fairly diligent, intelligent, and earnest in
seeking to do service to the Saviour, in whom we have
trusted, and to the flocks over which He has set us. But
what if, at successive stages — beginning early and re-
peating the process often—what if, when openings and
calls came to us to embrace a loftier standard, to pitch
higher and more worthily the key of service, to take the
harder and the nobler view of what a minister may dare
and do for Christ—what if we have slidden—alas! how
easily—along the lower path, transacted with our own
conscience, indulged ourselves—always, no doubt, in respectable and seemly ways—and set narrow limits to
sacrifice, to endeavour, to Christian ambition? I cannot
refrain from expressing my fear that some of us older
ministers—I do not say all, for I do not think so—but

some of us—have greatly lost and thrown away our lives; because, though we have spoken strong words and forcible thoughts, and done it sincerely, meaning all we said, yet we failed to back them with a straightforward, unsparing devotedness of life, answerable to the words we spoke. I am not thinking, of course, of a paraded devotedness, exhibited to catch the eye of others; but of that personal affirmation of the truth we hold in continuous deeds of self-forgetting practice, which should have lent its silent force to all our dealings with the souls of men. When we look at this aspect of Wesley's life, we seem to hear a voice saying to us, if it is not too late—and saying to younger men for whom it is not yet too late: "Be ye not unwise, but understanding what the will of the Lord is."

It is time to bring this to an end. We join with you in thanking God for the life and work of this great, true, courageous, and fruitful Englishman, this noble servant and apostle of Jesus Christ. We gladly own how well it is that in this memorable instance you should consider one that had the rule over you, that has spoken to you the word of the Lord, that you may follow his faith, remembering the end of his conversation. What you have learned and received and heard and seen in him, we shall rejoice to know that you go forth in God's strength more than ever to do. At the same time, we remember that this was God's special gift in the man we commemorate, that he was enabled to bring to the difficulties and the dangers of his day a fresh eye, and a new impulse of faith and hope, and a creative instinct in grappling with facts. Therefore we will pray that among you, and also in all our Churches, there may rise up men who in this highest, truest sense reproduce the spirit and the work of John Wesley.

The Prophet of the Eighteenth Century.

By the Rev. JOHN CLIFFORD, M.A., D.D.

———o———

> "*Ye are the sons of the prophets, and of the covenant which God made with your fathers, saying unto Abraham, And in thy seed shall all the families of the earth be blessed.*"—ACTS iii. 25.

THESE words form part of Peter's appeal to the Jews to accept and use the latest revelation of God to men, made in Jesus the Nazarene, who had been crucified on Calvary some eight or ten weeks before, and who, within the last few days, was so strangely and unexpectedly vindicated and glorified by the spiritual marvels of Pentecost. It is a supreme moment in the history of Jerusalem and of the world. The day of Pentecost has fully come ; and it is "the beginning of days," the dawning of a new era of light and life, not for one here and another there, but for thousands gathered from every nation under heaven. Nor is the mission of Christ limited to the human spirit. The ascended Redeemer is also the Saviour of the body, and in the man so notoriously and so long lame, but now perfectly sound, stands revealed before them all, in the wide sweep of His healing energies. That man's firm step is a visible argument for the despised Christ, and his exultant song an audible and persuasive appeal for the examination of His claims. What can you say against a gospel that heals lame men and quickens dead souls? Butler's *Analogy* you may challenge, and Waterland's reasoning on the *Eucharist* you may question; but what can you do with the indisputable logic of facts offered in crowds of godless miners changed to newness of life by the preaching of John Wesley?

But it is poor service, after all, only to silence an objector. He needs guidance. Probably he is a baffled seeker after truth, confronted by a new fact which refuses to harmonise with his interpretation of the revelation he already knows, and whose authority he has long recognised. Therefore Peter, moved by the Holy Ghost, says to the wondering people as they crowd the portico of the temple, " See you what the healing of this lame man means? Do you understand these signs? Don't look on us as though we had done it; we haven't. God, and God alone, has wrought this great marvel—your God, your fathers' God, the God of Jesus Christ. He has raised from the dead the Prince of Life, whom you killed, and here in this forty-year-old cripple made young again He reveals Him to you as the Prince of Life still. You are surprised; and yet, if you understood the heritage of prophecy you have received, you would have expected it, for this victory over disease is part of a predicted series of deliverances, and is of a piece with the call of Moses, the exodus from Egypt, and the departure from Babylon, and springs out of the faithfulness of God to the covenant He made with Abraham when He said, ' In thy seed shall all the families of the earth be blessed.' Remember, ye are the sons of the prophets. Recognise your noble heritage. See in these occurrences verifications of the original promise, exemplifications of the law of universal redemption, and welcome the message of salvation we preach. The grace of Christ is here fulfilling—that is, filling out—the programme, and actualising the ideal of ' the law which came by Moses,' and proclaiming to you that God has raised up His Son

Jesus, and sent Him 'to bless you in turning away every one of you from your iniquities.'"

WIDE RANGE OF WESLEY'S INFLUENCE.

II. Fathers, brothers, and members of the great Methodist people, have I not undeniable warrant to say to you on this memorable morning, "Ye are the children of the prophets, of the covenant which God made with your fathers," saying unto John Wesley, as clearly as He did to Abraham, "And in thy spiritual children shall all the families of the earth be blessed"? "*Ye*"*!* did I say? Surely I must say *we;* since we Congregationalists and Baptists of England and the world are sharers in the great Evangelical Revival, have received incomputable blessings from Wesley's ministry, and owe much of our present light and fire to the message he delivered with such convincing clearness and saintly devotion. Certainly I cannot forget that debt; nor can I cite a more decisive example of the immense service of the Founder of Methodism to the older Christian Churches of the last century, than that which is offered in the annals of the Society to which I owe my conversion to God. The General Baptists date from the opening decades of the seventeenth century, and from the first held and taught the infinite and universal love of God in Christ Jesus. But at the time of Wesley's conversion they were critical, contentious, and cold. The breath of the Puritan inspiration had ceased to stir their hearts and move their wills. "The word of the Lord was rare in those days; there was no widely-spread vision," and little experience of the quickening energies of the Holy Spirit. But it came to pass that Dan Taylor, a Yorkshire miner, heard the gospel from the great evangelist, and was converted to God. Soon afterwards he entered the General Baptist ministry, but was so infected with the zeal and passion of Wesley, that he could not rest till he had founded the New Connexion of General Baptists. This was in 1770.

The word of the Lord grew mightily and prevailed, and to-day we are a strong, glad, and victorious company of the followers of Christ ; for whom, if you are resolved to include in one federation all the Methodist offspring, you will assuredly have to make room.   I quote this page of history, because it is typical of that regeneration of the Churches of England accomplished by the ministry of Wesley. God's best gifts are for everybody. His choicest messengers speak an universal language. His chief prophets render a world-wide service. We are *all* the sons of the prophets and of the covenant of redeeming love which He hath made with our race, saying to its elect spiritual leaders, " And in your seed shall all the families of the earth be blessed."

WESLEY ESSENTIALLY A PROPHET.

III. The wise know that no heritage equals in value that which we have in the inspirations and toils of the God-given prophets. They are an authentic witness from the spiritual realm, — speak for God, think after His thought, throb with His pity, burn with His fire of justice, move with His calm patience, and work for men with His undespairing energy.   They stand for God ; for His motherly brooding over our chaotic life, to shape it into Divinest order and beauty. As the great mountains catch the sunshine, and radiate the light and heat, making the valleys fertile and the rivers sing, so the seers receive the rays of the Sun of Righteousness, and reflect His healing beams on those who sit in the shadow of death. They are conspicuously spiritual leaders of humanity, and therefore, whilst the Old Testament is full of them and their work, they also reappear in the New, and give energy and exaltation, spontaneity and spirituality, to the whole activities of the early Church. The Christ of the Cross and of the Throne has received gifts of men for men, some apostles and prophets, and some pastors and evangelists. And of those men He has in His grace bestowed in these later centuries, John Wesley holds a place as primary as it is arresting, and as unchallenged as it is immeasurably and prophetically fruitful. He is the chief Prophet of the Eighteenth Century. The prophetism of the New Testament in all its sublime qualities and successes reaches its maximum in him, and places him at the springhead of the spiritual life of our modern England.

Like many other men of original inspiration, Wesley has failed even yet to win the full recognition of his character and service. For though his name is as familiar as the words of daily greeting, yet few know him at first hand, and of those few not all know him accurately and in the secret of his inmost life and character. Intrinsically he is a prophet ; essentially he is a God-made, God-trained, God-inspired, God-ruled man. Leave God out of his life, and it is a riddle you cannot solve, a darkness you can feel.

He was a *student* equipped with wide and solid learning, a good classic, a forcible reasoner, a man of rare intellectual conscience and sincerity, ever alert in thought and uniformly balanced in judgment. It would be the grossest mistake to treat him as an ill-trained street-preacher, compensating for lack of brain by strength of lung, and setting fervour to do the work of thought and research. Had he not been so distinguished a prophet, he would have taken highest rank as a man of letters. He always spoke with the authority of knowledge ; but his scholarship was always his servant : his logic was fused by a burning love of God and souls, and his mental acquisitions were all severely subordinated to spiritual and practical uses. There was not the faintest trace of the scholastic pedant in this strong and serene prophet of God.

Moreover, Wesley shines with arresting splendour in the " glorious company of the *Apostles*." He laboured in season and out, going from Cornwall to Newcastle, and from London to Ireland, as a minister and a witness to the things wherein he for himself had seen Christ ; as a witness to the conscious and experimental facts of deliverance from sin, peace with God, and joy in the Holy Ghost.

But the marvellous successes that attended his preaching, when sinners fell prostrate beneath the power of the word, and stricken souls cried importunately to God for mercy, were due to the irresistible conviction that he came straight from the presence of the living God, and witnessed for an actual and *felt* Redeemer of men. The mere witness, however accurate and earnest, is always less than a prophet. But Wesley was the inspired apostle of experience, the real incarnation of a living and aggressive faith.

Not a few men talk of Wesley's *system;* graded and coherent, ubiquitous and centralised, supple and strong, as though his victories were won by machinery, and his chief distinction was his masterful genius as an administrator. But trace the growth of his institutions. See them start into life in his "Journals;" one at Bristol, a second at Newcastle, other portions here at City Road, each appearing as it is wanted, a practical response to a felt and obvious need, an appropriate garment for the growing and expanding life, advancing as a family advances, and full of the throbbing vitality of the creative man of God ; and you discover that the power was not in the machine, but in the *man.* The spiritual renewal of the world is not in systems, but in souls—souls filled with all the fulness of God.

Looking at the neatly-clad cleric, small of stature, calm in spirit, clear and simple in talk, logical rather than rhetorical, men have hesitated to assign him a place amongst the masters of vision and of speech whom the Eternal ever sends forth to lead His Israel to its predestined goal. But it is one of the charms of prophetic power, that it is so diverse in its manifestations, and clothes itself in such a variety of forms. It thinks in the scholar, sings in the poet, paints in the artist, preaches in the evangelist, fights in the hero, rebukes in the reformer, and pulls down and builds up in the men who lead the ages to victory. In Elisha it is gentle and genial, silent and strong, as the unperceived forces of the spring changing the face of the earth this morning ; and again, in Elijah it is sonorous and desolating

H

as a raging ice-storm. Soft and still, it moves like dew amongst fragrant bloom, and along the spear-like blades of grass; violent and surprising, it dashes forward with the swiftness of an earthquake, and the destructiveness of streams of burning lava. In aged John it speaks with tones of winning entreaty, and from the serenity of a masterly calm; in Paul it faces the "lion" Nero on his throne, and dares death with a victor's smile. It is retiring as a violet in a hedgebank in Melanchthon, and in Martin Luther it is as bold and obtrusive as a sunflower. In Leighton it is sweet and placid and persuasive; in bold Hugh Latimer it speaks as fearlessly to king and statesman as to peasant and labourer. In Wesley it appears in many forms. Like Abraham, he early catches a glimpse of the far-off issues of his life, and trembles and rejoices in the sight. As a modern Moses, he leads the English people out of a sombre and repellant theology, into a clime radiant with summer thoughts of God and His redeeming mercy. Like Samuel, he is the founder and head of a band of prophets, whose hearts God had touched through his faith, and whose lives God had enriched through his devotion. He has the intrepidity, but not the crushing fierceness, of Elijah; and, though it comes later, yet he attains at length the Isaiah passion for holiness. In consciousness of the resistless urgency of the Spirit, he repeats the experience of Jeremiah, and he follows John the Baptist in the total subordination of all his life and work to the glory of Christ his Redeemer. From first to last, then, he is a prophet of the Highest. He has a prophet's training, sees with a prophet's eye, moves in obedience to a prophetic impulse, and works to the end with a prophet's patient persistence, deep, calm, and reproductive fruitfulness.

GOD IN WESLEY'S HISTORY.

IV. No man with an eye for spiritual facts can look into Wesley's history without seeing God; and he who looks continuously is likely to feel, as Newton did after looking at the sun, that the image of God is so burned into his soul that he can see nothing else. At least seven signs of Divine preparation and training for a prophet's mission may be noted : his godly descent, his early and prolonged spiritual education, his pre-eminent prayerfulness and yearning to serve God, his pity for suffering and weak men, his whole-souled committal of himself to God in his conversion, his clear-ringing reality and unfaltering obedience to the Divine will.

Like Samuel, he had an inspired mother, came of a godly stock, and was separated from his birth to his high vocation. More propitious pre-natal conditions no prophet could have had. Inspired personalities inspire. Communion with his God-taught Puritan mother enriched and quickened his life to an unprecedented degree. The arousal of sympathy for the imprisoned, contact with earnest seekers for a holier life, the mystic touch of Thomas à-Kempis and Taylor and Law ; the bewildering and disappointing experiences in Georgia, the revelations of the Moravians, the flash of light from the soul of Martin Luther,—all prepared for the moment when He who sent Peter to Cornelius, and so initiated a new departure in religion, brought Peter Böhler into fellowship with John Wesley, and through him into consciously vital union with the Lord Jesus Christ, as the Redeemer from sin, the King of souls, and the Lord and Master of service.

THE PROPHET AS SEER.

V. From that moment Wesley was a SEER, "a man," as Carlyle would express it, "with an eye ;" a man living in the light as God is in the light, seeing things as God sees them, thinking His thoughts, echoing His message, and obeying His laws. He saw the *facts* of life in their spring and essence, beheld *God* in the face of Jesus Christ, got to the beating heart of *religion*, and started on his journey towards the realisation of the *social ideal* of Jesus.

1. Now he saw through the heaven-lit windows of his own soul that the radical want of men was God, the living and loving God, delighting in mercy, eager to redeem, and able to renew ; God revealed in His Son Jesus Christ, and revealed also in His pardoning grace and righteous power in man's own heart. This was the one thing needful. This was the panacea for England's ills. The whole head was sick, and the whole heart was faint, but here was the one all - sufficient Physician.   The nation's so-called peace was in Wesley's judgment an anticipated death, it's "sober piety" wicked apathy, its Churches a deception and a snare, and its religion a series of delusive ceremonies.   Stirred in soul by the God-given vision, he earnestly besought men, saying, "Come now and let us reason together, saith the Lord ; though your sins be as scarlet, they shall be as white as snow ; though they be red like crimson, they shall be as wool."

Wesley was not alone in the sight of this evil. Bishop Burnet saw it and lamented it ; Archbishop Secker deplored it ; but Wesley saw God as they did not, and men never know what to do with sin and wrong unless they see Him making an end of sin, by the sacrifice of Himself, and bringing in an everlasting righteousness. In fact, it is not too much to say that Wesley re-discovered the New Testament idea of God. Raleigh, in his *Elementary Politics*, says, "To change national customs and habits, we must change *ideas.*" That is the fact, Nothing is so potent amongst us as an idea, except a living soul. Ideas make our real world. As they are, so are we. Therefore, the man who changes the ideas of a community on the most momentous themes—God, Sin, Duty, and Destiny— does the most towards changing the habits and customs of that community. This is Wesley's real distinction. He is the foremost force in the most radical and far-reaching revolution in the thought and life of men since the Reformation of Martin Luther. We call it the *Evangelical Revival.* The language is most exact ; words could not be more true to fact. It is a revival ; not an

absolutely original movement, but a quickening into newness of life of old truths and principles,—that is, it is a
revival of the *Evangel*,—a calling into play of the ideas
and forces of the gospel as it is in Jesus Himself—a
preaching of it as the power of God, actually present,
saving, healing—saving on the *spot* and at the *moment*,
and so saving that you know it, and have an assurance
of the Divine peace, and of the gracious authority of the
Saviour over the whole man. It is a restoration of the
ideas of the gospel in their primitive simplicity, a new
advent of truth, as the truth is in Jesus.

For the most part the idea of God dominant at that
date, and regulative of the thoughts of men about religion, was that of a sovereign controlling power; absolute,
arbitrary, and awe-inspiring—fore-casting the future, fore-
ordaining the lot of man. Wesley lifted into authority
over the consciences of men the conception of God in
Christ reconciling the world unto Himself, not imputing
unto men their trespasses. In the reigning theology the
emphasis was placed on the eternal decrees of Jehovah;
Wesley shifted the emphasis to the redeeming aims of the
Divine rule, and the universal provision for the forgiveness
of sins in the Divine sacrifice. To most men God was
distant from the world of man—sat apart from its sin
and sorrow, its care and woe, observing, judging, ruling;
Wesley rose up to declare God in the actual life of
humanity, encompassing the human soul, seeking to save
and re-make it after the Divine ideal of what it should be.
Here was the major part of the secret of his power. The
old method separated society into its elect and non-elect
members; the new, into men who gladly accepted God's
mercy, and those who continued to reject it. That fixed
men's ideas on God decreeing, and started the question,
"Am I one of the elect?" This forced men to think of
God as living, and started the inquiry, "Do I repent and
sincerely believe the gospel?" That made debaters, this
produced penitents; that sterilised the sense of responsibility, this quickened it, and made it fruitful of action;

that was a paralysis of the will, this generated repentance toward God, and faith toward our Lord Jesus Christ. That turned an era of growing religious freedom into one of widespread decay of the spiritual life and increasing national corruptions; this led on to the newer and better England of to-day, with its broad philanthropies, growing brotherhood, and abounding beneficence.

Now that change was not in any sense due to philosophy, nor did it owe anything to logical acumen; it was God Himself who inspired and sustained the revolt against the benumbing traditionalism and blinding theology of the day, and flashed into the prepared soul of Wesley that New Testament conception of Himself revealed in Jesus, which contained all the forces of the spiritual revolution.

THE RECOVERY OF SPIRITUAL RELIGION.

2. Nowhere was this revolutionary idea more operative than in Wesley's recovery of the intrinsically spiritual conception of religion. Carlyle, misreading the man and the hour, exclaimed, "What is this Methodism, but a new phase of Egoism stretched out into the infinite!" No blunder could be greater, no judgment more wanting in historical and spiritual insight. This Methodist doctrine of conversion was an anticipation expressed in more luminous terms of his own teaching about the soul's passage from the "Everlasting No" to the "Everlasting Yea." It was, in short, an assertion that the essence of religion is not opinion, not Church relationship, but a going over of the soul to God in Christ Jesus, in penitence for sin, and in trustful venture for holiness, followed by the identifying of the whole life and thought and being with Christ Jesus and His world-saving purposes. Religion is of the soul, not of the senses; of the heart rather than of the head; of the temper and disposition, not of the lip; a wholly surrendered will, not an entirely accurate creed; a living faith in a personal Saviour, Himself

entering by His Spirit into the soul, and filling it with His peace and joy, so that there is a vivid and glowing consciousness of actually and now possessing the *eternal* life.

> " Whoso hath *felt* the Spirit of the Highest,
>   Cannot confound, nor doubt Him, nor deny."

> " Speak to Him, thou, for He hears,
>   And spirit with spirit can meet ;
> Closer is He than our breathing,
>   Nearer than hands or feet."

But the religion that commences in such an experience advances to a distinctly ethical goal, and is full of ethical inspirations. "*One thing I do,*" said Wesley, "*spread scriptural holiness.*" But what is that ? Let him answer : "Loving God with all our hearts, and our neighbour as ourselves, is the perfection I have taught these forty years. I pin down all its opposers to this definition of it. No evasion ! No shifting the question ! Where is the delusion of this ?"

Why, Matthew Arnold himself does not insist with closer reasoning or more pungent speech on religion as conduct, as practical obedience, than does Wesley ; and Wesley had what Arnold confesses he had not,—the spiritual impulse, the adequate impact and inspiration to obedience, which is the real secret of Jesus. " For the love of Christ constraineth us ; because we thus judge, that One died for all, therefore all died ; and He died for all, that they which live should no longer live unto themselves, but unto Him who for their sakes died and rose again."

THE SOCIAL IDEAL OF JESUS.

3. By way of that return to the New Testament conception of God, and of intrinsic religion, Wesley makes a decided and prophetic approach to the *social ideal of Jesus.* Reared in an atmosphere of High Churchism, supersaturated with ecclesiastical notions, it was only the height of his aim, and the sincerity of his spirit, which saved him the labour of *consciously* creating a Church system, and aided him in providing the best

nourishment for the spiritual life in the fellowship of the " class" and " band meetings ; " in the activities of lay-preaching and of general ministry to men.   He did not attempt to create a Church, but to save and nourish souls.   He was bent on practical ends.   Besides, he did not want to break with the Church of England ; why should he ?   But he created something far better than that Church, and rendered his followers for evermore independent of it.   That may be a most venerable edifice, constructed on the most approved principles of ecclesiast-ical architecture, and according to the most accurate measurement ; but if it yields neither food nor comfort to those who are to dwell in it, it is not surprising if earnest men should prefer to enter a simpler and less pretentious structure, that satisfies their felt and pressing needs.   To err is human ; but man has a singular way of surprising those sapient souls who denounce him, by refusing their advices, and electing what proves to be the best.   I cannot understand a man who knows and uses Methodism, and tries to follow his New Testament, preferring to dwell in our sacerdotal Anglican Church !

4. God's gift to Wesley of the true conception of His character, implicitly contained a covenant that in his seed all the families of the earth should be blessed. In God's purpose the individual and exceptional is always the evangelistic.   God never makes any man for himself, least of all a prophet.   No scripture is of any private interpretation.   Its sweep is world-wide, and its inspiration for humanity.   The Spirit of God is everywhere—underlies all humanity ; but the carbon-points from which the electricity which fills and bathes air, earth, and sky, streams out in lanes of brilliant light, are those elect souls in whom He dwells, and through whom He has free course, illumining and guiding all.   The true prophet has not a parochial mind, except when, after Wesley's pattern, he makes the world his parish.   He cannot work in chains. What are tribal distinctions and race-boundaries to the man who watches for souls as one that must give account ?

His motto is, like Wesley's, "To go not to those who want him, but to those who want him *most*,"—to the worst and weakest, as one who has found in Christ the true measure of man, and in His Cross the infallible standard by which to judge of the worth of the very chief of sinners in the sight of God. To the uttermost of human need he carries the provisions of the gospel.

> "Thou would'st not *alone*
> Be saved, my father ! *alone*
> Conquer and come to thy goal,
> Leaving the rest in the wild."

No!

> "Still thou turnedst, and still
> Beckonedst the trembler, and still
> Gavest the weary Thy hand ;
> Therefore to thee it was given
> Many to save with thyself ;
> And, at the end of the day,
> O faithful shepherd ! to come,
> Bringing thy sheep in thy hand."

These four formative ideas given by God to Wesley have gone far to the making of our modern England, and are now entering into the collective consciousness of the world, shaping thought, inspiring emotion, and creating character. Our best exegesis of the Scriptures vindicates them. Science and philosophy agree to sustain them. Experience attests their increasing power, and the widening of human life offers fresh opportunities for their application and use. We joyfully recognise them as amongst the best forces of the English-speaking people of to-day, and with devout gratitude we say, "God hath made us, and not we ourselves. We are His people and the sheep of His pasture ;" and amongst the shepherds He has sent us, and for whom we glorify and adore Him, none ever led into better and more nourishing pastures than John Wesley, the Founder of Methodism.

THE PROPHET'S CALL.

VI. If any student of John Wesley questions his claim to the place I have assigned him as a seer, no one can doubt that he felt the prophet's goad to service, heard the call of God to duty, and moved from point to point in his long career in obedience to that call. The word of the Lord was like a fire in his bones. He was weary with forbearing, and could not stay. He must speak. The truth of Christ was alive in him, authoritative and all-mastering, trampling down his prejudices and prepossessions, and making him at last a glad slave of Jesus Christ. He does not choose his path, but walks on, not always seeing the next step, but still advancing to the clearly-proposed goal. "God," he says, "thrust us out;" that conquers his repugnance to field-preaching, opens the door to the lay-ministry, and makes him a revolutionist in spite of himself. He has an all-pervading sense of the personal activity of God; and in his last words, "The best of all is, God is with us," he supplies the key to his entire ministry. For him God is all, and God is enough. The supernatural fills his life. It is not an accident in its course; not an occasional invasion; not a momentary interference: it pervades it, dyes it through and through, constituting him a potent witness to the fact of the real presence of the redeeming God; to the certain arrival of His cleansing and uplifting revelations to sincere and courageously trustful souls; and to the enormous power He infuses into individual men, freely given to him, for carrying forward the world to—

> "The one far-off Divine event,
> To which the whole creation moves."

CHRIST THE FINAL TEST.

VII. And now may I venture to echo Peter's teaching, that the first duty of the heirs of the priceless legacy of the prophets is to open heart and mind to the reception and application of the latest revelations of God, and the fullest energies of the Spirit of God. Wesley grounded individual religion on the present manifestations of the living God to the personal soul. There is no other basis for it. God lives now, redeems now, teaches now, and renews now. No doubt His work all through the ages is a unity. Christ does not contradict Moses; He fulfils him. The Epistles do not supplant the Gospels; they explain and illumine them. The present does not belie the past; it repeats and confirms it. The truths of the book of Nature are not in opposition to the truths of the Bible; they supplement each other, and therefore we ought to listen diligently to the things spoken to us by the Peters and Pauls of our day, comparing their words with the Scripture of Christ, to see whether they are in accordance with His redeeming purpose and kingdom, with His sacrifice and ethics, with His character and ideal. He is our infallible test, the complete and absolute revelation; other teachers were and are fragments, "broken lights." In Him dwelt the fulness of the Godhead bodily. He is the pattern and type of the fully-inspired life, and in this infallible Person we have the all-sufficing test, the one supreme means of verifying the teachings of men and the movements of the Spirit of God within us. Wesley was not averse to criticism. He did not act as if anything could be gained by refusing to examine truth, by veiling difficulties, and talking as if Christianity could not assure itself to the reason as well as to the conscience and heart. He was intellectually alert to the last, and as anxious to maintain intellectual sincerity and sanity as he was to secure practical holiness. In our age of intellectual daring, we must not alienate the young mind by mental cowardice, but be ready to "prove all things, holding fast that which is good."

THE TRANSLATION OF ETERNAL IDEAS.

2. Nor would either Peter or Wesley free us from the obligation of *translating* into the living and current speech of men the eternal ideas of God, instead of being indolently content with the forms of speech and moulds of thought consecrated by the use of centuries. The language

of science and of the street changes every fifty years ; so
ought that of theology and of the pulpit : for language,
like men, is born, and grows, and dies.   We are all in
danger of meeting living men with dead words, offering
the petrifactions of theology instead of the bread of everlasting life, and giving the scorpion of condemnation to
those who ask for the nutritious egg.   Phrases that
throbbed with life in this building at the end of the last
century, fail to touch the soul of this generation.   The
elect language of the godly, such as "the witness of the
Spirit," "full assurance of faith," "Christian perfection,"
are still sweet as honey to the aged, but such words are
puzzles and worse to not a few of the younger minds
about us.

Wesley was a master of words, saw their real meaning,
and both in interpreting the speech of men and in
speaking to them, recognised the necessity for the translation of the ideas of God into the actual and living words
of those he addressed ; and if we are to help in that great
readjustment of the Christian gospel with the stores of
knowledge given to us by God to-day, we must follow in
his wake, so that men may hear in their own language the
wonderful works of God as the Redeemer and Renewer of
lives, and be able to apply His gospel not only to the
individual, but to the social redemption of men.

SACERDOTALISM OUR FOE.

3. The prophets were often in battle against the
priests ; Peter's chief opponents were the priests ; Wesley
discovered in ecclesiastics his bitterest persecutors ; and
we shall not discharge our responsibilities as sons of the
prophets, if we do not fight with all our might against that
uncompromising and recrudescent sacerdotalism which
to-day fetters Christian liberty, saps Christian manhood,
and threatens the existence of the Christian religion.
We must maintain the essential spirituality and inward-
ness of religion, and seek to save all men, in the personal

assurance of the adequacy of the gospel we preach, and of the Christ we represent, for all the needs of man and all the ills of society. The Galilean is conquering. I read a few days since that Colonel Ingersoll had prophesied that in ten years' time Christianity would be so decadent that two theatres would be built for every church. A month or so ago, a zealous Methodist wrote to tell him that the time was up, and the Methodists alone were building four churches every day ; and he proceeded to make the almost unkind suggestion that he should help the churches by another prophecy. That challenge was based on the experience of the grace of Christ in us. We know whom we have believed. We have the witness within ourselves to the truth of our message, and to the power of Christianity ; and following Him who is at once our Saviour and Leader, we go forward to victory, assured that to-day, as one hundred years ago, " The best of all is, God is with us." All glory be to His name !

Divine Service.

By the Rev. F. W. MACDONALD, Wesleyan College,
Handsworth, Birmingham.

——o——

> "*Of these things put them in remembrance, charging them in the sight of the Lord, that they strive not about words, to no profit, to the subverting of them that hear. Give diligence to present thyself approved unto God, a workman that needeth not to be ashamed, handling aright the word of truth.*"— 2 Tim. ii. 14, 15 (R.V.).

THE Apostle here sets in impressive contrast the false and the true teacher of religion. History knows them well, these two types of theologian. The one "strives about words." He may be learned, laborious, ingenious, but he deals with *words*, not *things*. Logic, rhetoric, eloquence, instead of serving truth, become its substitutes, an end in themselves. And this the apostle calls "logomachy," word-strife, a term of just contempt.

And it is good for nothing. It serves no true end, it advances no real interest. It is neither pleasing to God nor profitable to man. Nay, it is worse than useless, it is positively mischievous. It "subverts the hearers." Instead of building up, it brings about their "catastrophe," or overthrow.

But the other, the true teacher, aims at being "approved of God." To this all other approval—popularity with the many, flattery from the few—is held subordinate. To be "unashamed" before God, day by day, while his work is doing, and at the last day when it is done,—this is at once his endeavour and his hope. And so he "gives diligence," "as ever in his great Taskmaster's eye," rightly to handle —that is, to set forth in order and proportion, and apply to men's hearts and consciences—the word of truth, which is the power of God unto salvation to every one that believeth.

Thus does the apostle describe the spirit and aim of the true theologian, and, without any further exposition of the text, I shall proceed to speak, as is fitting on this occasion, of Wesley the theologian, as of one to whom this description may be applied with perhaps as little reservation as to any Christian teacher who has lived and laboured amongst men.

1. *Wesley was a theologian*—that is, a student and a teacher of Christian doctrine. The Bible was his text-book. All his studies were made to converge upon its contents ; in all his teaching this was his basis and starting-point. He sought to combine, to classify, to draw out in clear and orderly statement, the teaching of Scripture concerning God and man, sin and salvation, and to show that the root and centre and reason of all is to be found in the person and work of our Lord Jesus Christ. He was essentially a Biblical theologian. "God Himself," he says, "has condescended to teach the way. He hath written it down in a book. Oh, give me that book ! At any price give me the Book of God." Whatever judgment may be passed upon this utterance, it expresses a spirit and a method which he consistently maintained.

Moreover, he must be counted amongst the most influential of theologians. What is, and what is not, influential in this world is to be ascertained by the test of facts. Wesley is one of the few teachers of religion who, after powerfully influencing his own country and his own age, has shaped religious faith, and the forms and manifestations of religious life, in many lands, and on a large scale, after his death. The influence of his teaching is visible to-day, not only in the definite, easily-recognisable theology of the twenty millions of adherents of the Methodist Churches, but it may be traced over a much wider area, if not as a predominating force, yet as one that has helped to mould, or modify, or give direction to the religious progress of mankind.

What a potent office is that of the theologian! Strange that its importance should ever be disparaged, that the work of the teacher of religion should be compared disadvantageously with that of the politician, the journalist, the financier, the man of business, as though they dealt with realities, and he with unrealities! But this can only be held consistently by those who deny the spiritual order, God and His kingdom, and the spiritual capacities and requirements of man. But if these are the true realities, compared with which earth's most substantial possessions are shadows, then surely we may say, "The proper study of mankind is"—God. In God the problem of humanity has its solution, and the aspiration of man its fulfilment. The heart and the flesh cry out for the living God. As long as man is what he is, in respect both of capacity and of incapacity, of desire for the good and enthralment to evil, of yearning for life and bondage to death, teachers of religion, though they may be despised, cannot be dispensed with; and if one generation cast them out, the generations that follow will build the tombs of the prophets, and garnish the sepulchres of the righteous.

I am speaking of the true, not of the false, theologian; and I say that, instead of being the last and least of workers, he is among the first and best. If he who teaches men to plant, and build, and work in metals, is a benefactor, what is he who brings glad tidings of great joy, who shows the way of salvation, and rightly divides the word of truth? If it is good to learn how to subdue the earth, and navigate the sea, and cultivate the arts and industries of civil life, surely it is the crown of all knowledge to know the true God, and Jesus Christ whom He hath sent!

It may seem to be enforcing a truism, but there are reasons which make it desirable that the true worth of spiritual work should be understood. The office of the preacher of the gospel, of the teacher of religion, cannot be disparaged without vast injury to human life as a whole. If the sensual and the intellectual between them succeed in crushing out the spiritual from the modern world, not all its wealth and wit will save it from corruption. The spiritual man was never more needed in the world than he is to-day,—the man, that is, who works in the spiritual sphere, who employs spiritual forces, and achieves spiritual results.

And are not spiritual results the pledge and procuring cause of other results which even the children of this world know how to prize? Spiritual results—conversion, renewal, sanctification—work out in character, and conduct, and history. All the world admits to-day that Methodism has exercised a great influence for good amongst the people of this country. It has been the parent of industry and thrift, of intelligence and virtue, of educational, philanthropic, and social progress, here and in America and in the Colonies, to an extent which no historian, however cynical, can overlook, and no critic, however hostile, can deny. As a wholesome moral force, at once conservative and expansive, and under both aspects beneficent in a high degree, the praise of Methodism is now a literary commonplace. But they who prize the fruit must not scorn the seed from which it sprung. Wesley put forth no large programme of social reconstruction. He preached repentance, faith, and holiness. " I will teach transgressors Thy ways, and sinners shall be converted unto Thee." That was his programme,—his plan of campaign, if the terms may be used,—and the rest followed. The sceptic, the man of the world, may despise the teacher of religion, but he must needs pay homage to his work, when, after many days, it is seen in amended lives and ennobled characters, in happy homes and a virtuous people, in the stability of nations and the progress of mankind.

I

2. *Wesley was a theologian with a spiritual history.* If it is true of the poets that "they learn in suffering what they teach in song," it is also true of prophets and apostles and great spiritual teachers, that they are fitted for their vocation through inward travail and discipline. Paul's conversion prepares for his apostolate. God must reveal His Son in him before he can become the messenger and witness of Christ to the Gentiles. Before Augustine can expound and defend the doctrines of Original Sin and Divine Grace, he must learn by experience the meaning of the words, " In me, that is, in my flesh, dwelleth no good thing ;" and, " I can do all things through Christ which strengtheneth me.". So with Luther; before he can preach the forgotten gospel of the righteousness of God which is by faith of Jesus Christ, his strong soul must wear itself in unavailing efforts to attain a righteousness by works of law. Then only was it revealed to his humbled and prepared spirit, that the just shall live by faith,—a revelation which brought to him at once the peace of God, and the inspiration and motive of his life-work. And Wesley is in the succession of strong men, whose personal experience of the things of God has been no mere private blessing, but the preparation for a great career. Not justification by faith alone, but the larger issue of salvation by faith,—salvation, not safety, but deliverance from sin, the renewal and sanctification of the whole nature,— this was the large, the glorious issue to which Wesley was irresistibly drawn, and in the solution of which was involved not only his individual happiness, but a new era of spiritual life for Churches and nations.

Up to thirty-five years of age Wesley was an Oxford Anglican of the best type. God-fearing from his well-trained childhood, he rose through years of rigorous self-discipline to a blameless manhood,—conscientious, self-denying, and devout, making religion the supreme end and master-principle of his life. He resolved to dedicate all his life to God, to mortify everything that bore the stamp of self, and set perfection steadily before him. So he rose early, fasted rigorously, frequented sacraments, lived on the merest pittance, and gave away the greater part of his income. He divided his time between public and private devotion, the visiting of prisoners and sick people, and the spiritual oversight of the kindred souls that gathered around him. The name of "Methodists" was first given in derision to the little band of University men who, under Wesley's guidance, were seeking to live holier lives—lives more strict, methodical, and religiously disciplined, than was usual in those days.

These first Methodists were above all things Churchmen and students. They revived the observance of long-neglected canons and rubrics; they moulded their lives on ascetic models; they thought and spoke much of Christian antiquity, and read the Fathers and Mystics, à-Kempis and Bishop Taylor, and the great High Church Mystic of their own day, William Law. This Oxford Methodism, with its almost monastic rigours, is a fair and noble phase of the many-sided life of the Church of England, and, with all its defects and limitations, claims our deep respect. *But it was not the instrument by which the Church and nation were to be revived.* It had no message for the world, no secret of power with which to move and quicken the masses. To do this it must become other than it was. It must die, in order to bring forth much fruit. And this death and rising again were accomplished in the spiritual change wrought in Wesley, the leader of the later, as he was of the earlier, Methodism.

That change has often been described. I cannot call it "conversion" in the full sense of the word, for I do not believe that Wesley was an "unconverted man" through all the devout years that preceded the change. But it is plain that his apprehension of salvation by faith in Christ had been imperfect and confused. It had brought him no rest to his soul. He longed to be at peace with God, and to have a sure trust and confidence that his sins were forgiven. Suffice it to say that the way of faith, which is the open secret of the gospel, at once hidden from the

wise and prudent, and revealed unto babes, was revealed
to him. He received the reconciliation, and rejoiced in
God. Whether rightly called " conversion " or not, there
can be no doubt as to the significance of the change
wrought in him. If not a "new man" in the deepest
sense, he was practically *another* man, possessing new
powers, and ready for a new work. Religion was no
longer a painful quest, an anxious endeavour, an arduous
discipline,—it was a life, bright with the infinite love of
God, and strong in its consciousness of acceptance with
Him through Christ. Peace with God, the witness of the
Spirit, the blessings of sonship and sanctification,—these
were no longer the distant goal of a painful pilgrimage,
they were included in the common salvation. Every
sinner might claim them in Christ ; every believer would
find them. All this Wesley now knew by experience, and
from this revival in him, the revival throughout the land
had its beginning. He himself was the first product, and
then the chief promoter of the rediscovered gospel of
salvation by faith.

Doubtless something was lost when Methodism moved
from its academic birthplace into the work-day world,
but more was gained. The Fathers and the Mystics were
laid aside, the calm seclusion, the alternating hours of
study, meditation, and prayer, the leisurely yet diligent
life dignified by great traditions, and set amid surroundings congenial to cultivated taste,—all this was left behind ;
but the poor had the gospel preached to them on Kennington Common and Kingswood Hill, in Gwennap pit,
and on Newcastle Moor. Lincoln College and Christ
Church, with

> " Their studious cloisters pale,
> And storied windows richly dight,
> Casting a dim religious light,"

were no longer a home for Wesley and his brother.
They lodged in poor men's houses ; they ministered in
barns and kitchens ; they preached in highways and
market-places ; they were pelted with mud and stones in

the streets of Walsall and Wednesbury, in Sheffield and
Newcastle. But meanwhile ignorant, unhappy, sinful men
and women were brought to the knowledge and love of
God, to peace of mind, to purity of life, and good hope
of heaven. So did the change wrought in Wesley
pass from his own soul to the souls of others, and by
the blessing of God bring about a world-embracing
evangelism, crystallising after a while into Œcumenic
Methodism.

3. *Wesley was the teacher of a spiritual theology.* Alike
in his writings and in his ordinary ministry, Wesley laid
emphasis on the offices and operations of the Holy Spirit,
and on the capacities of the spirit that is in man. In
both these respects the orthodoxy of his day was timid
and minimising. The office of the Holy Ghost was
practically limited to the inspiration of Scripture and the
founding of the Church, that is, to the establishing and
equipment of the order of things called the Christian
religion, with which, henceforth, He had little, if any, direct
relation. To think of Him as exercising direct, vital,
fruitful influence on men was—enthusiasm. In this way
the key of personal religion was lowered and rationalised.
It was made natural throughout, a thing of ordinary
motives, resources, and results. It lacked at once depth
and height, having no Divine quickening at its root, and
nothing that implied a Divine presence and power in its
fruit. It would hardly be too much to say that Wesley
reintroduced into popular and practical theology the
doctrine of the Holy Spirit. He showed that it is not
necessary to adopt the predestinarian point of view in
order to do justice to the work of the Holy Spirit in the
salvation of man. No Calvinist could surpass him in the
just emphasis he laid upon the fact that salvation is of the
Lord, yet no Pelagian or Socinian could teach more im-
pressively the reality of man's moral freedom, and his
personal responsibility as regards repentance and faith.
In Wesley's theology, the Spirit of God is everywhere a
living Spirit, and the Giver of life, the Author of faith,

regeneration, and sanctification, bearing witness with the
believer's spirit, and filling him with joy and peace through
believing.

Closely allied with Wesley's reassertion of the offices
of the Holy Spirit, is his vindication of the claims and
capacities of the spirit of man. Here also the prevailing
doctrine of his day was meagre and inadequate. It had
no confidence in the spiritual element of human nature,
and in its susceptibility to other than rational and pruden-
tial considerations. It did not believe in the existence of
an inward eye with powers of vision all its own, powers
dimmed and enfeebled it might be, but capable of
being revived and re-illumined. It knew nothing of an
inward ear, dull it might be from disuse, but only waiting
for the Divine *Ephphatha* to enable it to hear the voice of
God.

In Wesley's theology, the spirit of man recovers its
rights. It is a spirit fallen, alienated from God, guilty,
incapable of self-recovery, but a spirit created in the
image of God, still possessing, though in weakness and
dishonour, the powers and faculties of its origin. Man
was created to know God. Of that knowledge he is
capable ; he possesses the organs, so to speak, of such
knowledge as surely as he possesses the organs through
which he knows the things pertaining to the temporal and
visible order. Those disused, imperfect organs may be
restored. By the operation of God's Spirit, man's spirit
may be raised into newness of life. He may hear the
Divine voice, he may discern things spiritual, he may
know the things that are freely given to him of God.
And this Wesley taught, not in philosophical but in
scriptural language, not to students and thinkers as such,
but to the people at large. He threw himself fully and
fearlessly upon the very aspects of religion of which the
Church had been fighting shy. It fairly took away the
breath of learned divines to hear of a gospel preached out
of doors, under which Kingswood colliers and Stafford-
shire potters found peace with God, and rejoiced in Christ

Jesus. But Wesley was right. Can we not all see it now? It is of little use to preach a gospel timidly trimmed down to inoffensiveness,—a gospel that makes no great promises, and raises no high expectations. It is an altogether mistaken wisdom to be more parsimonious than God. The gospel is the power of God unto salvation, or it is not. If it is not, then no amount of learning or ingenuity can make it a real remedy for the sin and misery of mankind. But if it is, then let us treat it as such, confidently reckoning on its Divine efficacy as applied by the Spirit of God to the sinful but redeemed spirits of men.

An illustration of Wesley's spiritual method is furnished, by comparing his way of treating an important question with that of Bishop Butler. This is not done with a view to disparage the latter. It is a pleasure to bring these two great names together, not for narrow and invidious comparison, but as master-workmen in God's service, accomplishing each the work that was given to him, with the powers with which he had been entrusted by the Lord of all power and might.

Both Butler and Wesley had a profound sense of the vastness and mystery of things, and of the limits of human knowledge, arising from the limitation of our faculties. "It is not perhaps easy," says Butler, "even for the most reasonable men, always to bear in mind the degree of our ignorance, and make due allowances for it." "A man must really, in the literal sense, know nothing at all who is not sensible of his ignorance. . . . Nor can we give the whole account of any one thing whatever." In the same strain Wesley writes : "How little does the wisest of men know of anything more than he can see with his eyes! What clouds and darkness cover the whole scene of things invisible and eternal. . . . We have no senses suited to eternal and invisible objects. . . . A thinking man wants an opening, of whatever kind, to let in light from eternity."

With views like these did Butler and Wesley face the

question of religion, its evidences, its claims upon man, and the more or less of difficulty experienced in substantiating those claims by sufficient proof. On every side were those who said the case was not made out, that the evidence was inadequate, and that, to say the very least, great difficulties in the way of belief remained when the apologists had done their best. This neither Butler nor Wesley denied. Here they were at one. It is in the further treatment of the case that the characteristic difference between them appears. Butler replies, in effect: "The evidence may not be altogether what we could desire, but is it not sufficient to make it reasonable we should act upon it? We are in no position to insist upon demonstrative proof, which indeed is very rarely forthcoming in regard to practical matters. Probability is the guide we follow in the great majority of instances where we act at all. Ought we not to follow it in this matter also? Moreover, may not difficulties in respect of religious belief constitute for some persons the chief trial of life, a moral test on which much depends; just as, with other persons, common temptations to vice or folly furnish the tests by which character is disciplined and judged?" These are indeed weighty suggestions, very fit to be offered to those to whom they were addressed, and still demanding consideration from those whom they concern.

But Wesley's method is altogether different. He replies by shifting the whole question from one region of the soul to another, and making his appeal to a faculty that has not yet been consulted, a faculty whose powers have been underestimated, whose true office has been forgotten, whose very name is associated with feebleness and inferiority. He calls upon *faith*. Like the prophet, who, when the seven sons of Jesse passed before him that he might choose a king for Israel from among them, called for the youngest son, saying, "Send and fetch him; for we will not sit down till he come;" so Wesley looked in the face the whole array of intellectual forces engaged in the task of

making religion look reasonable, and, passing them by,
called upon *Faith* to awake, arise, and direct its vision to
the things of God.

" Faith," said he, " supplies the need, showing what eye
hath not seen, nor ear heard, neither could it before enter
our heart to conceive. It gives faculties suited to things
invisible. I now am assured that these things are so, I
experience them in my own breast. And this I conceive
to be the strongest evidence of Christianity. I do not
undervalue traditional evidence. Let it have its place and
its due honour. It is highly serviceable in its kind, and
in its decree. And yet I cannot set it on a level with
this." The Spirit beareth witness with our spirit. Whoso
believeth on the Son of God hath the witness in himself.

Such was Wesley's belief as to the province of faith,
and the power of spiritual vision possessed by the spirit
of man when quickened and illumined by the Spirit of
God. Such was his language to a learned and sceptical
correspondent ; and in strains like this it was sung by the
early Methodists at Moorfields and Kennington Common,
at the Foundery and City Road Chapel, and afterwards
by their children's children from the rising of the sun to
the going down of the same :

> " Spirit of faith, come down,
> Reveal the things of God ;
> And make to us the Godhead known,
> And witness with the blood.
>
> " 'Tis Thine the blood to apply,
> And give us eyes to see,
> Who did for every sinner die.
> Hath surely died for me."

Wesley and the Children.

By the Rev. FREDERICK J. MURRELL.

—o—

" Be ye followers of them who through faith and patience inherit the promises."—HEB. vi. 12.

MY DEAR CHILDREN,—

You all know that during the past week we have been celebrating the Centenary of the death of John Wesley, the Founder of our Church, whose spirit passed away to God from the house in which I live.

During the week, two, and sometimes three services, have been held in the chapel every day, and it has been crowded each time, from floor to ceiling, with people from all parts of the country, and from distant lands as well.

Many people have wondered at the great interest which has been shown in the life and work of Wesley. But I have not been surprised at all, because what has taken place here during the past seven days, I have experienced on a small scale for three years.

There is not a week passes but that people come from nearly all parts of the world to visit the house where Wesley lived, to sit in his chair, and stand in the room where he died.

One morning more than forty people from Toronto came to the house in a body, before ten o'clock in the morning, and as they stood in the little garden waiting for the door to be opened, they attracted so much

155

attention, that the cabmen and car-drivers stopped, and a tremendous crowd assembled, and when I let them in, grocers' boys and telegraph messengers came pressing in after them, thinking something dreadful had happened.

I will give you one incident which occurred in my house, to show you the interest people take in the place. About two years ago, a black minister called on me from South America. He told me he was born a slave, and that his father died in slavery. He said the Methodist preachers used to preach to the slaves in their cabins, and in the plantations, and do all they could to brighten and bless their lives, and a large and flourishing Church of black people was raised, called the African Methodist Episcopal Church. But he said, when he was twelve years old he received his freedom, and then he worked half the year and saved enough money he put himself to school the other half.

When quite a young man he became converted and joined the Black Church, and afterwards became a local preacher and a minister.

And at last, as an old man, his people had honoured him by sending him on a holiday to Europe and paying all his expenses. And they told him, as soon as he reached London, he was to visit Wesley's chapel and house, and tell them what he had seen when he returned home.

And he said, "There is one thing I want you to let me do. I hear you have Wesley's teapot. I want to have a cup of tea out of it."

"Oh," I said, "I am afraid I can't do that, as the spout is broken and the lid is gone. Besides, there has been no tea in it for a hundred years, and as a great deal of dust has got into it, I don't know what sort of tea will come out."

He said, "I don't care what comes out, I will drink anything."

He begged so hard, I at last had some tea made in my own pot, and poured it into Wesley's, and then gave it him in a cup. Before he drank it, he devoutly lifted up the pot and said the grace before meat which is on one side of it, and, after he had drank the tea and eaten a slice of bread-and-butter, he returned thanks from the other side of the pot.

Afterwards he asked to be allowed to write a letter on Wesley's bureau, and then to offer prayer in his study. And as I heard him thanking God for raising up a man, who had been the means of planting great Churches in distant lands, and breaking off the fetters, not only from men's souls, but from their bodies as well, and giving them liberty and life, I thought it was the most touching and pathetic sight I had ever seen, and felt amply repaid for all my trouble.

But why is all this interest taken in John Wesley? Simply because he was a good man, and gave himself to the task of making men better and the world happier and purer. People don't enshrine the deeds or take any interest in bad men,—they endeavour to forget them as soon as they can. You have had in these commemorative services an illustration of the scripture, " The memory of the just is blessed."

But all the other meetings were for men and women, and it was thought there ought to be one meeting specially for the children. And I think so too, and I will tell you why.

Because, in the first place, John Wesley was such a great lover of children. Dr. Stoughton told us the other night, his mother used to boast that when she was a child, John Wesley had kissed her. And she was not the only child Wesley kissed. Southey, the poet and biographer, tells us he remembered Wesley visiting his father's house, and as he was going down-stairs, Southey's little sister, a bright-eyed flaxen-haired child, was standing on the stairs, and as soon as Wesley reached her, he caught her up in his arms and kissed her, and then he laid his hand on little Southey's head and blessed him. And Southey says, until his death he felt the better for the good man's blessing.

And Wesley not only loved the children, but the children loved him. They used to climb upon his knee, look up into his beautiful face, play with his soft and silken hair, and nestle in his bosom.

He had a marvellously successful way in winning their love. I won't say he bribed them, but he adopted a method which made failure almost impossible. He used to save new sixpences and bright pennies, and then, when he went among his people, give them to the children. Mr. Curnock, who is sitting by my side, says he has one in his family now. And thus they always hailed his visits with delight, because they knew he had brought them something. I think preachers would be much more popular with you children if they acted in the same way.

Is it not right, therefore, that a man who so loved children, and who was so loved by them, should have his death commemorated by the children of to-day?

And I am delighted to find the Methodist children now have as much reverence and affection for him as the Methodist children had a hundred years ago. The magnificent statue of Wesley just erected in the front of the chapel, is their gift and tribute of love.

The idea originated in the mind of a little boy, and all the Sunday-school scholars at once took it up, and, with the help of the editor of the *Methodist Recorder*, they have already sent £800. And on Monday morning last, when the statue was unveiled. it was my pleasing duty to hand to the President of the Conference two beautiful wreaths of ivy-leaves and snowdrops, sent by a Sunday school in Cornwall, to be laid on the pedestal, on behalf of the children of Methodism.

And another reason why there ought to be a children's service is this :—

If in the next century the world is to be better and the Church stronger and more effective, it rests entirely with them. Wesley recognised this fact. He said, " I reverence the young, because I know how useful they may be after I am dead." Indeed, he felt if the Methodist Church were to continue, it depended upon the children.

One of his preachers once asked him how Methodism was to be perpetuated, and he said, "Take care of the rising generation. Look after the children."

And he did that himself. He prepared Scripture lessons for them, wrote and revised catechisms; and when in Bristol formed the boys and girls into Juvenile Society classes, and whilst in the city met them himself twice every week. And the year before he died, as an old man eighty-six years of age, he preached a sermon to children from this very pulpit; and to show you the great importance he attached to it, there is not a single word in it of more than two syllables.

He also believed in giving the children a good secular education, and for this purpose opened a day school, and allowed children whose parents were too poor to pay for them, to come free.

And as many of you think you have very hard lessons to learn and strict rules to keep, I will tell you what the rules of Wesley's school were.

"All the children had to be present at divine service in the chapel every morning at five. They had to begin lessons at six, and keep on until night. They were not allowed to play, and had no holidays." But even Wesley was compelled to admit this hard and severe discipline was not a success.

But above all, he was most anxious for the conversion of the children. He believed they could be converted and live to Jesus, and he ordered his preachers, wherever it was possible, to gather them together, and give them religious and spiritual instruction. And so you see Wesley had a great love for children, and tried in every way to do them good.

And now what I wish to do is this, I wish to hold him up as a pattern for you young people to imitate.

I know that Jesus Christ is the only perfect pattern, but, as the apostle says, "we should be followers of those who

through faith and patience inherit the promises," and therefore I want you to cultivate the qualities which made
Wesley great and good and useful.

And this is quite possible. You must remember John
Wesley was not a statue, a man made of bronze or marble,
but a living being, made of flesh and blood exactly as men
are now.

And he was not altogether perfect. As a young man,
before he was converted, like a great many other young
men, he had weaknesses and failings, but by the grace of
God he overcame them all, and became pure, and strong,
and noble.

I will very briefly sketch his life. He was born in a
parsonage at Epworth, in Lincolnshire. He must have
been a very proper baby, for his mother, who had nineteen
children, never allowed one of them to cry after it was a
year old, except in subdued tones.

And he must have been a very precocious child, for one
night, when he was only six years old, the rectory caught
fire, and his father and mother, in their haste to get the
servants and children out, forgot him altogether, and did
not miss him until it was too late to get to him.

But the noise woke him up, and he groped his way
through the smoke, climbed on to the top of a chest, and
in his little white night-dress presented himself at the
window, as much as to say, "Here I am, get me out," and
some men stood on each other's shoulders and rescued him.

After this he commenced his studies under the care of
his father and mother, and when he was only ten years old
was sent to the Charter-house School, London. And here,
being a little fellow, he was rather unkindly treated. He
tells us, at meal-times the big boys used to steal his meat,
and for months he had to live simply on bread.

Whilst at school he worked very hard, and soon gained
a high position, and he attributed his good health and
spirits to his running round Charter-house square three
times every morning. So you see hard work will not hurt
you if you have plain food and plenty of exercise.

After he had been at school six years he won a scholarship at Oxford, and proceeded to the university; and he at once did what I would advise every boy to do as soon as he goes out into life,—choose good companions. He associated with the best young men in the university, and gave himself up to a life of piety and good works. He studied the Bible consecutively, took the sacrament regularly, and visited the prisons and workhouses; and ultimately he graduated as a very brilliant scholar, and was elected a Fellow of Lincoln College.

After completing his university course, he was ordained a clergyman, and went as a missionary to the North American Indians. But after two years he returned to England, and whilst attending a service in Aldersgate Street, London, was savingly converted to God, and then his life-work began.

He preached with power and success in the churches. And when, because of his zeal and earnestness, the churches were closed against him, he preached in houses and barns, and in the open air; until at last, as an old man of eighty-seven, worn out with labour, he peacefully fell asleep in the arms of Jesus.

And now let me tell you, in a few words, what qualities characterised Wesley. They are the following:—

I. DECISION.

As soon as he was convinced of his duty, whatever it involved, he did it. And I want every boy and girl to imitate him in that particular. Dare to be singular; dare to do right.

Wesley paid no attention to sneers and derision. Perhaps there is nothing wounds a boy more than to be jeered at, nicknamed, and treated with scorn. But all this Wesley endured unmoved.

At Oxford they called him and his friends the Holy Club, the Good Young Men; and at last fixed on them, in contempt, the name of Methodist.

And he was not affected by slander and evil speeches. One day he promised to take his niece Sally with him to Canterbury and Dover. Her father, Charles Wesley, heard that some of Mr. Wesley's letters had been stolen from the bureau, which is now in my house, and had been so altered, that instead of conveying a spiritual meaning, as they were intended, became capable of a wicked meaning, and were then sent to a newspaper. As soon as Charles Wesley heard of it, he went to the Foundery, and begged his brother to stay at home and vindicate his character. John Wesley's reply was, " Brother, when I devoted to God my ease, my time, my life, did I except my reputation ? No ; tell Sally she shall not be disappointed. I will take her to Canterbury to-morrow."

Once, when he was preaching in Dublin, he said, " Every sin a man can commit has been laid to my charge except drunkenness." And at once a short squat woman in the crowd, with a tattered dress and a red plaid over her head, screamed out, at the top of her voice, " You old scoundrel, and will you deny it ? Did you not pledge your clerical bands with Mr. H—— for a noggin of whisky, and did not our parson's wife buy them ? you old rascal, you know you did." Instead of upbraiding the woman, he simply lifted up his eyes to heaven, and thanked God that his cup was full.

Do not be deterred by scoffs and jeers and hard speeches, but at all costs do what is right.

II. PERSEVERANCE AND INDUSTRY.

Wesley owed all his success to the blessing of God upon his own efforts. He entered the Charter-house School as a free boy because of his great proficiency. And he could never have entered Oxford had he not won a scholarship, for whilst he was there he was so poor he could not afford to pay a barber to dress his hair. And his success as a preacher was largely due to the same cause. Of course he was a great preacher and a wonderful

K

organiser, but it was his untiring energy and his refusal to be conquered by difficulties that made him so successful.

One afternoon Wesley was at Hayle in Cornwall, and was appointed to preach at St. Ives in the evening. The two towns stand on each side of a bay, and the only way in which he could get to St. Ives in time was by driving over the sands. When he started to cross the bay, the tide was rising and was fast covering the sand, and a sea-captain, apprehending his danger, begged him to go back at once.

"But," Wesley said, "I have to preach at St. Ives at a certain hour, and cannot get there in any other way; I will therefore cross over."

Putting his head out of the window, he shouted to the driver, "Take the sea." Very soon the horses were swimming and the carriage rocking with the waves. The poor coachman was afraid he was going to be drowned; but Wesley put his head out of the window, his long hair dripping with the salt water, and exclaimed, "Driver, what is your name?" "Peter," said the man. "Peter," he said, "fear not; thou shalt not sink." And they got over in safety.

The first thing Wesley did when he reached the other side was to see the driver comfortably lodged, provided with refreshments and warm clothing, and placed before a good fire; and then, totally unmindful of himself, and drenched as he was with the dashing waves, he went to the chapel and preached as though nothing unusual had occurred.

That shows you the determination and resolute purpose of the man. He allowed nothing to keep him from duty.

He preached fifteen times every week, travelled four thousand miles every year, was in the saddle more hours than any other man that ever lived, Napoleon Buonaparte not excepted, and was at work, winter and summer, the whole year round, at four.

Rely for success in life on the blessing of God upon your own industry.

III. COURAGE.

He had physical courage. In the presence of wicked men and howling mobs, he was as bold as a lion. He was related to the great Duke of Wellington, and he was as bold for Jesus Christ as Wellington was for the King.

Once a multitude of rioters burst into a house in which he was staying, determined to kill him; but instead of fleeing from them, he calmly walked into their midst, and asked who he had wronged and what he had done. And they were all so abashed and cowed, he passed through them without receiving a scratch or a speck of dirt upon his clothes.

At another time, a mad bull was driven into his congregation, and when, furious and bleeding, it reached the table on which he was standing, Wesley simply put his hand on its head, and went on with his sermon as though nothing unusual had occurred.

And he had moral courage. In public and private he rebuked men for sin, and witnessed for Christ.

Once, when riding in a coach with a young officer, who swore frequently, Wesley asked him to grant him a favour, and, when asked what it was, said, " As we shall be travelling together some distance, if I so far, forget myself as to swear, kindly reprove me."

The young man took the hint, and gave up the evil habit from that hour.

Never be ashamed of your principles, or to speak a word for Jesus.

IV. BENEVOLENCE.

When he was a young man, however much he received, he lived on £28 a year, and gave away all the rest. When he was at Oxford, with the other young Methodists, he helped to clothe and educate a number of poor children ; and one cold winter's day one of these poor children, a young girl, called on·him.

He said, " You seem starved. Have you nothing to cover you but that thin linen gown ? " She told him it was all the clothing she had. He at once put his hand into his pocket to give her some money, but found that he had scarcely any left. Then he looked at the pictures on his room, and the thought struck him, " Will the Master say, ' Well done, good and faithful servant !' Thou hast adorned thy walls with the money which would have screened this poor creature from the cold." And he at once took them down and sold them, and bought the poor girl warm clothing.

And he acted in this spirit throughout life. He established Orphanages for children, built Almshouses for poor men and women, and instituted a " Loan Society " to help deserving people who were in monetary difficulties. He gave away during his life more than £40,000 ; and, when he died, left behind him—two silver spoons and the great Methodist Connexion !

Cultivate a spirit of generosity to the cause of God and the poor.

Above all, imitate Wesley's devotion to God. He was great, and good, and useful, because he was filled with the power of God, and spent his life in the service of humanity. Last Monday morning, at ten o'clock, I went into my study, the room where Wesley died, and I thought, from this spot, at this hour, a hundred years ago, Wesley passed away to God. The place seemed holy ground, and in contrition and penitence upon my knees I asked God to baptize me with the same spirit that had filled Wesley, and to qualify me for whole-hearted service. Let me urge you all to offer the same prayer. Live as he lived, not for ease and pleasure, but to do good, and then your lives will be bright, joyous, and blessed.

The Charter of the Church in the Centuries to Come.

By Mr. S. D. WADDY, Q.C., M.P.

——o——

> "*And Jesus came to them and spake unto them, saying, All authority hath been given unto Me in heaven and on earth. Go ye therefore, and make disciples of all the nations, baptizing them into the name of the Father, and of the Son, and of the Holy Ghost: teaching them to observe all things whatsoever I commanded you: and lo, I AM WITH YOU ALWAY, even unto the end of the world.*"—MATT. xxviii. 18-20.

DURING the last few days you have often been reminded of John Wesley's saying, "The best of all is, God is with us." It was almost his dying cry; but it was no new and sudden inspiration then. It presented accurately what had long been the attitude of his mind.

On Wesley's lips these words conveyed two distinct and yet closely-connected ideas. On the one hand, they expressed the exultation of hallowed joy; and, on the other hand, they were the shout of holy triumph. "God was with us; and therefore we were filled with rapture." There it is, the cry of happy gratitude. "God was with us, and therefore we were crowned with success." There it becomes the humble ascription of all glory to God. Such was the temper of Wesley in his warfare and toil. As he neared his end he dwelt with increasing simplicity and earnestness on the two thoughts thus sacredly linked together. They had long inspired the labour of his life; they filled with ecstasy his triumphant death.

The century that has elapsed since that day has shown that this cry was not the boast of folly or the deception of fanaticism. The words were words of truth and soberness. They have been constantly illustrated and enforced by the personal experience of believers, and the growing history of our Church.

I do not, however, to-night desire to dwell entirely or even mainly upon the past. Those learned and godly men to whom you have lately listened with so much profit and delight, have fully reminded you of the mercy God has shown us, and the prosperity with which His presence has blessed us. I will not presume to glean where they have reaped. But in this last service of a series which will ever be memorable in the history of Methodism, I may not inappropriately fix your attention on the second century rather than on the first. Let us, on our gratitude for the past, found our warnings, our encouragements, our resolves for the future. From the exclamation of the saint exulting that God was with him then,—from our own thankful memories that God has been with us ever since,—we turn to a still fuller promise—a promise not for a generation or a century, but firm till time shall be no more—a promise proclaimed by the lips, not of the dying servant, but of the risen, the eternal Lord:

"LO, I AM WITH YOU ALWAY, EVEN UNTO THE END OF THE WORLD."

This blessed announcement is not only the hope and confidence of the believer,—it is the charter and inspiration of the Church; and to this application of the words I ask your prayerful attention.

I. TO WHOM IS THIS PROMISE GIVEN?

Matthew specifically mentions only "the eleven disciples." From this fact some learned and well-meaning, but not very liberal, men have assumed that the command and blessing were confined to the apostles, and that an argument in favour of "apostolical succession" may be found in this passage. Rest assured that in the second century of Methodist history, and in City Road Chapel to-day, I shall not waste your time in demolishing this arrogant trumpery. The mere existence of our Church at this celebration,—its marvellous growth during past generations,—its millions of faithful believers, on continent and island, the wide world over,—this crowded house of God, —these happy faces,—these saved souls,—are sufficient answer to all charges of heresy and schism, and to every feeble and narrow-minded attempt to limit or to fetter the grace and mercy of God. If, in truth, none but the eleven apostles heard these words from our Lord's lips, they heard them for us as well as for themselves. A promise which was to live till the end of the world, could not be confined to men who in a very few years would rejoin their Lord in His celestial glory, and they could no more claim a monopoly of His earthly blessing, than an exclusive title to the "many mansions" in heaven.

But there is good ground for believing that the apostles were not the only persons present on this august occasion. It is highly probable that the evangelist gives us here the details of the manifestation which St. Paul shortly describes in 1 Cor. xv. 6, where he tells us that Jesus "appeared to above five hundred brethren at once." This view is strengthened by an expression in verse 17. The earlier part of this chapter finds the apostles in Jerusalem. The narrative brings them thence into Galilee to the appointed mountain, and there "they worshipped Him." But it adds that "some doubted." Now, who were these doubters? Certainly not the apostles. They had been already convinced, and filled with holy and trustful joy. Ten of them.

we are told by St. John, had seen Him in Jerusalem, and "were glad when they saw the Lord." The eleventh, Philip, was absent at that time; but he had subsequently seen Him at the same place, and had adored Him as "my Lord and my God." The whole eleven had, in fact, travelled to Galilee in joyful obedience to His Divine command. The doubters must therefore have been some of the Galilean disciples, who had not hitherto beheld their risen Saviour; and the whole earthly Church, with but few exceptions, was probably gathered there when Jesus uttered this universal blessing. Whether, therefore, these words were spoken to the apostles as the representatives of the Saviour's flock, or to a more numerous congregation of the believers in Him, we equally claim them as our own,— the heritage of the whole Church of Christ, universal and enduring.

II. BY WHOM IS THIS PROMISE PROCLAIMED?

The inquiry is not an idle one; for the message is so majestic that on the lips of any man—mere man—however wise or good or great, it would be impertinent and profane. The speaker therefore begins by challenging our reverence on the ground that "all authority hath been given to Him in heaven and on earth." His words assert His divinity, for He claims eternity and omnipresence when He undertakes to bless and aid His servants through all time and in every place. But while the disciples were awed by the behests of a visible God, they remembered also that He was the risen Saviour. They recalled the life of sympathy, the atoning love of His cruel death, His tender forgiveness of their lukewarm cowardice and unbelief. He was at once the loving Saviour and the omnipotent God. It was this Being of infinite mercy and of infinite power who was about to demand much from them, and who therefore was about to promise them a perfect encouragement and a glorious reward. He would summon them to self-sacrifice and toil; they must undergo privation and suffering; they must battle with the powers of earth and the fiends of hell; they must abandon the joys of life, and crown their devotion by a martyr's death. And before He calls them to this tremendous strife, He heartens them by the promise that He whose perfect and enduring love has been so well proved in the past, and can be so absolutely trusted in the future, — that He who will never leave them nor forsake them,—is clothed with "all authority in heaven and on earth." Angels from above shall have charge over them, shall guide their steps and lift their hands. The powers of nature shall be swayed by His high control, the providence of God shall work on their behalf, and the constant presence of their Lord shall be their comfort in tribulation, their joy in sorrow, their life in death.

Brethren, our work is not so terrible as theirs. We have only to meet contemptuous indifference where they encountered cruel persecution. We have to bear sarcasm and sneer where they were chained to the stake or thrown to ferocious beasts. But the promise in all its richness is ours as well as theirs. And through the rolling centuries the words are as fresh and as true in the nineteenth as in the first. They ring blessed and glorious in our ears to-day, and they shall be the charter and inspiration of our Church in the ages to come,—"Lo, I am with you alway, even unto the end of the world."

But there is one subject still to be considered before we thus appropriate the promise:

III. THE CONDITION ON WHICH THIS PROMISE IS GIVEN.

It is dependent on the performance of duty. The authority is an authority to commission us for our work. The heart of the passage is the command to do it. The grace is a grace given to assist us, and succeed us, and bless us in its doing.

The central purpose of a Christian Church is a Church to do Christian work. The nature and scope of this duty are broadly but accurately given in the nineteenth verse. Undeterred by the perils and difficulties of distance, we are to "go" to the nations ; undaunted by the immensity of the task, we are to go to "all the nations." With un-wearied patience and devotion, we are to "make disciples" of the most brutalised and barbarous, or of the most sceptical and sensual. We are not merely to confer upon them civilisation, political education, or social improve-ment,—we are to bring them definitely into the Church of Christ, "baptising them into the name of the Father, and of the Son, and of the Holy Ghost." We must not rest satisfied with their formal or intellectual acceptance of the doctrines of religion, but must "teach them" in purity of life and consecration of soul "to observe all things whatsoever Christ commanded us." This is to be the work, not of a few, however rich or godly or learned, but of all ; and in face of this gigantic and apparently hopeless task, our strength, our comfort, our assurance shall be the abiding presence of the Redeemer, who will be with us "alway, even unto the end of the world."

This was the mission of the early Church. The wide world tells the tale of its success or failure. It was the mission of Wesley and his sons, and millions of glorified saints and of happy believers to-day are the result of their labours. You and I are amongst the trophies which those founders of our Church have won, and I refrain from the long record of their toil and triumph, only because during the last few days you have been so fully reminded of their hallowed struggle and their glorious success.

But I am compelled to emphasise one principle,—God requires that *all* should work. It is our duty and our privilege to be good. It is equally our duty and our privilege to do good. In Mosaic times, the prayer of the great lawgiver was, "Would God that all the Lord's people were prophets, that the Lord would put His Spirit upon

them" (Num. xi. 29). Our Lord sent forth not only the
twelve apostles, but the seventy disciples. The growth of
the primitive Church was largely due to the fact that the
evangelising spirit and practice were not exceptional but
universal. It is true that in the Acts of the Apostles
we find scanty records of the work of more than six or
seven men. The towering pre-eminence of a few colossal
evangelists dwarfed and almost obliterated the record
of the steady, pervasive, but comparatively unobserved
work of the mass. But St. Paul contemplated with
satisfaction a state of Church life when "all could prophesy one by one, and all might be comforted," and the
very disasters that threatened to destroy Christianity were
overruled for good, because they that "were scattered
abroad" by persecution, "went everywhere preaching the
Word."

When Methodism was young, the same principle and
practice prevailed amongst us. One characteristic of our
forefathers was that they were *all* at work and *always* at
work. Humanly speaking, this was the secret of their
success. Let me ask you in all faithfulness, Are we loyal
sons of such noble sires? I believe that I am here to-night
as being in somewise a representative of the lay-preachers
of our Church. Then let me stand by my order for a few
moments. The admirable speech delivered here last
Thursday by my brother Clough, the President this year
of our Local Preachers' Association, renders it unnecessary
and unwise for me to dwell on the enormous work that
laymen have done, and nobly done, in bygone days.
The great point is this: that while they have always
been a necessity of our Church's existence, and are still
indispensable to its continued life and usefulness, we are
sadly deficient in numbers; and, moreover, our ranks are
deserted by the very men whose help we most specially
desire.

I call to-night for recruits! You will not so far misunderstand me as to think that this appeal involves the
slightest reflection upon the "regular" ministry. My only

desire is to rouse *our educated laity* to undertake this work. The fact is that we are drifting into a habit of leaving the preaching of the gospel almost entirely to the ordained ministers, as though they were exclusively qualified and appointed to be heralds of the Cross. This is fatal to ourselves, and mischievous to others.

It is fatal to ourselves. A lazy Christian is a dying Christian. If we are not working *for* Christ, Christ will not long work *in* us. I believe that we have here the reason of much which has lately caused "great searchings of heart;" and that one great peril of Methodism (perhaps its greatest) lies in our losing the habit, as a people, of earnest, healthy work. If we do this, we shall soon by steady and fatal stages lose our love for it, then the power to do it, and at last our whole spiritual life.

But, in addition to its malignant effects on ourselves, this tendency to narrow evangelism into a profession or business, is ruinous to others. Humanly speaking, the world can never be saved by the clergy. It has never been possible at any period of the Church's history. Two obvious reasons show that it is not possible now.

Consider, on the one hand, the purely missionary work of the Church at home and abroad. The darkness of our own country and the vastness of foreign heathenism present a field too wide, obstacles too mighty, a harvest too plenteous, for labourers so few as the ordained ministry must continue to be. As well might you hope to win a campaign by the struggles of the officers only, while the rank and file look idly on. "The field is the world," and "the labourers are few."

But there is a further difficulty. The ordained ministry could not do the work if they tried; but they are not allowed to try! We expect them to devote themselves to a sphere of duty quite distinct, and which is apparently the inevitable consequence of our past success. Our preachers have become pastors,—absorbed in the cares of the Church. If, for the edification and delight of congregations of converted people, the pastor is boxed up in his pulpit, or assigned to pastoral visitation, the meeting of classes, and (alas!) the management of funds, he will have but little time left in which he can go after the outcast and lost. But they will not come to us. They will not bring their squalor, their sorrow, or their sin into close contrast with the light and harmony, the purity and joy of the people of God. We must go to them and "compel them to come in."

Who then must do this great work? *The whole Church of Christ.* We want an army of sensible, earnest, godly talkers. Call them local preachers, or lay evangelists, or missioners, or what you will. Never mind the name. We want the men, and in no stinted measure. For if the world is to be won for Christ, " ALL THE LORD'S PEOPLE" MUST BE PROPHETS. Our sermons need not be preached in church or chapel, or under any roof at all. Our audiences need not be counted by the hundred, or even by the score. We must follow the people wherever they go, and proclaim the glad tidings wherever we find them. This was the work of our forefathers; and, in order to make our second century match our first, men of all professions and trades, and from all classes, must come to the front, and carry the war back into the enemy's country. If I could once plant this conviction firmly in the minds of our educated and godly laity, this centenary celebration would have glorious results. And the emergency is pressing! For observe how for want of some such organisation, Methodism already suffers. Many of our most venerable sanctuaries in the midst of London and other large towns, once crowded with worshippers, are now comparatively deserted. Their former occupants and their children have achieved wealth, and have moved into the suburbs or the country; and their empty places have not been refilled. We, alas! are becoming accustomed to this state of things, and reconciled to it. And we satisfy ourselves by murmuring helplessly that "the population has left London." True, one population has done so, but there is still a population there. If one Methodist family has gone to Brixton, and another to Chiselhurst, and a third to Enfield, are there not thousands of human beings still living around this very chapel ? They have not perhaps the same education or rank or Methodist history as those who have gone—but they have souls ! It may be that you cannot reach them by the same means as were effectual with yourselves. Then let us try others. There are hundreds of converted people here,—at this moment,—in this chapel,—who are admirably qualified for this work, but who are doing, in fact, little or nothing in the way of active Christian evangelism.

I know the "stock" excuse which many people make in answer to such a challenge as this. "Oh," they say, " I really cannot preach or speak in public, or 'canvas' strangers. I have not the gift !" This is only mock-humility. Watch this shy and dumb Christian. His wealth increases; his influence widens; his ambition expands. Some kind friends suggest to him that his opulence, rank, and talent clearly mark him as a fit and proper man to be a member of the House of Commons. His own desires are flattered by the thought. He accepts the invitation. And in a moment he develops a power of public oratory and resources of personal persuasion which are a miracle to everybody but himself ! My brother, try your experiment first of all in the service of Christ ! Preach—not politics—but the gospel ! Canvas—not for votes—but for souls !

If, however, our hesitation is the true child of humility, our text is our perfect answer. Take courage ! The work authorised by His Word, guided by His wisdom, done in His strength, filled with His presence, cannot fail ! Let Christ be with us in the study and in the pulpit, in the cottage kitchen and among the outdoor crowd,—let Him sway our hearts, fire our emotions, inspire our words and tones, and we must conquer ! And this rich blessing shall assuredly be ours; for He saith, " Lo, I am with you alway !"

IV. LASTLY, THEN, THE PROMISED PRESENCE OF CHRIST IS THE CHURCH'S GREAT INCENTIVE TO DUTY.

When we are brought face to face with our task, we need some mighty motive to brace us for an enterprise so glorious, but so awful. We look abroad over our own country, and its unsaved millions; we observe its social vices, its perverse ignorance of Divine truth, its contempt of God and His laws, its drunkenness, blasphemy, infidelity, and lust, — and we are appalled. We gaze on other lands, and the prospect is still more ghastly. Nations claiming to be civilised, whose polish is rottenness, whose theologies are a mockery, and whose religious hope is despair, drive us sadly to own that it is still true that the world lieth in the arms of the wicked one. We may almost be forgiven if our hearts sink within us when we are called to such a warfare as this.

The same temptation assailed the apostles, and to them the outlook was even more terrible than it is to us. History gave them none of the encouragements which have brightened our hopes. The marvellous blood - bought triumphs of the Cross, which cheer our hearts and sustain our faith, were still unwon. The word of God had not been translated into every tongue, and preached in every clime; learned men had not laid their talents, and mighty kings their sceptres, at the feet of Jesus. Inconsiderable in number, rank, and wealth, the disciples were called to overthrow the philosophies, heresies, and tyrannies of the world, and our Lord foresaw their probable dread. He heartened them, therefore, beforehand. He prefaced His command by the " authority " which pledged Almighty aid. He followed it by the promise which rounds and perfects the whole, with the pledge of an enduring presence and an infinite love.

The assurance of God's presence with His servants has always been their chief comfort and stay. When Jehovah bade Moses bear His message to Pharaoh, the patriarch quailed before an embassy so hazardous. " Who am I ? "

said he in trembling excuse. " Certainly I will be with thee," was the all-sufficient answer of the All-Sufficient God. When, at a later crisis, he pleaded, " If Thy presence go not with me, carry me not up hence," his anxiety was anticipated by, " My presence shall go with thee, and I will give thee rest." So also under the New Covenant. Jesus cheered the disconsolate apostles with the promise, " I will not leave you desolate, I will come unto you." And the charter of the Church is still the same. The trust of the disciples when Christ ascended from Olivet was the strength of Methodism in our first century,—the watchword with which we begin our second,—the source of our growing hope, our deepening faith, our brightening joy. Christ's presence *with* the Church and *in* the Church has always been, still is, and ever shall be, its *strength* and its *life*.

Let us illustrate this by a few particulars.

1. Our exalted Christ is our *strength*. As the God of Providence He supplies our every necessity.

He is not only the Head of the Church, He is also " the Head over all things to the Church " (Eph. i. 20). Restored to His imperial throne, He sways all things for the accomplishment of His saving purposes. Thus, He prepares our *way*, our *instruments*, and our *men*.

With infinite wisdom and power He prepares our *way* before us. He moulds the history of the world for the furtherance of the gospel. The designs of good men, and the overruled plots of bad men, subserve His gracious purposes. He bends the intrigues of politics, and subdues the ambition of conquerors, till even " war proclaims the Prince of Peace." " The wrath of man shall praise Him, and the remainder of wrath He shall restrain."

Moreover, He prepares our *instruments*. With what merciful accuracy has He timed the progress of discovery so as to serve His sovereign will. Inventions have sprung to light just when they could do least harm and most good to Christianity, and science and art have been the unconscious handmaids of the gospel. One familiar example of this is the printing press. If man had possessed this engine at an earlier date, it is hardly too much to say that it would have been a curse rather than a blessing. Of the literature of Greece and Rome, it is fair to suppose that the best has survived, and some of it is not without nobility and beauty. But how large a proportion is corrupt! If the filth of Aristophanes, Catullus, Horace, Ovid, Petronius, and a host of minor writers, had been multiplied by the press, the flood of contamination would have been frightful. But the art of printing came just in time for Tyndale and the translation of the Bible; and its whole history has been ennobled by the work it has done in sowing broadcast the Word of God.

Christ is the strength of the Church, lastly, in this—He prepares and gives us *men*.

The first disciples were chosen by Him who " knew what was in man," summoned by His own voice, and trained by His own care. From age to age He has continued to provide the men for the day. He found the early fathers and martyrs. He inspired the leaders of the Reformation. He shaped the characters and guided the lives of the founders of Methodism. He adorned and fortified the infant Church with the administrative sagacity of John Wesley, the raptured poetry of Charles Wesley, the burning eloquence of Whitefield, the seraphic devotion of Fletcher. Through the whole of the bygone century He has never failed us. These walls have echoed to the voice of Benson the divine, Coke the missionary, Clarke the scholar, Bunting the statesman, Watson the theologian, Newton the evangelist, Punshon the orator. The names of Reece, Fowler, Treffry, the Jacksons, Hannah, Farrar, Scott, Lomas, West, Young, Prest, Rattenbury, Jobson, Gervase Smith, Shaw, Romilly Hall, and scores of other men as majestic as they, rush from our hearts to our lips. With them we think of eloquent laymen equally worthy of memory. William Dawson, the Yorkshire farmer; Charles Richardson, the Lincolnshire thrasher; Drew, the learned shoemaker; George Smith, the Cornish historian; the scholarly Dr. Melson; the village blacksmith Hick. Merchant princes have brought their wealth to Christ's feet: Farmer, Heald, Lycett, Chubb, Macarthur. He has moved some to consecrate their talents and their lives. He has moved others to sanctify their riches. The Christlike spirit, the actuating presence of Christ, has given us the strength of the heart, of the wealth, of the learning, of the life. Nor can we refrain from thanking God for some still in our midst, who, with a long record of noble work nobly done, tarry yet awhile listening for the Master's call. We sympathise with that victim of his own tireless zeal and self-sacrifice, the erudite and profound theologian of modern Methodism. We rejoice over the venerable man who, twice our President, champion in bygone days of warfare, storehouse of our history, teacher of hundreds of ministers of the gospel, rests from the long and worthy labour. And we are filled with gratitude as we cry, Thank God for William Arthur and the Tongue of Fire!

All these men have been given to us by our Head. He made them what they were. He gave them the victories they won. Their names, and others which I must not recall, are an inspiration to us this day. As we hush our own words, we almost think we can hear those well-remembered tones which in past years have thrilled all hearts in this house of God. We seem to catch once more " the sound of the voice that is still," hushed in this world for ever, but ringing with a clearer and gladder note before " the great white throne."

Now, all these men had one prevailing characteristic. Christ was in them. They had the abiding presence of our Lord. Differing widely in almost everything else, they agreed in this, they believed firmly in Christ as their Saviour; the ambition of their lives was to do His work, to be endued with His image, to have " Christ formed in their hearts, the hope of glory." And the more you study their lives and characters, the more clearly and forcibly will you recognise that the blessed presence of Christ with them was their motive and their argument, their inspiration and their strength, their joy and their crown.

And He who gave us them will give us others. The second century will bring us men as richly endowed, as truly ordained, as these were. Shallow ritualism may impertinently question their " orders" or their succession. Their "authority" comes straight from headquarters ; and he who receives his commission direct from the King's own hand, and who, in the strength of it, has fought and conquered the powers of evil, may afford to smile at those who find fault with him because he has never taken the enlisting shilling from the recruiting sergeant.

2. But the presence of Christ is not only the strength of the Church,—*it is its very life.* We depend upon Him not only for what He does *for* us, or gives *to* us, but for what He is *in* us. This is the personal experience of every believer—"I live ; and yet no longer I, but Christ liveth in me." And that which is true of the individual, is true of the collective body of believers.

He is the life of our *doctrine.* Our creed rests on Him, and is filled with Him. The atonement, resurrection, ascension, and intercession of our Redeemer form the centre round which all our theology is gathered, the foundation on which all our religion is built. No philosophy however subtle, no morality however pure, can supply the place of these doctrines. If we refine them into poetry, or lose them in abstraction, the life is gone. The doctrinal life of Methodism has ever been derived from our clear acknowledgment of our need for Christ and our dependence upon Him.

The characteristic feature of our teaching has been the constant exhibition of the Cross. Our preaching has been one long, earnest cry, " Behold the Lamb of God ;" and this has been the great secret of its freshness and power. We have had amongst us scholars, poets, orators, divines ; —but their success has been proportioned not to their genius and learning, but to their loyal devotion to Christ ; to their emulation of the apostle, who "determined not to know any thing save Jesus Christ and Him crucified." If in the coming years we are to succeed like them, we must hold the same faith. Jesus Christ, in the atoning efficacy of His blood, in the triumph of His mediatorial reign, must be the life of our pulpits, the foundation and centre of all our teaching. Any graces of style or developments of culture will be dearly bought if for them we neglect or conceal the Cross.

Lastly, He is the life of our *experience*. The characteristic feature of our experience has been a predominating and passionate longing for conscious fellowship with the Redeemer. We describe our seasons of holy joy most naturally by saying, "It was good to be there, for we met with Jesus." This desire fills our prayers and inspires our songs. Every phase of religious experience, every step of our spiritual life, is in our hymnology linked with and made dependent on our personal union with Him. The "mourner convinced of sin" cries :

> "Take this poor fluttering soul to rest,
> And lodge it, Saviour, in Thy breast."

Hungering for present salvation, we plead with redoubled appeal :

> "My heart would now receive Thee, Lord!
> Come in, my Lord, come in!"

The yearning for entire sanctification foretells with confident faith that

> "When Jesus makes my heart His home,
> My sin shall all depart."

When convinced of backsliding, we pray

> "Open the intercourse between
> My longing soul and Thee;
> Never to be broke off again
> To all eternity."

Wearied of the cares and vanities of the world, we sing :

> "My heart ever fainting
> He only can cheer :
> And all things are wanting
> Till Jesus is here."

For shelter from storm and sorrow we cry,

> "Take me, Jesus, to Thine arms,
> And keep me ever there."

Death loses its terrors when we seek to

> "Live happy in my Saviour's love,
> And in His arms expire."

Celestial joys brighten into fresher glory as we exclaim :

> "Thy presence makes my paradise,
> And where Thou art is heaven."

And we exult in the prospect of everlasting blessedness in Him :

> "Spring Thou up within my heart,
> Rise to all eternity."

This experience must still be ours. It is our *life*. Just as a Christless theology would soon become not only useless, but absolutely mischievous ; so a Christless experience is lethargy deepening into destruction. It is true that emotion alone is not enough. Religion without knowledge is superstition and fanaticism ; but religion without a felt Christ is despair and death. The indwelling Saviour, whose presence is ever recognised, and whose influence is ever felt, is the strength against temptation which brings us purity ; and the security against doubt, which gives us peace.

This has been the history of our first hundred years. May God repeat it in the second ! We want no new doctrines to coax people into our communion, no new experience to shape their lives. Fighting the same battle as our forefathers fought, wielding the same weapons, marshalled by the same Captain, we look with firm faith for the same blessed and eternal victory.

Thus, then, we start on our new century. We do not know what its unfolding will reveal, what fresh spheres of labour will invite our effort, what times and causes of peril will test the Church. New doors are even now opening

on every hand. At home and abroad souls are longing
for the truth. The partly explored regions of Central
Australia await us, the hundreds of millions of China are
awaking to the light, and the mysteries of darkest Africa
challenge our research. In this wide and varied strife, of
which at present we know so little, there will be unforeseen
but awful struggles with the powers of evil ; and in that
stern fight and long-drawn toil the promise of the text
will often be our surest and almost our only support. For
however fierce the battle, our weakness need never falter,
and our ignorance need never fail. Christ is "the power
of God and the wisdom of God ;" and with all that power,
and all that wisdom, He will be with us "alway, even unto
the end of the world."

In the work of the Church take this as your watchword.
Patient evangelist, in the midst of darkness and misery, in
the home of despair, in the den of infamy, He is ever at
your side. Brave missionary, in the far-off islands of the
sea, in your solitude and your exile, you are not alone !
He is "with you alway !" Simple believer, tried by the
scoffs of the scornful or the persecution of the malignant,
He will be at your right hand, and you shall not be
moved ! In bereavement, in sorrow, in trial, in care, in
agony, He will never leave you nor forsake you. And
when at last the end shall come, when strength of body
and mind begins to fail, when with wasting frame, throbbing
temples, and parched lips, you draw nearer and nearer to
the valley of the shadow of death, still His rod and His
staff shall comfort you. In the darkness and agony on
this side of the river, your last memory shall be the words
of the promise, " I am with you alway." Clinging as the
stream rises—clinging to that loving hand which has never
let a believer fall—clinging to Jesus all the way across,
He shall land you on the eternal shore ; the words begun
on earth shall finish in heaven, the promise shall become
fruition, as with fulness of revelation and fulness of glory
you hear at last His own voice, " Lo, I am with you alway,
even unto the end of the world."

The Wesley Centenary.

—∻—

PART II.

Other Religious Services,

HELD IN CITY ROAD CHAPEL.

Saturday Evening, February 28th,
THANKSGIVING AND PRAYER.

Monday Morning, March 2nd,
THE UNVEILING OF THE WESLEY STATUE.

Monday Evening,
MEETING: REPRESENTING THE METHODIST CONNEXIONS.

Tuesday Afternoon, March 3rd,
THE SACRAMENT OF THE LORD'S SUPPER.

Tuesday Evening,
A REVIEW OF METHODIST WORK.

Wednesday Afternoon, March 4th,
OPENING OF THE ALLAN LIBRARY.

Wednesday Evening,
METHODISM AND SOCIAL WORK.

Thursday Evening, March 5th,
THE PRIVILEGES, DUTIES, RESPONSIBILITIES, AND OPPORTUNITIES OF THE YOUNG PEOPLE OF METHODISM.

Friday Evening, March 6th,
METHODISM AND THE SISTER CHURCHES.

Saturday Evening, March 7th,
THE CENTENARY LOVE FEAST.

Thanksgiving and Prayer.

---

*The Services in Commemoration of John Wesley's Death
opened on Saturday evening, February 28th, with a
Devotional Meeting, conducted by the Rev. Richard
Roberts and the Rev. H. Douthwaite*

Address

By the Rev. RICHARD ROBERTS.

RECALLING the circumstances of Mr. Wesley's departure,
and alluding to his quotation of the hymn, "I'll praise
my Maker while I've breath," Mr. Roberts said : His days
of praise are not yet past. God granted to Mr. Wesley
his oft-repeated desire to "cease at once to work and live."
Every Christian is called to work for Christ, and the
humblest toil for Him is an unspeakable honour. Mr.
Wesley's message may be compared for its universality to
that of the great Apostle of the Gentiles. Like the angel
flying in the midst of heaven, he had a message to all
nations, peoples, kindreds, and tongues. It was : Redemption for all men through faith in Jesus Christ. In
many pulpits of Wesley's early days that was a doctrine
forgotten or denounced. John Wesley was called to

deliver the Churches from the swathing bands of a limited salvation. The opening hymns of our Hymn-book show this.

Another doctrine of the Wesleyan Revival was that of Christian Assurance. It was held, even by good men, to be presumption; and denounced by pulpit and press as fanaticism. Others said it was a special privilege, granted but to a favoured few in apostolic days. Mr. Wesley had preached for years before experiencing this blessing himself, but as soon as he did he boldly proclaimed it as the heritage of every Christian. The doctrine of the Witness of the Spirit is prominent in the hymns.

> "We by His Spirit prove
> And know the things of God."

Mr. Wesley made religion a thing of joy. Such hymns as "Come ye that love the Lord," "My God is reconciled," etc., are proof of this.

Another doctrine emphasised was that of Christian Perfection. It startled the Churches to hear that the grace of God could deliver from all sin, inward and outward; that grace was mightier than sin — Christ stronger than Satan.

> "He wills that I should holy be:
> What can withstand His will?"

May the day never come when, in our congregations and class-meetings, meaningless drivelling ditties shall take the place of these grand old hymns.

While thankful for Wesley and Methodism, we cannot help casting a glance forward to the day of the Lord's coming, when an innumerable throng of saints shall be directed by the Saviour to take possession of the thrones purchased for them. They will come from India, China, and Japan; from Europe, Africa, and Australasia; and Wesley, overpowered at the sight, may be imagined crying :—

"All thanks be to God,
Who scatters abroad,
Throughout every place,
By the least of His servants, His savour of grace."

And as the last is conducted through the gates of Paradise, I see Wesley and Whitefield bowing low before the Redeemer, saying, "Not unto us, O Lord; not unto us, but unto Thy Name give glory, for Thy mercy and for Thy truth's sake." Some of us will be there. I am thankful to be a Methodist, converted to God fifty-six years ago, and conscious ever since that I am Christ's, and Christ mine—able to sing,

"My God, I am Thine;
What a comfort Divine,
What a blessing to know that my Jesus is mine."

Address

By the Rev. CHARLES GARRETT.

It is a great privilege to be present at the first of a series of meetings, which will, I trust, bless not only Methodism, but the world. It is peculiarly fitting that we should begin with a prayer-meeting. Prayer-meetings have been our strength and glory from the beginning. They are still the true tests of the spiritual condition of our Churches, and I trust that a strengthening and stimulating influence will go from this meeting to every prayer-meeting in Methodism. I am perplexed as to the best way of using the few moments at my disposal, but I am anxious to say a word or two that may promote our gratitude to God, and lead us to devote ourselves afresh to His service. We have reason to be grateful for the boundless, priceless blessings which we have received through John Wesley. Some have thought it strange that we should celebrate the death of a man. But I hold that this is in perfect harmony with all our traditions. When Mr. Wesley's mother lay dying, she said to those who surrounded her bed, "When I am gone, sing a hymn." And when her son went home, his friends stood up and sang,

"Waiting to receive thy spirit."

Our Hymn-book seems specially fitted for such a purpose. The grandest hymns in the book are such as might be sung by death-beds and at the grave-side. No music ever impresses my heart so much as those beautiful hymns sung on such occasions to our old-fashioned minor tunes. These are infinitely better than the doleful trappings that are sometimes thrown around the king of terrors, making him more hideous than he is. There are two ways of looking at death—the selfish way, which thinks only of the loss we have sustained; and the joyous way, which thanks God for the good work done by the departed, and for the pleasant memories they have left behind. The Methodist way is the latter, and it is in this spirit we are met to-night.

I am glad to know that we have not a monopoly of this joy. In large numbers of churches and chapels celebrations similar to our own will take place to-morrow and through the week. It is fit and proper that it should be so, for John Wesley was the Morning Star of the Second Reformation; the Herald and Inbringer of a new era of blessing for the Church and for the world. To look beyond him is to look into the dark ages, when men had no rights, and God no honour. All the great religious and social movements, which are the glory of the nineteenth century, were in John Wesley's mind, and he attempted to carry them out. As to Foreign Missions, he made the Methodist Church a Foreign Missionary Society, with the motto, "The world is my parish;" while the Home Missionary system he established was such as the world had never seen since the early days of Christianity. Sunday schools were started by Wesley before Raikes was born. He founded a Bible Society before the Bible Society had come into existence; and wrote Tracts and put them into circulation long before the era of the Religious Tract Society. He established Schools for Poor Children before the British and Foreign School Society had been founded. He was a Temperance advocate long before the time of the Seven Men of Preston; and if the Church he founded had held to his principles, the curse of drunkenness would long ago have been swept away. A hundred years before my dear friend Dr. Stephenson was born, John Wesley established Orphanages. He was the pioneer of the work of disseminating cheap books; and of founding Dispensaries for the Poor. He visited the prisons before John Howard entered on his mission of mercy. He was an energetic enemy of the Slave Trade before Wilberforce took up the subject. He established a Benevolent Loan Society long enough before General Booth. In a word, he did his utmost to destroy the kingdom of Satan, and set up the kingdom of Christ. But while remembering with gratitude the great work which God has done through John Wesley, it is equally necessary that we should remember our own tremendous responsibility. A cowardly soldier in Alexander's army, who bore his name, was told by the general that he must either change his name or his conduct, and I would say the same to every selfish, idle, or worldly Methodist. God means our Church to be in the forefront of His victorious army, and with such examples, warnings, stimulus, and opportunities, woe to us if we shrink back. Wherever there is a work of the devil to be destroyed, a want to be supplied, an evil to be removed, a sorrow to be soothed, there is work for Methodists to do. The character of the next century depends largely on us; and if as individuals and churches we lay ourselves upon the altar that sanctifieth the gift, next Sunday will see our pulpits filled with flames of fire, and "multitudes will be in the valley of decision." To kindle our zeal let us look at our forefathers. Look at their simple faith! George Dawson once said, "The world wanted a church for doubters." It will not be the Methodist Church. Our Hymn-book has no provision for such an event. There are hymns for believers rejoicing, fighting, working, suffering—but none for believers doubting! Look at their ardent love!—It was not sentimentalism, but "the love of God shed abroad in their hearts by the Holy Ghost given unto them." They taught the working men of England to shake hands with each other. In the class meeting the squire and the labourer were brothers, rich and poor met together; they had liberty, equality, and fraternity of the highest kind. Look at their quenchless zeal! They shrank from no toil and no sacrifice, if by any means they might bless man or glorify God. Look, lastly, at their heaven-born joy! An old-fashioned Methodist was a living proof that religion does not make people miserable. They did not need the theatre or the ball-room to make them happy. They had a joy unspeakable and full of glory. I well remember, as a lad, walking along the lanes with some of those early preachers, after they had done a long, hard day's work, and how joyously they sang:

> " In the heavenly Lamb
> Thrice happy I am:
> And my heart it doth dance
> At the sound of His name."

We have a noble ancestry: let us seek to catch their spirit and imitate their example. Then will the next century be filled with the glory of the Lord.

The Unveiling of the Wesley Statue.

———✦———

THE Statue presented by the Children of Methodism was unveiled by the President of the Conference on Monday morning, March 2nd, being the One-hundredth Anniversary of John Wesley's Death.

THE REV. DR. MOULTON said:—

The statue is the work of Mr. Adams - Acton, to whom also we owe the beautiful sculpture of the Wesley Monument in Westminster Abbey; it is the gift of the children of Methodism. The glory of the children is their fathers, and this gift expresses the loving and filial devotion which they owe to him who, under God, was the father of them all. It is a fitting thing that, close to a crowded thoroughfare of this great city, on the spot consecrated by Wesley's hallowed toil, there should be placed a statue of one who was so great a benefactor to London, and to England at large. The attitude of his person, and the book in his hand, show that it is the Evangelist Wesley who is now displayed before us. It was by his active evangelism that he did the work for which every disciple of his and every English citizen must always revere his memory. The statue presents to passers-by a good idea of Wesley's form and lineaments. I hope and pray that many on viewing it may be led to think of Wesley's character and labours, and that in generations to come it may still be said that " He, being dead, yet speaketh."

After the ceremony, a Religious Service was held in City Road Chapel, at which the following addresses were delivered :—

The PRESIDENT of the CONFERENCE.

The services that have been arranged for this week, the various meetings that have been announced, have most of them direct reference to the evangelistic work of the Rev. John Wesley—the foundation of all his work—that part of his work which is continually in our thoughts. Hence it is well for us at this first meeting to remind ourselves that the interest extends far beyond our own community ; that the interest is shared by all the Churches of the land, for we believe that there are very many who cannot be personally present with us this morning, who are with us in spirit ; and that this interest is carried beyond the ranks of those who would profess to belong to any religious community, but who are careful students of the history of their own country. The historian of the eighteenth century, whoever he may be, cannot pass over the social, moral, and, I may say, the political effects of the work which John Wesley carried out. I should consider it a most unfitting thing on my part to detain you, under the special circumstances of the day, by any lengthened observations of my own, but I should like to commend this particular thought to all those who are here met in John Wesley's chapel. We compare most thankfully the circumstances of England in the last century with those of other countries ; we are deeply thankful that we were spared much that brought trouble, and almost ruin, elsewhere ; and we, at all events, have no doubt that the great work which was accomplished through Wesley and his coadjutors—first the evangelistic work, and then the

results of that work—had very much to do with the
liberty and peace and freedom from sore trouble that our
country enjoyed during the last century.

THE VENERABLE ARCHDEACON FARRAR.

MR. PRESIDENT, LADIES, AND GENTLEMEN,—

It is about a month ago, I think, since our friend Dr.
Stephenson did me the honour of asking me to be
present on this occasion; but for many reasons—partly
because for some time I have not been very well—partly
because recently it has been God's will that I should pass
through a great and crushing sorrow—and especially
because of my great dislike to make public speeches—I
thought myself justified in refusing the invitation. But
when our kind friend wrote to me again, and said there
was a very natural and earnest desire that on this occasion
at least one clergyman of the Church of England should
be present to do honour to the name of John Wesley, and
when he added further the wish—far too flattering to me
—that that clergyman should be myself, I felt that it was
a duty that put aside every other consideration, and I beg
your pardon for my impertinence in asking you to accept
my presence as a sign that the hearts of all representatives
of the great Church of England are warmly with you.

Sir, I must not appear here under false pretences. We
are here to do honour to one of the most disinterested of
those benefactors who " have raised strong arms to bring
heaven a little nearer to our earth." But I am a presbyter
of the Church of England, the son of a presbyter of the
Church of England, the father of a presbyter of the
Church of England. To that Church I have been, and am,
and always shall be, devotedly loyal. I would say in the
well-known words of Edmund Burke, " I desire to see
the Church of England great and powerful. I wish to see
her foundations laid low and deep. I wish to see her open

M

wide her hospitable gates by a liberal comprehension. I
desire that she should bring a message of peace to mankind, that a vexed and wandering generation may find
refuge and deliverance in the bosom of her maternal
charity." But for that very reason I have always felt it to
be my duty to hold forth the right hand of brotherly
fellowship to the members of all truly Christian communities, and to do this—not grudgingly, not superciliously,
not patronisingly ; God forbid !—but to do it in the spirit
and in the words of St. Paul, "Peace be to all them that
love the Lord Jesus Christ in sincerity."

Sir, I regret—I have no doubt that you regret—that
it was a part of God's mysterious providence that there
should be this great separation between the Wesleyan
community and the Church of England. It is a delicate
task—it is an ungracious task—it is for us an impossible
task—to apportion the blame for that separation (if blame
there be); but we may believe and hope that God has
overruled the separation for His own high purposes, and
the furtherance of His kingdom in the earth. But, as a
Churchman, I may at least express my regret that to the
Church of England of a hundred years ago, perhaps for
her warning, perhaps for her punishment, perhaps, after
all, for the promotion of her essential work by those who,
not being against her, are on her part—the grace was not
given of a wisdom which has often been shown under
similar conditions by the Church of Rome—to use,
incorporate, assimilate the mighty enthusiasm which gave
its momentum to the Wesleyan community. I do not
blame, I do not judge—I leave all those decisions to the
day of judgment; but I may say, if the bishops of that
day had only understood that the free river of the grace of
God must often overflood man's strait-dug ditches—if
they had only had the insight and magnanimity to accept
the mighty self-sacrifice of Wesley—to make him the
General of a great Christian Order within the Church of
England, or a Bishop *in partibus infidelium*, for the
evangelisation of the waste places, so to speak — the

Methodist separation would never have taken place. Sir, it was not so, and we must accept facts as facts.

But this I say: If heaven be large enough for us all—if with members of every sect we may stand, as many of every sect will stand, as fellow-saints in the presence of God—it does seem to me astonishing; I go further—it seems to me shocking and disgraceful—that Christians bound together by a common Christianity should treat each other on earth with mutual coldness and disdain. Wesley, at any rate, set us the example of a splendid tolerance. It is said of him that no reformer whom the world has ever seen so united faithfulness to the essential doctrines of revelation with perfect charity to men of every Church and of every creed. The same charity has been expressed and felt by the best men in all ages, and we always think with pleasure of those words of William Penn, that "the humble, the meek, the merciful, the just, are all of one religion, and they shall recognise each other in another world when the mask is taken off."

But why should I appeal to human authority when we have the authority of the Lord of all time, and of all worlds Himself? We know that he came to a Church that was perfectly filled with a chaos of arrogance and disdain, yet He chose the heretical Samaritan as a type of the goodness that loves its neighbour as itself. And therefore I shall repeat once more the story which many of you know so well—the story which our dear friend Dean Stanley used to tell. And let me say that if that great and good man were living to-day, I am quite certain that he would have been standing here as an infinitely more worthy representative of the Church of England than I am. He used to tell a story which he called "Wesley's Dream," to the effect that Wesley in his dream went to the gates of Gehenna, and there asked, "Have you any Romanists here? any Anglicans? any Baptists? any Calvinists? any Independents?" and in every case he received the answer "Yes, a great many!" He then asked, "Have you any Wesleyans here?" and the answer was still "Yes! a great many!" Stunned by that answer, he went back to the gates of heaven, and asked, "Have you any Romanists here? any Anglicans? Baptists? Calvinists? Independents?" "None whatever," was the reply. "Have you any Wesleyans here?" he asked. "None at all!" Then in amazement he asked, "Whom, then, have you here?" The answer came, "We have none but Christians here, and we recognise no other name." Wesley, at any rate,—whether he had that dream or not, or whether it was a pleasant allegory of the Dean's or not, —Wesley was the author of a sermon on the "Catholic Spirit," which would have the honour of being thought shockingly lax by bigots of every denomination. And Wesley used to say, in words which every true Christian man may borrow from him, "I desire to have a league offensive and defensive with every true soldier of Christ. We have one Lord, one faith, one baptism, and we are all engaged in one common warfare."

Sir, there is no reason why, on this occasion, the most rigid and the most icy Anglican might not feel it an honour, as I do, to be present here to-day. For we are present to do honour to the memory of a pre-eminently holy man, and we honour ourselves in honouring him. He was, as you know, a presbyter of the Church of England. He loved the Church of England, he recognised the Church of England every day in the grace which he said at his daily meals—he died in her full communion; and I think, therefore, that on that ground alone no clergyman need hesitate to be found here. But undoubtedly he did meet with hard measure from, and only tardy recognition, by the Church of England. The bishops of that day delivered charges against him. Vicar after vicar closed his church to his ministrations at first; and some were so base as to head the mobs of his assailants, and to shower upon his defenceless head a whole literature of anathema and acrimony. As a boy I remember to have heard how the great Bishop of Oxford, Samuel Wilberforce, speaking in Exeter Hall, amid thunders of applause, in "rolling words, oration-like," mentioned the day when the Church of England "showed a semi-vitality, or rather an anti-vitality, in expelling from her bosom that saint of God, John Wesley." Those words were a strong indictment—they were not literally accurate—but, at any rate, let us forget these memories, and say that we have changed all that. I doubt not that many of the Wesleyan ministers who are now present were present ten years ago, when, in the solemn aisles of Westminster Abbey, there was erected the cenotaph of John and Charles Wesley, with the memorable words inscribed upon it : "I look upon the whole world as my parish ;" "God buries His workmen, but carries on His work ;" and "The best of all is, God is with us !"

Sir, I think with something of awe that I am standing in the very chapel where the body of the great evangelist was laid in state, and hard by the humble tomb where his remains await the resurrection of the just, and I thank God that the vast movement that he inaugurated is still continued, that the force of it is not yet spent. Were his spirit with us, he might recall the very text from which he preached when the foundation-stone of this chapel was laid one hundred and twenty years ago, and he might again exclaim, "What hath God wrought !"

Let me say a few words about John Wesley. Although the Church and the world have learnt at last to be comparatively generous to John Wesley—although the roar of contemporary slander has long since ceased—I do not think that even now we have learnt adequately to appreciate the immensity of his services. Consider only his disinterested munificence. There may have been men who were equal to him in talent, in imagination, in learning, and in genius ; but where was there a man of that age who came up to him in beneficent, self-sacrificing generosity, and who left behind him such an example of moral lustre to the world ? Consider his charities. How many men have there been who chose to be absolutely poor throughout their lives—living on an income little more than that of a curate, and yet giving away a sum not less than £40,000 ? Consider his courage. The physical courage of the soldier and sailor is cheap and common compared with the courage of a scholar, a clergyman, and a gentleman, who, in that age, day after day, and year after year, faced raging and hostile mobs, and underwent what was then the humiliation of preaching in the open air. Physical courage was nothing to the moral and spiritual courage which enabled men like the Wesleys and George Whitefield to

> " Stand pilloried on infamy's high stage,
> And bear the pelting scorn of half an age."

When letters and extracts from his Journals were forged to the defamation of his character, John Wesley remarked to his brother Charles, " When I devoted to God my life, my ease, my time, I did not except my reputation ! I will not stay to defend my character. I will go to Canterbury to-morrow, and pursue my work."

Consider, besides, the extraordinary continuance of his indomitable powers. Consider that he preached 42,400 times after his return from Georgia—often at the rate of fifteen sermons a week. Consider those 225,000 miles that he travelled, often many hundreds of miles a week on the execrable roads of those days. Consider the record of the meetings he attended, the fierce controversies that raged around him, his endless publications, his many anxieties, his burdensome care of so many communities ; and when you have thought of all this, I will ask you whether the clergy of the present day have not reason to make confession of what Mr. Price Hughes has not hesitated to call our laziness, our ease, our supineness? When you consider the extraordinary energies of Wesley, what clergyman of any denomination might not feel honoured to stand here, to do honour to one who so heroically lived and who so nobly died ? I say that even now I do not think we have done sufficient honour to the work which Wesley did. Consider the fact that he gave an impulse to all missionary exertion—the British and

Foreign Bible Society, the Religious Tract Society, the
London Missionary Society. Even the Church Missionary
Society owes much to his initiative. The work of Education and the work of Ragged Schools—the work of Robert
Raikes the Gloucester printer, and John Pounds the
Portsmouth cobbler—were partly anticipated when the
sainted Silas Told taught at the Foundery. Wesley was
the first to encourage the cheap press, with all its stupend-
ous results; he was the first to make common in
England the spread of religious education; he was a
pioneer of funeral reform. Besides all these things, he
was the inaugurator of prison reform, for he visited prisons
and sought to improve them long before John Howard
made that his special work; and the very last letter he
ever wrote was a letter written to Wilberforce to spur him
on and encourage him in his brilliant advocacy of Emancipation for the Slaves. We may therefore feelingly
endorse the estimate of one who said that almost everything in the religious history of modern days was fore-
shadowed by John Wesley.

But even now we have not touched upon that which is
his most distinctive work—the preaching of the gospel to
the poor. Let Whitefield have the honour of having been
the first to make the green grass his pulpit and the blue
heavens his sounding-board; but let it not be forgotten
that that daring example was followed from the first by
John Wesley, and he continued in it, so that at the age of
eighty-one he preached at Kingswood under the shadow
of trees which he himself had planted, and to children's
children of his disciples who at that time had passed away.
Overwhelming evidence exists to prove what was the
preaching of that day, and what was the condition of the
Church and people of England. How dull, how soulless,
how effete, how Christless was the preaching! How
vapid, how Laodicean was the general character of the
Church! How godless, how steeped in immorality was
the general condition of the nation! Wesley was the first
man who revived the spirit of religion among the masses

of the people, and who roused the slumbering Church. His was the voice that first offered the great masses of the people hope for the despairing, and welcome to the outcast ; and his work is continued under changed forms, not only in the founding of the great Wesleyan community, but also in the Evangelical movement in the Church of England itself; and even at this moment in the enthusiasm for humanity which is shown by the poor, humble, and despised Salvationists. All that is best in their efforts has been learnt from John Wesley, because, as the late Bishop of Durham said, "the Salvationists taught by him have learnt, and have taught to the Church again, the lost secret of the compulsion of human souls to the Saviour."

Sir, when I think of John Wesley the organiser, Charles Wesley the poet, George Whitefield the orator of the Wesleyan movement, I cannot fail to see that they were special instruments chosen by God for the revival of true Christian religion in this land of ours, and I thank God for them. We still need such men. Blessed be God ! we have among us not only in the Church of England, but in all Christian denominations, men who, though they may be regarded as "lazy" in comparison with those who preached fifteen times a week amidst such innumerable toils, are still faithful and earnest workers. But if the revival of religion, if the slaying of dragons, if an irresistible enthusiasm for the redress of long-seated and intolerable wrongs is needed, we cannot employ the services of ordinary men like ourselves. Worlds and Churches are not saved by Committees or by Conferences, or by men who live and walk in the hard-beaten paths of custom and the deep-made ruts of routine. Those revolutions are created, and those revivals are again called into existence, by men who escape the average ; by men who come forth from the multitude ; by men who, as our Lord bade us, go out into the highways and hedges ; by men who have the love of God burning like a consuming fire upon the altar of their hearts ; by men who have become themselves electric to flash their lightning into the dying embers, their burning words, their irrepressible zeal, into other workers, —these men are the richest boon which God gives to Churches, to nations, to societies. But such men in every age and generation are necessarily rare, and such a man pre-eminently was John Wesley.

THE RIGHT HONOURABLE H. H. FOWLER, M.P.

MR. PRESIDENT,—

In the graceful and eloquent speech in which the Venerable Archdeacon of Westminster has paid so ample, so just, so fair a tribute to one of the greatest sons of the Church of England, he said he was here to-day as a presbyter and as the son of a presbyter of that Church. I am here to-day, Mr. President, as the son of a Methodist minister. My father was the only Methodist minister who, from John Wesley's day till now, died in John Wesley's house, and his remains lie in this *campo santo* of Methodism; and I deem it a high honour that I should be permitted, in this the first service connected not only with our denominational, but our national tribute, to represent in a very feeble degree the laity of the Methodism of to-day.

Seventy years ago, the ablest of John Wesley's biographers wrote these words:—" There may come a time when the name of Wesley will be more generally known, and in remoter regions of the globe, than that of Frederick or Catherine." Sir, the day has come. In the remoter regions of the globe, the vast extent of which never crossed the brain of Southey—the remoter regions of a greater Britain than John Wesley ever knew—of 40 millions not only of the English-speaking race within these islands, and of 60 millions of the English-speaking race across the Atlantic—but of the tens of millions of the English-speaking race in our great Colonies, and among the missionary converts of India, and of China, and of Africa, and of the sunny islands of the Southern Seas, where the name, the

history, the crimes of the Prussian despot and of the
Russian Empress are absolutely not only forgotten, but
unknown history—the name, the influence, the power of
John Wesley are a living and effective force.

It is right to cherish the memories of men whose lives,
whose examples are among the most precious possessions
of Churches and of nations. Heroes, saints, martyrs, we
all delight to honour, but they are gone—their work is
done—"well and faithfully done." "Good and faithful
servants," they have "entered into the joy of their Lord."

But we do not celebrate a memory to-day. John
Wesley is a greater force in the nation to-day, in the
Church to-day, than he was a hundred years ago. We
have not yet to write the last line of his epitaph ; we have
not yet to put the top-stone on to his monument ; he
influences powerfully and effectively our national history,
our national character, our national position.

It is easier—far easier, I think—to estimate the progress
and the position of the work which John Wesley began,—
a work which, though a century older, is stronger to-day,
better to-day, than when he left it ;—it is easier to do that
than to form an impartial judgment of the man himself.
Somebody has said that great men are like great mountains,
—a long interval must be spanned before you can estimate their true proportions and their real magnitude. I
do not know whether the interval of a hundred years is a
sufficiently wide chasm to intervene between the death of
Wesley and the just estimate of his character. I am not
sure that we have yet reached the standpoint from which
we can view in all their fair proportions his personality,
his genius, his greatness, his failings, his blunders,—they
have all yet to be judicially summed up. John Wesley's
biography has yet to be written. We have had portraits
painted by personal friends, we have had the eulogies of
devoted followers, we have had the criticisms of foes, or at
all events of those who are assuming to be friends, but
who have no sympathy with his movement ; but the cool,
the final judgment of history has to be written. And while

we value what we have had,—brilliant rhetoric, keen and cutting controversy, admirable pictures of certain phases and characteristics of John Wesley's life,—while we value the vast accumulations of material which some day or other will form the storehouse where the biographer of Wesley will find his best resources,—I still think, sir, that the real man has to be portrayed by other hands in another fashion. We have had full-dress lives ; we all see John Wesley as you see him there in that statue to-day, with his gown and cassock, and in what may have been his natural hair or his wig ; but the man, the little man in physical stature, the great man in mental stature, the everyday man with all his peculiarities, has to be photographed on the English mind.

We shall therefore, perhaps, best discharge to-day's duty by looking more at the work than at the man. His work stands out in the history of our faith, in the history of our nation, as clearly as the dome of St. Paul's stands out on the horizon of London. Let me go for my evidence not to one of John Wesley's friends and admirers, but to one who has little sympathy with John Wesley's creed,—a man who looks upon John Wesley's work with a cool, discriminating eye—a fair, impartial historian—the greatest, perhaps, of living historians, viz. Lecky. " Although," says Lecky, " the career of the elder Pitt, and the splendid victories by land and sea that were won during his ministry, form unquestionably the most dazzling episodes in the reign of George II., they will yield, I think, in real importance to that Religious Revolution which had begun in England by the preaching of the Wesleys and Whitefield."

Now, why does a secular historian give Wesley's work this political pre-eminence over even the work of the Government of Lord Chatham ? Why does he give it to John Wesley ? Because that Religious Revolution was in the highest sense of the word a political revolution. It has affected, it has controlled, it has dominated our national policy.

Two great men in the eighteenth century were contemporaries. There is not much interval between the dates of their births and the dates of their respective deaths,—Voltaire and Wesley. You trace the influence of Voltaire through the French Revolution—for that Revolution was practically originated by him—that influence is seen to-day in the legislation, in the Government, in the morals, in the irreligion of France. The same description can be applied to Wesley. We trace his history through the same period of time, and we see his influence to-day in the legislation, the Government, the morals, and the religion of Great Britain. And if we take the range of the century (for a long time is needed to test a contrast between two great lives),—if we group the results of those two men's teachings through the generations which have flitted across the human stage since they left this world, —I say boldly, I say it without fear of contradiction, that if this world were all—if this world, with its physical happiness and its physical suffering, was the limit of the comparison—I say the teachings of the one have been as great a blessing as the teachings of the other were an unmitigated curse.

Archdeacon Farrar has alluded to the state of England in the eighteenth century. You can have four tests which are within the range of every member of this congregation, by his access either to the national libraries, or to the cheapest forms of literature. Take the pictures of Hogarth, the novels of Smollett, the letters of Lord Chesterfield, and the *Newgate Calendar*. These records tell you what England was in the eighteenth century,— sunk in moral apathy, buried in sensual corruption. I think it was a great French writer who said there was no religion in England at all. There were only four or five members of Parliament who ever went to church on Sunday. In the House of Commons to-day, we talk of "the honourable and gallant gentleman," and "the honourable and learned gentleman;" but I think the House would be very much astonished if some member were to speak of another, as Wilberforce was once spoken of, as "the honourable and religious gentleman!" Ay, and worse than all, because this vice above, this corruption above, descends, the poor were outside religion as they were outside civilisation. You had cruel laws—cruelly administered, and that made a cruel people. I cannot sum up John Wesley's work in connection with that state of society more justly or more completely than in the words of another great English historian of the present generation, J. R. Green: "The Methodists themselves were the least result of the Methodist Revival."

I hope my friends who are going to speak this week will remember that, and throw their minds across the boundaries of our own denomination. The result of the Methodist Revival—the noblest result, was "the attempt, which has never ceased from that day to this, to remedy the immorality, the ignorance, the physical suffering, the social degradation, of the profligate and the poor. The Church was restored to life, a new philanthropy reformed our prisons; infused clemency and wisdom into our penal laws; abolished the slave trade, and gave the first impulse to national education." Wesley preached, Wesley taught in his chapels, in his class-meeting, in his Journals, in his practice, the true application of the great saying of Burke, that "whatever is morally wrong can never be politically right." And from the days that John Wesley, as a Fellow of Lincoln College, Oxford, visited the poor degraded prisoners in Oxford gaol, to the last days of his life, when he wrote his final letter, to which allusion has already been made, bearing his dying testimony against that most execrable of all human villanies, the slave trade —John Wesley never faltered in attacking cruelty, ignorance, intemperance—in alleviating all the forms of sorrow and suffering, and in upholding the Christian man's obligation to bring his Christianity into his daily performance of public duty in all its branches.

What was the result of such a gospel as that?—(I will not go over the ground that has already been traversed so ably and so eloquently)—the result of the position of the English mind, of English public opinion through the great cataclysm of the French Revolution? If you refer to your history, you will find that there was an attack all along the line on property, on authority, on morals, on religion—and England escaped. Why? I believe it was the Methodism of the lower classes, the Methodism of the middle classes, their intense antagonism—and, mind you, they feel it as strongly to-day — to antichristian teaching, which saved the nation and the constitution of England: and during the century which is now drawing to a close, gradually, slowly, but surely, the teaching of the New Testament is becoming year by year a stronger force in our national life—stronger far than when in her proudest days the undivided Western Church dominated the thrones and principalities and powers of Christendom. John Wesley's Methodism "hid the leaven in three measures of meal," and to-day, without distinction of class, or party, or creed, our public life is being leavened with that blessed influence.

To-day — I say it as a politician — as a Christian politician—the strongest argument to the final court of appeal is not pride, not revenge, not aggrandisement, not gain, but " Is it right ? "

Part of the secret of this influence, still so powerful, was John Wesley's genius in the adaptation of vital principles to surrounding circumstances. He did not believe in— he eschewed and abhorred — a cast-iron uniformity of means and institutions. His religious organisation was spiritual engineering of the truest and highest type. He built his bridges, he excavated his cuttings,—yes, he sometimes drove his tunnels, just according to the nature and extent of the difficulty which at the time, and under the circumstances, then confronted him. He was always abreast of his age—generally in advance of his age—and never behind his age.

This week we shall record (it has been recorded already in that masterly article which appears in the *Times* of this morning) the numerical strength of Methodism; but, whilst we do that, let us never forget, what the Archdeacon has so powerfully brought before us this morning, that one of the noblest features of John Wesley's Methodism was the absence of bigotry, of sectarian rivalry, of ecclesiastical animosity. His catholicity was limited to no Church and no creed. I think one of the most typical instances of this in his later life is to be found in the anecdote, that on one of the feasts of the Church, which he always reverently observed, viz. All Saints' Day,—he mounted that pulpit (to which Mr. Fowler here pointed), and in solemn silence, in meditation, in prayer, to the astonishment of his congregation, he remained for several minutes. Then, as if giving expression to the thoughts that had passed through his mind, he gave out that noble lyric of his brother's which sums up the communion of saints in the words:

> " Come, let us join our friends above,
>   That have obtained the prize ;
>
> One family we dwell in Him,
>   One Church above, beneath,
> Though now divided by the stream,
>   The narrow stream of Death."

High Churchman as he no doubt originally was—and if Dr. Rigg will forgive me, I am not quite sure whether he ever got rid of his High Churchism, even up to the very last ; but, at all events, irregular Churchman as he was, declaring, as he did, within two years of his death, that he had never varied in any point of doctrine from the Church in which he lived, and in which he died—he held out the right hand of fellowship, I was going to say to all who loved the Lord Jesus Christ in sincerity, I may say reverently he held out the right hand of fellowship to all who feared God and worked righteousness. Read his wonderful comment on the teachings of the great Emperor Antoninus; read his prediction that that enlightened heathen would be among those who sit down in the kingdom of God with Abraham and Isaac and Jacob, when many professing Christians will be shut out. I am old enough to remember that one of the favourite domestic books of devotion of the former Methodists was John Wesley's abridgment of the work of the Roman Catholic saint, Thomas à Kempis. He held out the right hand of fellowship, again, to orthodox and heterodox Nonconformists.   He declared that Methodism required of its members no conformity either of opinion or modes of worship ; one thing only was required, viz. to fear God and work righteousness.   I think his last definition of the test of admission into the Methodist Society was this : "Is the man a believer in the Lord Jesus Christ ? is his life suitable to his profession ?"   He hated controversy, although he was continually involved in a great deal of it.

And we claim to-day to be his true and faithful followers. If we inherit but the smallest portion of his spirit, we shall claim to be "the friends of all, the enemies of none."   His conflict was with vice, with ignorance, with intemperance, and with sin.   His motive and his aim was to destroy the works of the devil ; and all who are fighting that battle— no matter what uniform they wear—are the comrades of "the people called Methodists."

I would, in closing, in one sentence recall the scene around that death-bed a century ago.

What was his last confession of faith ? What was the creed in which he died ?—

> "I the chief of sinners am,
>   But Jesus died for me !"

What was his last hymn ?—

> "I'll praise my Maker while I've breath,
>   And when my voice is lost in death
>   Praise shall employ my nobler powers."

What was his last prayer ?—"Bless the Church and the king.   Grant us truth and peace through Jesus Christ our Lord."

And what were his final words of thanksgiving for the

past and hope for the future ?—" The best of all is, God is
with us !"

In that confession of faith, in that litany, in that inspiring motto, you have an epitome of the Methodism
which to-day reverently, thankfully, hopefully gathers
around John Wesley's tomb.

ALEXANDER M'ARTHUR, Esq., M.P.

MY CHRISTIAN FRIENDS,—

I can assure you that I feel it both an honour and a
privilege to be permitted to take any part in these deeply-
interesting and important memorial services, and if I could
say anything calculated to interest this meeting, or promote the great object we all have in view, it would afford
me much pleasure. But, after the able and admirable
addresses we have just heard, I think I shall best consult
my own feelings and your wishes by not occupying very
many minutes of your valuable time on this occasion.
You will, however, I presume, expect me to say a few
words. I once had the pleasure of hearing Dr. Talmage
of New York deliver his popular lecture on the Bright
Side of Things, and he commenced by saying he thought
this was the best world God ever made, that he believed
this to be the best period of its existence, and that he
was glad he got on board at this particular time.

Well, sir, it is of course impossible to prove that this is
the best world God ever made, but I suppose it will be
universally admitted that this is the best and most
enlightened period of our world's history. We have
heard and read much of what we call the dark ages, with
all the ignorance, superstition, persecution, and cruelty
which characterised them ; and, although the disposition
to persecute still exists to some extent, we may well feel
devoutly thankful that it is our happy privilege to live in
a better and more enlightened age, in which life and
immortality have been brought to life by the gospel, in

N

which we can worship God according to the dictates of our consciences, none daring to make us afraid, and in which we enjoy so many Christian privileges and advantages which our forefathers did not enjoy one hundred years ago. It is also gratifying to know that we live in an age of progress. I suppose it will be admitted by all, that during the present century greater progress has been made in art, in science, in literature, in the education of the masses, in the condition of the working classes, in promoting temperance, in civil and religious liberty, and in numerous discoveries calculated to promote the health, comfort, and happiness of mankind, than has ever been made in any previous century of our world's history. And surely we must all rejoice in the progress and extension of our common Christianity throughout the world, in the success of the British and Foreign Bible Society and similar institutions, through whose agency many millions of Bibles and Testaments in all languages have been put into circulation. Nor should we omit the Religious Tract Society, and other institutions for the diffusion of useful and Christian knowledge. In the success of our various missionary societies, the progress of the Christian Church at home, and above all, the marvellous progress of that section of the universal Church to which most of us have the honour and privilege to belong—a Church which was only in its infancy one hundred years ago, and which, if we include all branches of Methodism, is now said to be, and we think correctly said to be, the largest Protestant Church in existence. When Mr. Wesley died there were not 60,000 members of Society. Now, we are informed, there are in the United States of America alone, 31,765 ministers, 54,711 churches, and a membership of nearly 5 millions, which we suppose may be safely doubled or trebled if we take the number of hearers into account ; and when to those we add the Methodism of Canada, Australasia, Africa, the United Kingdom, and other parts of the world, we may well adopt Wesley's own language, and exclaim :

" Who, I ask in amaze,
Hath begotten me these,
And inquire from what quarter they came ?
My full heart it replies,
They are born from the skies,
And gives glory to God and the Lamb."

Surely, sir, when we take all this into account, we cannot fail to perceive what a mighty influence for good Methodism exerts, and what a blessing it has been to the Church and the world ; what a civilising, purifying, and elevating influence it has exerted, not only in rural districts of this and other countries, but also in more crowded centres of population, where vast numbers have been brought from darkness to light, and to serve the living and true God, rescued from ignorance, irreligion, and in many cases from profligacy and vice, and have been raised up to become useful members of society, to occupy important positions in the Church and the world, and to prove by happy experience that "godliness is profitable unto all things, having the promise of the life that now is, and of that which is to come." We might also refer to the fact that Methodism has greatly stimulated and enriched other Churches, many of whose most earnest and energetic members, and most able and successful ministers, received their first religious impressions and early training in our Sunday schools, or as class - leaders or local preachers. Again, it can easily be proved that the State has been greatly benefited ; for we have it on the highest authority that "righteousness exalteth a nation, but sin is a disgrace to any people." And we believe that whatever tends to promote education, temperance, morality, truth and righteousness, promotes good order, lessens taxation and increases national wealth. This, we believe, Methodism has been instrumental in accomplishing to a much greater extent than many, who know comparatively little about the numerous and varied agencies she employs, are aware of. Indeed, it is astonishing how little is known about Methodism, even by many well-meaning and professedly Christian men : what erroneous opinions are entertained respecting it, and how bitterly it is opposed and persecuted by many from whom we might expect better things and more Christian conduct. Numerous instances might be given in proof of these statements, and we too frequently find them in the daily papers.

I was on one occasion travelling in a railway carriage with a gentleman, a member of a Christian Church, and in the course of conversation I happened to say I was a Wesleyan Methodist. Judge my surprise when he said, "But don't they deny the divinity of our Lord Jesus Christ?" I might also give an instance of the ignorance, bigotry, or intolerance which exists, even in the House of Commons, although, I am happy to say, to a very limited extent. On one occasion I was writing at a table in one of the lobbies, at which two other members were also writing, when one of them, addressing the member sitting beside him, said, "I am writing one of the Nonconformist ministers: do you give them the title of Rev.?" But notwithstanding the ignorance of some, the indifference of many, and the opposition, if not persecution, too frequently encountered, Methodism still claims to be the friend of all, the enemy of none; and whether we reflect upon the past, survey the present, or anticipate the future, we have abundant reason to thank God, take courage, and go forward.

Many years ago, Dr. Osborn said he thought the prevailing sentiments should be gratitude, humility, and hope. Those should be our sentiments now. I trust that one of the results of these services may be to unite the various branches of the Wesleyan family and all other denominations of Christians more firmly in the bonds of Christian love and charity.

Meeting: Representing the Methodist Connexions.

THE PRESIDENT OF THE CONFERENCE.

THERE is peculiar interest in this meeting. We are a company of relatives, who, through force of circumstances, do not often come together. You know how often it is the case in the ordinary relations of life, that cousins and brothers are separated by circumstances or by accident. It is from no desire on our part that this separation exists.

This first speaker of this evening is one of ourselves; and the warmest welcome will be granted always by an English Methodist audience to a representative of Ireland. But these other brothers have set up housekeeping on their own account. Each has built a house; and I think I may say, without any injustice to their power of originality, that each has built it very much after the old pattern. They have, of course, introduced improvements—they would not have made alterations unless they thought them to be improvements. It has been said by some that it would be very much better for all the brothers to come and set up housekeeping together. Of that I am no judge; but in order that we should understand one another, it is essential that we should come together more frequently. The interest felt in John Wesley and this celebration is equal on their part to anything that we can

express. I will venture in your name to give one general
hearty welcome to them all, and I am perfectly sure that
they will express the same hearty welcome to you.

Methodism in Ireland.

By the Rev. O. M'CUTCHEON,

VICE-PRESIDENT OF THE IRISH CONFERENCE.

I ESTEEM it a privilege to be permitted to represent on
this occasion that branch of the great family of Methodism which the late Rev. Charles Prest always insisted
should be called Methodism in Ireland, and not Irish
Methodism. We have a patron saint called St. Patrick,
and our custom has been to celebrate his death instead of
his birth. On this account we have been subject to some
kindly criticism, as if the custom partook of the character
of an Irish bull; but now we shall at any rate be able to
comfort ourselves by your example, because you are
doing the same with regard to John Wesley. The Protestant Evangelical Churches meet together under the
union flag of the Evangelical Alliance on our saint's day,
to pray for God's blessing on His kingdom in that
country and throughout the world. In the same way we
are met to-day to celebrate the death of John Wesley, not
as a mere memory, because he still lives, and the influence
he generated still prevails throughout Christendom.

It is no part of my business this evening to delineate
the character and labours of John Wesley. It is as unnecessary as it would be impossible to add to what we
heard this morning. However he may have been misunderstood during his lifetime, however he may be misunderstood still, his labours were self-denying. Though
his name is pre-eminently the heritage of Methodism, the
fruits of those labours are to be found in all the Christian
Churches of the United Kingdom. A distinguished country-

man of mine published some years ago a very appreciative
sketch of John Wesley. Giving a very eloquent description of Rome, and calling St. Peter's an ecclesiastical
Eddystone, he said that John Wesley occupied towards
his age the same commanding position. There could be
no doubt whatever as to the deep interest which John
Wesley took in Ireland. He crossed the Irish Channel no
fewer than forty-two times. In those days there were
no magnificent steamboats as there are now ; even the
sailing vessels then in use were very inferior. And yet
John Wesley counted it no hardship to visit Ireland so
frequently ; and perhaps it would be better for both parts
of the United Kingdom if there were more intercourse of
that sort to-day. I do not know by what providential
circumstance John Wesley's thoughts were first directed
to that part of the kingdom. At the Conference of 1746,
held in Bristol, this question appears on the " Minutes :"
" What ought to be regarded as a providential call to
some new sphere of labour ? " The answer is : " An
invitation from some person who would have a house to
receive us, and the possibility of doing more good than
by staying where we are." In the following year he
visited Dublin, spent some time there ; and in the year
1748 Ireland appears upon the " Minutes of Conference,"
divided into four circuits, each province for a circuit ; and
in the same year appears the name of " Charles Skelton
from Ireland," received as one of the Assistants. So early
did the good seed sown in that country bear fruit.

It would be impossible on the present occasion to follow
out in detail the remarkable history of the Methodist
movement in that country. At John Wesley's death
there were 28 circuits, with 66 ministers, and about
14,000 members of Society, or about one-fifth of the
entire number of members then in the United Kingdom.
We must look upon that as a remarkable success. The
population of Ireland at that time was estimated at about
4,200,000. It is generally acknowledged that that estimate
was far too low. It was made for purposes of taxation.

and therefore was not intended to be the outside figure. The population to-day is well known to be under five millions. So that, for all the purposes of a rough comparison, the population may be taken as much the same as it was a century ago. We have now 131 circuits, 190 ministers engaged in the active work, and some 26,000 members of Society. It is true that in many places our cause, to visitors from England, will seem very small and feeble. But there is scarcely a part of Ireland where Methodism is not to be found. In the course of my ministerial life I must have visited and slept in every county. We are not confined to one part of the country, —our influence is very general.

You may perhaps know very well from other sources, that there has been a vast emigration from Ireland to other parts of the world. It is not necessary to speak of the causes of that emigration ; they are various, and they affect the population in various ways. I have no intention of trenching upon the field of politics. We did not commence to take any account of the number of emigrants from our Societies until 1830. Within these sixty years 35,000 members of Society have left us by emigration. If we take into account the children and other adherents, we have lost not less than 100,000 of our people within that time, and yet we have two-thirds more members in Society to-day than when John Wesley died. The marvel is, not that we are so small, but that, despite these adverse influences, we still maintain our position and influence, for the good of our country, and the glory of God.

Let me say here that our country is unique in one respect, and our brethren in England will appreciate this. We over there get the credit of being factious and quarrelsome, and disposed to divide. That may apply to certain parts of the population ; certainly it does not apply to Methodism. We have never had but one division in the Methodist family in our entire history, and that one division we have healed. We are one united Methodism throughout that country, with the exception of the few congregations belonging to the New Connexion and the Primitive Brethren of England. I believe the providence of God brought that about. For five years I was one of the secretaries of the Union Committee. We did not go about the thing rashly; but, after the Church was disestablished in Ireland, our Primitive Wesleyan brethren felt that the reason for their separate existence was removed. It was necessary to obtain an Act of Parliament in order to remove certain difficulties out of the way to the union which we both desired. I believe, in the most remarkable manner, God's providence favoured the obtaining of that Act of Parliament,—a measure which took out of the hands of local trustees the power to control the disposition of the chapels if two-thirds of the Conference sanctioned the union with another religious body. The union was effected in perfect peace; and I am thankful to say, not only that United Methodism has passed through the crisis of that difficulty without injury, and without any sacrifice of principle on either side, but that the state of the Connexion generally, financially, spiritually, and in relation to the population, is far better than it was previous to the union. I do not believe that any one would desire to go back to the former state of things.

There is another matter which I think is unique in the history of Methodism in Ireland. The late Dr. E. O. Haven, of America, visited Ireland some years ago, and gave to the world his impressions of our cause. He said: "The Methodists are the only Christian denomination that have ever gained a strong foothold in Ireland without an emigration of membership from abroad, without Government aid, and drawing their numbers alike from the ancient Celts and Saxons. This is a phenomenon that challenges attention. Wesley and his associates were voluntary missionaries to Ireland. They did not carry with them a colonisation, as the Presbyterians did. They did not enter Ireland under the protection of an armed soldiery. Their first converts, ministers and people, were alike from all classes." You cannot estimate its influence upon the population merely by its numbers. There is another testimony which perhaps will be better appreciated here. We envy our brethren in England nothing, except their free access to the masses of the population. Reference was made this morning to Southey and his *Life of Wesley*. Whatever may have been its faults, he strove to get the best information he could. He wrote to Bishop Jebb of Limerick, and asked how it was that Methodism in Ireland had been a comparative failure. The bishop knew something of the work, and, writing back to Robert Southey, he said he was not prepared to admit that Methodism in Ireland had been a failure. He said that if they looked to the Protestant portion of the population, which was the only portion to which Methodism had access, and compared its numbers with that portion of the population, they would come to the conclusion that it had been quite as successful in Ireland as in other parts of the world. He looked upon it as "a powerful resuscitator;" and said, "The disproportion, I will allow, between the gross population of Great Britain and Ireland exceeds the disproportion between the gross population of Great Britain and Ireland. But then I doubt whether the Roman Catholics can be fairly taken into account; and in that case, Methodism may be truly said to have made a greater progress among the legitimate objects of it here than in the sister island." I think the bishop made a mistake when he said that Methodism in Ireland had access to only one portion of the population. Dr. Coke, at one of the Conferences, suggested to the preachers to bring to the next Conference an exact statement of the number of Roman Catholics who had been converted to God; and, after careful inquiry, the report to the next Conference was that upwards of 700 members of Society were converted Roman Catholics. These are matters which we are not accustomed to blazon abroad, because, if we did, they might block our way in some cases; but despite political complications, perhaps even because of them, the barrier which has prevented our access to the people is being gradually broken down, and I do not know that at any former time we had more access to the people. We have no intention of living on the reputation of our fathers. In John Wesley's lifetime, there were some leaders in London who expressed their regret that Mr. Wesley and his brother Charles should expend so much time in Ireland, and send so many preachers there; the leaders in London would be wiser now. But Mr. Wesley replied, "Have patience, and Ireland will repay you." Has it not done so? Ireland yielded to him some of the most eminent of his coadjutors, — Thomas Walsh, Adam Clarke, William Myles, William Thompson, Henry Moore, and others. Has not Irish Methodism founded, or aided in founding, Methodism throughout the world? The fruit of our labours fills the earth. We rejoice with you in your successes; and unite with you to-day in thanksgiving to God for the gift of John Wesley to the Christian Church. We hope that for our own country, and for God's cause throughout the world, a brighter day has dawned. May it be found so!

Methodist New Connexion.

By the Rev. JAMES LE HURAY,

PRESIDENT OF THE METHODIST NEW CONNEXION.

I AM here to reciprocate the brotherly sentiment which your invitation implies, cherishing as I do the hope that the meeting may be the pledge and promise of closer approximation, of kindlier fellowship, and of more serviceable co-operation in the future than in the past. Surely such aspirations are in harmony with the place and purpose of our meeting. We meet in the mother church of our beloved Methodism, to do honour to the memory of our great Founder. At the father's grave the children's differences are forgotten. In such a hallowed atmosphere one cannot think of sect for love of the brethren. All human adjustments seem to vanish, and one sees but the heavenly side of our Methodism, and on its heavenly side there are no differences. Its Divine principles hold us all in unity as gravitation holds in one Atlantic the billows of the sea. Up in our spiritual sky one rainbow arches in benedictions over us all. We all breathe the same atmosphere, drink from the same fountain, and break the same bread. In the spirit of gospel truth, as in the bonds of gospel love, all the family are one. As I look into your faces and join in your songs, Methodism seems broader and more beautiful to me than ever before. It has all the radius and radiance and charity of a Divine reality.

In Wesley's life and influence we have a common heritage. His name is fragrant to us as the flowers of spring, and his history inspiring as mountain breezes.

> " The actions of the just
> Smell sweet, and blossom in the dust."

And the hallowed dust that reposes beside us—

> " Until the eternal day shall break,
> And the night shadows of earth shall flee away "—

that dust has blossomed in beauty for many a year, and is still fragrant with perfumes that make every English breeze from Wesley's grave a welcome messenger to Methodists the wide world over. He needs no marble to perpetuate his fame. What avails the sculptor's art to him whom the holy Church throughout all the world has embalmed in her everlasting remembrance? His monuments are reared in millions of glad and grateful hearts; monuments built up by the prayers of the penitent and the praises of the redeemed; monuments that are numbered by the harps swept by immortal fingers; monuments that will endure when the marble has crumbled, and the bronze has melted, and the heavens rolled up as a scroll have passed away. " They that turn many to righteousness shall shine as stars for ever and ever."

Even outside our Methodism, no true lover of his country

will willingly let the name of Wesley die. Other sons have saved her from the enemy without; not counting their lives dear unto them, they have hurled back the armed legions that would have crushed her beneath their heel, as her uncrumbling rocks have hurled back the inrush of the storm-driven billows. But Wesley, with other God-raised men, saved her from the enemies within; the moral foes who were insidiously undermining her greatness and threatening her with ruin, dire as that which has overtaken others, on whose broken pillars and blackened ruins time has long since written "Ichabod." The century which witnessed Wesley's birth has been described as "a dewless night succeeded by a sunless morn." Whilst literature flourished, religion drooped and died. A faithful few still trimmed their lamps in "a darkness which might be felt," but their feeble light only served "to make the darkness still more visible." The Church was designated "a fair carcase without a spirit," and the clergy had less authority, and were under more contempt, than those of any other Church in Europe. Christianity, systematically invested by an alliance of all her foes, scientific and sensual, philosophical and frivolous, was perhaps more fiercely and forcibly assailed than at any previous period of her history. And the defenders of the faith, all too few and far between, kept puffing out, half despairingly, from behind their paper bulwarks, their replies to the well-directed volleys of their phalanxed foes. The upper classes were avowedly infidel and shamelessly profligate; the lower stupidly ignorant and grossly irreligious. Says Hannah More, "We saw but one Bible in the parish of Cheddar, and that was used to prop a flower-pot." In the face of such facts, is it unreasonable to suppose that swiftly and surely the darkness would have deepened, and the depravity gathered strength, until Christianity would have been proscribed, and, under the sway of a brazen, brutal atheism, England, like her neighbour France, would have been plunged into the agonies of a revolution, in which order would have fled before anarchy, and the land been deluged in blood? If the nation was to be saved from riot and ruin, then it had become time for God to work ; and now the mighty, merciful work began. In this hour the men were born on whom tongues of fire were hereafter to descend, and in whose lips the old truths of a dead orthodoxy were to become keen and powerful—the very sword of the Spirit. God, in His mysterious providence, was about to make Methodism the counteracting salt by which the nation was to be preserved from putrefaction.

Three men stand out foremost and tallest in this marvellous work, *i.e.* Whitefield and the brothers Wesley,—men who, in contrast to the sinful and sceptical and superficial around them, were animated by a piety which went deeper than the face, and farther than the words, and left behind it a fragrance fresh from the Rose of Sharon and the Lily of the Valley. Under the same Divine inspiration, they were as diverse in gift as in face, symbolising respectively soul and system and song in the new movement. "All force and impetus, Whitefield," we are told, "was the powder-blast in the quarry, and by one explosive sermon would shake a district and detach materials for other men's long work. Deft, neat, and painstaking, Wesley loved to split and trim each fragment into uniform plinths and polished stones. Whitefield had no aptitude for pastoral details ; Wesley, with a beaver-like propensity for building, was always constructing Societies, and, with a king-like craft of ruling, was most at home when presiding over a class or Conference." Whilst John was the founder of Methodism, Charles Wesley was its sweet singer ; whilst the one brother laid the foundations and reared up the pillars of the new tabernacle, the other filled it with melodies—melodies which fed the flame of piety from the purest oil of the sanctuary, renovating worn-out spirits, and quickening hearts benumbed by sordid cares, and winning everywhere a listening ear for the higher harmonies of heaven. Methodism was builded rapidly, but the walls would never have gone up so fast had they not been built to music.

No new truths had these to give to the world. Their movement was not a creation; it was only a revival. They simply burnished up old truths which they had found rusty and hidden beneath encrusting errors, and held them up in all their brightness before men's astonished eyes. They took the very gospel, which had become palsied and powerless in the hands of others, and made it mighty through God. On their Heaven-inspired lips, the message which had hitherto produced no more impression on men's consciences than a rippling wave on a granite rock, became potent and penetrating as the arrow shot from the bow of a strong and skilful archer, which hits the point at which it is aimed, and quivers there with unspent force. Like a fierce tornado sweeping across the deep, their soul-stirring appeals reached the deepest emotions in men's natures; strings long silent were swept as by an unseen hand; wells long sealed were opened, and the waters stirred to their innermost depths. The scoffer was silenced, and the infidel convinced. The oath died unuttered on the lips of the blasphemer, and the fiery cup was dashed from the lips of the intemperate. The man that came to revile remained to pray. "I came to break his head," said one of Whitefield, "and he has broken my heart." In a word, whenever and wherever they preached, there the scenes of Pentecost were re-enacted, and bitter tears rained plentifully from broken hearts. Widely and swiftly, as fire in stubble, the movement spread. Penitents transformed into preachers went forth to proclaim, as with a trumpet-note, the faith by which they were saved. Every renewed life was converted into a lever to elevate and ennoble other lives around. Believers banded together in spiritual brotherhoods against the world, the flesh, and the devil; gathered together into small companies for counsel and communion, that they might perfect holiness in the fear of the Lord; and from these class-meetings went forth, as live coals from the altar, souls intent on kindling a fire which earth and hell might strive to quench, but strive in vain. And from that time

to this, the work has grown the world over, and the years
through, until to-day the sons of Wesley are found in
nearly every land. Once a by-word, Methodism has now
become a praise and power in the earth. Though its
first adherents scarcely numbered more than the family
shut up in the ark, it gives its name to-day to over
twenty-eight millions of souls, gathered out of every
nation, and people, and kindred, and tongue. Well may
we exclaim, with its great Founder: "What hath God
wrought!" And still it lives and thrives. Like the bones
of the prophet in Old Testament story, which gave life
to the dead body cast into their sepulchre, the divinely-
blessed words and works of Wesley are still quickening
multitudes into spiritual life, though the lips which spoke
them, and the hands which wrote them, have long since
crumbled to the dust. Being dead he yet speaks, and will
speak, for whilst Methodism lives Wesley can never die.

And now, sir, the question comes, How can we, the
children, use most wisely and well the splendid heritage
handed down to us by our fathers? How make the future
of our Methodism greater and more glorious than its past?
It has been said that we are in danger of being ruined by
our prosperity; that, richer and more respectable than
our fathers, we have become weaker and more worldly
than they; and that, unless we are watchful, this worldliness will bring our Methodism into the character and
condition of Sardis, which, under the name of life, had the
coldness and palsy of death. I dare not say the charge is
unwarranted, though I do believe it is exaggerated. We
admit that in too many instances the pulses of our
spiritual life are feeble and fluctuating; that our piety is
not commensurate with our privileges. We have to mourn
too often over home lavishness and church parsimony;
days given to pleasure and hours grudged to God; energy
in the world and indolence in the church; tongues
eloquent on all things but Christ and Christian experience; visits of etiquette never omitted, and visits to the
fatherless and the widow in their affliction never paid!

All these things prove that the old Methodist fire has been allowed to burn too low. And what is the remedy? We want quickening. We need life—more life—and still more life. It is not new machinery we want, or even a readjustment of the old,—we have it in abundance and in perfection. What we require is a larger inspiration; a mightier spiritual force to set it in motion; a fresh baptism of the heaven-born ardour which sent Wesley and Whitefield amongst the people as a flame of fire which leaps up among dying embers. Without this our Methodism may be " rich and increased with goods," and yet be only a Dead Sea, into which rivers of wealth may flow, but from which no living waters go forth to enrich surrounding wastes. If we wish to repeat the successes of our fathers, we must largely run on their lines ; drink deeply and often of the fountain whence they derived their strength. The great Methodist Revival was born in the little Oxford prayer-meeting. Having there obtained power with God, they went out, and, through Him, obtained power over men. The preaching, which like a hammer broke the rocky heart, was nerved with the energy of agonising prayer. As expressed in your admirable pastoral, sir, this is our want to-day. I fear that the hard-kneed race of Methodists is becoming extinct. In the busy and anxious life most of us are living, prayer is in danger of being crowded out. One thing after another comes in and thrusts it aside. It is like the impotent man at the pool of Bethesda : while it is coming another steps down before it. I know that it has become a fashionable thing to sneer at prayer as a weak and worthless thing — "a passionate wail flung to the viewless winds ; " but as Methodists we know better than that. Our history from the beginning has taught us that it is an appeal to the sympathetic heart and the resistless arm of a living, loving God. Let those laugh at prayer who will, we know its worth too well to be laughed out of it. The problem of prayer is not to be solved from the professor's chair. It has been solved already a thousand

O

times on the bed of languishing and in the upper chambers
of devotion, in dark hovels and darker dungeons, where
Methodists have prayed till the heavens have opened.
Let us pray, then, and pray often; pray in secret and pray
in concert; do not let us forget the assembling of ourselves together for prayer.   Remember that spiritual
warmth is communicated by contact.   The warm heart
kindles the cold.   The living faith quickens the dead.
The heart may grow too cold for the fire burning on its
own altar to thaw it, but the gathered heat of many fires
will quickly melt it into streams of sympathy and service.
How often in our history have a few earnest souls in a
class-room kindled a fire which has set a whole circuit
in a blaze.   Oh, sir, we mourn over the hardness of men's
hearts, and the slow spread of Christ's kingdom.   Let us
rather mourn over our timid faith, which only touches
the angel's wing with the tips of its fingers, instead of
hanging upon him with Jacob's death-grip, exclaiming,
" I will not let Thee go except Thou bless me."   Endued
with such power, difficulties would melt before us like
snowflakes before the sun, and, like Wesley and Whitefield
of old, set on fire of God, we would go forth as cleansing
consuming flames to purge the dross and burn up the
stubble of sin.

Early Methodism was evangelistic in its spirit.   It
inaugurated the " Forward Movement " in modern Church
work.   The new departure, of which we are now hearing
so much, is really only a return to the old paths.   Wesley
felt the burden of souls upon him, and he went out to seek
and save them.   Not willingly at first, but under Divine
constraint.   He would rather have delivered his message
in a church and from a pulpit, but God shut the church
door in his face, and compelled him to go out into the
highways and hedges.   It needed no little fortitude for
such a man as Wesley to do this.   The courage which
could lead a forlorn hope is inferior to that which led
Wesley, with the refined and scholastic atmosphere of
Oxford about him, to mount waggons and tables by the

road-side, and address low-bred, vulgar mobs; but he did it. It needed almost seraphic sweetness to endure unruffled the coarse onslaught of brutal colliers,—men who, brought to bay by the fiery arrows with which he transfixed their consciences, were sometimes more savage than beasts at Ephesus. Yet in the midst of the wildest tumults, pelted with foul missiles and fouler oaths, bruised and bleeding, he maintained a sweet serenity, the outshining of a Christ-like compassion which overlooked the scorn in its solicitude to save the scorner. He saw, beneath those rough and often ragged forms, souls capable of being raised by Divine grace from the lowest depths to the loftiest altitudes of Christian saintliness and splendour. They were to him prodigals, who, though reduced to utterest beggary and steeped to the lips in swinish impurities, were to be brought back to the Father's house, clad in festal robes, and made to swell the music of holy mirth. And so he patiently endured insult and anguish, and pleaded and prayed with them, with what result let history tell. As he did so we must do, if we desire his success. Our responsibilities are as great, and our opportunities are as many as his. Men still stand aloof from the means of grace. As there was a rough desert not far from the Holy City, so round about our splendid chapels, with their respectable congregations, there are moral wastes which need to be rescued from weeds and worthlessness; multitudes without God and without hope in the world. The fact is notorious: it glares upon us in the crowds that flood the streets of our cities, or flow out into the suburbs; it chequers the sunshine and disturbs the joy of the day of rest. With many, eternity has disappeared from the sphere of motive. To-day is all in all. Sense sways spirit, and the shows of time eclipse the realities of the future. What, then, is our duty as Methodists to these poor outcasts, who are as sheep without a shepherd? To bring back one, the great Good Shepherd left His ninety-nine; and shall not we go forth to seek the lost when half a nation lies outside the Church's pale? Too long we have waited for the

people to come to us. Now, like the Master, let us go to
them. We must, if we wish to be true to the spirit of
our Methodism. The greatest achievement of her early
history was the gathering in of the outcasts ; and the work
from which she derives her greatest glory, and to which
she owes her existence, must be continued if she is to be
multiplied and enlarged. Let us go, then, as Wesley went,
with compassion in our hearts and with Christ on our lips ;
Christ crucified, the expression of eternal love, and the all-
sufficient refuge for sinful men ; the Christ who touches
human life at every point, and in so touching it lifts earth
to heaven. Such a message will bring the weary and
heavy-laden around us, like thirsty travellers around a
newly-discovered well. It matters little whether the
draught of living water be given in an earthen cup or a
golden chalice.

> " The main thing is, does it hold good measure ?
> Heaven soon sets right all other matters."

And, sir, let us enforce our evangel with our lives. The
age which saw the rise of Methodism was one in which
religion had fallen into contempt ; it had degenerated into
a thing of empty form. The inconsistencies of professors
had made it a smoke in men's eyes, and a stench in men's
nostrils. Methodism rose up in protest against these
things, and sought to counteract them by "spreading
scriptural holiness through the land." It demanded a
higher spiritual life in those who were called to witness
for God, so that they should not only profess the truth but
practise it. By such men—men whose lives enforced the
teaching of their lips—men who were "happy in their
holiness, and holy in their happiness"—Methodism sought
to fulfil her mission. And, sir, if our future is to resemble
our past, that is what we need as Churches to-day,—men
who not only hold the truth, but who are held by the
truth ; men whose lives are deeply rooted in Christ, and
uniformly crowned with the fruits of holiness ; men who
live in Christ and for Christ, as those who are alive from

the dead. Depend upon it, if we have such life in our midst, it will make itself felt in the world around us. The piety which can be kept in the dark, and no one be the wiser for it, is not worth the keeping. It is worthless as the barren fig-tree, which withered under Christ's curse. But, sir, it cannot be hidden, even if we would. Invisible in its essence, it will be patent enough in its result. You could no more suppress it than you could prevent light from shining. Imprison Peter, and the darkest dungeon will blaze at midnight with more than midday glory. Thrust Stephen out of the city gate to stone him, and whilst his life ebbs away beneath the cruel, crushing blows, the light will flash up within him till his face shines like the face of an angel. And so in any case, if a man has grace within him, it will flow forth spontaneously as heat from a fire or fragrance from a rose. Like the box of ointment which Mary broke, it will shed a perfume all around. Ah, and like the wind which swept over the valley in which the prophet stood, it will turn dead, dry bones into living men. It did in Wesley's day, and it will do in ours. These are the sort of lives Methodism wants to fit her for her world-wide mission. Thank God she has had, and still has, such lives. Still, they are all too few. Our need is that such lives should be multiplied—that the exception should become the rule. Our need is that the average Methodist should be as our present best, and our best such as we have never seen. Let all pray as some pray, and there would be a plentiful and permanent rain of blessing. Let all work as some work, and no part of the field would be unoccupied, and no sheaf of the great harvest ungathered. Let all live as some live, and that old battery of the enemy, Inconsistency, would be silenced for want of ammunition. And our beloved Methodism everywhere would become what her sainted Founder intended her to be, and what we his children long for her to be—a Church whose voice will be as a trumpet, her example as a light, her influence as a sword, and her life as a sermon to wake the dead.

Primitive Methodist Connexion.

By the Rev. J. HALLAM,

PRESIDENT OF THE PRIMITIVE METHODIST CONNEXION.

I AM glad to be here when City Road is beginning to renew its youth, and I hope the renewal of its youth will be something more than concrete foundations and marble pillars and better seatage. I hope the Church that worships in this sanctuary will renew its youth with greater fidelity and love to Jesus Christ.

One hundred years ago to-day, John Wesley breathed his last; forty years ago to-day, William Clowes died— the potter who gave up his work, and took one-third of what he was getting at his trade, in order to preach the gospel. I have been glad here to-day, sir, to see behind me in this beautiful window, that the central representation is John Wesley, standing under a green tree and in the free open air, with Bible in hand, preaching to the people; so William Clowes was the field-preacher of our Church, who, under the green tree, in the market-place, anywhere, told poor lost sinners that Jesus Christ died to save them. There may be some here to-night who do not know that William Clowes is one of the men whom we call our founders,—a man who not only could preach the gospel, but could shake a congregation when he began to pray. And you value prayer, unless I much misunderstand your expressions of sympathy with what the previous speaker has said in that singularly chaste and beautiful address. You believe in prayer; and if City Road and all Methodists will go more to their knees, we shall have a revival, and we shall all renew our youth.

At the time when John Wesley was just coming to the front, it is said that Voltaire, the French sceptic, visited this land; and when he got back to his own countrymen, he said that the English people were so disgusted with the Christian religion, that neither the old faith revived nor a new religion would make its fortune. This meeting gives the lie to that. If John Wesley could stand to-night on this platform, I think his heart would be gladdened. He might well say the time had come when the world was his parish.

And now, sir, what are we here for to-night? Are we here to congratulate one another, to rejoice that the Mother Church of Methodism is hale and hearty? She is not a wrinkled, decrepit, withered old woman. Her quiver is full of arrows; her children are multitudinous. There is "abundance of corn on the top of the mountains." This is the hope we have, the confidence we feel here to-night. But while we are here to congratulate ourselves, shall we rest and be thankful? Is the work of Methodism finished? If the work is not finished, and Methodism has not completed its mission, we would like to say, Let us more than ever go at it. We discuss methods, we spend time in criticising plans, we differ about schemes, we compare the respective virtues of Abana and Pharpar with Jordan, and all the time the leprosy remains. It is time that we tried to rise and go forward. If John Wesley could speak, he would repeat, I think, some of his own words: "Observe that it is not your business to preach so many times, but to save as many souls as you can, to bring as many sinners as you can to repentance, and with all your power to build them up in that holiness without which no man can see the Lord." We are sometimes crushed with our rules of procedure in our Methodistic work. It has once or twice come over me in my ministerial life, that I would like to burn my plan, and ask myself where best to go. I am not sure that such an expression may not be thought heterodox in a meeting like this; nevertheless, I have so felt at times. We want to go go with the old watchwords, and to sing the old hymns, such as,—

> " He breaks the power of cancelled sin,
> He sets the prisoner free :
> His blood can make the foulest clean,
> His blood availed for me."

Wesley had an idea that his mission was to sinners, and in the energy generated by such a conception, Methodism must open her gates, and she must go out, and send her preachers to preach the gospel wherever the people are.

Is this all we must do? What is our work in regard to the great social questions that are outside us? What is the attitude of Methodism to some very critical questions that are round about us to-day? Have we just to preach the gospel? Is our work finished with doing that? No, sir! Outside this chapel there are the seething lapsed masses, men and women perishing by thousands; and also in other cities and towns in this land, where the only difference is that the sinners are fewer in number, the evil remaining the same in degree; and there are questions involved that touch the hearts of good men, and Methodism cannot sit still and be silent. We want to attend to the temporal needs of men, and we ought to act as John Wesley acted,—to do good to all men. You remember the story of John Wesley's coach sticking in an Irish bog. I do not know whether our friend Mr. M'Cutcheon has ascertained its precise geographical situation or not; but while Wesley was in difficulties himself, an Irishman passed by with a dejected air,—he was about to be evicted from his hovel. To his surprise, Wesley put a pound into his hand. The poor man gave expression to his gratitude and joy as only an Irishman can. That was John Wesley's social Christianity. A local preacher once went home after a service he had been conducting, and found a message that a poor man of his acquaintance had no coal in the house to make a fire. Though weary with a long walk of many miles, he took off his coat, in which he had preached the gospel, and put into a sack as much coal as he could carry, and walked two miles, in order that the poor man might have a fire. I call that Methodistic Christianity. It is the Christianity of Christ.

We must also present a united phalanx as Methodists. We are different regiments; we must all be one army. We may be different tribes; we must all be one Israel

Issachar and Judah may have their respective positions as well as Zabulon and Naphtali when the camp is pitched; but we must have in the middle one tabernacle, one law, one Shekinah, one cloud of glory, and if we cannot realise that our work must be a failure. I am glad to think we are one upon these points. Some people talk of schism; and, while we are rejoicing, some are terming us schismatics and telling us our duty. · Well, let them call us schismatics, it will not hurt us; and I think we will not do each other much harm here to-night, and we do not wish injury to the National Church, only we would like all the Churches of the land free Churches. As for you and us, speaking for my own Church, I may say that we have nothing to forgive —no hatreds to remember. I am here to-night, not only with my personal good-will, but with the hearty consent of the Church I represent. We have broad lines of demar-cation. They may, they will get rubbed out. Perhaps some may think them broad, but there is no impassable gulf. That has yet to be created, if it ever is. I would like to desiderate that we should get to know one another a little better sometimes. You, sir, intimated that it was an accident. I think you are right. I believe that it is due to our itinerancy. It is not dislike, hatred, jealousy, envy, which hinders closer relation; it is the accident of itinerancy which precludes it so often. Then, sir, there are anomalies which I think should not exist, and which freer intercourse might remedy. For instance, last week I went to preach at a Northumbrian village; in the same week another Methodist preacher fulfilled his appointment there. During the preceding week other two Methodist ministers preached in the same village. That is the regular fortnight's work at this particular place; and the whole four of us in the fortnight did not muster fifty people. I do not want to damage village Methodism, but I want to know if that is the right thing for village Methodism. I do not think it is. I do not tell you on this united platform which Church had the biggest congregation—I leave that for you to find out.

The Bible Christians.

By the Rev. W. HIGMAN,

PRESIDENT OF THE BIBLE CHRISTIAN CONNEXION.

WILLIAM O'BRYAN was born thirteen years before John Wesley died, and he was converted four years after that event. His mother was a truly pious woman, who aided the Methodists, and helped them to establish preaching in her own and neighbouring parishes. The home was a home for the ministers and their followers. William O'Bryan, as soon as he was converted, at once sought the salvation of others. He exhorted men to flee from the wrath to come. A press of business led him to neglect the duty, but a time came when he felt humiliated. He held a prayer-meeting in a distant village. A Society was formed; and for the first time, on Christmas Day, 1795, he took a text and preached a sermon. Up to that time seventy souls had been led to Christ through him. He felt drawn to give himself to the work of the ministry.

In July 1809, in the absence of the circuit minister, Mr. O'Bryan was asked to do his work. While thus engaged, he heard that in New Quay there was no evangelical preaching, and on being relieved from circuit work he proceeded to that place. Here his labours were greatly blessed, and he was thus encouraged to proceed in this irregular way. He established preaching in many places, walking many miles on the Sabbath day. He had difficulties and opposition, and in November 1810 he was formally excluded from the Methodist Society, his irregularities being his only offence. As he was a married man, he could not be admitted into the regular ministry. At this time he heard there were many places eastward which were destitute of evangelical preaching, and in a true missionary spirit he went to them. Mrs. O'Bryan, like a brave and earnest woman, began to conduct meetings at home. Multitudes of souls were converted. In the early part of 1814, Mr. O'Bryan gave up his business, and laboured in many places. After trying for six years to be employed by his own people, he resolved to go on with his work, and to leave the results with God. At Shebbear he was much pressed to form a Society, and twenty-two persons gave in their names. Not one of these knew of his severance from the Methodists. All who joined had been regular attendants at the parish church. The first quarterly meeting was held on January 1, 1816, at his own house in Holsworthy, the members in church fellowship being 237. The first local preachers' meeting was held at Week Orchard, and it was decided to employ a second preacher. James Thorne accepted the position. The first Conference was held on August 17, 1819, and a form of chapel deed was decided on. Women-preachers were unanimously accepted. The missionary society was formed in 1821. The name of Bible Christian was theirs by gift. Their preachers would preach ; and one day, under the broad canopy of heaven, a mob collected. There was a pile of broken stones close by, and these they used freely, some using their fists with stones in them. The preachers had their heads and faces and hands cut, and yet they preached. Souls to them were more than stones, and the infuriated mob said, " Surely these must be Bible Christians." The name is a gift from our enemies, and we accept it as such. The Lord has blessed us greatly. We have our rules of Society, our code of doctrines, our magazines, our hymn-books, our missionary society, and still "the poor have the gospel preached to them." I have known men give all their salary to keep a station alive. Is not this true Methodism ? And if Wesley to-day could speak to all who are in any true sense his followers, would he not say : Economise your time, talent, and resources of every kind, and at any rate keep out of one another's way. Do not ride four horses to one village, and send four men to do the work that could be better done by one. And surely Hugh Bourne and William O'Bryan would give the same advice.

And so would James Thorne and Dr. W. Cooke, whose strong sympathy with every proposal tending towards Methodist union was so well known. Union is strength, and a United Methodism would be an immense, incalculable power for good. The world is to be saved, and the power of sin to be everywhere broken and destroyed. As instruments in God's hands, our first duty is to save the people. Let us join hand in hand to fight for the Lord of Hosts, and success is certain.

Wesleyan Reform Union.

By the Rev. GEORGE GREEN,

PRESIDENT OF THE WESLEYAN REFORM UNION.

I LOOK upon Methodism as a great family, and consider it no mean favour to be counted one of its humble members. I trust this Centenary Celebration may enable us to understand each other better, and that we may separate with stronger attachments even than when we assembled. We are met to-night under circumstances at once solemn and joyful.

1. *Solemn*, because we call to mind the great loss Methodism sustained in the death of her Founder. And John Wesley not only belonged to Methodism, but was a true benefactor of mankind at large. Our Church did not suffer alone: all England suffered, humanity suffered, and heaven alone was the richer for his death. We are reminded, too, of the rapid flight of time. Since our Founder's death a century has rolled away; and still how much work remains undone. There is surely much land yet to be possessed.

2. But we are met under *joyful* circumstances, because of the success we have thankfully to record. How true are the words, "God buries His workmen, yet continues His work." We have to rejoice that the work has not been in vain. The splendid success of the great Methodist

movement calls for our gratitude to-day, and should encourage us to increase our diligence and fervour and faith that the future may be yet more successful.

Methodism is not played out. Perhaps I represent the most radical wing; but we are loyal, we love Methodism. We are proud of our parentage; we do not forget our origin; and we feel a profound reverence for John Wesley's memory, and for the Mother Church of Methodism.

Though Methodism is divided, its sections are not hostile. The strongest possible ties bind us together. In all essential things we are one—one in our origin, one in our usages, one in our work. We ought not to feel, as we have felt, that we are so far separated. Humanity is in a hopeless condition, but there is hope to be proclaimed to the worst, and none need despair. We have to carry the gospel of hope, and deliverance, and sympathy to men everywhere, and to seek to improve their lives. It is not her organisation, but her recognition of the ever-present power of the Holy Spirit, that has been the strength of Methodism in the past, and that is her hope for the future, if we are to evangelise mankind. I trust that we shall grow closer together as the years roll on, and that the coming century will eclipse the past in success and triumph.

United Methodist Free Church.

By the Rev. M. T. MYERS,

PRESIDENT OF THE UNITED METHODIST FREE CHURCHES.

IT is one hundred years to-day since John Wesley finished his earthly course. It is very appropriate that services should be held in commemoration of the event, and that all the branches of the Methodist family should unite in such a work.

Since his death, great changes have taken place in the religious, scientific, commercial, and political world, and in the general condition and improvement of mankind.

The Bible Society, as an auxiliary of the Church, has scattered the leaves of the tree of life—which are for the healing of the nations—broadcast among the people, and the England of to-day is not what it was one hundred years ago. That wave of spiritual light and life, which passed over this country during the latter half of the last century, has proved the truth of the saying of Neander: "All national greatness depends upon the tone of public feeling and manners, and that on the influence which religion exerts on the life of the people." Gradually, step by step, we have risen, until the best education is now within the reach of every child of the poorest family in the land ; the rights of citizenship may be enjoyed by every man of sober and industrious habits ; liberty of conscience has been secured ; a commercial and maritime position has been gained, such as finds no parallel in the history of all the human family.

Within three years of Wesley's death, William Carey went out to India, and commenced the work of modern Protestant Christian missions. And now, what a different prospect does the world present to the view of a believer in Christ ! We have access to Rome, and all the kingdoms of papal Europe. The Bible has been translated into the languages of the swarming millions of the Celestial Empire, and the missionary has crossed its rivers, scaled its mountains, and traversed its plains, carrying the lamp of life. The ports of Japan have been opened, and practically its inhabitants have accepted the gospel of Jesus Christ. India is held by a Christian power, and strenuous efforts are being made to preserve its infant race from immolation, raise the female to her proper position in social life, destroy the influence of caste, abolish idol temples, and convert the abodes of cruelty into homes of peace and love ; and all Asia begins to recognise His throne who is Prince of the kings of the earth. Africa is now explored, and the Missionary Societies have undertaken the question of its evangelisation, by which its sable sons shall be free, and enjoy the liberty by which Christ blesses all His people; and Ethiopia stretches out her hands unto God, and the Isles of the Sea wait for His law. To Mr. Wesley, if to any man, and more than to any man, is to be given the credit of this change in the condition and prospects of mankind.

During the Centenary celebrations, Mr. Wesley is considered as a preacher, writer, organiser, patriot, philanthropist, etc. Now, it is not my intention to touch on any such questions, but to consider other phases of the subject, different, but just now equally as important.

1. We need, and might have, a little more united action. We have peace. We have no need to hoist the flag of truce. There is not a jar between us. We can meet in committee, look each other in the face, recognise each other, shake hands, understand and bid each other "God-speed" in our work. The Œcumenical Conference ten years ago did a great deal for us; this meeting will strengthen the cords; and the Conference to be held in Washington next October will add its influence. Methodism in this country is split up into many sections, each having its own peculiarities, and each doing a great work, no doubt; but there needs a little more united action on the part of all these sections on all public questions affecting the interests of the Church and the well-being of the masses of the people. I do not mean organic union. That will come; but for that we are not yet much prepared. I wish we were. When David was an old man, he desired to build a "house for the Lord in Jerusalem;" but he had been a man of war; that disqualified him, and the work must fall into other and cleaner hands. "It is the Lord's doings, and it is marvellous in our eyes." A United Methodism will come, but some of us old warriors will have to be laid in the sepulchres of our fathers, if it be in sweet odours and divers kinds of spices made by the apothecaries' art, and in great mourning.

But in view of the difficulties of the hour, and the need of strength to meet the growing emergencies of the moment there is something we can do. We can at least prepare the ground, and collect some of the material, or favourably dispose the people towards building this temple of the future. Methodists of all shades of opinion should be willing so far to unite for the common good. A United Methodism would be the strongest bulwark of Protestantism in this country. When high dignitaries of the Church and official documents can unblushingly say that the Reformation was a mistake, and that the righteousness of God which is by faith unto all them that believe, is a delusion and a snare, we need again some Luther to nail his theses to the door, not outside, but inside the Church. It is amazing what a few men can do when they are united and determined, especially when they are right. The poor Waldenses, notwithstanding the power of kings and the fulminations of the wrath of the Vatican, kept the pure fire burning in the mountains of Piedmont for hundreds of years. One million Methodists, with all our organisations and an open Bible, would be far more certain of success than Leonidas with his 300 brave Spartans in the Pass. Not only should we be able to hold the gates of the Hot Springs, but pour the tide of light and life over a ransomed race. " And who knoweth but that we are come to the kingdom for such a time as this?" Is it too much to ask or suggest that some means be devised by which all the sections of the Methodist family can federate, so that we can move steadily and unitedly in any case when the Ark of the Lord is in danger. I ask for nothing impossible. I ask for nothing in my own personal interests, or the interests of the community I have the honour to represent. I ask for nothing but in the name and interests of the Great Head of the Church and the welfare of mankind. This is a fitting moment to inaugurate some scheme which would rally all the hosts of our Israel, and present such a front as would deter those who are wrong, and strengthen and encourage those who are right, and are trying to benefit our race. Men of light and leading, judge ye what I say!

2. To do this, we must understand and have strong confidence in our weapons. We are engaged in a great moral conflict. All the conquests of the past have been won by the proper and judicious use of these two weapons —the Word and the Spirit. Starting out from Jerusalem, after the day of Pentecost, it was the Word which ran, and the Spirit which glorified that Word by giving efficiency and success to its publication. It was not till the Papacy had succeeded in withdrawing the Word from the people, that they succeeded in deluding, and imposing upon them all the nonsense that cursed the ages and ruined the prospects of the Churches. The era of Luther was the first great revival of letters. The Reformation under Wesley was the second revival of letters. The most distinguishing feature of the early Methodists was the attention they gave to, and the knowledge they had of, the Word. Many of the mothers of Methodism had a better knowledge of the Word than some of the most learned men of the time. From Genesis to Malachi, but especially from Matthew to Revelation, they were acquainted with every promise and prospect. That was the strength of the early Methodists; and the Word, in the hands of the Spirit, became the power of God unto salvation to thousands who believed. In modern times the tendency is to dilute the one and ignore the other. A strong confidence in these weapons, which still are mighty, is essential to success. Opening our eyes, we can see this any day by illustrations which clearly indicate the Divine plan and purpose. Just in proportion to the clearness of the vision, and dependence upon the work and power of the Spirit, is the success of any person or Church. We may depend upon other means, and have some kind of success. There are social and moral elements in human nature, which, if properly nursed and developed, are strong enough to bring young people together in friendship and in fellowship. But to build up a spiritual house, you must have these two divinely-appointed means, the Word and the Spirit, in active and constant co-operation. There

P

may be aids and auxiliaries, but there must be no substitutes, or it is the wood, the hay, and the stubble which
will be consumed by fire. That word is the Word, and
that spirit is the Spirit of Life! With these we have
nothing to fear. They are omnipotent. We hear of "The
Bitter Cry," the "Submerged Tenth," and "Darkest
England" and Africa. Heaven's appointed means to
meet the wants and woes of a sorrowful world are the
Word and Spirit. These never fail, when properly used
in the full assurance of faith.

3. But there is another quality wanted, without which
much of what we possess is ineffective and useless. And
that quality is courage—that quality of mind and heart
which carries a man through danger and difficulty without
fear; so distinct and strong in the early disciples and
saints of older times—a quality as essential in the moral
world as on the field of conflict and death. You read of
those three youths on the plains of Dura. When called,
upon pain of a death of a most fearful kind, to fall down
and worship a golden image, their reply was, "We will
not worship that image: our God whom we serve is able
—if He sees fit—to deliver us out of the fire; but if He
does not see fit—if we have to suffer—well! be it distinctly
known that we will not worship that golden god." That
is courage, courage which never fails to win, especially if
the cause is right. Such courage is as essential to-day on
the part of the minister, the merchant prince, the trades-
man, and every young man and woman who has to go
into any of the workshops of this great city and the towns
in the country, as on the plains of Dura. To be ashamed
of Christ is more than a weakness or a failure, it is a sin,
and a sin which soon works out its own end.

One of the tendencies of the times is to compromise
matters, until there is little distinction between what is
right and what is wrong, between what is true and what is
false. "Oh, leave it alone, all will come right in the end;"
and the condition of the world to-day is just the result of
this unjust and lukewarm condition and action of the

Church. Looking around us, we can see churches, chapels, and preaching-rooms without name and number. We have cardinals, archbishops, bishops, canons, deans, rectors, vicars, and priests. We have ministers, local preachers, leaders, deacons, and Sunday-school teachers by hundreds of thousands. What an army! We have services in cathedral, hall, and temple. We have organisations of all sorts, from the grand Missionary Society, the Bible and Tract Society, to the village Band of Hope. Many are running to and fro, and knowledge is being increased. But yet sin abounds, and unblushing profanity walks and stalks through our streets in open day. The revelations of our Divorce Courts, the scenes on our racecourses and in gambling dens, and the condition of the slums in our great and little towns from the drink traffic, are a disgrace to the name of Englishman wherever the record flies.

Surely there must be something wrong, when all our multiplied and varied agencies fail to keep in check the ever-increasing flood of ungodliness and iniquity. What is it? Let me ask you to ask yourselves, What is it? Are our weapons of warfare not as mighty as in former times? Is the word less powerful to-day than when it was said to be the "power of God"? Is the Lord's arm shortened that it cannot save as in the days of Wesley and Whitefield? A thousand voices answer, No! a thousand times No! Then I ask you, What is it? The fault must be somewhere. Where is it? If it is not Divine, it must be human.

> " Tender handed stroke a nettle,
> And it stings you for your pains ;
> Grasp it like a man of mettle,
> And it soft as silk remains."

It is courage that is wanted on the part of those who love the Lord Jesus Christ to-day. The very exercise will teach the need of seeking to be replenished at the fountain. Many of the greatest reforms ever effected were at the commencement treated with contempt, and their advocates subjected to all kinds of abuse and persecution. What courage it required forty years ago on the part of Charles Garrett and others to advocate teetotalism in the Methodist Churches! Their success to-day is an evidence of what courage can do. The old Spartan mothers used to train their boys, that when they went to war, if they found their swords too short to reach the enemy, they were to add a step to the length. A fire broke out in the East-end of London, and in fifteen minutes every engine in the Tower Hamlets was upon the spot, and the danger and damage was rather from flood than fire. Semiramis, at her toilet, hears of a rebellion in Babylon. In a moment, with dishevelled hair, she mounts her chariot, puts down the rebellion, and returns to finish her toilet. When a French army was crossing the Alps to the assistance of Napoleon in Italy, an avalanche carried a drummer-boy almost 1000 feet into the yawning gorge below. The general seized a rope and threw it around his waist. His veterans besought him with tears not to venture into the depths of the chasm. "Wipe your tears and seize the rope," said the general, and in thirty minutes he placed the boy upon the road safe and sound, amid the plaudits of the whole army. Energy and courage such as these on the part of all those who profess the Christian name, would place a ransomed world at the feet of Christ before the opening of the twentieth century. We want more courage—courage to acknowledge that we believe in the divinity of the Word, in the efficacy of the death, and in the sufficiency of the grace of Christ—courage to confess Him before men, and preach the truth, however unpopular it may be.

To-day we need a little more united action on the part of the Methodists, a strong and unwavering confidence in the Word and the Spirit as the means of enlightening and saving mankind, and a courage commensurate with the work we have to do.

We had an old man in Leeds who safely reached his hundredth birthday; and when asked the day after how he was, he said, "Well, I am better on my feet to commence the second hundred than I was to begin the first." Methodism is on its feet, is in good health, and active in all its movements. It is as necessary to-day as in the middle of the last century. The world has not got into a condition to do without it. We commence to-morrow under better conditions and brighter prospects than ever before. The fields are white unto the harvest ; thrust ye in the sickle. Great changes have taken place during the century, and Methodism has been an important factor ; but what it may do in the future remains with ourselves. Let us resolve, the Lord helping us, to carry the Word by the Spirit to the uttermost extremity of the human race, and its vivifying pulsations shall be felt and seen in the purity, the joy, and the happiness of a redeemed and saved people.

Sacrament of the Lord's Supper.

By the Rev. JAMES H. RIGG, D.D.

———o———

DEAR BRETHREN,—

We are gathered together on an occasion entirely
without precedent, with a solemnity, tenderness, and
emphasis all its own, so far at least as our Church
is concerned. We meet as followers of John Wesley,
rejoicing in that gospel which he preached, believing
in the doctrine of a conscious life in Christ, and understanding that that life is one to flow from heart to heart,
from lip to lip,—that we are not only to be recipients,
but witnesses. The fellowship of Christ's people, after
the primitive pattern, is a hearty, free, uttered, diffusive,
generous, compassionate missionary fellowship. That
is the fellowship in Christ in which, thank God, we all
believe—the doctrine and experience and life taught us
by our Father and Founder; and it is as still holding that
doctrine, and participating in such an experience, and
prepared to witness to these truths, and as representing a
fellowship founded on these truths, that we are gathered
together in this holy sanctuary. We are here—for this is
indeed a representative gathering—not merely as belonging to City Road or to London, or to our own proper
Church,—in which we glory,—but as representing the
followers of Wesley in every country, on every continent,

beyond every sea, and of many different races. How many hearts are in unison with us to-day; how many eyes are converging upon this point! Multitudes of prayers have been offered that we should be assembled, not only in the name of Jesus, but with the presence—the real presence—of Jesus in the midst of us. This is a representative assembly, gathering for a holy commemoration in memory of one whom, on this day and in this place, we can scarcely name without our hearts being filled with deepest emotion, and our eyes almost ready to overflow. It is in memory of Wesley that we are gathered here to-day. He is not only a name, a memory, to us—though dead, he not only speaks, he lives under God, through Christ Jesus, by His Spirit. The power that John Wesley wielded in Christ's name still holds its place amongst the great influences of this earth. For us the solemn thought is, that it depends more or less on us, and each individual bears his share of responsibility, whether the power shall abide in its pristine energy, its true Divine and spiritual purity, or whether it shall through our own fault decline from generation to generation. God forbid!

This celebration, we trust, will be one means of preventing such a decline, and bringing us back to those original springs of doctrine—to those fontal truths—those primitive laws and energies—which belong to Pentecost, and which are not yet exhausted. We are gathered in memory of Wesley. Oh, what a hush there is throughout the Churches of Methodism at home and abroad. We have tasted of the holy power in the services that have preceded. Let us lift up our hearts to God, that there may be the very quintessence of the power for the sacred service of to-day.

We are gathered here on this spot. Yonder Wesley died; here his remains were laid. Within this neighbourhood thousands came to take their last look upon the great apostle of his time. Here we are in the chapel which he so dearly loved. Twelve years before his death he had the bliss of seeing it finished. How delighted he was to preach in it! How his soul rejoiced and was revived when crowds came to listen to him here—crowds that increased as his years grew! But, above all, how he rejoiced to administer the Lord's Supper in this sanctuary! That was his chiefest, most exquisite joy, to see people coming in crowds to consecrate themselves afresh to God. Those saints were choice spirits—most of them, at any rate—a consecrated people, a peculiar people, not fashioned according to the course of this world, but transformed in the spirit of their minds, setting a pure and godly example in the midst of an untoward generation. Are we their true successors? Let us lift up our hearts in prayer to God, that that Spirit which rested upon them may rest yet more abundantly upon us. Yes, brethren, *we* are here. Is it too daring to ask whether John Wesley is here, whether his spirit is near us? Is it too bold to believe that still the spirits of those who have departed hence in the faith and fear of God, do care for the things which are done in this lower sphere, especially for the causes they watched over, and for the work which it was given them to begin? I know not whether it is right to speak of it. But I think all of us will have some such thought as that now, when the hundred years are completed, that the blessed saint is not far from us, that he is permitted to joy in beholding our order, and that even his bright spirit is more abundantly refreshed when he sees thus that his works do follow him.

Wesley delighted in Sacraments, and especially in the Sacrament of the Lord's Supper. He loved it beyond every other means of grace. He was never weary of insisting upon the duty of frequent communion, even speaking of constant communion. He counted it a privilege not only to have weekly, but sometimes, though rarely, daily communion of the Lord's Supper. Let it not be said by any that this was mere ritualism. Wesley doubtless was brought up a strict son of the Church of England. He loved the order of the services in the Church. He found them to be wells of salvation, springs of joy and peace. But there was no slavery, no mere mechanism, in the ritualism of John Wesley. He kept many of the fasts of the Church—not all; he rejoiced in her feasts; he delighted in the anthems of the cathedral, the fair order of the shrines of his Church, when indeed it was fair, when the truth and the spirit were there. His ritualism had its springs in a soul penetrated by Divine light and love. There was indeed a time, even in Wesley's history, when his ritualism had too much the character of a servile observance. But when he embraced Christ by spiritual faith, all that ritualism passed away. Thereafter he loved the services of the Church, because he found Christ there, and his soul was refreshed. It was so with the festival of All Saints, to which reference was made yesterday. He loved All Saints' Day. He always kept it. And why? Because he thought of the blessed saints of all ages, the great cloud of witnesses. He delighted to meditate on them, and he looked forward to the time when he should join a still greater cloud of witnesses above. That was spiritual faith and refreshment, and not a mere servile ritualism. When he administered the Sacrament, his delight was to think that the saints of heaven were in sympathy with the saints of earth; and if the Holy Communion was administered on All Saints' Day, his joy in that respect was redoubled.

He was not a modern ritualist. He did not love the Sacrament because he thought the Sacrament was the one and exclusive source of life for the soul. He did not love it because he felt he must go to the priest and Sacrament, if he would have the indwelling Spirit in him, and could not otherwise have that unspeakable privilege and right. There was nothing of that sort about Wesley's love for the Sacrament. No! He had learned better in Aldersgate Street. He learned better when he found peace through believing. He tells us that whilst some one was reading Luther's Preface to the Epistle to the Romans, his heart was strangely warmed, and he felt that he did trust in Christ for salvation; that his sins were taken away, and that he was made free from the law of sin and death. That did not come to him from the blessed Spirit through the Sacrament of the Lord's Supper. Wesley had been learning the secret of this great salvation for some time before at the feet of Peter Böhler, but on that particular occasion he proved it. Wesley knew better than to think for a moment that the Spirit was chained, chained to a succession of ministers—chained to a process of Church ritual. He knew better than to believe after his conversion (he never, indeed, believed it at any time), that the Spirit could only come through elements upon which the priest had laid his hands—that the line of spiritual influence was absolutely limited, and limited in that mechanical and servile way of ministration. That was not Wesley's faith. He knew in whom he had believed. He knew that it is by faith—the faith of the operation of God—that life comes into the soul. Wesley was no ritualist in the modern sense. He knew that the "Spirit bloweth where He listeth." Please to take that for granted. And why do I refer to that now? Because at this moment there are people trying their utmost to insist, or using every device to insinuate, that Wesley was a ritualist in that modern sense, and that all his love for sacramental occasions was a part of such ritualism as the priests who hold superstitious and popish doctrine teach upon this point. I will refer to a few passages in Wesley's own writings, for I would like to take this opportunity of slaying that error effectually and finally for those who have ears to hear.

In 1733, Wesley was at the very highest point of his ritualism. He never was higher than then, and he preached a sermon upon the Lord's Supper in 1733 for the use of his pupils. He reprinted that sermon in 1788; and he says when he reprints it, that he had never varied in his teaching from the teaching laid down in that sermon. Then what does that sermon teach which he wrote in 1733, and reprinted in 1788? Does that sermon contain any trace of the modern Anglican teaching as to sacramental efficacy? There is not a trace of it. He says, "As our bodies are strengthened by bread and wine, so are our souls by these tokens of the body and blood of Christ." "These *tokens!*" In these words there is no doctrine of the corporeal presence of the Divine-human Saviour in the elements. Again he says, "The design of this Sacrament is the continual remembrance of the death of Christ by eating bread and drinking wine, which are the outward *signs* of the inward grace of the body and blood of Christ." Again he says, "All Christians were obliged to receive these signs of Christ's body and blood." How careful he is to retain and to repeat the words "signs" and "tokens"! Never for a moment did it enter into his mind to use language that savoured of anything like the superstitious doctrines of to-day—doctrines that were then held by some of the Non-jurors, but which he absolutely refused to hold or have anything to do with. Again, "The bread and wine are commanded to be received in remembrance of His death to the end of the world." That was his teaching in 1733. He has a sermon on "The Means of Grace" (one of our standard sermons). In that sermon he says a very few words about the Sacrament of the Lord's Supper. He quotes the Lord's own words, "Take, eat, this is My body." "That is," he explains, "the sacred *sign* of My body." Can anything be more express or Protestant than that? "And He took the cup, saying, This cup is the New Testament (or Covenant) in My blood." "That is," says Wesley, "the appropriate *sign* of that covenant." They are signs—not, because the priest's hand has passed upon them, and his lips have uttered sacred words, are they changed into the very body, blood, soul, Divinity, and humanity of the Lord Jesus Christ. No such doctrine as that was held by John Wesley. He was no ritualist. Again, after quoting the words, "As often as ye eat this bread and drink this cup, ye do show forth the Lord's death till He come," he says, "By these visible signs ye manifest *your solemn remembrance* of His death till He cometh in the clouds of heaven." He does not say, "You feed upon the sacrifice which we have prepared for you." He does not say, "You take the Lord Jesus into your very system and frame of body, soul, and spirit." Nothing of the sort. He speaks of "signs" and "tokens," but not a word that savours of the modern popish doctrine can you find in anything that he has written upon this subject.

But there is still one more passage, which is, perhaps, the most striking of all. He was writing to his mother— and this, too, some years before his evangelical conversion, when he was at Oxford, a High Churchman—but not in the modern sense. In his letter to his mother he says, "One consideration is enough to make me assent to my father's and your judgment concerning the Holy Sacrament, which is that we cannot allow Christ's human nature to be present in it"—that is, in the bread and wine— "without allowing either Consubstantiation or Transubstantiation." He refused to accept the doctrine which some of the men whom he knew held, viz., that the very human nature of Christ was put into the bread and wine. "It is not in it," he said, "and we cannot hold that it is in it, without holding either Consubstantiation or Transubstantiation." Let no one say Wesley ever held high doctrine of this sort.

Well, but the other day I observed that a High Church paper quoted a passage from Dr. Brevint's *Manual of the Lord's Supper*, which Wesley allowed to be printed as a preface to his brother Charles's Hymns on the Lord's Supper; and this particular High Church organ, after quoting a passage, says, "Hence it follows, Wesley held all our High Church doctrine in regard to the Lord's Supper." Let us see how that really stands. Dr. Brevint (as Dr. Osborn has shown in his published volumes of Wesley's poetry) did write a tractate on the Lord's Supper. Wesley did allow it to be a preface to his brother Charles's wonderful Hymns on the Lord's Supper. But what does Dr. Brevint say? This is the passage quoted : "The Lord's body and blood have everywhere, but especially at this Sacrament, a true and real presence." Can that be confounded with the *creation* of the localised presence by the manipulation of the priest, and by the words that he utters? "The Lord's body and blood have *everywhere*, but especially at this Sacrament, a true and real presence." That is a very different thing from saying that it is *made* to be present because the priest has consecrated the bread and wine. *We* believe that Christ's presence is everywhere, but especially is Christ spiritually and really present with us here and now. Further, Brevint says, "He" (*i.e.* the Lord) "sends down to earth the graces that spring continually from His everlasting sacrifice and His continual intercession." Where in all this is there any teaching of Popery, or of modern ritualism? Surely the Lord "*sends down*" the graces, and we are waiting for them. But their doctrine is that the *Lord Himself* is put into the bread and into the wine, so that every particle of the bread (ah! you will hardly believe it, some of you) contains and is instinct with the whole presence of the incarnate Christ in His Godhead and in His humanity. And further (I never try to explain what is believed on this head without something like a shudder), they say that when the recipient takes at the hand of the priest the bread and wine, he receives them into himself, into his living system, and that then there comes the thrill of Divine life into that system —the very living Christ, because of the eating and swallowing the very body and blood of Christ! and that that is the only way Christ in His most essential graces, in His true spiritual life, can ever find a place in the soul, the identity, the nature of any one of woman born. Ah! brethren, such is not our doctrine, and such was never the doctrine of John Wesley. Take it from this meeting, wherever you go, that when any one tries to persuade you that John Wesley had the slightest taint of modern ritualistic superstition in regard to the Lord's Supper in his teaching, it is an assertion totally, absolutely without foundation.

Here let me say, in passing, it is doubtless a great part of the power of the High Church party that they say,

"Christ Jesus is here on this altar." They elevate the Victim when they dare, when they are not afraid of the law and its consequences, and then what they wish is that there should be adoration paid to the transformed —I must say transubstantiated—bread and wine, because the person of Christ is there. Some of them go so far as to indicate by signs when the entrance of Christ into the elements takes place, so that all the people may know the very moment. There is a wonderful power in this. It is the power of a present faith, though it is an ignorant and superstitious faith. But then, blessed be God! when we are as we ought to be, we have all that power in combination with the simplicity of truth. For what is our doctrine? That the Lord is verily present—that here and now He is not very far from any one of us. But it is not only at the Lord's Supper that He is present with us. His promise is, "Wheresoever two or three are met together in My name, there am I in the midst." Again He said, "Lo! I am with you alway, even unto the end of the world." We believe in the real presence of our Lord wherever there is a spirit yearning after God, wherever there is a solitary soul seeking after Jesus.

But you may be asking, Why, if Wesley were no ritualist, did he regard the Holy Supper with such extraordinary love and reverence? What then is it which makes this Sacrament so precious? It is a part of the same great truth which belongs to all God's dealings with us, to all Christ's ordinances, viz., that it is through the spiritually apprehended truth and the Divine Spirit that men's souls are saved, enlightened, and quickened. It is just because this Holy Sacrament is so full of aggregated, combined, crystallised truths, gathered and united in one blessed institution, that it is so precious, and is made such a blessing to those who know how to receive it. You come to the Table. You look upon it. You see nothing but the fair cloth and the simple elements, and you may say, How should there be such a blessing coming from it? My friends, you look at the transparency which lies on one of your own tables in your sitting-rooms. That transparency, as it lies in the shadow on the dark cloth, looks like a mere dead, plain piece of glass. But hold it up to the sun, and you will find that it is marked with exquisite lines, that it contains beautiful, delicate, richly-coloured pictures, and in the sun the beauty comes out, and you see what that transparency was meant to show and to teach. Even so it is with the Sacrament of the Lord's Supper. You look at it. It seems to be a simple ordinance. But come to consider its meaning, and you will find it full of instruction—of suggestion—of scriptural truth—of blessing untold. What is it that we are taught there? We are taught: (1) That Christ is one with His people—most condescendingly one with them—that He puts Himself, as it were, upon a level with them—He is their Saviour, Brother, Friend. (2) That the people of the Lord are one with each other,—

> " One family we dwell in Him,
>   One Church above, beneath."

(3) That it is by feeding upon Christ in your hearts, that Christ Himself spiritually passes into your nature, and that you become "one spirit" with Him. "The words that I speak unto you, they are spirit and they are life." "We feed upon Him in our hearts, and find that heaven and Christ are one." (4) That the Lord triumphed over death; for we are reminded of His own precious words, "I will no more drink of the fruit of the vine until I drink it new with you in My Father's kingdom." He was looking from that table towards what awaited Him beyond all the darkness and sorrow outside. He knew that the cross was close at hand, but He was looking to the feast at His Father's right hand. (5) We learn also that those to whom Christ has given His Spirit will be His guests at the table of His everlasting kingdom. These are some of the truths (and there are others) that are gathered together in this holy ordinance. Oh! if we come with our hearts rightly prepared, what a

depth of meaning; what riches and treasures of instruction; what volumes of spiritual quickening; what consolation; what lighting up of hope,—there is in the Sacrament of the Lord's Supper!

And now, do not let us forget, when we come to this table: (*a*) That we come as the Lord's own chosen and consecrated disciples, those who have walked and talked with Him, and are prepared to bear witness of Him as their Christ and King. We do not come here to *be made* disciples. In that upper room there were faulty men—Thomas who doubted, Peter who denied his Lord, and others—but they were all disciples (Judas had left). In like manner there are faulty men here, but you are the Lord's disciples, and you mean to be His. Therefore you come to this Supper of the Lord—

> " The badge and token this,
> The sure confirming seal,
> That He is ours, and we are His,
> The servants of His will."

(*b*) That at the Table of the Lord faith is the organ by which we are brought into spiritual connection with all the living realities of Christ's gospel. (*c*) That at the Table of the Lord we shall find the Object of our faith. The bread and wine will remind us of the atoning sacrifice of Christ. We shall not only see the Sacrifice, we shall look above and beyond, and on the wings of faith soar—

> "From Calvary's to Zion's height."

There we shall see our great and glorious High Priest —"who ever liveth to make intercession for us." Our privileges are greater than were those of the disciples in the upper room. Their Saviour was then about to go to Calvary. Ours comes down from Zion to preside at our gathering, and makes Himself one with us. And when we kneel at the communion-table, it is the King of saints that our faith recognises.

(*d*) Once more: If our faith is as it should be, we

shall not only be thinking of time—dwelling upon our present needs—we shall look to the great eternal Supper of which I have spoken—the Supper at which, when our Lord by His Spirit has done His final work of love upon us, has "washed our feet" from every spot and stain of the world and its ways, we shall sit down with Him as His brethren and drink the new wine in the kingdom of His Father and our Father. Our faith will realise that also.

Dear brethren, we are the spiritual Israel, we are Christ's chosen ones. Those apostles in the upper room, what was their work? To go out baptized, consecrated, to be the Lord's witnesses, and to fill the world with His saving truth. So we are to be Christ's witnesses. We are the host of God's elect. Let us renew our vows and consecrate ourselves afresh to God's service. Ought not this to be a deep and memorable solemnity—one never to be forgotten? Ought we not all—especially those who are ministers—to look for such a baptism of power as we have never had before? We are on our way to the land of promise; Egypt is behind us; we have left its darkness. The world is outside—the world that crucifies the Lord. In the streets of Jerusalem there are the Pharisees and Sadducees, men who scorn and rage against the Saviour. *Within* let there be consecration—peace, devotion. Let the Lord Jesus and ourselves be united in a covenant sealed and blest as never a covenant between Him and us was sealed and blest before. May God give us His blessing, for Christ's sake!

A Review of Methodist Work.

——o——

WE deal this evening with special topics, and these topics
are those to which John Wesley attributed the very utmost
importance. Last evening we represented John Wesley's
succession ; to-night we represent his own work. You
know how he loved the villages. The connection of Mr.
Wesley with education, also, is quite familiar to us, and
the gentleman who will speak to us this evening on
education has been most closely connected for a number
of years with a school which bears the name of that which
Mr. Wesley founded. It is not necessary for me to say
to any Methodist anything about Kingswood. As to
Methodism and literature, you know that Mr. Wesley was
reading all his life. In all the intervals he could snatch
from preaching and evangelistic work, he read, but not for
himself, for he was continually bent on finding out what
he could abridge or extract for the benefit of the people.
He provided a wonderful literature, at a wonderfully cheap
price, for the use of the Methodists. As to foreign missions,
there was no great and organised society during the greater
part of Mr. Wesley's life, at any rate. You know that the
very first event in Mr. Wesley's public life was his going
to Georgia to preach to the Indians. He did not go to

preach to the colonists; he was much surprised when he arrived there to find that he could not go to the Indians. Hence the close connection between all the subjects of this meeting and our great Founder is most evident.

You will, I know, wish an expression of your warm-hearted, prayerful Christian sympathy to be conveyed to Mr. Champness and Dr. Jenkins. From Dr. Jenkins I had a letter last night, in which he expressed his great regret at not being here. The name of one of the speakers suggests the name of Dr. Osborn. We have his nephew here, but Dr. Osborn is one of those who would have most heartily rejoiced in this celebration. I should like very much to be authorised by you to send a special message to Dr. Osborn. His wonderful labours in the hymnology on which we have been speaking, his intense interest in all that interests us, must call for this. With his name I should like to mention those of the only other ex-Presidents who have not been able to be with us—the names of Mr. Arthur and Dr. James.

Methodism and the Masses.

By the Rev. PETER THOMPSON.

I PERSONALLY regret that I have to be here to-night instead of to-morrow night, in consequence of Mr. Clapham's absence. There is not any special phase of the subject which comes before us during such a week as this, with which I myself have greater sympathy, or in which I have more definite personal, practical interest. I rejoice in the creation and history of Methodism, and in our present position and purposes and hopes with reference to the vast multitudes of the people of this country. I have felt again and again during the past few hours, how completely John Wesley was the apostle of the masses, how utterly God fitted him and furnished him and sustained him in that marvellous ministry for the vast crowds of people that heard his voice, that felt his powers, and that were blessed through his preaching and work.

I have realised what you, Mr. President, have referred to, how wonderfully the hymns with which they were then familiar, and with which, thank God, we are now familiar, put in the very clearest way those experiences which were the very foundation of all Mr. Wesley's strong efforts throughout this country. A phrase came to my mind this afternoon connected with him, about that inner working of God within him, not far from here, when he felt his heart "strangely warmed," and when he realised for himself the full blessing of personal salvation :

> " Salvation in His Name there is,
>   Salvation from sin, death, and hell,
> Salvation into glorious bliss,
>   How great salvation, who can tell ?
> But all He hath for mine I claim,
> I dare believe in Jesus' name."

And then I thought of another, as I realised him going forth, possessed of that rich gift—that great salvation from God :

> " Sent by my Lord, on you I call,
>   The invitation is to all."

I understood, as I thought of these words, which have become so familiar, how deeply he realised that he was sent of God, accredited by his Lord, with a message for the multitudes of the people. The gospel which he preached was a message for the poor, and for the crowds that gathered around him. He preached Christ.

> " His only righteousness I show,
>   His saving truth proclaim :
> 'Tis all my business here below
>   To cry, ' Behold the Lamb ! ' "

Realising all this blessedly in his own heart, and thereby strong and fearless and full of courage, he went among the people, and faced all that was involved in the hostility as well as the approval of the multitudes around. Crowds thronged to hear him, and as they heard they received from his message that which he had gained, and became converted and holy in life unto God. The masses of the people in the days of John Wesley needed the gospel, and needed the ministry of love, and righteousness, and mercy. The records that tell of the condition of life in those days are startling. Most of you, no doubt, are perfectly familiar with the details of the description that represents the irreligion and the viciousness and the criminality of the people of that time; and how there was terrible severity, and even cruelty, in the administration of the law. And yet it was utterly powerless to bring terror to the hearts of evil-doers. Often those who represented the Church— the clergy, and those who were regarded as the teachers of religion and the representatives of the New Testament— were unfamiliar with the Word of God. Those who had read some books seemed to neglect the Scriptures; and right throughout the multitudes of the people there was found ignorance and separation from the love of God, that involved infidelity, viciousness, and vile living. And so, as Mr. Wesley and those who were his fellow-labourers went in and out among the people, and got to know their histories, their past experience in the workings of evil, and discovered the causes which were at work, bringing such wrongs into their lives, they were found strong and full of earnest purpose in waging war with the causes of iniquity and ruin that then obtained. And one of the impressions that we get, as we try to take in a full view of the position, is this, that side by side with all this man did in exhorting sinners to turn from their sins to God, he recognised his responsibility as a minister of Christ to rebuke those who had authority and responsibility, in those arrangements in social life which worked destruction to the masses of the people.

His marvellous utterances against slavery stand out pre-eminently strong, and he could not recognise the actual life of the slaves, without speaking out in un-

measured terms against that iniquitous system. And the
definite action he took with reference to our own Church
in the West Indies, in requiring the members to separate
from any part whatever with slavery, is a most striking
fact. Even beyond his words against slavery were his
strong words against the liquor-makers and the liquor-
sellers. As he knew the actual lot of the people involved
with the drink, and all the workings of the public-houses,
he believed and spoke in the name of God, that these were
destroying His Majesty's subjects wholesale. His sermon
on the "Use of Money" contains probably the strongest
condemnation of the liquor traffic that has ever been
spoken or written. And in his letter to the Right Hon.
William Pitt, as well as in his "Thoughts on the Scarcity
of Provisions," he asserts and maintains the most powerful
Christian appeal that could be made to any responsible
Government against deriving revenue from that which
brought only ruin to the people. The interests of men,
as men, had taken hold of him. He felt the preciousness
of those redeemed by Christ, and whatever injured men
and women he was prepared to denounce with fierceness
and fearlessness. And while he was thus speaking out,
with utmost clearness, against all these workings of sin,
he was claiming for the people all the rights and all the
privileges that God has ordained for our humanity. He
claimed for them immediate personal access to God, immediate personal knowledge of God, conscious enjoyment
of salvation, deliverance from the guilt of sin, and the
possession of the might of holiness. He announced these
as the opportunity and privilege of every man, wherever
he found him. He had a gospel for the people that
secured their emancipation from the thraldom of sin, their
introduction into the family of God, and their possession
of eternal life. Hence it is said that wherever the
Methodist preachers went, they carried with them the
message of hopefulness, and encouragement, and blessing.
Wherever they fulfilled their ministry, good of every kind
followed them in their course.

Another aspect of our Founder's relation to the masses of the people has impressed me in this way. He looked out upon the people. He got to know, from actual contact with them, all their ignorance and sin, and the vast extent of the work that needed to be done ; and while it was possible for him to include such an enormous amount of ministry as he put into his life, he felt that it was not at all adequate for reaping the plenteous harvest that he now looked upon. Unknown to him, and without his special effort to call it forth,—even against his prejudices,—there were being thrust out, to be co-labourers, the local preachers and the class-leaders ; those who would be able to supply his lack of service, and to supplement his abundant labours. They received the same love, the same conscious power, the same joyful assurance, and they went and told their fellow-men of the saving power of the gospel. As God was with him, so He was with them ; and there grew out of the recognition and use of these helpers a network of agency covering the whole land, that the people might be reached. The masses were rightful claimants of the gospel, and of all that grows out of the experience of godliness. The fruits of this organised work were seen on all hands, and have been recognised by all those who have carefully referred to the actual life that resulted from the enterprise, or rather, that work of God.

Side by side with this new organisation, there was the quickening of the thought and interest of all the Churches in the condition of the people. I am sure all of us rejoice to-day, in looking back upon the later period of this last century, to note the marvellous way in which the great bulk of the Christian Churches have become Methodist. I challenge any one to find me a Church that is not now looking at the masses ; that is not now considering the people ; and that is not now arranging its energies, and making its plans to get at the people. I wish we could say that, while the streams of blessing have been multiplied, they had all continued to flow strongly and deeply. Alas for some of us, we have not kept on steam ! With some of us there has not been a surrender of all plans and methods and means of working to the one paramount necessity of getting the people saved. I rejoice to believe that better days are upon us. I hope this week will quicken the fervour and strengthen the purpose of all of us, so that, however multiplied may be our agencies, there may be put into every one of them the same passion of love, the same practical ministry, that characterised the work of our fathers. I feel to-day that the people are calling aloud to us, that the masses of the people are presenting their claim, and we shall have to be very hard-hearted if they do not compel us to regard their plea, and to answer their call. They are crying out for Methodism. They are stretching out their hands for Christ.

I rejoice greatly, especially with reference to London, that we have had "the bitter cry of the outcast," so effectively uttered by Mr. Mearns' pamphlet. I am thankful for the marvellous labours of Mr. Charles Booth. His book, *Life and Labour in London*, with its cold, hard, stern statements of fact, ought to stir the very depth of every Christian soul. It reveals the poverty, the oppression, the drunkenness which exist among the vast populations of the East-end. In proportion, similar conditions of life obtain throughout the country. Then, again, I am thankful for the religious statistics which have been got together by Mr. Mearns, showing the provision made for public worship in proportion to the population. I am sure all of us ought to become very earnest supporters of every Chapel Building Committee. The *British Weekly* has added to our indebtedness by the publication of the Religious Census recently taken. We find that, although the actual provision is utterly inadequate to the population, the provision is double what is actually necessary for those who are so far in sympathy with religion as to attend a place of worship. My dear friends, it is a lamentable fact that on a Sunday night there are only a quarter of the people worshipping God, who, on any reasonable expectation, ought to attend. Surely there is work to be done. The liquor traffic still walks impertinently before us; the makers and consumers of drink unblushingly take their place with us in our civil and commercial and religious life. We must be as faithful as our Founder. He knew that the liquor traffic was a curse: we know it so tenfold now. He denounced slavery. I know of a slavery—I have seen it!—as cruel, as ill in its manifold results as any slavery recorded in history. One of my own members was making garments for 2½d. a dozen, because she could not see her children perish. Another poor woman, whose babies were crying round her for food, met her employer, and offered to do them for 2¼d., if he would let her have them, and so the 2½d. work was taken from my member, and given to the poor woman who would do them for 2¼d. to keep her children from starvation. I had as soon work in the presence of the lash as work in the presence of such cruelty as that. The cry of the oppressed is filling the air. The cry of the enslaved and crushed is going up unto the ear of God, and if His servants will not hear, shall He not visit for these things? Methodism must do for the masses what our Founder did. We shall have to denounce the competition which means a curse, to denounce the sweating which means the degradation of the poor. How terribly we are getting involved in Sunday labour! Visit our docks at home. Nay, alas! visit them in Scotland, the land of the Sabbath, and you will find there the steamers leaving the docks, entering the docks, and the men commanded to work. Why? Because the vessels are so valuable, they cannot afford to allow them to lie fallow for twenty-four hours. The blood of men and women is worth more than the biggest steamship ever built. Our tramcars, our 'buses, our railways go at full speed, that men of leisure may be gratified, that men and women who have time and money may take their pleasure at the expense of the workmen's Sunday. Methodism, in lineal succession and spiritual succession, must speak out everywhere against these things. Marvellous changes have come during the past century. Some of those changes have been fraught with very great peril to the entire community—the aggregation of people in our large towns, the severance of a great number of the people from the soil, the unhappy separation between rich and poor. No longer can it be said that the rich and the poor live together. The poor are herded together, the rich have left us for fairer climes. Both suffer from the separation. The rich grow selfish and narrow in sympathy, the poor grow reckless and bitter. I know not how these things are to be dealt with, but I felt I could not be silent about them. We shall have to go where Mr. Wesley went, and get our hearts "strangely warmed,"—to go to the old Book, and learn what the Master says, and what the Master's mission is. We shall have to abolish the old labels, "the masses," the "working classes," and the old terms with which we may be familiar. I want Methodism to write over the forehead of every harlot, across the face of every poor docker, right in the front of every man and woman of any class and every class—"My brother," "My sister." Then the liquor traffic will end. Then the slavery of sweating and greed and competition will be annihilated; then the Sabbath, which was made for man, shall be guarded for man; and then the right of improvement, of music, of literature, of all the arts, shall be enjoyed by all, and be laid at the feet of the Master. Then shall home-life become elevated, pure and sweet; church-life universal, sacred, and spiritual; and the brotherhood of man and the Fatherhood of God shall be real, because all have become "sons of God," who "worship the Father."

Methodism and Education.

By Mr. T. G. OSBORN, M.A.

WE read in the columns of the leading journal to-day that the Methodists have not hitherto been remarkable for the breadth of their intellectual culture, and in this respect furnish a curious contrast to the Founder of their communion. John Wesley enjoyed the privilege of public school education. He had the learning and resources of a great university at his command. His successors for many years found the universities shut against them ; and what wonder, sir, that they had to begin at the beginning. I admit that some of the greatest men that have belonged to our Church did not do all they might have done for lack of that culture, but the blame rests elsewhere.

In dealing to-day with the question of Methodism and Education, we must not forget the different circumstances in which both were found in England a hundred years ago. Methodism, it is true, was born and cradled in a university, but she soon left her native place, and it took a verylong time to get her back again. Education was then a luxury for the rich, secured, even if somewhat extended, by a monopoly of the clergy. All the grammar and public schools were in their hands, and all the avenues to our great seats of learning were closed to Nonconformists, and, after a little while, to Methodists, while the days of popular education were yet far away. Thus to our fathers there were presented the proverbial three courses : they might let their children grow up in ignorance—they might surrender them to the enemy—or they might found and maintain their own schools. The last course was difficult for a poor people, the second was awfully dangerous, but the first was impossible. So education and Methodism were closely connected from the very first. Indeed, before the actual genesis of Methodism, Wesley had recognised education as part of his great mission work, and it was much the best part, too, of his work at Savannah. But after his conversion education, as well as evangelisation, was placed at the very root and basis of his great work.

Just take a date or two in confirmation of this. On April 2, 1739, Mr. Wesley preached for the first time in England in the open air. On May 12, in the same year, the foundation-stone of his first preaching-house was laid ;

and in June 1739 the foundation - stone of Kingswood School was laid. In these successive months you have the outdoor evangelism, the chapel, and the school. And so it was throughout Mr. Wesley's lifetime—he never faltered in his efforts to work these three great instruments together. And I think I might make bold to say that education, even higher education, was part of the primitive—the earliest tradition of Methodism. At any rate, I find this remarkable statement published, with high Methodist authority, about thirty years or more after Mr. Wesley's death:—"It has always been understood that good schools for the literary, scientific, and religious instruction of the youth of the Societies, was a part of the original plans of Methodism,—a part which has been unavoidably postponed by the necessity of circumstances, but never finally given up."

The germs of every one of those departments of education are to be found in the work of John Wesley himself. In Kingswood School, for instance, we have Wesley's first attempt at primary, and afterwards at higher education ; while we see from the life of Adam Clarke, as well as from the early "Minutes," that this was also at first regarded as a seminary, a theological college, for the preachers. In the Foundery School in London, and the Orphan House in Newcastle, as well as in Miss Bosanquet's (Mrs. Fletcher's) Orphanage at Leytonstone, we have the seed sown which was to remain out of sight buried for long years, but eventually to reappear in the Children's Home and Orphanage which we all rejoice in to-day. The Sunday School started by Hannah Ball, a Methodist, at Wycombe in 1769, and by Robert Raikes and Miss Cook at Gloucester in 1781, was warmly welcomed, and adopted by Wesley in 1784 and 1785 ; and thus we have not an educational institution among us to-day which we cannot more or less distinctly trace back to its germ and origin (though in some cases only very embryonic) in Wesley's own day.

But to look back more definitely to the state of Methodist education one hundred years ago. In 1791 there were existing a considerable number of good Methodist private schools, but beside Kingswood, which was still open to all Methodists (being restricted to ministers' sons in 1794), there was no Connexional institution, and only a few elementary charitable schools at Bristol, Newcastle, London, and perhaps some other places. Sunday schools had spread fast. So far as we can gather, there were throughout England, in connection with all the Churches, about 200,000 children, and perhaps about one-eighth of these were in Methodist schools. There was no theological institution, no training college. To-day there cannot be less than five millions in Methodist Sunday schools throughout the world. In England we have not merely a large number of primary day schools, but we have already founded, somewhat at haphazard, a number of graded boarding schools for higher education, which only need to be grouped and linked together to make a great and powerful system ; and we have four theological colleges for the special training of ministers, and two training colleges for teachers, while the number of Methodist students and graduates now at Oxford and Cambridge and other national universities is by no means insignificant.

If we include in our view America and Australia, the result is much more striking. In 1881, and I have not been able to get later details for all the Churches, there were about 300 colleges and seminaries reported in the two great sections of American Methodism, and 30 colleges in Australia and New Zealand ; and to these should be added the high schools and colleges in our own mission work and those of the American Mission, and all the colleges and universities of Canadian Methodism. All this has grown from this little seed a hundred years ago, and it surely argues real life in the seed, and careful culture since the sowing.

It would be (to me at least) most interesting to trace the development of our different branches of education from the germ till now, did time permit, but it would be

far too long a task. Set apart in 1794 for ministers'
children only, and supplemented in 1812 by Woodhouse
Grove, Kingswood has not merely been a school in the
forefront of educational institutions, and abreast of its
rivals of other names and other aims, but it has been a
seed-plot, a nursery for schoolmasters and ministers. No
money, I believe, has ever been better laid out for Connexional purposes than the old familiar Kingswood and
Woodhouse Grove School collection, or has brought in a
better return. The men who have devised and guided our
Methodist education schemes of improvement and advance
have, in a very large proportion, been drawn from our oldest
Methodist high schools. That means that what advance
there has been is due to an impulse from within rather
than from without ; it is natural growth, and not ex-
traneous addition, that has made our educational system
what it is. This, I think, is one of the most striking and
most hopeful features in the whole case.

As we watch the development of the different branches
of this work, we find, I say, the initiative from men who
were at Kingswood and Woodhouse Grove. Without any
endowment but the generous interest of the Methodist
people, this school has carried on the best traditions of
Wesleyan scholarship ; it has given at least eight Presidents of the Conference to the Connexion, among whom
we count our Chairman of to-day; it has supplied our
theological institutions with some of their ablest teachers
from the very first, and there is not one of these institutions to-day that has not high on its staff at least one from
the same source. The principals of both our training
colleges, like the head-masters of our large schools—the
Leys and Wesley College—at least half the masters of
our other quasi-Connexional schools—Truro, Trowbridge,
Canterbury, Congleton, and the like—came from the same
source.

And if we look abroad, we can trace the same influence
—from Colombo and the Mysore, to Wuchang, or to
Melbourne, the educational work is under similar guid-

ance. The value of this school to us as a Connexion, especially in former days, was perhaps more clearly seen by our enemies than by our friends. I believe it is true, at any rate it is stated in Methodist lore, that the two Universities of Oxford and Cambridge both passed resolutions to the effect that no one educated at Kingswood School should be admitted to either university, and that resolution has never been rescinded to this day. In the face of a fact like that, it is interesting to know how strong a foothold Kingswood has in both universities to-day. In the last comparatively few years, not less than sixty Scholarships and ten or twelve Fellowships have been taken by Kingswood boys at these same universities ; and, now that our head-master at Kingswood is a distinguished alumnus of both Kingswood and Cambridge, I think we may conclude that this resolution has surely been forgotten. I rejoice to see in the last University Lists that the old school shows no sign of feebleness or decay.

I wish emphatically and gratefully to express my own conviction that John Wesley was divinely guided when he put the school as well as the chapel at the foundation of his great enterprise. Take away Mr. Wesley's school and its influence from the Methodist history of the past century, and there would be an immense blank.

The next step that was taken to advance higher education on Methodist lines after this was, so far as I know, taken in the year 1831–1836. This led to the establishment of Wesley College, Sheffield, the first Methodist High School of the new foundation, and was due to the sagacity and foresight and earnestness of one of the grandest Methodist preachers of the last generation. I shall be forgiven by you, Mr. President, I know, as an old Sheffield boy yourself, and surely by any Methodist audience in City Road, if I stay one moment, though unworthiest of his old pupils to do so, just to pay a brief tribute to Dr. Waddy. He was a man before his time in this great question of higher education in our Connexion.

He was before his age, as Mr. Wesley was, on this subject. He maintained the true tradition in times when there were few to support or to sympathise with him, and his earnest efforts are still bearing fruit in the wider and truer success to-day of the great cause he tried so hard to serve. His name is inseparably linked with the school of which he was the real founder—it has done great things for Methodism. Not to mention some that bear *his* name so worthily to-day, let me recall from the memories of one brief school generation the names of the founder of the Children's Home, the Richmond Commentator on St. Paul's Epistles, and the author of *Daniel Quorm*.

Wesley College, Sheffield, was soon followed by the College at Taunton, and, despite all changes and adaptations to the new times, they are both doing good service to-day in the same great cause.

It would ill-become me, Mr. President, to say much in your presence about the last great movement in Methodism for the highest education. I believe it was in 1874 that as a Connexion we faced the question of a Methodist Public School, and by the energy and liberality of a few the Leys School was established. Of course it is but an infant among the great old schools of the country, but it is an infant that has won an honourable recognition among them, and even distinction. It is through the Leys School that we have as Methodists found our way into the last of those charmed circles from which we were so long shut out. There are, I know, statistics of its success that I could quote, but statistics can never be fair to a new school. The main fact is that the Leys has solved a great problem for us—the question as to the possibility of reconciling Methodist training with the breadth and freedom of English public school life ; and I have no doubt that, in the review of the next century of Methodism education, one great feature will be the story of the Leys School and the name of its first head-master. But about the same time attention was drawn to the needs of a particular class of our own people. It became clear that in self-defence we must retain the children of Methodists who were unable to pay the high fees.

In hastily reviewing the history of education among us, I can hardly touch for a moment on our endeavour to fulfil our Founder's own promise of colleges to insure us an educated ministry. We cannot forget that our fathers had to work out this question amidst difficulty and opposition, but their work has abundantly justified them, and to-day we are all of one mind as to our theological colleges, and their importance and value to us as a Church. Their educational influence has reached far beyond the ranks of the ministry. To mention but one of the indirect ways in which these institutions have been influential throughout the whole range of Methodism, let me name the writings of Mr. Beet and Dr. Pope.

As we review Methodist educational history during the past century, it is impossible to omit all reference to our efforts to secure and advance primary schools. The Churches were naturally alive to this duty before the rest of the nation. Our fathers did right nobly when there was no aroused national conscience to support them, and they established schools in different parts of the country that, besides being bulwarks against all sorts of intolerance, will bear comparison as purely educational agencies with any others. I think I am right in saying that, whatever may be our views of future policy, we are all agreed that these 839 schools, with their nearly 200,000 scholars, are a heritage of noble work, especially when we consider with them the 800 day schools, with well-nigh 50,000 scholars, in our missions abroad. But we have also undertaken the not less important work of training teachers for our own schools in our own way; and our two training colleges to-day, Westminster and Southlands, will bear comparison with any. No thoughtful man among us can doubt for a moment that by this work we are most effectively bringing religion to bear on educational work. And while it is impossible to name many of those who have done such good work, it would be wrong not to notice the sagacity and devotion of Mr. Scott, so long a Methodist pioneer in this direction, and the public work and public writings of his extremely able successor, Dr. Rigg, which have yet to be fully understood and appreciated as they should be, and as they will be some day.

To review our Sunday school work in this last century would be long and difficult. For the most part it would be an uneventful story of continuous progress and improvement in methods and arrangement, as well as aims and their accomplishment. The Connexional recognition and direction has been constant throughout the whole period, although it is only in comparatively recent years that a minister has been appointed to supervise the Sunday schools. Our own Sunday School Union has been a great success, and it may safely be said that never at any previous period were our Sunday schools so well equipped and effectively worked.

One other great department of our educational work— one of the youngest—claims more time than we can give to it to-night. There has been no more rapid and hopeful growth in Methodism of late years than the Children's Home and Orphanage. Though not overlooked by Wesley and his contemporaries, the very tradition of this work seemed to be lost among us until it was revived by a young minister rather more than twenty years ago. The wonderful success that has attended Dr. Stephenson's efforts — the many different branches that are now in active operation, and the far-reaching, almost world-wide influence of this work as a whole—show clearly enough that the scheme filled up a vacant place in our Methodist economy, and I think I may reverently say that it shows also that the Divine blessing has rested upon it.

I have thus, sir, very briefly, and I am conscious very imperfectly too, touched on all the various branches of our Methodist education. If I have said anything that has seemed to be boastful, and inconsistent with the tone of humility and modesty which you yourself have marked out as most suitable for this occasion, I should deeply regret and retract it at once.

But as we look at the state of things a century ago, and the history of advance through the subsequent years, it would be wrong not to rejoice gratefully in the past, and look forward trustfully to the future. We are bound to praise Him who has done great things for us, and as a Church it is surely not unbecoming on an occasion like this to recognise the work of those who have gone before us. One soweth and another reapeth. Other men laboured, and we have entered into their labours ; but surely we may, for just one brief moment at least, joyfully anticipate the time when he that soweth and he that reapeth shall rejoice together.

If the time allowed, I should be glad to say a few words as to the future of our work. I believe, for instance, that our Children's Home and Orphanage work must be greatly increased if we are to do our duty as a Church. Noble as that institution is, it is insufficient. Those of us who believe that the solution of the great pressing social questions of the day lies with those who have and train the children, must recognise the imperative need of making more earnest efforts in this direction. Forty or fifty " Children's Homes " might save the great cities of the next two or three generations. Will any man tell me anything else that will, humanly speaking? Then, as to our Sunday schools—I think we must recognise that as they are likely to be more and more the only place for direct religious teaching and influence for multitudes of children, the teaching must be better and more practical, and the influence more spiritual. I do not think we realise how much we owe in this matter to outward circumstances, which have now for a century given to the Churches wonderful opportunities of reaching the children of indifferent or godless parents. It is a serious consideration, that a comparatively slight change in the habits of life among the working classes might change all this. I sometimes think I see signs of such change, and wonder if the Sunday school system, as known among us to-day, has begun to alter, if not decay, at the very height of its great success. Change I do not fear, but I do fear decay. If we can maintain the life, the living organism will soon adapt itself to changed conditions, but systems die.

> " They have their day, and cease to be."

We must be on our guard. With respect to the education of our ministers, our course in the past is justified not merely by its results, but by the imitation of our friends. The great religious body that had for so many years the monopoly of the universities and all their learning, as well as their revenues, has found that general education is insufficient, and the tendency among them is more and more toward theological colleges. Still, we might learn a lesson from them in return, and if we were so to avail ourselves of modern improvements as to secure our ministry having their general studies with our young laity, and only their theological work under separate training, I believe they would gain in breadth and sympathy.

This topic, of course, touches on our future relations to the universities. There was a time when the nationalisation of Oxford and Cambridge was thought to have met the needs of all the Churches. Has this proved to be so? The immediate result has been the multiplication of denominational colleges in a way altogether unprecedented. Hertford, Keble, Ridley, Selwyn, Mansfield, all these point to a very different conclusion. Are we not to have our Wesley or Moulton College? But I believe this is debateable ground.

There is, beyond dispute, one great gap in our educational system that I trust to see filled up before long. The last five-and-twenty years have seen more advance in the higher education of girls than in any other department. We have not as a Connexion held aloof from this movement : our preachers' daughters have noble schools, and there are flourishing middle-class schools for girls at Jersey and Folkestone, and Penzance and Penrhôs, and elsewhere.

Moreover, Methodism is rich in private schools for girls, inferior to none, giving just the special training of a cultured home that we most covet for our daughters. But for those who pass on to higher educational work we have no place. There is no college as distinguished from high school. We cannot afford to lose our most cultured women ; they have been the life and strength of Methodism. No other Church has recognised them so fully, and been so much indebted to them, as the Methodist Churches, and we have greater work yet for them to do. And yet at present we are losing them in numbers, by obliging them, just when most impressionable, to live and work under hardly neutral, probably antagonistic, influences. Our brethren in America do not do that ; even the young Churches in Australia are wiser than that. And I trust the time shall soon come when we shall have a Ladies' College for Methodists.

I wish that something could be done among us to link our Methodist schools closer together, and to make a plain and easy path for a poor child of ability from the bottom to the very top of our system. By this I mean a Methodist path. There are such paths that are non-Methodist and anti-Methodist; and our own able and ambitious children have been left to the temptations of endowments, which are so used as to be practically—I had almost said prizes for apostasy—at any rate, rewards for desertion. I leave particulars. But if we are to do our part in the next century in the great work of education, we must have a clearer vision and a nobler ideal towards which to work. We must aim more especially at the cultivation to the highest degree of *all* the faculties of *all* our children. Usefulness rather than money-making must be our aim. In education, as in all else, our Lord's rule is supreme : " Seek ye first the kingdom of God and His righteousness, and all these things shall be added unto you."

I have little doubt that there is a grand future for Methodism, as well as for education. I believe the next century will be one of great progress in knowledge ; there will be keener research and nobler triumphs. But knowledge puffeth up; it is by itself proud, and selfish, and hard. Intellectual education by itself only means more polished pride and more refined selfishness. We must have more than this, or it is worse than nothing. I covet earnestly for our loved Methodism, if indeed she be "Christianity in earnest," that best gift of teaching men that there is no inconsistency between the highest intellectual and the highest spiritual culture, but that these two agree in one. It is our earliest Methodist tradition, that evangelistic fervour, intense religious feeling, the loftiest spiritual experience, the most thorough fidelity to God's Word, the fullest sympathy with the needs and the difficulties of the poor and the ignorant, *can* be united with intellectual breadth, with fearless love of truth, and with a noble enthusiasm for learning. This is the tradition that we have received from our fathers, and this we would hand on to our sons. And then I believe that Methodism and education, like one of those great twin orbs that the telescope has revealed to us in the realms above, revolving round one common centre, each supplying light and stability to the other, will shine forth through the ages to come, giving light and blessing to men and glory to God.

The PRESIDENT said : Perhaps I may add one word to Mr. Osborn's most useful and powerful speech, to illustrate the change that has come over England in a comparatively short time. I believe I am right in saying that when Mr. Osborn himself was at the University of Cambridge, he was the only Methodist there. I have known in recent years sometimes as many as fifty there. When I was a boy, a very weakly, sickly boy, my father made inquiries to see whether I could go to the Grammar School in the large town in which we lived. He found that the prejudice against the son of a Nonconformist minister was so great that he had to give up the thought. For myself, of course, I am most thankful, as I was sent to Woodhouse Grove, where I obtained health and everything else.

Methodism and Literature.

By the Rev. W. L. WATKINSON.

MR. THOMPSON challenged any one in this company to contradict him ; he is just the man to do it. We shall all be sorry for the man who contradicts him. But it would not do for me to challenge any man in this congregation.

I must cast myself on your indulgence, if, not to waste a moment, I excuse myself for once from the liberalities of rhetoric, and speak to you under the guidance of rather extensive notes ; and, as my subject touches literature, it may perhaps not be altogether inappropriate that we honour letters in this shape. And you have this confidence in listening to me with these notes—there is an end to them.

The modern Greeks have a legend, that, as the soul resides in the human body, so every building is inhabited by a spirit, and the character of this spirit for good or evil is determined by the character of those whose shadow fell on the foundation-stone of the building. Naturally, any institution is largely influenced by the temper of its founder, and this is manifestly true of Methodism in many particulars. The special genius of Wesley persists in the Methodism of to-day, and displays itself in every direction. This is true in regard to the question of literature. Wesley was an intelligent man, a scholar, a passionate lover of literature, a man of light as well as of leading,—things that do not always go together ;—and this bias he gave to the Church which by the grace of God he was permitted to establish. If Whitefield had formed a Church, he at least would scarcely have given to it so marked a literary and educational character as did John Wesley. The Church founded by the Countess of Huntingdon has certainly not been wanting in culture, but, I conclude, it owed little in that particular to Whitefield. But Wesley, calling himself a man of one Book, was in fact a man of very many books. His literary character was always revealing itself, and his literary activity was simply marvellous. During his long life he never ceased producing books, and publishing books,—theological, historical, classical, poetical, philosophical, and medicinal. Many of these were written by Wesley himself, many of them were revised and condensed by him, and many of them were issued by him at cheap prices for the sake of the public. For John Wesley knew the value of the working man before the working man had a vote.

When Wesley left the Moravians in Fetter Lane, and went to the Foundery, he went to the right place. He had a great deal of that kind of work to do; and whilst with all his might he smote the anvil, and occasionally smoothed with the hammer, his books were thrown off like sparks to illumine the thick darkness of the age. Wesley's preachers in this matter caught his spirit and followed his lead.

We may at once acknowledge that Methodism is not a literary Church in any such eminent sense as is the National Church. It has produced little of that massive literature which is the glory of the Establishment. And this can be counted no disgrace to Methodism. Methodism provides no lettered ease. It exacts from all its ministers so much immediate active service, that they have little opportunity to become influential scholars, profound theologians, literary artists. When we remember that ours is a working Church, absorbing all our time and energy in immediate claims of duty, the wonder is rather that we have accomplished so much in the direction of literature, and not so little. Our ethical writers remind us that there sometimes occurs in life a conflict of duties ; and many a Methodist preacher has found himself in this dilemma between literary aspirations and pastoral duty, and it is greatly to their credit that many of them have put aside their intellectual speculations for the sake of homely, simple service among the people. And if it is satisfactory to know why many books have not been written, it is also pathetic to think at what immense self-denial much of our literature has been produced.

But whatever may have been the literary limitations of Methodism, it has produced some noble writers, and made the intellectual world its debtor. Commentators like Adam Clarke and Joseph Benson, theologians like magnificent Richard Watson and Richard Treffry, controversialists like Thomas Powell,—these, and many others, are recognised as princes in the intellectual realm.

And these masters have worthy successors to-day. It has been well said, "That will be a degenerate age when we must go to the cemetery to find our greatest men." All our greatest men are not there. Modern Methodism has no reason to be ashamed of commentators like Agar Beet; of popular writers like Mark Guy Pearse; of noble legalists and statesmen like Dr. Rigg; of theologians like Dr. Pope; of Dr. Gregory, at once poet, theologian, and philosopher; of eloquent logicians like William Arthur.

And there is another name that it would misbecome me to praise, and that it would be equally unpardonable in me to ignore. A man who has the rare privilege of translating the Scripture, has indeed singular honour and felicity; he becomes henceforth in a sense identified with the immortal literature he translates, and stands, like John's angel, in the sun. If John Wesley could revisit us, nothing, I believe, would give him greater pleasure than the fact that modern Methodism had been honoured in the person of one of her most gifted sons to take a place on the Board of Translators, which has given to the whole English-speaking world the Revised Version of the Holy Scriptures.

These writers and many lesser lights—for God made the stars also—brighten the firmament of Methodism, and give light unto the world. The man who affirms that Methodism has cared little for the intellectual life of the people, that it is altogether Philistine, proves that he is a Philistine. Its literary work has aimed high, and it has been steadily and ardently pursued through all the century since Wesley fell asleep. And this is not only true of the Mother Church of our common Methodism. The Primitive Methodist Church, the New Connexion, the Bible Christians, the Methodist Free Church, have each been true to the genius of Wesley, and carried out his aim with splendid, unflagging energy.

The literature of Methodism is the literature of a working Church, and as such it bears certain characteristics which we may note. Many of our publications have been of an experimental character. Wesley was a great student of psychology, and he loves to give accounts of the conversions and experiences of people of all types and conditions. Many a page of the Journal, on which the reader would wish to have recorded some of the stirring incidents of Wesley's life and generation, is occupied with the detailed experience of some child, some poor woman, some converted collier or convict. The *Magazine* followed in the same direction. The late Mr. Percival Bunting very graphically designated the *Magazine* "The Westminster Abbey of Methodism." And Methodism has been exceedingly rich and abundant in biography. In the work issued by Dr. Osborn some twenty years ago, it is shown that out of the 2554 works issued by Methodist preachers from the beginning, 320 (or about an eighth of the whole) were biographical. And Methodism has made no mistake in thus giving large recognition to Christian experience. We all know the story of the origin of the miners' safety-lamp. George Stephenson and Sir Humphry Davy were contemporaries, and both were engaged in designing a lamp which might be used safely in mines infested with fire-damp. Stephenson was engine-wright at a Newcastle colliery, a man with the least technical scientific knowledge; but, with a practical head and a daily experience of mines, he felt his way empirically to a triumphant result: without any knowledge of chemistry, he invented an effective lamp. Sir Humphry Davy was a brilliant scientist, he understood the nature of the various gases, and by a series of learned experiments he perfected at length a lamp of great merit. In fact, the lamp of the rough engine-wright and the brilliant scientist were substantially identical. The two discoverers had followed different lines—the one theoretical, the other practical;—but the one being a logical reasoner, and the other being a close observer, they arrived at a similar result, and their invention is not displaced to this day. Religion may be demonstrated from two sides — reason and experience, logic and life ;—and hence we have apologetical literature and biographical literature, but surely the latter is not inferior to the former in power and conclusiveness. The thousands of honest men and women who have had experience of the things of God, who have tested the truth of Christ in all life's chequered scenes,—these are witnesses for the defence of the faith certainly not inferior to Pearson, Butler, or Hooker. Here Methodist literature has rendered great service to the Church of Christ,—it has been a witnessing Church in a very eminent degree, telling out what it has felt and seen of the grace of God.

The literature of Methodism has also been to a large extent of a practical character. It has been in a very slight degree metaphysical, or speculative, or imaginative, except occasionally, perhaps, in some of its theology; and being always in such close touch with the life of the people and the facts of evangelisation, it has been saved from many errors and heresies. Dr. Lardner, a theorist, wrote an able and conclusive book, to prove the impossibility of a steamship crossing the Atlantic, and the first steamer that crossed from Liverpool to New York carried that book with it, and everybody except scientists believed that Dr. Lardner was refuted. Life, experience, fact, spoilt many a fine theory ; and the fact that Methodism has been a working Church, has given its literature far more practical worth than speculative interest.

Much of our literature has been devoted to the building up of the people in personal goodness. Much of it has been devoted to recording the development of the kingdom of God at home and abroad. And even when the

publications of our Church have been on subjects of a
more general character, they have usually been designed to
the moral improvement as well as the intellectual pleasure
of the reader.   The poet, the metaphysician, even the
scholar, may be disappointed with our literature, but it has
its vast value notwithstanding.   Kew Gardens are very
interesting and very delightful, but after all the nation finds
its life in the orchards of Kent, the pastures of Yorkshire
the harvest-fields which clothe the landscapes with cloth of
gold.   Our literature has also been popular in its character.
I am not sure that it has been popular exactly in the
modern sense of that word, but in the best sense of that
word it has been popular, aiming at the instruction of the
many rather than at the culture of the few.   The grand
feature of the nineteenth century has been the popularis-
·ing of the best things.   Music has descended from the
Olympus of opulence, and the toiling million is charmed
with the concord of sweet sounds ; Art has quitted those
palaces which for ages have been her prison, and the
multitude is bewitched with the hypnotism of beauty ;
Knowledge has stepped out of the great libraries into the
street, and the masses declare it a pleasant thing to see
the light.   I have no hesitation in saying that for the last
privilege the people are greatly indebted to John Wesley.
Newton discovered the law of gravitation ; Columbus
discovered America ; Watt the steam-engine ; and John
Wesley discovered the million.   Long before Lord
Brougham and his friends essayed to bring out a cheap
popular literature, John Wesley had sought, with much
success, to do the same.   He had a great notion of cheap
books, and he was the very pioneer in the cause of
popular literature.

Being of this popular impressionist character, much of
the literature of Methodism has been evanescent.   But a
sunny day is evanescent, so is the dew of the morning,
so is the shower and its rainbow ; but they make the earth
beautiful, and fill it with fruit, and the often slight and
vanishing literature of Methodism has done its precious

and grateful work, strengthening from year to year the best life of its people. After the lapse of a century, we have no reason that I know of to be ashamed of our literary history. Our press has gone on unceasingly sending forth useful and valuable books in considerable variety; monthly publications touching the current life of the Church and the world, and containing many an article of beauty and genius. We have two newspapers, of which I may confidently say that they do no more harm than other newspapers. We issue millions of tracts, whose simple but sublime virtue none may declare; a missionary literature, which to sincere and earnest students is more surprising and romantic than all works of mere imagination; a Review, which treats great themes in a broad and philosophical temper; and lastly, a literature for the Sunday school and the young people, exquisitely calculated to attract and exalt the intelligence of the coming generation.

We have no reason to be ashamed of our literature, for it has always been on the side of truth, of righteousness, of temperance, of freedom, of humanity, of holiness, and of happiness.

But what of the future? May not Methodism in the time to come do far more even in the direction of literature than she has already done? The development of religious literature on all sides does not free Methodism from literary responsibility. We have always had an organic Methodist press; we owe a vast deal to that press, and we ought to do far more in this matter in the future, and not less. Unless the Churches occupy the ground with pure and noble literature of every kind, doubtful and pernicious literature will spring up and flourish with disastrous luxuriance. Our Church, then, must enter into the modern spirit, and intelligently and enthusiastically cater for the million.

It seems to me that our Book-Room occupies a very peculiar and trying position. It is expected, on the one hand, to supply the Connexion with a superior and popular literature, and, on the other hand, it is heavily taxed in the interests of various Connexional Funds. And there is a strong tendency in some quarters to cease appealing to our people for the support of various institutions of our Church, and to look to the Book-Room to make up the deficiency. For my own part, I think this a great mistake. I say, let us directly and honestly appeal to our people for the support of the Old Preachers', and Widows' Fund, and every other fund, and we have no reason to fear the result of such a frank appeal. But let us not put the incidence of what may be thought an unpopular fund on the Book-Room ; let us not handicap our Steward by any severe requisition. I know very well that the official men shake their heads, but I am not alarmed by that. I have been to Conference, and I notice that they always shake their heads there. It is a sort of departmental palsy.

Publishing is not always such a lucrative business as some people seem to think ;—John Wesley found that out. An American was addressing a number of young men, when he said : " Look at me, gentlemen, and see how I have got on in life. When I first came to this country, I was not worth sixpence, and now I owe 200,000 dollars." There is a passage, a humorous passage, in Wesley's Journal, that reminds one of this anecdote : " Wednesday and Thursday I settled my temporal business. It is now about eighteen years since I began writing and printing books. And how much in that time have I gained by printing? Why, on summing up my accounts, I found that on March 1, 1756, I had gained by printing and preaching together a debt of £1236."

Still a fair profit may be made, I suppose, in the publishing trade ; let us then expect no more than a modest dividend from this quarter, let us put no M'Kinley tariff on the intelligence of the Connexion. Nothing will serve the world better, nothing will serve Methodism better, than that our Book-Room should be effective. Whatever else the Book-Room is, it must be effective. Its function is glorious, its possibilities are great, and it must not be limited or exhausted by financial responsibilities. Our Book Steward at this moment has the confidence of the whole Connexion, and from him we all expect great things. But our Steward can only realise our hopes as we patriotically and enthusiastically sustain him. We shall not help him much by criticism, but we shall help him greatly by sympathy. Some in Methodism may aid our Steward by giving him the opportunity of bringing out their best work ;—the other parties I need not exhort. Some one said of our country that it was a reservoir of talent ; certainly there is a vast amount of literary talent in Methodism. I would appeal to all my brethren in this matter : let all those who can aid our Steward in sustaining and raising the literary reputation of our Church, do so, and even if they make some sacrifice in doing this, well, we ought to be willing to make some sacrifice for a Church to which we owe so much. And all our people must aid by encouraging our literature. We have not been a literary Church, perhaps we never can be, but there is a sphere in the intellectual and literary world that we ought to fill, and must fill, if we are to be true to the spirit of our Founder, if we are to do fully the great work that God gave us to do.

Methodism and Missions.

By the Rev. G. W. OLVER, B.A.

IT will be very evident to all who hear me, that it would be impossible for me to attempt to do what Dr. Jenkins himself would have done had he been present. I could never hope to say what he would have said, nor to say it in the manner in which he would have said it. I have no doubt that Dr. Jenkins will in due course revise his manuscript, already in my hands, and I trust he will be allowed to place in the memorial volume the paper he would otherwise have given to us this evening. At the same time, I feel that it would scarcely be fitting if I were to sit down without saying something on the subject of Missions by way of conclusion.

I have felt this all the more, because I have been persuaded, as I have sat upon this platform, that the relation of Methodism to Foreign Missions is the one great secret which must guide us in grappling with and in solving the many problems that await us in our own land.

I need not take you back to the time when Mr. Wesley went out to Georgia as an agent for the Society for the Propagation of the Gospel in Foreign Parts. He was then a missionary, but not a Methodist missionary. He returned, and very soon found himself in the midst of a great movement, the far - reaching extent of which the generations to come will be better able to judge than we can even now. It would be very interesting to try to trace how many Christian Societies that exist in our own day, dealing with the people at home and dealing with the needs of the heathen afar, were brought about by the influence of the Methodist movement. For, when we are speaking this evening of the Methodist movement, I do not understand that we are speaking simply of our own Church, or of the Connexion of Churches of which our own is ever recognised as the mother ; but it is a wider movement, that which I will venture to call the great movement of the eighteenth century.

But, sir, the Christian Church in England had been stirred and moved before Wesley and Whitefield arose. Three great movements have swept over the religious life of this country since the middle of the sixteenth century —the Reformation, Puritanism, Methodism. Wherein lies the secret of Methodism, that it most of them all should not only stir the heart but abide in its influence, gathering might as the generations pass? I think we may understand it if we will ponder for a moment.

When this question has come before my own mind, again and again I have gone back to one passage of

Scripture: " In Jesus Christ neither circumcision availeth anything, nor uncircumcision, but faith that worketh by love." The great theme of the Reformation was Justification by Faith ; and the Christian Church took up the parable, and read : " Neither circumcision nor uncircumcision, but faith" —and it stopped. Not that it did not pass further in practical life, but the attention was riveted there. And then gradually the Churches went back, and the movement began to fail. Another hundred years, and Puritanism arose, and read : " Neither circumcision nor uncircum- cision, but faith that worketh." It set itself in sternness and loyalty to do its acknowledged work ; and those who have read the history of the Puritan movement know what it wrought in political, in social, and in family life. And then again the Church settled down. Another hundred years passed, and Methodism appeared, and took up the old parable, but finished it well : " In Jesus Christ neither circumcision availeth anything, nor uncircumcision, but faith that worketh by love."

So, sir, I read that great message of Methodism,—the love of God to man, by man, in man ; the love of God as the substance of truth, the secret of experience, the rule of practice. And it was when the heart of Wesley opened to the blessed truth, " My Father, God," that he was able to look out upon the world, and to recognise the Fatherhood of God, the Sonship of the race, and the Brotherhood of man. If we will understand Methodism, we may see how that great truth, the Love of God, fixed itself in every part, in its doctrine—the wonderful redemption, the witness of the Spirit, the perfect life ; in its experience—joy in the Lord, consecration of service, consecration of substance ; in its economy—the Methodist class - meeting, the love feast, the prayer-meeting, not as obedience to an ecclesi- astical rule, not as a mere fulfilment of a personal duty, but as the outflow of a brotherly kindness that seeks to help the feeble and the needy. And it found expression in the outward life, as you have heard,—in the Orphan Schools at Newcastle, the Dispensary at Bristol, the Poor's

S

Fund within the Church, the Strangers' Friend Society
without it,—everywhere it was the consecration of a living
love in the service of the common brotherhood. And it is
no marvel, therefore, that Methodism has found its place in
mission work.

I love to turn to the old Hymn-book, and to note in
what different ways Mr. Wesley was wont to deal with sin
as a personal matter, and with equal sin in other sinners.
You want a terrible hymn :

> "How shall I leave my tomb,
> With triumph or regret ?"

Or :

> "Terrible thought, shall I alone —— ?"

But when he is looking out upon the world of sinners
(have not you been singing it to-night) :

> "Come, O my guilty brethren, come."

That was the outcome of his heart. Did not he feel the
sinfulness of sin ? Did he minify the wretchedness of
wrong-doing ? Never. But if you want the missionary
tone of John Wesley, as he looked out upon a world of
sinners, it is here :

> "Oh that the world might taste and see
> The riches of His grace !"

Or, again :

> "Oh for the trumpet voice,
> On all the world to call !"

The mission work with John Wesley, the mission work
with the true Methodist, is not merely the fulfilment of
a duty ; it is the outcome of a loving heart that longs
to bless the world. It is no marvel if, as the result of
this, every Methodist Church throughout the world is a
Missionary Church. If the love is there, it cannot be
otherwise ; and the Church can never cease to be a
Missionary Church, unless the members of it first lose
the love.

I will not occupy your time this evening by many

statistics, but I may say that there are in England five Missionary Societies more or less Methodist,—the Wesleyan, the Bible Christian, the New Connexion, the United Methodist Free Churches, and the Primitive Methodist. In America there are the Methodist Episcopal, the Methodist Protestant, the Wesleyan Methodist Connexion, the African Methodist Episcopal, and the Methodist Episcopal Church South. Wherever there is Methodism the wide world over, it is the result of mission work. These Missionary Societies just mentioned have altogether a membership of 69,600. Of these the American Societies number just over 24,000 members in their Foreign Mission Churches, and the five English Societies something more than 45,000. There is no room for boasting; but it would be a shame—would it not?—if the old Methodist Church were not the leader, if we gave up the heritage that we have received from our fathers, and were not in the van of all the Methodist Churches in this work? And so in connection with your own Society, after having formed so many Conferences in different parts of the world, you have even now upon the mission field more members than all these other Missionary Societies, both here and in America, put together.

Those who have gone before me have asked, one after the other, "And now, what of the future?" I thanked God as I sat there and listened to Peter Thompson, and I said to my neighbour, "I only wish I could take a hundred men out of this congregation, and put them to work where Peter Thompson works, and see what he sees. There would not be a man of the hundred that would not come back and stand side by side with him." At home we have the great social problem, and abroad we have the crying need; and where is the solution to be found? In speculative philosophy? No. In legislation? No. It may help, but it cannot cure. It is to be found in the old secret of Methodism—a truth, an experience, and a practice—in love of God and the brotherhood of man. Did John Wesley ever think all men were equal? What, in muscle, in mind, in morals? No; nor do you. All men equal? No, but all men are brethren. The big brother and the little brother, the strong sister and the weakly sister—brothers, sisters all—the strong to help the weak, and God to help us all. And therefore let us learn the lesson: If we are to reach the brethren afar off, and if we are to help the brethren at home, there is one way, and only one. It is for every one of us, without exception, to betake himself to the secret place, and look once more upon the face of God. It is for every one of us to win back, by His mercy, the consciousness of the indwelling love. It is then, in His name, to go forth and live the life of Christ.

I spoke of three movements. I will only say a word about a fourth. There are two great facts that concern the life of our land and of the world to-day. The one is in the Church—the other outside it. In the Church a yearning for the higher life, a longing for holiness, for consecration, and, thank God for it, a recognition of personal services. Yes, and outside, socialism—ay, let the ugly word alone if you don't like it—a great wail of suffering humanity; the world waking up to a consciousness of its misery; society groaning by reason of the burdens that press upon it. Where is society to find its answer? I verily believe, as I do that there is a Father in heaven to-day, the answer is here. When the Church takes up its theory of the real brotherhood of man, and goes out into the world and lives its creed, socialism will hide its head; for its wildest dreams will be more than fulfilled when the teaching of Jesus of Nazareth reigns in the homes of the land.

Two lessons, then. One for the Christian, the other for the sceptic. Amongst the working classes there is not more scepticism than elsewhere. My conviction is that under the profession of scepticism there is a strong yearning after truth and after God. At all events, we may let scepticism take care of itself. Human nature will never rest in a blank negation. You let scepticism alone, conscience will do its work. For the Church the lesson is to live the life of love. For the working man, what? Be he who he may, he cannot adopt a policy more suicidal than to set himself against the gospel of Jesus Christ. The hard-headed working men of England are finding that out, and God grant they may find it out very fast. If they are to help one another and themselves, their common-sense must lead them to stand side by side with those who are trying to uphold the doctrine of Jesus.

The Opening of the Allan Library.

———o———

By the Chairman, Mr. ALEX. M'ARTHUR, M.P.

THE service in which we are engaged is one of very great interest and importance. The Library that is about to be opened is very much more valuable than many persons have any idea of. Only a year or two ago the British and Foreign Bible Society paid £3000 or £4000 for a collection of old editions of the Bible, and I am quite certain that if the valuable books which have been presented to us by Mr. Allan had been offered for sale they would have realised a much larger amount. I think, therefore, that we may congratulate ourselves on their possession. During the last few days we have heard much of the great work which Mr. Wesley accomplished during his eminently useful life, but I think that there has scarcely been a sufficient acknowledgment of the great services he rendered in the cause of education. It is well known that John Wesley did more in his day for the cause of education generally, for the uplifting of the people, for the education of the young and of his fellow-workers, than any other man at that period of the world. But education in Mr. Wesley's day was very different from what it is now. At that time the people of England were shamefully ignorant. Two-thirds of the population of this country could neither read nor write, whereas now it would be difficult to find a young man or woman of twenty or twenty-five years of age who cannot both read and write. But just in proportion as the standard of education in the nation is raised, it is essential that the education of ministers should be raised; for it is their duty not only to keep abreast of the people but to lead the people. On that ground, therefore, I think we have great cause to congratulate ourselves on the acquisition of so valuable a Library. You are aware that many of our local preachers and young ministers have not very large means, and cannot afford to have large libraries; and to them it will be a great boon to have a Library of that kind to fall back upon and to consult when they desire to do so.

The History of the Allan Library.

By Rev. JAMES H. RIGG, D.D.

Mr. Chairman,—

At the beginning of the present century Mr. Allan, who was at that time perhaps the most safe, cautious, and trusted adviser of the Connexion, in regard to legal business, occupied a pew in this chapel. In that pew, besides the father, there were two sons, who were accustomed from their earliest years to worship in this chapel. The father was a careful, conscientious, loyal Methodist, from the North of England. The sons were sent in early life to one of the public schools of London, and, after having distinguished themselves there, they went to the University of Cambridge. One of them died—a most promising and devoted young man; the other, Mr. Thomas Robinson Allan, became the Founder of this Library. He grew up as an exceedingly shy and timid man — diffident to an almost unexampled degree, but clinging continually to his recollections of Methodism, to his love for the Conference. The family, after leaving

City Road, went to Blackheath, where possibly there may be some, even now, who will remember him. I believe they lived at the " Paragon," and attended the Old Deptford Chapel.

Mr. Thomas R. Allan was not made for the conflicts of life. His health and tastes combined to make him a traveller. He visited a great part of Europe ; and whilst he was travelling, and looking at book-shops, the thought took hold of him that the Church of his childhood ought to have a great Library. He nourished that thought for thirty or forty years. During that time he was looking out for books which could be put into such a Library, and he spent a fortune on them. He had booksellers in Vienna, Berlin, Amsterdam, and other places, who were continually on the look-out for rare and valuable books. Nothing was said to any one until the year that Dr. Waddy was President, some thirty years ago ; and then Mr Allan wrote a long argument and statement which he sent to Dr. Waddy, urging that the time had come for our Connexion to undertake the founding of such a Library. At that time, however, we were not ripe for that work, and nothing came of his representations, although the MS. containing them was put into my hands by Dr. Osborn not many months ago.

In the year of my Presidency this good, devoted, humble man—this lover of learning, of good men, and of Methodism—came more than once to see me. That was the year of the Thanksgiving Fund; we did not meet, and at that time nothing was done. In 1884, however, when his travels had come to an end, he called on me again, and, not finding me at home, wrote to me. Eventually we met, and he stated to me his views. I pointed out to him the difficulties that would be likely to arise with regard to the acceptance of his proposals—that we should have to build a place in which to house his books, etc.; and I hinted, as gently as I could, that his gift, grand as it was, might prove to be one that we could not easily take advantage of. But I did not discourage him from giving the books, although

I tried to prepare him for some delay in our arrangements to take full advantage of them. After much needful and careful preparation, I brought the matter before the Conference ; and at the Conference of that year—1884—the necessary consent was given to accept the books, which had been lying, most of them for years, at Tilbury's warehouse ; and a suitable acknowledgment was sent to Mr. Allan of his splendid gift. They were then removed to the Book-Room, where they have been ever since. Well, it was a beautiful thought that the Church of his childhood ought to have such a Library. In the original document, in which he argued the case, he referred to the Sion College Library of the Church of England and the English Presbyterian or Dissenting Library (Dr. Williams'), and he expressed the hope that the Methodist Church would, in this respect, be equal to the Established and Dissenting Churches.

In order that this hope might be realised, he spent many thousands of pounds in the purchase of rare and precious books—some of which were of extraordinary value. Thus the foundation has been laid for a Library of inestimable worth to Methodist ministers, local preachers, students, and lovers of books throughout the whole Connexion. Do they want to study the early history of the Church? They will find there magnificent copies of the writings of the early Fathers, and other productions of rare and incomparable worth. Do they wish to study the history of the Reformation, and some of the ages that were antecedent? They will find a wonderful wealth of literature appertaining to those periods. As to the Popish Controversy—that seems to have been a peculiar study of Mr. Allan's ; and the works relating to it, and to the history of the Councils, are very numerous and very valuable indeed. The standard works of the Reformers on the Continent—German, French, and Dutch—are to be found there in a very large collection. Also the works of our own national theologians and divines, both of the Church of England and of the Puritan schools. Our Methodist writers, down to a fairly recent period, are also worthily represented. The works of many of our best historians, such as Grote and Macaulay, are to be found there in most magnificent bindings. These are only samples. There is a rich contribution of hymnology of various schools—our own included. There are medals and coins, and engravings of emperors and of distinguished divines of the Church of England. The collection of Bibles is very wonderful—including, as it does, ancient and modern editions in almost every one of the ancient and modern languages. There are Polyglots there, Mr. President, that would make your eyes shine to look upon.

Now I know that all this is of comparatively little worth to those who care for nothing except modern books. But you can't have a Library without such a foundation, that is to be worth anything at all for a great Church. And it is worth a great deal to us to have such a foundation on which to build. Generous friends are adding to the Library. Mr. Buller has contributed the wealth of literature collected by the late Dr. Rule. Mrs. Bunting has given us the remains of her husband's library ; and, both for their intrinsic value and their precious memories, those books have been most thankfully accepted. Mr. Pocock, a man of literary culture, has also made us a present. Mr. Whitehead, of Guernsey, has sent us a valuable series of volumes. Also the library of the late Mr. Foster, Newton, has been added. By reason of these gifts the original Library of 12,000 or 13,000 bound volumes, besides thousands of unbound but very valuable dissertations, has been considerably increased. Mr. Allan knew that the choicest theological and exegetical discussions of the Continent are published in pamphlet form—they are not bound ; and that is the form in which Continental scholars are accustomed to issue their own learned researches and the researches of others. Therefore, he collected for us treatises on the most important questions of theology and interpretation. Thousands of those pamphlets which he collected are there in readiness for the use of our theological tutors and of our exegetes. Don't let any one say that they are all of no use because they are old—because it will be found that the ancients have robbed us of a great many of our thoughts. A great many of our theological puzzles, which are supposed to be quite modern, were anticipated by the ancients. And the same is true, though not to so large an extent, even of many of the questions of Biblical exegesis. There they are, and they are a part of the learned and noble apparatus of study which has been provided by the generosity of our venerable friend.

I visited Mr. Allan during his last months of life. My friend the Secretary of the Conference and Mr. Telford occasionally went with me. We were thankful that, before he became so weak, he had completed the legal documents by which this gift, which he had so long set his heart upon, was made fast and sure to our Connexion. The old man between eighty and ninety years of age had seen the dream of his heart put in the way of accomplishment when he was taken to another world. For many years he had not had a home of his own. He had spent his life in wandering from place to place. He had no wife, no sister. He mourned the loss of his brother. He thought of the past, and for us he thought of the future. You will now know something of the origin of the ALLAN LIBRARY.

We are quite aware of the need of having modern books. The books that Mr. Allan gave to us may be said to bring us down not later than forty years ago. Of course we need to have recent books. We have begun to purchase. We have made some very capital contributions both for ministers and for local preachers. For instance, we have obtained the *Commentaries* of Meyer, also the whole series of the *Expositor's Bible*. You will now find there the Cambridge Bible for Students, the *Story of the Nations* in all its parts, and many other books of the like description. The *Speaker's Commentary* is ordered, but it is not as yet upon the shelves. We are bringing in many of the standard histories of our times.

Nor are we neglecting philosophy. We have got some of
the finest philosophical works of the last twenty years;
and we have authorised the President and Professor
Davison to superintend the selection of other books.
But we are at the end of our resources; and the question
to-day is, whether this grand foundation is to be left without an adequate superstructure — whether this great
opportunity is to be brought to us, and not to be made
available for the Connexion at large? We need to spend
£700 on modern books. With that sum at our disposal
we could supply all that is pressingly needed on that head.
I do not mean to say that we should put nothing there
except the gravest possible books. We shall have poetical
works, and also some other works of imagination. But
they must be choice books, such as go to the completion
of a literary education for men who have to do their duty
in these mixed times.

But, in order to carry out this proposal, we must have
money. And, after all, £700 is a small sum to be raised
by a great Connexion like this. If we had had to appeal
to the Connexion for a suitable building for such a Library,
we could not have asked for less than £10,000; for Mr.
Allan bound us, by his deed, that the Library should be
within the limits of the City of London or of Westminster.
And I think he was right in so binding us. Under the
circumstances, the Connexion would have honoured such
a demand. I cannot doubt that. It would be unworthy
of us to doubt it. But now, owing to the great generosity
of which we have been the subjects, we are enabled to
place these books in the rooms which you will see this
afternoon in connection with the Book-Room. We are
bound, however, to pay some rent. Altogether we calcu-
late that our expenses cannot be set down at less than
£600 a year, exclusive of some present aid that is
necessary in order fully to equip the Library. That is
what we ask the Connexion for; and, if you think of the
history of this movement, you will say that we have a
right to ask it. We are looking for a generous response

to this appeal, both in the way of donations and subscriptions.

As to "subscriptions," let me remind you that the
donation of Mr. Allan was a donation to the ministers
of the Conference. He thought the ministers needed such
a Library. I believe they do; and if all is true that is
said by some about us, as ministers and as a people, we
need the means of enriching and enlarging our learning
and culture very much indeed. (A laugh.) Mr. Allan
presented his gift to the ministers of the Connexion; but
the Pastoral Conference, to which this matter was first
referred, at once agreed that the local preachers should
share in the advantages of this Library, as soon as it could
be started, on equal terms with the ministers of the body;
and it is upon that basis that our arrangements were made.
Of course, they were only too glad to say also that they
would like their lay-brethren, other than local preachers,
to share in the benefits, because we want the laity to help
us with the funds. Our committee, therefore, is a mixed
committee. We want our lay friends to be with us all
through—we want them to become guinea subscribers—
the subscription for ministers and local preachers being
half-a-guinea.

The Library will always be in two parts. One part of it
will be circulating, and the other stationary. It will be
readily understood that volumes which have cost £50, or
more, cannot with safety be allowed to be taken away. A
certain proportion of these books will be books of reference,
and will be retained in the Library; but all the new books
are intended to be diffused; and many a minister in country
town or village, who is not at present able to obtain valuable books on theology and history and research, will have
them placed within his reach.

Now, this is an audience that ought to do the business.
It is large enough; it is intelligent enough. It is, moreover, in a gracious mood. The blessing of the Lord has
come upon us; the Spirit has touched our hearts. This is
the Centenary of Methodism. It is a time for doing some-

thing generous, and simply to renovate this chapel, greatly
as it is needed, will not fill up the measure of what might
well be done on this Centenary occasion and in connection
with this City Road gathering.

By the Rev. W. F. MOULTON, M.A., D.D.,
PRESIDENT OF THE CONFERENCE.

I AM glad to know that there is at this moment in the
chapel a near relative of the donor of this Library. I am
glad that he is present to hear with what gratitude we
acknowledge the very great generosity of his cousin, Mr.
T. R. Allan, in presenting this magnificent Library to our
Connexion. Dr. Rigg has fallen into what I am afraid is
a very common habit of his ; he has so spoken as to show
that he forgets an old rule that used to be laid down for
reapers—viz., that no field should be so closely gathered as
not to leave something for the gleaner. I may, however,
mention two things.

1. The book which I hold in my hand will show you
that the greater part of the 20,000 volumes (besides 8000
pamphlets of very great value) has been most carefully
catalogued.

2. In connection with this Centenary celebration it
should be remembered that John Wesley gave a Library
to the Wesleyan Connexion, which he did his utmost to
circulate as widely as possible. Wesley's " Christian
Library " was brought to the doors of his people, and he
lost a great deal of money by it.

Either of these facts might serve as a text to-day. Mr.
Wesley's plan of publishing and circulating "extracts"
from important works could not be pursued in the present
day to any large extent—students would not be satisfied
with that ; but it is well to note that Mr. Wesley showed,
in many ways, how much he valued the diffusion of
literature amongst his ministers and people, and that we

are simply following his lead when we are considering this question of a Library.

But how to bring the literature which we have acquired to the doors of our people is a difficult question. Dr. Rigg has shown that what has been given to us is not so much a Library as the foundation of a Library. That foundation is a very magnificent one, but it is not one that could be used to great advantage except by a limited number of specialists; and, therefore, if we resolve as Methodists to found a Library, it will be necessary for us, at some considerable expense, to acquire a large proportion of books such as Dr. Rigg has mentioned. We ought to make up our minds to this—to accept this gift as the nucleus of a large and most useful Library, the books of which may, on reasonable terms, be circulated in various parts of the country. I take it for granted that the Library will, to a large extent, be a Library of solid literature. In most towns it is easy to obtain the lighter literature, but it is not an easy thing for a local preacher to get a large number of books that particularly interest him. Not long ago an earnest request was presented to the Conference, on behalf specially of our local preachers, that there might be drawn up, by some competent authority, a list of books suitable for reading in the different parts of Theology. Such a list was prepared accordingly; and that list—supplemented from year to year—might be included in the catalogue of this Library, and used with it.

A good library catalogue has in itself an educational effect, and if we had not simply an alphabetical but a classified catalogue, it would be a great benefit to our Connexion for many years to come.

I may venture to say that there are those on this platform—some of whom have been connected with this Library from the first—who are prepared to pledge themselves that no effort shall be wanting on their part to make the Library all that it must be made for the use of Methodist students and the Methodist people. A great deal depends upon the response which you make to our appeal this afternoon. I can confirm what Dr. Rigg has said that the Allan Library is at present housed on most liberal terms. I only hope that the Book Steward is as well contented with the terms, as representing the general book department, as those who look at the matter from the side of the Allan Library are satisfied. I hope this Library will grow to a far greater extent than its present limits will suffice for. We are accustomed to do things on a large and generous scale, and I do not believe that the Methodist people will hesitate to do this now that they see the need of it.

Methodism and Social Work.

—o—

The PRESIDENT OF THE CONFERENCE.

IF ever we had need of serious and earnest prayer, and of all the courage which belongs to the service of the Lord Jesus Christ, it is in connection with the questions which occupy us this evening. If we cannot so fully quote the direct example of John Wesley as we could in our last meeting, the spirit of John Wesley is in every part of the subject which will come before us to-night. But in some respects it was impossible in his age to do what has become possible in ours. Above all others, our age has been distinguished by the privilege which has been conferred upon the Church of Christ in some of these all-important questions. Questions will be brought to our notice this evening with which your own hearts are in deepest sympathy. Our hearts have been filled at times with fear and horror, and at times with hope and joy ; and nothing can so appeal to the deeper feelings of our nature as those matters of which I am now speaking. In our meetings hitherto, very distinct references have been made to the future, but the present and the past have naturally occupied our main attention. This evening we have the future before us. I believe the future is in our hands. We have the means of carrying on this work through

T

God's blessing. But if we have the power we have also the responsibility. No body of Christians ever had the responsibility for dealing with social questions which those who live at this time undoubtedly have. Therefore I call upon you, with all your hearts, with earnest prayer to God, and with profound consecration of yourselves, to sing this hymn:—

"Soldiers of Christ, arise."

Methodism and the Working Man.

By the Rev. H. T. SMART.

I THINK myself happy that I have the honour to speak to you on the relation of Methodism to working men, and the more so because working men are not so much a class as they are the nation, seeing that three-fourths of our population are made up of wage-earning people. It is well known that amongst no section of the community was Mr. Wesley so successful as amongst this class. Oxford don though he was, he loved to preach to the miners of Kingswood and Wednesbury, and from them and their order he got his most useful converts and the largest number of his triumphs. The names of John Nelson the stonemason, and Tom o' Jack's lad may be taken as the representatives of many thousands of honest working men of whom Wesley could say, "In Christ Jesus I have begotten you through the gospel." Whilst in Voltaire's country this class was engaged in making tanneries for human skins, in Wesley's country the same class were engaged in singing all over the land:

"Oh, that the world might taste and see
    The riches of His grace!
The arms of love that compass me
    Would all mankind embrace."

And it was very largely due to the influence of Wesley and his coadjutors that England was not visited by those

disasters which befel our neighbours across the Channel.
What saved England in the eighteenth century will save
her in the nineteenth; and therefore we do well to
address ourselves with all possible energy and devotion
to the work which Mr. Wesley set us the example of
doing—namely, promoting the evangelisation of the great
body of the community.

Where John Wesley's body lies we all know very well,
but his soul is marching on. And, blessed be God, his
soul has been marching on all through the century. For
this reason, therefore, we do not meet this evening to
discuss how we can win our first triumphs amongst this
class, but rather to consider by what means we can best
extend the triumphs which, by the Divine blessing, Methodism has already achieved amongst working men. The
Rev. Edward Smith's little book, *Three Years in Central
London*, may, I think, be worthily mentioned on the same
day as Wesley's Journals.

But not only in Clerkenwell have we to rejoice over
converted working men. In other London circuits, as I
have myself lately seen, we have a fair representation of
this class; whilst in Lancashire and Yorkshire, in which
counties I have spent the last twelve years of my ministry,
we have in our Societies large numbers of converted working men, who are seeking not only to save their own souls,
but also to save the souls of their fellows. I have been
the pastor of working men who have counted it no hardship to walk four miles after a hard day's work to some
centre of evangelistic work, and then to walk four miles
back again to their home. I have been the pastor of
working men who have been so concerned for the conversion of their mates, that they have denied themselves
sleep for four nights running, in order that by prayer and
fasting they might cast out some unclean spirit. I have
heard a man say in his pew to his neighbour, "John, you
know what a blackguard I was, and God has saved me—
He can save you." And I have seen with what exuberant
joy these men enter into possession of that blessing of

conscious salvation, of which Dr. Dale spoke to us this morning. I have witnessed the delight which they have experienced when, like Wesley, they have felt their hearts "strangely warmed," and they have realised that Jesus Christ loved them and gave Himself for them.

Yes, we are very thankful for the success that has attended our labours during recent years; but we know that Ramoth in Gilead is ours, and we cannot be still, but must go and take it. We are anxious to win the working men of England, and therefore we must address ourselves during the closing years of this century to their evangelisation.

To secure this object, our reliance must be placed entirely on the gospel of God's grace, made effectual by His Holy Spirit.

At the same time, we must not forget that it is our duty to promote the temporal well-being of the working classes. And if we endeavour to discharge that duty, we shall find ourselves in the happiest accord with the spirit of our Founder, who was quite as enlightened a philanthropist as he was a devoted evangelist. In many ways Mr. Wesley promoted the temporal well-being of the people. He actively supported the Society for the Reformation of Manners, of which he said, that if it did not directly lead to the salvation of souls, yet inasmuch as it lessened sin it promoted the glory of God.

Having some medical knowledge, he opened a dispensary, and gave away medicine to all comers, many of whose faces he said he never expected to see again. He established a Loan Fund, which was a rather dangerous experiment, and one which I have not myself imitated. Then he found that there were many people without work, and so he actually became for a time a sort of labour-master—a middleman, but not a sweater. During at least four months one of the rooms at the Foundery was turned into a workshop, which was going farther than any modern Methodist preacher has gone; for I do not know that any of my brethren have turned a Methodist vestry into a workshop; but John Wesley did this, and he did it because he believed that it was most important that workless people who were willing to work should have work found for them.

In a time of national distress, Mr. Wesley issued a long and an earnest appeal to the nation in *Lloyd's Evening Post*, in which, having investigated the poverty which then prevailed in England, he advocated certain remedies for the existing destitution. He gave the people of that day a graphic picture of " Darkest England " as it then was. Nor did he refuse to go into details ; for he condescended to write about beef, mutton, milk, and eggs, and to discuss the question why those articles of diet were then so extremely dear. He actually went so far as to call attention to the high price of lard, and he recommended a plan by which work was to be found for the unemployed. He showed his generation a way out of " Darkest England," but they refused to follow it, as indeed the nation has refused to follow it until this day. For he advised his fellow-countrymen to " prohibit for ever that bane of health, that destroyer of strength, of life, and of virtue— distilling."

No doubt that was a drastic remedy to propose, but it was Wesley's plan for relieving national distress. As you are aware, a Ministerial Temperance Secretary will be set apart at the next Conference, and for the first time in our history we shall have a minister whose sole duty it will be to promote the spread of temperance. If, therefore, you should hear of Mr. G. A. Bennetts going so far as to recommend the entire prohibition of distilling, you may say that the spirit of Elijah rests on Elisha.

In order to promote the temporal well-being of working men, it is necessary that we should see that they are wholesomely housed. I have myself seen, not only in large towns but in some of the most beautiful parts of England and Scotland, large numbers of people, made in the similitude of God, living in such dwellings that if I had any horses I would disdain to put those horses where British men and women and children are put from day to day.

I do not know how far the Methodist people are acquainted with these facts ; but if they wish to grasp the whole problem of the uplifting of the masses of the people, they should be told that many of our fellow-subjects are living in " kennels," as I have heard their dwellings described by themselves, and in " coffin-cottages," as I have heard them described by clergymen of the Church of England. The truth is, that the poor do not so much live in these dwellings as die in them, as may be proved from the fact that the death-rate of the district in which my last chapel was situate was double what it was in the district in which my house was situate.

To bring up children in habits of decency and morality in such houses is most difficult, not to say impossible. And it must be remembered that almost all home-pleasures are beyond the reach of these ill-housed people. Furthermore, the monetary loss they sustain through preventible sickness is very heavy ; and, as a working man's health is his capital, I wish to say that he should be maintained under wholesome conditions of life. I am aware that it is said that the habits of this class are degraded ; but, granting that that is so, we ought to improve their dwellings, were it only for the sake of their children. In the admirable address which Mr. T. G. Osborn gave us last night, he suggested that the only effectual way of dealing with our social problems is to rescue the children from evil surroundings. Certainly that is one of the best methods—if it be not the only method—of improving the social and moral condition of the people; but if it is to be carried out, the children of the poor must be provided with homes in which the sexes may be brought up separately, and in which decency and morality may be possible. In your day and Sunday schools, and in your Bands of Hope, you are teaching the children principles which, I fear, it is next to impossible for them to practise, seeing that their environment is so degrading. Let us, then, declare that Englishmen shall not live in fœtid alleys, and foul garrets and cellars and in single rooms, but that they shall be decently and wholesomely housed. I am glad to be able to tell you that during recent months meetings have been held on Methodist premises to promote this object. Whilst the class-meeting has been going on in one part of the building, in another, dignitaries of the Churches of England and Rome, members of Parliament, and working men, who fear God and work righteousness, have been consulting on Methodist property as to the best means for abolishing slums.

If we can but succeed in getting the people suitably housed, we shall find it much easier than we now do to make them sober, righteous, and godly.

There is another work which needs to be taken in hand by Methodism, and that is the work of effecting a reconciliation between capital and labour. Our industrial wars are causing great sorrow of heart to all who wish to see the classes reconciled to each other. I am well aware that the subject is a delicate one ; but is Methodism to be dumb upon the relations of capital and labour ? Have we nothing to say to employers and employed about their respective duties ? Surely it is right that we should exert some influence in order to guide a movement which intimately concerns the welfare of the community.

I should like you to dismiss from your minds what you often hear, that working men are so discontented that it is impossible to satisfy them. It is true that they are as a class discontented ; but are they the only class that are not content ? Mr. Bryce says that it is an age of discontent, and no doubt he is right. Certainly capitalists are as dissatisfied as labourers. Shareholders in public companies — Allsopp's Brewery, for example — are not exactly a pattern of contentment. Only the other day I noticed that at the meeting of the London General Omnibus Company a shareholder was far from satisfied. The dividend was only ten per cent., and he thought it should have been twelve and a-half per cent. Prince

Bismarck said, in the day of his power, that Providence had denied to working men the faculty of contentment, and that, therefore, it was the duty of governments to enforce acquiescence. But working men only share the discontent that prevails amongst all classes, and I earnestly wish we could turn the winter of our people's discontent into "glorious summer" by bringing the kingdom of God into their midst. We must curb the greed for money which marks all classes. We must insist upon this truth, that a man's life consisteth not in the abundance of the things which he possesseth, and that men must look not on their own things but on the things of others also, and that every man must seek not his own but another's wealth. We must tell employers that it is the indefeasible right of workmen to combine to protect their own interests ; and we must tell the employed that it is the right of workmen to refuse to combine if they are so minded.

It is often said that working men are led by unworthy leaders, but, if this is so, is it not because they have not been able to secure better leaders? When the trees desired a king, they first solicited the olive tree to reign over them. But the olive declined the honour. They then approached the fig tree and the vine, but with no better success. As a last resort they accepted the bramble tree. If the bramble is reigning over some trees that we know, is not the reason this—that the olive and other trees have disdained them? We must find leaders for the workmen, who shall teach them to attach sanctity to contract, to avoid all that is unfair and illegal, and to rely on the Divine method of self-defence. We must tell them that if they will trust to reason and expostulation and conciliation and arbitration, for obtaining their legitimate demands, we will stand by them. Secularism must have no reason for existence, for we must be as secular as the Old Testament ; and Socialism must be shown a more excellent way, by all of us becoming as socialistic as St. Paul, who bids us "bear one another's burdens, and thus fulfil the law of Christ."

We must also go among the employers, and teach them to give unto their workmen that which is just and equal, and to be ambitious first to be good masters, and then to be rich masters, if that may be possible. As ministers of religion, some of us have this great advantage, that we can put our hand across the gulf which separates employers and employed, and bring each class nearer to the other.

During recent months work of that kind also has been done on Methodist property. Whilst class-meetings have been going on in some of the rooms connected with the Wesleyan chapel in question, in another room labour representatives, trade unionists, and unskilled workmen have been meeting once and again, in order to promote the amicable adjustment of labour disputes. I had the privilege some time ago of leading a body of picked workmen to the office of the Manchester Chamber of Commerce, where they were met by a number of capitalists, and where they discussed the question in which they had a common interest with the employers. As I watched the workmen conduct the business on equal terms with the capitalists I thought I saw some of those foolish and hurtful class-prejudices and class-hatreds, which are doing so much mischief in this country, subside before my eyes.

We must bring the classes closer together. At present they are almost as much apart as are first-class and third-class railway passengers ; and, as it is not good for any class to dwell apart, we must undertake the task of welding the classes together—a task than which there is none other of greater importance, and one which will bring about, when once it is finished, that delightful time when " violence shall no more be heard in our streets, wasting nor destruction within our borders." Last night Mr. Watkinson suggested that some persons now-a-days were interested in the welfare of the working man because he now possesses a vote. But we do not want his vote, for Methodism does not exist for party purposes. But I am free to say that my interest in the working man is all the greater because he

has a vote. For weal or for woe you have entrusted to
him the destinies of the nation, and therefore, if it is to be
well with this country, the democracy must be sober and
God-fearing. The only way to secure a righteous House
of Commons is to secure a righteous electorate, and that
can only be done by active aggressive work amongst the
masses of the people. I hope, therefore, that we may be
able in the years that are before us to combine fervid
evangelism and active philanthropy.

Pressing Social Questions.

By Mr. P. W. BUNTING.

It is with no little diffidence that I attempt to speak to an
audience like this on so vast a subject as the relation of
Methodism to the social problems of the age. Mr. Smart
has made my task a little easier, by speaking of one or
two of the great questions which agitate our time.

It is a great time into which we are going ; and, as a very
experienced statesman said two nights ago in my hearing,
we are really, in no inflated language, on the very verge
of a new era—a new era in politics, because a new era in
social questions. For politics, day by day, are coming to
be social questions ; and, if I have not the slightest hesitation on an occasion like this in speaking of politics, it is
because the politics of this day are no party squabble, but
touch the deeper, profounder issues which all parties are
feeling. It is true that one party may be a little less
hopeful, and another may be over-sanguine and allow
theories to prevail over practice. The President told us
that our business was not a servile imitation of Wesley,
but the application to new times and problems of the
spirit in which he lived. With this in our hearts we are
able to go forward with as much confidence into the work
of the twentieth century as, under his guidance, we went
into the work of the nineteenth.

It is, indeed, a great era into which we are going; an age in which there are not only practical questions which no age has ever yet had to deal with, but in which great theories are being launched of the future of politics, and the future construction of society. One thing I want to observe—that, as in all great political crises, the true foundations are to be sought in religion. The modern political world is the direct offspring of the Reformation. The reason why men are Democrats to such a large extent to-day is that the Reformation announced the spiritual equality of men in the presence of their Maker, and gave to each individual soul the franchise of the spiritual kingdom. Men are very apt to translate the terms of ecclesiastical polity into those of civil polity. It was when the divine right of the pope and his notion of the Church were gone that the divine right of the king followed.

What is our attitude as Methodists to those great underlying principles—to the principles, in a single word, of the brotherhood of man, and the possibility of realising that brotherhood in a social kingdom of God upon earth? I hold that we have very great and special advantages for dealing with these theories and their practical outcome.

It almost takes us back at a step to the time of John Wesley to say that the first qualification we have is our profound and enthusiastic belief in universal redemption. In Mr. Wesley's time that was the fighting doctrine by which he would have died. I think it is a doctrine for which we ought to fight, and by which, if necessary, we ought to be ready to die to-day. For I believe that the political and social salvation of the world, as well as its religious advancement, depends upon it. Under the doctrine of universal redemption you put an end at one stroke to the privilege of individuals. That doctrine of Mr. Wesley's is no far-off and metaphysical dogma. Universal redemption is the very life and breath of our religious principles, and we go forth to every man with the declaration that he is a brother of Christ, whether he knows it or not; that he has been redeemed; and that he has only to exercise his privilege to be a man as good as any.

And, again, we have the principle of immediate and conscious conversion. That again is a great political and social principle. For what does it really mean? That there is no long process of training which requires expense, labour, toil, and trouble, to enter upon our spiritual privilege—that the door is open for every man immediately. From the very principle of redemption it is a birthright, in spite of any want of conditions on his part, simply on the terms that he is prepared to go in and exercise it. That is a matter of the most vital consequence; for we have to deal, in social problems, not with a theoretical body of men, but with the whole mass of mankind before us. You allow no property qualification, just as you abolish as far as possible the qualifications and conditions and barriers and restraints which prevent men from entering upon the advantages of society. We base all that upon our religious principle—that a man may at once, whatever his past, whatever his present, on the condition merely of justification by faith, enter upon his privileges; that he may, upon immediate repentance, take up his birthright and become a full citizen.

I hold, therefore, that just as historically the Christian doctrines of the Reformation have produced the modern ideal of society, so we, who hold them in their strongest form, are the best able to give them effect in the social sphere. Again, we have had a hundred years of close and practical experience in putting these different theories into operation. The reason why you find wherever you go, in village or town, so many Methodists coming into public life is, that they have been accustomed in the spiritual sphere to preach and practise those theories. We have the habits of business. We have the habit of expecting immediate results. We have a business-like style, which qualifies us above all others to enter upon these social problems.

I am reminded that it is from a Methodist that the most important regenerating scheme of these days has proceeded. They say we are under the umbrella of General Booth ; but, the truth is, General Booth is under our umbrella. He gets his inspiration from the very doctrines which he and we have always preached and practised. He happens to be the most audacious and powerful of single Methodists, and he has therefore produced a scheme which has challenged the attention of the world ; and I shall be very much disappointed if he does not make it the stepping-stone to a great social reform.

With these principles in our favour—the principle of the right, the immediate right, of every man, and the best method of getting that right into exercise, we, the Methodists, may go into these social schemes of the future and the present with the greatest confidence.

For a moment or two let us look at some of these problems.

The first is the problem of poverty. If we are going to deal with that, we know what is the real and ultimate cause of poverty. We know the true cause of poverty is ungodliness. In our own Church there is not much, and what there is we can easily deal with. If half the population were members of society there would be no poverty at all. But, while I adhere to every word that Mr. Smart has said about the housing of the working classes, I know—we all know—that to make clean the outside of the cup and platter, to give a nice four-roomed tenement, papered and furnished, is of very little use if your father of the family is going to come home drunk, and break the windows and the furniture too, and tear the paper off the walls. I am for the housing of the poor, because I believe things act and react upon one another ; but we, as Methodists, have this great advantage, that we shall never forget the other side of the question. And while some persons seem to think that a fresh coat of paint is all that is needed to regenerate London, we know that, while we are willing to have the paint-pot in one hand, we must have the Bible in the other.

Over against that we have the problem of wealth. I sometimes wonder when I read some things that our friend Mr. Carnegie has said upon this question whether he was not after all a Methodist in his youth. Mr. Carnegie says that, whether or not you can get rid in the social sphere of the possessors of large wealth, at all events a possessor of large wealth is, and must consider himself to be, a person placed in a position of exceptional trust ; that he is not at liberty to devolve his trust upon the chance that his children will carry out his ideas to the extent that he has felt them ; that it is socially wrong for millionaires to leave millionaire children behind them. You have no right to suppose that the desire to carry out such a trust is necessarily hereditary any more than you have a right to suppose that the ability to legislate is necessarily hereditary. Therefore, the trust is not discharged by simply leaving your wealth in large quantities to the children that come after you. It is best for them to exercise the same qualities by which you arrived at your wealth ; and you do them no good, and fail in your public duty, if you leave them with large wealth. I do not say it is wrong to make reasonable provision for foreseen needs. I think we should sufficiently carry out the spirit of John Wesley if we left something to Providence. The danger is, when a man can no longer look up to God—when he loses the spirit of the Lord's Prayer, which asks for bread day by day. Something must be left to the chances of the future ; and your soul should feel that, for this world also, you are a dependent being, waiting upon the providence of God. You are not to be so elevated above your fellows as to be unable to sympathise with their life. If this were carried out how mightily our Church agencies might expand, how easy it would be to multiply our Church appliances ; how we might take in hand the missioning of the world in serious earnest ; how we might set an example to others of the devotion of wealth to great public ends—not necessarily ecclesiastical.

The influence of Methodism upon society is not only the influence exercised upon Church premises. The particular functions of society which the Church should undertake differ in different ages. The Church is the pioneer for the State ; and, when the Church has educated the State into taking up any particular work, the Church is free to start afresh in any direction. Look at this great scheme of General Booth's. Do you suppose that the benefits of that scheme are to be confined within the four walls of the Salvation Army? The great effect will be that he will reform our whole method of the treatment of the poor. Already the reform of the Poor Law is going to be a practical question very soon. The danger is, perhaps, that some of our sons and daughters may find the claims of public life so strong that we may lose them from our own work. If, somehow, we could check the ambition, which the young feel so very strongly, to get to the top of the tree and die rich, we should be able to conserve some of those energies for the service of Christ and the State. We might avoid becoming rich at all.

Many other branches of social reform are beyond our special dealing with as Methodists. We may do something to reconcile the disputes of capital and labour, by the efforts of individuals here and there. But our Methodist Church cannot do very much to solve, as a Church, that great social question of the day. And as for the great transformations which are taking place in wealth, the better distribution of wealth that is coming to us—that is due to great economic laws which are beyond the touch of any individuals. There we recognise the good hand of our God, who is so working that, at the same time that He is showering upon us the gifts of nature, wealth is getting better spread over the great mass of the people. I do not know that rich people are getting richer, but the poor are not getting poorer. The great mass is beginning to get divided more equally. I do not know why we should not share the good gifts of God freely with each other, as far as is possible. Equality may be a long way off; but that there should be a greater equality, that we should stand more upon one level, is a profoundly Christian thought, and that is what Christ is leading us to.

Wesley is a brilliant example for the eighteenth century. But we may go eighteen centuries farther back for a greater Example. It is difficult to say whether our Lord spent more of His time and trouble upon preaching than upon healing. But what I say is that when He took to His social work it was done on a large scale. He was in the constant habit of healing the sick in crowds, and dispensing His gift of health, as it were, with the free hand of a sower ; and when He thought fit to distribute free meals, it was done on a large scale—five thousand at a time. There is a precedent for your free breakfasts and dinners. There is a great passage in which our Lord depicted, with a large and broad hand, the scene of the Last Judgment : and He laid down there what was the ultimate criterion by which men were to go into salvation or damnation. What was it ? It was the test of active benevolence. The men who are blessed of the Father are those who visited the sick and the prisoners, and fed the hungry and clothed the naked : and the men who go into everlasting destruction are the men who refused to do these things. These are our Lord's plain and unmistakable words. We need not stop to enquire how this is consistent with justification by faith. The old question of faith and works seems to me to have been argued upon a somewhat mathematical basis. Modern science has given us metaphors, by the aid of which we may go a little deeper than these plannings out of departments of Christian duty. Faith and works are in organic relation to each other. Our Lord tells us that by these works of charity and mercy, and apparently by these alone, we are to be judged at the last day. It was said by one that "our life is in Christ ; " but that great passage will allow us to use the words in the reverse sense, and say that "His life is in ours." If Christ be the Representative of humanity, the great organic Centre to which we all belong, then everything that is done to His brethren is, in fact, done to Himself; and He feels the act done, and from Him comes the thrill of gratitude! And if in these works we are unable to separate the Master from His brothers, or the Lord and Saviour from the human race that is being saved, every good done to the human race is done essentially to Him, and it is impossible to do good to any man without doing good to Christ Himself.

There is our theology; we are one in Christ, and He lives with us and conducts the whole, and is in sensitive connection with every touch of social reform. Christianity is a radical revolution. It begins with a radical revolution in the heart, and goes on to a radical reformation of society. We have not only a Judge, but a Saviour who, gathering up the whole of our works, brings us all, the saved and the saviours, to share His glory of a complete salvation, in which we have all received and have all given, and in both capacities are one with Him.

Methods of Rescue Work.

By LEWIS WILLIAMS, Esq., J.P., Cardiff.

THE topic assigned me to-night is "Methodism and Rescue Methods." Our Founder's aim was not to establish a proselytising society, but a great Rescue Mission. It is true his master-purpose was to proclaim free, full, and present salvation for every man; but, in addressing the Church, he distinctly taught the duty of every member to seek most earnestly to rescue men from present as well as future misery, "or ye are not living members of Christ."

The study of Wesley's rescue methods are fraught with as much interest for the nineteenth as they were for the eighteenth century, and the most vigorous Methodism of " to-day " is where they are approximated or adopted. Wesley organised his forces to grapple with the miseries of his age, recognising the individual qualification, and providing work for each and all — setting before his followers an example unequalled, since the days of the Apostle Paul. He believed in Mr. Moody's maxim, " If you do a thing, do it."

His mission was to the classes as well as to the masses. The poor and outcast had his special care. He went amongst them not as a patron, but a brother. Bradburn says that " no poor man ever thanked him for his charity, but he took off his hat in graceful recognition." To his stewards Wesley said, " Put yourself in place of every poor man, and deal with him as you would God should deal with you." He went to the outcasts, in those prisons which he depicts as the " darkest seats of woe this side of hell." He read, prayed, and wept, paying the debts of imprisoned ones, and setting them free. We cannot gain admission to the prisons as he did,—we must ere long ; but what are we doing in the police courts or at the prison gates ?

A Christian worker met at our prison gate a man who last year was in one of your London banks, a victim of drink. He found his way to our mission room, and to-day is the centre of spiritual influence amongst two hundred and fifty men. Godly Methodists are realising that noble rescue work can be accomplished by their friendly hand in the police courts.

Wesley went to the poorest of the poor—what did he find ? Unclothed, unfed—what did he do ? Like his Master—gave his all. Wesley's views and sermons upon giving need to be re-stated and re-preached. Not content with giving, as we are told, £35,000 in charity, which he never delegated when able to dispense himself, he traversed the city to find help for the needy ; he gave the penny a week in the classes, for forty years to the poor ; he required all the members to bring what garments they did not need, for their poorer brethren ; in 1748 he established a Loan Society, a Labour Bureau, and that Strangers' Friend Society which distributed money not to Methodists only, but to people of all sects, and of no sect at all.

These rescue methods are needed as much to-day as ever, the more so as the near approach of universal suffrage makes it imperative, if the country is to be saved from socialism and communism, that we devote ourselves more earnestly than ever to genuine philanthropy and religious activity. Wesley gives us a pattern of broad, sympathetic practical charity. Care for the poor of the Church, by all means; and it should be deemed the highest discredit to allow a godly saint to die in the workhouse. But let the world feel that the Methodist Church has a sympathetic heart and hand, wherever need and suffering exists. A Stranger's Friend, a Merciful Society in every Church, a Helpful Society for old garments, Dorcas societies—yea, and even a Loan Society, that shall be an antidote to the pawnshop, a help to the Work Society. In all, ever remembering our Lord's "Inasmuch . . to the least . . it is to *Me*." From this meeting may we catch something of that inspiration going forth, as Whittier so tersely says—

> " To make the world within our reach
> Something the better for our living,
> And the gladder for our human speech."

Have you noted that Wesley arranged for the visitation of the sick by setting apart twelve in the Society to see that all the needy were supplied, that they met weekly to report what had been done and consider what more could be done?

Wesley established the first dispensary for the poor. The present want of the Methodist Church is a nursing sister in in every Society or Circuit. The High Church party have been wise in their generation. They have worked this method. The largest employer of labour in this country said to me, two years ago, " Mr. Williams, can you get me half-a-dozen Nonconformist nurses?" He could not. What a sphere opens up in this direction! It is my joy to have one of my own daughters who has consecrated her own life voluntarily to this work. What rescue work might be effected too in our infirmaries or workhouses!

Then there is the rescue of child-life. I hardly like to speak of this in the presence of Dr. Stephenson, but I am thankful that he has wiped away the discredit from our Church which once rested upon it in this direction. We are told that the germ idea of the children's homes, ragged schools, and mission schools is to be found in the Orphan House at Newcastle. We are thankful for all the grand work Wesley did in that direction, how he cared for the orphans, and how he lived amongst the poor in the Foundery yonder. We cannot attach too large importance to this work. Six weeks ago to-day, I was sent for by the Mayor of our town, Lord Bute. A woman and six children had been found in a brothel, huddled together in one room. As chairman of our School Board, I knew there were powers under the Act which could be put into operation. I sent for the mother. One little fellow came to the office with his "Good day, Mr. Williams." Inquiring, "How do you know me?" "Oh, I've been to the mission school, in Miss Williams' class." "If so," I said, "you are not going to an industrial school." Driven by sheer want, the woman told me, through the boys going off, fearing the bailiffs would come, to save her little furniture she flitted, and took refuge in this place, not knowing the character of the house; and there she was found. There was a girl, as fair and graceful as any daughter in this assembly to-night. When I saw her first of all dark fears were suggested. But I was soon reassured. She, too, had been at the mission school. One of my staff went out and got a new suit of clothes for the boy, and when a friend met me with him, looking so bright, he said, "Mr. Williams, is this your little fellow?" To-day he is sheltered in the Home of our good friend, Dr. Stephenson, and that fair, beautiful girl is sheltered in a kindly home too. That is the kind of work we want to do. " Child life, amidst such surroundings," as Lord Bute said,—"what can save them, booked for hell!" I do rejoice that we have such agencies. Give them your generous support.

Then there is the rescue of the drunkards. Given Wesley's ideal of a Church, with its ministers and members abstainers—that day we become the mightiest rescuing army in this kingdom. Do not give up any case. We have seen cases followed ten and even twenty years, and glorious results have at length been obtained.

We must face our duty, too, in rescuing our poor fallen sisters, in the same tender spirit, with which Wesley pleaded for the poor Magdalene ; not forgetting it is as much our duty to warn and rescue our falling, fallen brethren. Let us be brave and tender to warn and save our young men from a life of lust and passion and untimely death. In rescue work let us have mission-rooms connected with all our large places of worship, but let them be under the control of the parent Church. I wish to emphasise that—not two rival institutions, but one, working in harmony with the Church, and helping to fit its members to become useful members of the Church. Let these places be in our destitute localities. Let us have adult Bible classes. I know something of that work. I have seen cases most hopeless, men who would not go to a society class, who would come with you to read the Word of God, and have seen some of the most abandoned drunkards in our town converted. Have your girls' parlours, your boys' brigades, your recreative evening classes ; and—let me say—do not be afraid of teaching cookery. I had a very stubborn Board to contend with on that point, and I invited a lady to meet them. She said, " The chairman of our Board in Liverpool opposed it tooth and nail, but, being a very active magistrate, he thought he would try to ascertain the causes of the family broils which came under his notice. He found as a result that one-half the family broils brought before the Liverpool magistrates had their origin in the want of good cooking. If we want to rescue people from going down, depend upon it, we shall do good work in this direction, and elevate home life.

If there is any Church that owes more to outdoor preaching than any other, it is the Methodist Church. Let that be as much as possible in the back and destitute streets. I believe, for my own part, it is better to get services in the back streets than to get crowds in the large thoroughfares. A dying Roman Catholic heard our mission band across the street one day, singing " Jesu, Lover of my soul." He sent out to ask them to come and sing under the window. He died singing " Jesu, Lover of my soul."

If there has been any work in my own life that has repaid me more than another, it has been the sending of books to men with whom it was not profitable to argue. In fact, the two most intellectual men I have ever known in my town were brought to God through the gift of *Daniel Quorm*—a book which Mr. Moody said has been made almost a greater blessing than any other within the last twenty years.

Let us reduce the difficulties of the pew system to a minimum by our most influential men taking their place in the porch on a Sunday and giving a welcome to strangers. A man came into our porch one day, a man very well-known in London, who had had an income of £5000 a year,—a writer for the *Times*. He had fallen through drink, but he was rescued. A young man came, and, when spoken to, said, " I don't want to become a Methodist." A fortnight after that he was saved in a prayer-meeting, and to-day he is the sub-editor of the most influential paper in Australia.

Wesley organised the laity. The hearty co-operation of our Methodist laity is all-essential to our future success. But Wesley also recognised an influence which we are just beginning to recognise again—he recognised woman's gifts and influence. I believe that this is the greatest

power for rescue work that the Methodist Church possesses.
We rejoice in the splendid work, the splendid illustration
which our friends Mr. Hughes and Mr. Thompson and
others are giving us of the work of women. We are not
acting as copyists in the country exactly, but we are
striking out a line for ourselves. There are provincial
sisterhoods to-day doing a good work. I said to one
sister last week in my library, " Which is the best way to
get at the people ? " She said, " Methodism must go to
the people in a brotherly spirit. May I illustrate what I
mean ? " She was a teacher in one of our Board Schools.
One day, noticing a little child looking rather wan and
pale, she said, " Jenny, what is the matter ? " She replied,
" We have had nothing to eat this morning, and father is
very ill—he is dying." As soon as school was over that
godly woman found her way to the home, and found an
abandoned drunkard in a state of delirium, and dying.
He had been injured in a fight, and erysipelas had set in.
She went and got some food in, and fetched the doctor,—
never a word about Methodism all the time. There are
some bright exceptions among the sisters of the Anglican
Church, but with most it is nothing but " Church, Church."
Thank God, our sisters are taught to put Christ first. That
man got better, and when he was well he found out the
mission hall at which the sister worked to whom he owed
so much, and used to tramp a mile and a-half every
Sunday night, " clothed, and in his right mind," to hear
our " Dinah Morris " speak of Christ's power to save.

Let us consecrate ourselves to this work ; that we
may be

> " Like a chalice of dew to the weary heart,
> A sunbeam of joy bidding sorrow depart :
> To the storm-tost vessel a beacon light,
> A nightingale's song in the darkest night :
> A beckoning hand to the far-off goal,
> And an angel of love to each friendless soul."

Methodism and Temperance.

By Mr. T. MORGAN HARVEY.

I AM an abstainer, and the son of an abstainer. This meeting carries me back many years to the time when this temperance question was not quite so popular as it is to-day. I have repeated the story more than once, in speaking to our friends on temperance matters; but I think in this gathering it would not be out of place if I referred to the early days of the temperance movement in Cornwall. My father became the exponent of temperance principles in theory and practice. He received James Teare, one of the Preston men, when he came amongst us. He devoted a great deal of his time to the advocacy of the cause. Naturally he received some opposition. There was the opposition, for instance, of a publican. One day, riding through the town of Camborne, he passed a public-house, and the publican was at the door. As my father rode past, the publican gracefully lifted his hat. Some one standing by asked if he knew who that was. "Yes; Mr. St. Aubyn." "Oh, no," was the reply, "it is Frank Harvey, the temperance lecturer." At this the publican was beside himself, and snatching the hat from his head threw it to the ground, and said, "I'll never put thee on my head again."

At that time temperance meetings could not be held on Methodist trust property. I am glad to say the powers that be have been much enlightened since those days. We have, in our President beloved, a man who has spoken out on this great question. As to the widespread evil and the disastrous effects of the liquor traffic, all are agreed. The drink bill for 1890 gives £139,500,000. I should like to ask how much was contributed by our Church. I know some ministers and laymen who are not responsible for a single penny of it. This gives an average of £3, 13s. per head of the population spent in drink. We spend on religion £18,000,000. Twenty shillings to

Bacchus, half-a-crown to Jesus Christ.[1] I would remind you of sentiments expressed in the *Times:*—"Drink baffles us, confounds us, shames us, and mocks us at every point. It outwits alike the teacher, the man of business, the patriot, and the legislator. Its devastating effects are seen in every class, it affects all sorts and conditions of men." I appeal to all Christian workers, I mean those who do not stay at home at ease after the day's work is done, but to those who are doing something in the Master's name. I am quite sure they will confirm my testimony when I say that this drink question confronts us at every turn. You would not have the condition of bad housing—referred to by previous speakers—if the people were abstainers. Two gentlemen said a little while ago to Mr. Caine, "We are going down to the East end, Caine, to see about these things, *vide* the *Bitter Cry*—can we do anything for you?" He replied, "Find me a teetotal family in the slums." They could not. I was in conversation with the son of a landlord, one who owned tenements of this sort, and he said, "My father has tried again and again to improve the condition of certain dwellings, but the moment a lead pipe or anything that can be removed is put in, it is taken away to be sold for drink." Until you can alter the condition of society in this respect, you will not very materially alter the existing condition of things.

I could speak of the ravages of this drink in connection with commercial life. I have seen much of the sad effects of indulgence in intoxicating liquors on the part of those who have been in commercial circles. When I came over in 1869 I knew only one friend in London, and he said, "I know your principles, but I don't think you will be able to stand the fag of city life unless you take a little wine." I tried, however, and I tried successfully.

We have to report, in reference to our work, that we have 3,569 Bands of Hope, an enrolled membership of 370,681, while of adult temperance societies there are 652, with 43,481 enrolled members. But the committee report the

[1] Quoted from Letter by Dawson Burns.

adult societies "still feeble and unsatisfactory," and I think
it is so. But one reason may be given. These figures do
not represent the number of total abstainers in connection
with our churches. One reason is, a great many of our
people are working either as free lances, or in connection
with the Church of England Temperance Society, or other
organisations. What is the remedy? I say God speed to
all! but, as a Church, let us come up to our true standard—
it will help us, and encourage us when we see the grand
total of our numerical strength. I venture to suggest that
we want abstaining ministers in all our circuits. When
that is accomplished—and we are on the way, we are
increasing—our work will be immensely assisted. Whilst
the dual platform is altogether unsuitable for actual work
amongst the people, we can unite on great social and
political questions, such as the closing of public-houses on
the Sabbath. If it be true that the drink traffic exists for
the benefit of the people—and that is often asserted—then
let the people have the control of the drink traffic. If all
our ministers could be persuaded to be abstainers, and
would take the lead in connection with our adult societies,
we need not wait for another hundred or fifty years, but
five or ten years would produce such results as would not
only astonish us but would evoke heartfelt praise and
gratitude to Almighty God for the altered condition of
things in this country.

We have taken part during the year in a very important
question—the memorial presented at the Brussels Conference for the suppression of the liquor traffic in Africa. It
is a tremendous evil, and that continually. In reference
to the Sunday-closing appeal, I hope we as a Church shall
be decided on that question. Then as to compensation to
the poor publicans. Well, if that is dead and buried, I
believe the Methodists had a great deal to do with the
interment. By God's help it shall never get on the
statute book. Our last move has been the appointment
of a Connexional Secretary. This is a triumph in the
right direction.

What are we to do for the future? Refuse to profit by the drink in any shape or form; and if any of you have invested in breweries and distilleries I hope you will lose not only your dividend but your principal. A friend here suggests that they did lose their principle, or they would not have put their money in. Come out distinctly on this question. It rests very largely with the Methodist Churches, because you have heard again and again that we have influenced other Churches in the past, and are influencing them to-day. They copy us. Why, even the Church of England so-called—the Church in England would be a better expression—is copying us all round. This is no time for indifference and apathy, no time simply to be horrified by what you read, or to express a godly sorrow and a hope that a better state of things will come about. The time for decisive action has come. Individual responsibility rests upon us. We are either helping or hindering. He who drinks is helping the drink traffic. It is a question to ask ourselves: Are our hands clean? Some of my friends say, "Do not you keep anything in the house for visitors?" Many abstainers think it would be inhospitable and wrong to force their principles upon their visitors. I have escaped these trammels. Whilst it may be perfectly safe for some of us to take the drink, it may be ruinous and disastrous for some of those who follow our example. Think of the influence of our example exerted upon our servants. That is a very important point. I believe that hundreds of servant girls are ruined by the example of their employers. Encouraged by the successes of the past, and assured of ultimate victory, let us *as* a Church follow the example of John Wesley, and have nothing to do with the "selling, buying, or using of strong drink." One of the ditties we used to sing in the early days of the temperance movement was this:—

> " We have fought the battle many a day,
> And still will fight whoever says nay ;
> For while strong drink shall lay men low,
> It will never do to give it up so."

The Sunken Strata.

By the Rev. T. B. STEPHENSON, LL.D.

I PROPOSE to put the notes of my speech into an old secretaire I have at home, and perhaps when the next Centenary comes round, some one will buy it in Wardour Street, and then write a homily, showing what imperfect ideas people had a century before. [The audience, however, decided otherwise, and Dr. Stephenson proceeded.] I have not time to discuss the amount of the vice and wretchedness which lies at the bottom of the social scale. I do not agree with the current estimate of that mass, that it is a tenth of the population. I rather accept Mr. Giffen's estimate of six or seven per cent., and could give many reasons for this if I had time. That is an important difference; it means the difference between two and three millions. Yet, even so, the number is appalling. Whence comes this almost hopeless mass? Many of them are hereditary paupers. We have a pauper class that dates back to the time of the monasteries. Then we have people pressed down by misfortune—the death or disablement from disease of the bread-winner. Great numbers are pressed down by competition, by the competition of the pauper foreigner coming in; and, most of all, of the unskilled labour which floods London and other great centres from the country districts. And then there are the people brought up without a regular occupation. Thousands of lads, between fourteen and seventeen, can do nothing better than help a costermonger, or wait for the chance of carrying a parcel. They must live, at best, a casual life. Then there are people ruined by drink.

But I maintain, in spite of all that has been said, these are not people who never had a chance. For seven years I invited sixty such people to tea every Sunday afternoon. More than once, after giving them a tea, I remember some saying, when I read a chapter, "You remember what that is in the Greek, Sir?" Some were University men ; they had had their chance. How many are there of these people who were never in the Sunday school? Not many. It is not true, speaking of the sunken strata as a whole, that they are composed of people who have never had a chance. Hence, half the things that are said about the Churches neglecting them are a libel. But this is no reason why we should refuse them another chance. We do not so treat our own people. How many in our congregations have had a thousand chances, yet we go on preaching to them. If these people have had chances, and wasted them all, it only makes the case stronger for trying to help them to the utmost of our power.

Here, then, is a vast mass of vice and sin and suffering. Let everybody try to deal with it. Let General Booth try. I say, God bless him! He will probably make a great many mistakes — but God bless him. Let George Hatton try ; let Benjamin Waugh try. It will require us all to deal with this social problem. No one set of forces will suffice. The statesman, the social reformer, the Christian enthusiast, are all wanted in this work. But who are the statesmen? the men who talk at Westminster? Yes ; but who are the men who send the men there to talk, and say what they shall say? The people of England : the whole people of England, who have votes at elections. And the duty of Christian citizenship is one of those obligations which must be preached until people are ready to practise it before we can settle this vast social problem.

Did you ever read John Wesley's *Word to a Freeholder?* " I hope," says he, " you have taken no money." If that wish is no longer required, let us ponder his next words : " Act as if the whole election depended upon your single vote, and as if the whole Parliament depended, and through it the whole nation upon that." I hope Methodists everywhere will remember these words, on every recurring parliamentary and municipal election, because we cannot deal with this great social question without dealing with some of the great political questions which must be solved within a few years.

The land laws of this country will have to be seriously modified, the transfer of property must be made easier and cheaper, the law of primogeniture must be abolished, the leasehold law must be modified, small holdings must be increased in number, allotments on a vast scale and under a generous system must be created. Why are the towns crowded? Because it is becoming harder and harder to get a living in the country. Make it worth men's while to stay on the land. Then we must have our education laws modified very largely. A free education must be placed within the reach of every child in the country without his having to pay blackmail for it to the parson or the squire, either in the form of compulsory attendance at a place of worship, which neither he nor his parent would have chosen, or in a cringing servility which makes it impossible for him to discharge freely and fearlessly his duties as a citizen. The brightest young fellows feel the pinch of this system, and are eager to get out of the villages into any atmosphere that is freer than that of the places in which they were born. In dealing with these and many like questions Methodism has a great part to play. Many other questions, more or less municipal in character, also demand solution. We must have much cheaper methods of passing from the centres of the great cities out to suburban parts, where workmen's cottages can be built. This bears on the question of overcrowding. As the nation gives great privileges to railways, we have the right to say that travelling for the workman to the only place where he can get a cottage should be made as cheap as possible. In Glasgow, the Corporation built a model lodging-house. The experiment answered so well that subsequently several have been built, and to a great extent the question of lodgings for the working people is solved there. The London County Council has resolved upon a similar experiment.

Such matters as these bring nearer to Christian men and women their direct responsibility for all that goes on within the area of the County Council, and by its authority. We must help to send the right men to the County Councils, and we must protect the men we send there and who do their duty when they get there. I am very proud that the only man who has been burnt in effigy for anything done in his work on the County Council is a Methodist. Sure I am it is the clear duty of every Christian, and therefore especially of every Methodist, to see that John M'Dougall and every man who took a right stand on the music-hall matter, and on all similar questions, shall not want a hearty, loyal support when the next election comes round.

How are we to deal further with the drainage of this vast moral swamp? We must have a great extension of woman's work. God forbid that our sisterhoods, or our more organised attempts in the way of the professional employment of women, should supersede or discourage that free, loving labour which thousands of Methodist women have been giving for years past. But, in the peculiar circumstances of our times, let us send a great army of godly and intelligent women into the abodes of poverty and sin, to carry life and light and healing there.

We must have a vast multiplication of mission efforts in connection with our powerful congregations. We must have big missions, but little missions too. The big missions are the counter-attraction to the great public-houses. The little missions are wanted to counteract the little public-houses. It is not the big public-houses that do all the mischief. Without going five yards from their own door people can get drink. We cannot get all our people into huge halls. We must have the little mission-halls up and down in the dark alleys, into which a woman can come in her rags; and where a work, not very showy but very real, can be done.

Again there must be a great popularising of our religious services throughout the country. I would not like to have all our services on the type of St. James's Hall or of the Salvation Army. We must have a great variety, and adapt the services to the wants of the people. It is of no use saying, in a suburb where highly cultivated people dwell, "We will come here with our big drum and you must have this kind of service," any more than it is wise to say to people who are not trained to it "You shall have the morning prayers, whether you like them or not." The principle of adaptation to the needs of the neigbour-hood must be most sedulously and carefully observed.

And, let me say, we ought to be prepared to undertake missions that will never pay financially. Ordinarily, I grant we ought to have regard to such considerations. But if we are to deal with the slums, we must be content that our voluntary love and sacrifice shall do for Metho-dism what endowments do for the Church of England. We must be prepared to work for Christ in certain low neighbourhoods, where we shall never have a self-support-ing Church, but where we shall have people won for the Redeemer.

Last of all, we must do a great deal more for the children. For there is the true chance for Christianity. Given 10,000 sunken men and women, above forty years of age. Take hold of them; do all you can with anxiety, with patience, with love, with faith, with prayer; watch them—and what percentage of result do you hope to get in twenty years? Will you be satisfied with fifty per cent? Looking at human nature, if, at the end of twenty years, you have tried to save 40,000, and had succeeded with 20,000, it would be a large proportion. But give me 20,000 children and let me expend upon them the like energy and expenditure for twenty years, and let me report to you. I have tried it, and therefore speak from experience. For every hundred children that you let us deal with, you may rely upon at least ninety-five per cent. of good results. Both on the ground that we want the highest possible result to our work, and because we want to bring to an end as speedily as possible this dreadful state of things that shocks and distresses us, in God's name let us save the children.

The Young People of Methodism.

———0———

By the PRESIDENT OF THE CONFERENCE.

THE PRESIDENT read a letter he had received from Dr. Osborn. The Bishopsgate Congregational Chapel sent a message of kindly greeting. I have had (proceeded the President) an intimation this evening that such messages would have come in considerable number had it been known that we were ready to accept these brotherly expressions of goodwill. Few things have been more remarkable in these celebrations than the heartiness with which those who belong to the sister Churches have responded to any communication that has been sent. I think it only due to make special reference to this intimation. We have not been announcing contributions, but I may mention a cheque for £5 from J. T. Waterhouse, of Honolulu. A Presbyterian friend has placed in my hands a cheque for three guineas. Our subject to-night is " The Privileges, Duties, Responsibilities, and Opportunities of the Young People of Methodism." Anyone who knows anything about John Wesley will know how he yearned over the young people, how deep and constant was his sympathy with them, and how ready they were to flock round him and receive his teaching and his counsel. May the young people always be

X

drawn towards the leaders of our own Church with the same sympathy and confidence they feel towards our great Founder!

The Lessons of the Early Time.

By the Rev. THOMAS ALLEN.

A GOOD friend once said to a gentleman who was about to enter Parliament: "John, thou art about to enter the House of Commons; no doubt thou wilt often speak there. There is one piece of advice which I should like to give thee. Always have the end of thy speech ready, for thou wilt never know the moment when thou mayest need it." Now, with such a programme as we have to-night, I feel that the end of my speech must not be far away; and therefore, if you will pardon the mixture, I will plunge in and swim across, and if I do not get drowned in the process I shall come up dripping on the other side.

I want to do one thing to-night, and only one, and that is, to send the young people of Methodism, and the old people too, back to the historic life of our Church.

I have been talking lately to one or two Methodist historians, and one or two Methodist antiquarians, and they all say one thing, that they are astonished and pained to find that the people of this generation know really so little about Wesley and early Methodism. If our young people will read the Journals of John Wesley, and the *Life of Wesley* by Tyerman, and if they find that great storehouse of facts taxes their patience rather too much, I will venture to substitute Telford for Tyerman; and if they will read Stevens's *History of Methodism*, they will find that, not to touch deeper questions, these books will refresh their intelligence vastly more than many of the milk and water—nay, the water and milk—stories which are in circulation at the present time.

But, as we all know, history is not merely a chronicle

of facts—history is a process, a growth ; and therefore the historian needs to be followed by the philosopher, whose work it is to trace facts to the causes which produced them. Now, I rejoice to know that, during the past twenty-five years, the period of the Evangelical Revival has commanded the attention of philosophical historians, and if the young people of Methodism, and the middle-aged and the old people too, will read Stoughton's *Ecclesiastical History of England*, Lecky's *History of England in the Eighteenth Century*, and *The Church in the Eighteenth Century*, by Abbey and Overton, they will be able to estimate the great spiritual movement which we celebrate to-night. They will be able to understand the purpose which it has served in the scheme of Divine Providence, and the contribution it has made to the development of the kingdom of God on the earth.

But outside the main story of our Church life there is a vast amount of local history, of family experience of a Methodist character,—in a word, a vast amount of spiritual folklore, which has never been committed to print. What is more enjoyable than to sit by the fireside while some old man—and if you want an illustration I will name Dr. Gregory—describes the scenes in which he has acted, and tells anecdotes which are full of the simplicity and humour of the olden time. One regrets very much to think how much of this spiritual folklore perishes with every generation. There are old people here; your associations have been connected with Methodism. You have got recollections in your souls out of which volumes might be written. I ask you to communicate this interesting folklore to your children and grandchildren. And there are young people in this audience to-night— may I ask them with all affection to sit at the feet of these fathers, these old people, and to listen to what they have to say? And then they will have the opportunity in years to come of helping to continue the blessed traditions of the Methodist Church: and God grant they may be continued !

Sir, the life of Methodism has been a wonderful life after all. Some people may not think so, but our opinion is perfectly clear and definite as to this point. The life of Methodism is the outcome of those providential and spiritual forces which are the life - blood of all communities, whether ecclesiastical or civil. The early Methodists, for example, had a wonderful faith in Divine Providence. Methodism is the child of Providence, from beginning to end. You are familiar with the old Methodist Magazines. In those books the Providence of God is illustrated in a very remarkable manner. It may be a little heresy of my own, but I am rather disposed to think that their conception of Providence tended to develop in the early Methodists a touch of self-complacency. Some of them were disposed to think they were the favourites of the Almighty, and better than other folks. There is nothing like a true conception of Divine Providence for chastening a spirit of that kind. I am not going to say that Divine Providence is never special; but we have found out in these latter days that the care of God is expressed to a great extent in the constitution of the world, and in the laws of nature, which operate with so much regularity and certainty, and we have to study these laws and conform our action thereto.

When we consider the origin of Methodism, the external opposition it has conquered, the internal difficulties it has mastered, and the proportions to which it has grown in the various countries of the world, none can doubt that, as in the life of Israel so in the life of Methodism, the Providence of God has been an inspiring and directing force, and I am perfectly certain it will so continue to be.

Then the early Methodists were wonderful believers in the power of Divine grace. Thank God for that. Those good men never stayed to ask whether men differed in spiritual capacity, or how far Divine action was accommodated to the constitution and laws of human nature. They believed that the grace of God could produce something like equal results in all men, and therefore they used to insist that men of all types should pass through the same spiritual mould. Thousands of men in the early times developed capacities of life and service of which they had been utterly unconscious themselves. Very likely a certain number were injured by the pressure which was brought to bear upon them. People of peculiar individuality were unable to conform their experience and testimony to the common standard, and sometimes they were looked upon with doubt and suspicion. Sir, I rejoice to say that our spiritual theory is wider to-day. We do not expect every man to sound precisely the same spiritual note. We are content that every man should be developed by the Almighty on the lines of his own constitution and nature.

But while we have grown in breadth, I am afraid we have lost in force. It seems to me that the conversion of men, their sanctification, their testimony in prayer and praise, are not so definite as they used to be fifty or sixty years ago. I am quite aware that education has developed human taste and sensitiveness, and this has chastened the expression of Christian feeling. But let us be sure that we have the feeling. It seems to me that a great deal of experience in our Churches to-day is very indefinite, and that is the reason so many fight shy of spiritual fellowship. Their life will not bear description, and if that sort of thing is to spread it will turn the Churches of Methodism into mere congregations. If this Commemoration shall be the means of helping us to get back our original enthusiasm, I will tell you what it will do. Thousands of men will be developed in the spiritual line as men used to be developed. They will find out their spiritual capacities, and that is precisely what thousands of men and women in Methodism to-day need to do ; and they will use these capacities in the highest and most spiritual forms of Divine service.

The life of Methodism was marked by wonderful simplicity in the early times. It was originated just at the time when Puritanism had modified the artificial ceremonialism of ecclesiastical and civil life. It concerned itself with inward realities, and not with outward display; and yet, thank God, it did display itself in forms that were most original and striking—in the bitterness of penitence, in the joy of forgiveness, in outspoken testimony, in triumphant song, and in practical efforts to bring men to the feet of our Lord Jesus Christ. The Great Revival fetched men out of the most unlikely places, and it influenced them most profoundly. Think of Thomas Olivers, the shoemaker and poet. Think of John Nelson, the stonemason; Robert Carr Brackenbury, the country squire; the Countess of Huntingdon, the aristocrat; Dr. Adam Clarke and Joseph Benson, the commentators; Sammy Hick, the village blacksmith; William Dawson, the Yorkshire farmer; and John Hunt, the ploughman. These are names that have been household words in our families for generations. We remember the three Jacksons; Thomas and Samuel occupied the chair of the Conference, and Robert was a most active minister for many years. The Great Revival fetched these three men out of the cottage of a farm-labourer. There is not a Church outside Methodism that could have done for those three men what Methodism did. In the early times there were men in our Church of remarkable spiritual originality; in speech and action they were as fresh as the breezes of the morning in summer time. Somehow we don't seem to produce such men to-day. We have more educated men than we ever had, and we are not lacking in prudent men, men who know how to conform to the regulations and habits of Church life. But I feel that we need original men—in the spiritual sense. The social influences of this age are conforming us to a common type. Our danger to-day is spiritual monotony; we need a fresh baptism of the Holy Ghost, such as will bring out everything that is fresh and individual in men. The resources of human nature are not exhausted; they are only latent, like the life of plants in winter time.

When the heightened temperature of summer comes, all the flowers begin to blossom, and they seem to vie with each other in the contributions they make to the general display of life. And so it should be in the Church of Jesus Christ. If the spiritual atmosphere were only as warm and genial everywhere as it ought to be, men of all sorts would blossom under its influence, and the display of life in the Church would be as varied and fresh as the efflorescence of nature in tropical climes.

We hear a great deal to-day about the future of Methodism, and as to whether Methodism is to continue, and so on. Well, if Methodism is to continue, we must get the young people of Methodism converted to God. I cannot develop this point; but I will say further that, if we are to keep the young people of Methodism, we must not be afraid of saying to the world that we are a Church of Jesus Christ. We are discharging all the functions of such a spiritual institution. Of course the Anglicans, the extreme men, question our authority, but then their authority is questioned by the Romanists. I am disposed to dispute the very conception of historical channels through which alone Divine grace has flowed to men. The principle of Protestantism is that all men may come to God through the one Mediator, and receive Divine grace without the intervention of any particular order of men. That is a broad principle, and it has landed us in excessive freedom. But I would a great deal rather have that than the opposite extreme—a rigid uniformity and a repressive priestism.

Methodism, they say, is not ritualistic enough for people to-day. That is a matter which needs to be looked at and considered. There can be no doubt that, as a reaction against the false taste of the seventeenth and the eighteenth centuries, a wave of historic and artistic sympathy has gone over nearly the whole of Europe, and all the Churches have taken advantage of it to improve their architecture and worship. Why should we not do the same? People have filled their houses with musical instruments and pictures; they have even improved the ritual of the dinner-table. And why should we not improve all organised expressions of Christian faith and life? Culture is the handmaid of Jesus Christ. People say you may care for the outward until you sacrifice the inward. We know that perfectly well. Indeed, it is possible for a Church to become a sort of Madame Tussaud's, a show made up of beautifully dressed figures, but figures with no life in them. But however we may seek to improve the spectacle of Christianity, we must always remember that our first duty is to cultivate it as inward and conscious life; and, when we have done that, let us display it in worship and in institutional forms. But, first and foremost, let us display it in those forms of practical religion and social fellowship and evangelistic enterprise for which our fathers were so distinguished.

As to the future of Methodism, I will leave that. Let me say that I rejoice in the new outburst of life and zeal which we have in our Methodist Church. There is a great deal that is pessimistic in this age. The age is disconsolate. But the early Methodists were a bright and happy people, their life went up on the wings of song to the very gates of heaven. And so it may be with us. You should read Charles Wesley's birthday hymn during this time—

> " Away with our fears,
>   The glad morning appears
> When an heir of salvation was born !
>   From Jehovah I came,
>   For His glory I am,
> And to Him I with singing return.
>
> " In a rapture of joy
>   My life I employ,
> The God of my life to proclaim ;
>   'Tis worth living for this,
>   To administer bliss
> And salvation in Jesus's name."

By means of the evangelism which is abroad everywhere we shall bring the people by thousands into our Church ;

and let us try to conserve these results by discipline and wise administration. Then we shall not merely extend our Church during the next century, but we shall build it up, and it will be like Jerusalem in the olden time, a "city that is compact together." God grant it may be so!

Methodism a Church of Jesus Christ.

By the Rev. J. SCOTT LIDGETT.

WE have not only to commemorate the past, but to make the history of the future, and, as Mr. Allen has just told us, we claim to be one of the Christian Churches of this country. It is a great thing to make good the claim to be a Church of Jesus Christ. We cannot do it by tracing pedigrees, by taking one by one the doctrines of our creed, and proving that we have scriptural authority for them. We cannot do it merely by proving that the constitution of our Church is a scriptural constitution; and we cannot do it even by showing, as we have often done before and as we shall often do again, that the rise of Methodism was natural, was necessary, was providential, a century and a-half ago. It is the living Spirit which makes the living Church; and there are certain tests which must constantly be applied to those who claim to be a Church of Jesus Christ.

The first great test is this, Are you possessed by, are you in possession of, the living personal Jesus Christ? Have you caught His central meaning? Are you setting that central meaning forth? And have you, by the gift of the blessed Spirit, the power to bring that living Jesus Christ face to face with men?

Next, have you the power to come into relationship—the spiritual power I mean—with all men; to inspire the whole of man's life; to foster and to direct; and, so far as spiritual influence can do it, to perfect every human

330 CENTENARY SERMONS AND ADDRESSES.

power, and to order every social relationship in and for Jesus Christ our Lord?

And the last test, it seems to me, is this, Can you pass from the past to the future? Can you close the record of one century and pass on to the record of the next? Can you enter into new conditions, and change them and be changed by them, and yet in the midst of them be constant, losing nothing of the old but coming into securer possession of it all? Can you change and meet the difficult requirements of new ages, and yet have all the more the living Christ and the power of His presence realised in your midst?

These, sir, it seems to me, are the great tests which every Church must meet ; and they are the tests which will be applied most rigorously by the age in which we have to live, and the age which is yet to come. For, mark you, all the changes which are going on around us at the present time—the downfall of antiquated forms of thought and belief, the inrush of new conceptions and new knowledge, are only making men ask more urgently for the living personal Christ, for His meaning, and for the Divine touch and power upon the hearts and consciences of our time. We have an age to meet which knows the preciousness for all men of what are called the humanities, as no other age has realised it before ; and we have an age which, owing largely to the influence of our fathers and of John Wesley, while remembering the transcendent importance of the individual, begins to see the questions of society and the community coming into view. We are coming to see that individuals and Churches must find their true life by losing it, in and for the kingdom of Jesus Christ, as it is to be realised on earth when His will is done as it is done in heaven.

And if these tests are going to be applied to all Churches, how will Methodism meet them? I should like to say that there is one thing which our age is asking for— it is ultimate realities; and if you will go back to early Methodism, to its theology and life, you will find that the characteristic mark of Methodism is just that reality which this age seeks; the reality of men's union as a race created and redeemed in Jesus Christ; the reality of the terrible, the awful fact of sin; the reality of a living, conscious, transforming relation to a personal Saviour, Jesus Christ— a real reconciliation, consciously felt—a real salvation from a real sin—a real and blessed and brotherly Church fellow-ship—a real, practical Christianity, seen in the fruits of far-seeing philanthropy—and a real, far-reaching, practical efficiency to deal with the changing circumstances of our time.

I say that the more we study this Methodism of ours the more we shall come to see that in its living faiths, principles, and aims, we have not the gospel of the yester-day of our fathers, not the gospel of the day in which we live, so much as the gospel of to-morrow and the days which are after that. We shall see that the great privi-lege, duty, responsibility, and advantage of the young people who are Methodists is just this—that our precious heritage is the gift of that gospel with which the coming age must be met, and by which its demand must be satisfied, that you have not to spend your time in unlearn-ing half that which your fathers in the gospel have handed down to you.

The coming Church will be the Church which lives most consciously in the presence and power of Jesus Christ. The Church of the future will be the Church which catches from Him His broad and blessed and universal human sympathy. The Church of the future, confronted with the great social problems with which we have to do, will be the Church which is instinct with hope, and has the worthiest conceptions of the coming of the Kingdom of God to all men; which faces most bravely, in the light and strength of that hope, the terrible social and moral and religious wrongs amid which we live; and which has the greatest power to call forth the enthusiastic self-sacrifice of those who are its members. And I ask this evening, in the presence of God and of this congregation, Why should not this Methodism of ours be that Church in the twentieth century? And the answer depends on this— *Will* its young people realise and bravely accept the glorious trust which is handed down to them from those who have gone before?

But if they are to do that they must be led. I believe there never was a time when the young people of Methodism were more ready to follow. But they must be led.

If we lose our young people it will largely be because they find more inspiring and more capable leaders elsewhere, or because, instead of satisfying them, our ministrations have deadened them and have dissatisfied them. We want leaders in the ministers, in those who shape the policy of our Churches—for Wesley was a leader to the very last moment of his life. He was in advance of the whole army that followed him. And if you and I are un-Christlike, slovenly, narrow, self-satisfied, easy-going, then the cause is hopelessly and for ever lost. We want leaders—men of wide, lofty, Christlike aims; men of self-sacrifice, of practical wisdom; men who are not content to do a tidy, decent little bit of business in the Church of Jesus Christ—but men who know that this world is to be transformed, and who will not rest on the earth till Christ in heaven has His rights. We want the men to lead of whom their enemies may say, " The men who have turned the world upside down are come hither also." And if we get such men, endued with the power of the Holy Ghost —God grant we may have them to-night, God grant every one of us may be made such a man and such a woman—then I have no fear but that the young people will enthusiastically rise to our call, and the deposit of blessed and saving power will be brought forth and handed down to the times that are to come.

There is a great message to be addressed to the wealthy parents of Methodism in the present day. Many a Solomon has carried his wisdom with him to his grave; but, in the worthlessness and ruin of a Rehoboam, his ostentation and careless indifference have borne their fruits. Many a

son of Methodism has borne out the evil result of the
folly of his father. Are we to train our children to the
pursuit of wealth or honour? In that case the atheism in
which they will end is lurking already in our hearts. Are
we going to put them to the service of Jesus Christ, bringing them to His altar, training them in godly simplicity
as Wesley was, with many prayers and with unsparing
watchfulness? Are we going to pray that the flower of our
young ladies may join the Sisters of the People, that our
best-educated men may vow themselves to the cause of
God and the people for ever? Then shall the parents of
Methodism discharge their responsibility. And then, young
people, the responsibility rests fully upon you and me.

Wesley has won us a vantage-ground for the work of
the coming generation. He has not only founded the
Methodist Church, he has uplifted the general level of
faith. But he has only won us a vantage-ground. The
Book of the Wars of the Lord of Hosts is not completed
yet. Its greatest chapters are yet to be written in the days
to come, perhaps while you and I are yet alive. We want
men who, in the faith of Jesus Christ, will use evangelism,
theology, science, philanthropy, to carry the battle with
sin and Satan to the gate, in every department of human
thought, of politics, of economics, of social and spiritual
life. And the great message of this Centenary to-night is
that we, in the presence of our fathers, encompassed by so
great a cloud of witnessess, should yield up ourselves as
they did to the all-saving Jesus Christ, and then go forth
to quit us like men and be strong.

Methodism and Local Preachers.

By Mr. W. OWEN CLOUGH, F.R.G.S., F.S.S., Etc.,

PRESIDENT OF THE LOCAL PREACHERS' MUTUAL AID ASSOCIATION.

I DO not think this celebration would be complete if a
department of Methodism which has done much to build

up its success were not represented ; and especially, I think, is it appropriate that the office which I hold this year—by the accident of an accident—brings me here on an evening when the young are especially appealed to. I propose to-night to build up certain facts, with a view to show that local preachers will continue to be an absolute necessity in the Methodist Church, and then I intend to appeal to the young men who are present, and to that larger congregation who may read the proceedings of this evening.

The Founder of our Church did not willingly admit lay-helpers. He was a stickler for law and order. Having to be absent from London, he left Thomas Maxfield, in 1739, to take charge of the Society, to meet the classes, and to give such attention as might be necessary. Maxfield went a little further than was intended, and went on to expound the Scriptures, and *to preach*. This was represented to Mr. Wesley, and he very quickly turned his face towards London, to put a stop to this irregularity ; and you can understand how stern he would be. Coming back to London he came into the presence of his mother, who saw he was much distressed, and asked him what was the matter. He said, " Thomas Maxfield has turned preacher, I find." His mother replied, " John, you know what my sentiments have been, you cannot suspect me of favouring readily anything of this kind. But take care what you do in respect of that young man, for *he is as surely called of God to preach as you are.* Examine what have been the fruits of his preaching, and *hear him also yourself.*" She sent him to do what I would like the educated Methodists of this generation to do, to go and hear the local preacher. Wesley went and heard him, and all Wesley could say was, " It is the Lord's doing, let Him do as seemeth Him good." His prejudice gave way. Thomas Maxfield was the first local preacher of Wesleyan Methodism.

As the Church extended, the necessity for such help increased, and so Thomas Maxfield was followed by Thomas Richards, and he by Thomas Westall, and so on until to-day. And the necessity for lay help which existed in

1739 is not only as great to-day, but vastly greater. I affirm that Methodism is impossible without its local preachers.

I hold a plan of the Louth Circuit, where I was last Sunday week, a plan with thirty-seven preaching-places, and there are three itinerant ministers, as we say, "to work the circuit." This circuit of Louth is twenty-four miles across. The circuit of Sleaford covers seven hundred square miles, and there are three ministers to work that circuit. Extend your vision a little farther. I have selected six circuits out of the many in Methodism— Retford, Louth, Pateley Bridge, Malton, Salisbury, and Leek. I am determined to build up my position safe and sure in order that my appeal may be irresistible to the young men of Methodism. These are the figures :—

	Ministers.	Local Preachers.	Pr. Places.	Services.	Conducted by	Local Preachers' Sermons to one Ministerial.
					Min. L.P.	
Retford, . .	3	52	35	59	9 .. 50	3½
Louth, . .	3	67	37	45	6 .. 39	7
Pateley Bridge,	3	43	27	44	7 .. 37	5
Malton, . .	3	51	34	33	8 .. 31	4
Salisbury, .	3	60	27	54	7 .. 47	7
Leek, . .	3	55	27	43	6 .. 37	6
TOTAL, .	18	328	187	264	43 ..241	6

Let us take our own, our Mother Church. In the Wesleyan Methodist Society the local preachers are eight times as numerous as the travelling preachers. Out of every seven services taken throughout this country in Methodism, five are taken by local preachers. I am speaking now of what we call "the old body." There are 5,500 pulpits dependent every Sunday upon local preachers. What would it cost Methodism to supply these services? I will put a local preacher's services as worth five shillings a sermon. If they are not worth that they are not worth anything; and I may say that is the estimate many people put upon them. That would be a cost to Methodism of £2,750 per Sunday, or £143,000 for the year. What would it cost to supply these places if, for instance, local preachers were to go on strike?

On Monday evening there was a meeting held in this place, representing the Methodists of all the Connexions. I am going to tell you the number of chapels there are to supply in each Connexion :—

	Preaching Places.	Ministers (including O. T. and Supernumeraries).	Local Preachers.
Wes. Meth. (Grt. Brit.), .	8,000	2,004	16,038
" " (Irish Conf.), .	2,087	232	1,856
Meth. New Connexion, .	430	171	1,114
Primitive Methodist, . .	5,858	1,042	16,037
Bible Christian, . . .	467	141	1,146
United Meth. Free Church, .	1,333	343	3,646
Wesleyan Reform Union, .	204	18	465
TOTAL, . . .	18,379	3,920	39,972

Estimated in same ratio as Great Britain.

That is a proportion of ten local preachers to one itinerant minister. In 1796, fifty-six years after that first local preacher began his work and five years after Mr. Wesley's death, for the first time in Methodism there was a meeting constituted which is still known as the local preachers' quarterly meeting—a very anxious time for some brethren, because on that occasion certain questions are put from the chair (the superintendent minister presiding) which may be referred to as "searching." They apply to the doctrine of the brother, his attention to duty, his fitness for the work, and his moral character. The man who can run the gauntlet of that "searching" for forty or fifty or sixty years, as many do, is worthy of being listened to. To become a candidate he must satisfy the superintendent minister as to his knowledge of the Second Catechism and the elements of English Grammar. He must pass a twelve-months' probation. He must be "heard preach," and then he must have read the fifty-three "Standard Sermons" of Mr. Wesley, and Mr. Wesley's "Notes on the New Testament." One of the most beneficent things the Conference ever did was to impose that condition. At the end they "hear" him ; they appoint some one to listen to him, who reports ; and if the report is satisfactory he is subjected to an examination, and if he satisfies the superintendent minister and the local preachers' meeting—and there is generally some brother with some technical theological question—he is then received on "full plan," *and from that day all care for the intellectual life of the local preacher disappears.*

If you take the itinerant ministry, the candidate must pass certain examinations, go through a course at College for three years, and even then must be under the supervision of Conference for four years, must read certain books, and pass an annual examination until the time of his ordination. I want to do something to raise the intellectual status of the body I represent. Is it fair that nine-tenths of the preachers in the Methodist Connexions to-day should not have their intellectual life over-looked, and their studies directed, by the Church to which they give their services ? I hope that one result of this celebration will be that there will be a centre formed in every circuit where the local preacher shall submit himself to a course of wisely directed study, adapted to his life, ultimately bringing him into the position of being able to stand up before all the good results of the Education Act of 1870.

The influence of our Church is very great. The *Times* of March 2 said : " It follows that in Great Britain the Wesleyan Methodist Churches, taken as a whole, constitute the largest Protestant Communion next to that of the Church of England ; while if other parts of the world, and especially the United States, be taken into account.

Wesleyan Methodism may not unreasonably claim to number a larger body of adherents than any other Protestant Church." If this be so I claim for the men whom I represent here to-night, that they have, under God and under the guidance and direction of our ministers, aided in the work of building up this great Church, and of bringing us to-day to our glorious position.

The local preachers' services are gratuitous. I mention this lest any brother may think that he can lay up a good store of this world's goods for his old age in this work. They do not even thank you and reappoint you, as they do trustees and other Church officers. We are simply expected to go on, and we are glad to go on. I met a brother at the door of a chapel one Sunday who, learning that a Mr. Gilbert was going to take the service, said, "Oh, I shan't stay—it's only a local." I said to him, "Did you ever lend him a book? Did you ever try to direct his studies? I will undertake to say, if this is the Mr. Gilbert that I know, that you will hear a sermon that will do more to build up your spiritual life than all you will hear in the City, at your club, during the next month."

There was, in connection with the Thanksgiving Fund, a fund formed to aid necessitous local preachers, and last year £298 was voted by the Committee of that Fund for that purpose. For I am glad to be able to say that, although Methodism does very little for the intellectual life of her local preachers—as regards the physical life, there is some attempt made to help them in extreme old age. Those who have the Official Handbook will see that I am associated with what is called the Local Preachers' Mutual Aid Association. In 1849 this Association was established, and consisted of local preachers in Wesleyan Methodism, the United Methodist Free Churches, and the Wesleyan Reform Union. These three bodies were one at that time, and for the purposes of this Association we solved all problems of reunion by never being separated. Its object is to afford relief during sickness and old age,

to provide a sum of money payable at death, and to relieve
local preachers' widows. We believe that

" They also serve who only stand and wait."

The amount disbursed up to the present in this way has
been £106,175. At the present time there are upon the
funds of this Society 377 aged and utterly penniless
annuitants, including 97 widows. There is being paid,
mainly out of the free gifts of honorary members and
collections. the sum of £4,712, 10s. per annum; so that
some attention is paid to necessitous local preachers.

The local preachers of Methodism have specially done
their duty in respect to sound doctrine, and to maintaining
the Protestantism of our Church. A letter was sent by
Mr. Champness the other night, and I propose to read
from it one sentence : " I look upon every village chapel
as an outpost of Protestantism ; and I say to all who care
for the right of genius, liberty of speech and hearing. stand
by those who preach the gospel to the men who live by
the plough." I want the young men of Methodism to
come and help us to do it.

I would like to tell you of some cases which appear in
our report. Here is a poor old man who, after eighty-two
years of life and fifty years of service as a local preacher,
is in destitute circumstances ; another, eighty-three years
old, who has given fifty-three years of service ; another, of
ninety, who has given seventy-one years—and now,

" In age and feebleness extreme."

they are without the necessaries of life. I might tell you
of the widows of our local preachers—one of seventy-six
years, whose husband was a local preacher for forty-seven
years ; another of eighty, whose husband preached for fifty
years.

We want brethren who will go into this work, and bring
to it their wealth, their education, their social position ;
every power and influence they possess ; their burning zeal
for men, the noblest passion that can fill the human heart.

We want your help—at your peril stand aside!   There is
a responsibility resting here on every educated Methodist
to go into this work and help the Church.   Through this
strait gate all the ministry of this Church has gone.   If
you have felt this burning zeal for mankind, give your
hearts to God and your lives to His people.

> " Thou must be true thyself
> If thou the truth would'st teach ;
> Thy soul must overflow if thou
> Another soul would'st reach.
> It needs the overflow of heart
> To give the lips full speech.
> *Think* truly and thy thoughts
> Shall the world's famine feed ;
> *Speak* truly and each word of thine
> Shall be a fruitful seed ;
> *Live* truly and thy life shall be
> A great and noble creed."

The Past and the Future.

By the Rev. THOMAS E. WESTERDALE.

WE have heard a great deal about the history of Methodism this week, but the future of Methodism lies in the
fascination and unused power of that section of Methodism
this great meeting represents.   If this Commemoration
means anything, it means that Methodism is not decaying.
There are many things in history and in nations to
support the theory of the historic passing away of great
forces, and if you apply the test to Church systems and
Church beliefs, you will find the same development,—
periods of great prosperity followed by periods of almost
complete effacement ; and so confused and bewildered are
some people by this historic process, that in the midst of
all the enthusiasm of these great meetings, there are those
who persist in saying that our special mission, as such,
is ended, and that we must now simply take our place
as one of the ordinary Churches of the land.   And the
strangest thing of all about this modern delusion concern-

ing Methodism is the complacency with which some of
our own people are mentally consenting to the effacement of a system, which not only shows no signs of
decay, but indications that it is still but in the infancy
of that moral regeneration God purposes to accomplish
by its blessed agency.

I have nothing in my heart to-night but the fullest
hopes concerning our coming Methodism. It is not in the
mind of God or in the nature of things that great spiritual
movements must of necessity break up and pass away.
God's promise unto you is, "I will do better unto you
. . . than at your beginnings," and when the present
indefiniteness concerning modern Methodism has worn
itself out by the glow and fervour of that new life which
is breaking out, thank God, in all our circuits, the slow
of heart amongst us to believe, will be the very first
to admit the deception of their senses. What we are
suffering from just now is the result of our magnificent
success in days gone by. When there was no inner
Church in Methodism—when the Church was made up of
units, each unit representing a new conversion—fire, love,
zeal, holy enthusiasm were the order of the day; they
ruled the pulpit, they ruled the pew, they took possession
of the class-meeting, the leaders' meeting, and every bit
of Methodist plant throughout the Connexion, and the
land was filled with soul-converting energy. But during
the last thirty or forty years a new order has arisen, so
reserved and restrictive that some of us hardly know
what to do when Sunday comes round. But it will work
itself right; the old times are coming back, there are signs
of abundance of rain; and you may depend upon it,
when Methodism is convalescent once more, the God
of our fathers will come down and bless us with yet more
abundant power.

I heard a man say the other day that the Forward
Movement would ruin Methodism. Well, it will ruin his
view of Methodism, and the sooner the better. It is an
outrage on historic fact to say that if John Wesley were

here amongst us now, he would not bless our Forward Movement. John Wesley had a large bump for order and system and organisation, and things of that sort, and succeeded in keeping certain men in their proper places much better than any Conference has succeeded since. But the more the vision of his glorious life bursts on our view to-day, the more certain is it that John Wesley was the greatest religious reformer and ecclesiastical amender the world has ever seen ; and until men can convince me that the two processes for which God called him into existence have been exhausted—*first*, the purification of organised Christianity by the leaven of a converted ministry, and, *secondly*, the saving of that great outside world which organised Christianity never reaches—I will never assent to the proposition that the mission of Methodism is ended.

Don't let us be dazed by the stationary position of Methodism in some neighbourhoods, or the prophecies of despairing men. If Methodism is anything it is supernatural, the gift of God to our lost and ruined world ; and so long as there are abuses to be exposed in the established religions of the world, and multitudes of unsaved people whom no Church ever reaches, just so long will the supernatural call and mission of Methodism be alive as verily and as certainly as when God first sent John Wesley forth to spread scriptural holiness throughout the land. If we could throw ourselves back for a hundred years, amid those scenes which took place in this very chapel, when they buried him in early morn, for fear of a tumult if they had buried him later in the day,—I say, if we could place ourselves amid those scenes,—John Wesley gone, a Church of 80,000 members and 500,000 church followers without a personal leader, mutinous trustees abroad in some circuits ready to defy the Deed of Declaration, we might tremble then for the ark of God, and wonder whether our mission would not collapse. But since God has brought us through a full century of trouble and of glory since then, and established our goings until we are numbered now by at least 30 millions of followers throughout the length and breadth of the world, nothing but an inconceivable breakdown of capacity can ever dislodge us from the glorious place God intends us to fill in the destiny of the world.

I am going to make no apology for the semi-dazed condition of Methodism in some directions, its restless tendency towards new and dangerous experiments, its longing desire in some cases to escape the class-meeting test. For true it is that, in spite of all our empty chapels and apparent incapacity to fascinate certain particular neighbourhoods, Methodism is the greatest Protestant evangelical power in the world to-day ; and I am one of those who believe that when the ancient barriers which now block the way to perfect religious equality in this country are swept down by the advancing tides of the new democracy, Methodism, not only in America and in our Colonies, but in the land of its birth, will stand forth possessed with the first charm and claim to the confidence of those new and liberated forces. God made us not to die, but to live, and to go on increasing until glory shall crown what grace has begun. I do not want to indulge my soul, or the spirit of this great meeting, with any undue exaltation ; but if the nineteenth century is the best century the world has ever seen, it is because John Wesley and his faithful followers have made it so ; and if this leaven of blessing is to continue and increase, we must get back to the simplicity of our forefathers, both as to their trust in God and the manner of their daily Christian living. I am getting sick and tired— I know thousands are—at the distractions and confused counsels of modern-day Methodism. As far as fundamental and constitutional Methodism is concerned, there is very little that young Methodism desires to see altered ; if we change at all, let us change backwards, back to those forms and ways that made the children of our early Methodism so intense and spiritual in all their ways. But, as far as practical modern duty is concerned, there must be a great change. Our card-playing and our dancing, our going to the Sacraments on Sunday night and the theatre on Monday night—away with it! It is not Methodism, it is not religion, it is not Christianity; and if we cannot do the work God has given us to do without such alliances —well, the sooner our glory is taken from us and given to another, the better!

There were plenty of religions in the world before John Wesley was born, magnificent modifications of the finest modern thought of their day; and if you simply want Methodism to come down to one of those regular Church orders and systems, with no other end in view than to compete with some neighbouring church or chapel for the greatest amount of local Church patronage and support, that is no more like John Wesley's Methodism than black's white; and the sooner the Archbishop of Canterbury absorbs us once more into the bosom of his own communion, the better. But if you want to see the world saved, the Church purified by a holy ministry, the masses of the people brought down under the convicting power of God's Holy Spirit, then pray for the old times to come back again.

What we want is another Pentecost, a glorious revival. Very nearly the last words that Mr. Beauchamp left to the Methodist people were these. He said, "We have everything that is magnificent in Methodism just now—beautiful chapels, a marvellous organisation; all we want is a glorious revival." Brethren, let us pray for it. If you love Methodism, young men, pray for it. If you want a revival in your own heart, in your own home, in your own circuit, pray for it.

> "The praying spirit breathe,
>   The watching power impart;
> From all entanglements beneath,
>   Call off my anxious heart."

I pray that the blessing may be universal,—that wherever there is a Methodist heart to pray, a Methodist home to bless, a Methodist chapel to fill, it may come down in showers of blessing. If so, the temple of the twentieth

century shall surpass in glory the most radiant forms of
the building we are now completing, and the cry will still
go up to heaven, "The best of all is, God is with us!"

An Appeal to Young Methodism.

By Mr. GEORGE J. SMITH of Truro.

I HAVE experienced this evening some of the advantages
and some of the disadvantages of being one of several
speakers to whom is committed the same text. Coming
thus late, one has this awkwardness, that some of the
provinces which one fondly hoped were one's own copyright have been already invaded; but, on the other hand,
one is certainly spared the necessity of any introduction.

I need not now prove to you that young Methodism
has *opportunities* and *privileges* which involve *duties* and
responsibilities. I will simply, in the briefest terms, try
to announce some of what seem to me to be the chief
privileges of Methodist youth to-day.

There is, first of all, the glorious privilege of our spiritual
ancestry. The echoes of this building, and all the services
of this week hitherto, absolve me from the necessity of
dwelling on the life and labours of the great man whose
Centenary we are celebrating. We derive our strength from
no human name; but young Methodism shall never be
ashamed of him whose name we record in our distinctive
appellation as a portion of the Church Universal. No
religious community need desire a more glorious source
for its distinct existence than that great revival of one
hundred and fifty years ago, which awoke the churches as
well as the world around, which reared again the banner
of the truth, which renewed the face of the land, and
which, as impartial and secular historians remind us,
saved England from the perils of a revolution such as
that of France. And now, with one hundred and fifty

346 CENTENARY SERMONS AND ADDRESSES.

years behind us and with a new era before us, young Methodism pledges itself to follow those who have gone before us, as they followed Christ.

And, sir, if we bless God to-night for our spiritual ancestry, and for our heritage from the past, not less will we bless Him for our present,—that we have the old doctrines still in our midst, that we have a "free, full, and present salvation" still sounding from our pulpits, and that "Christianity in earnest," the name our fathers earned, is not yet a misnomer for their sons.

A further privilege has been briefly touched upon by Mr. Allen. In this age in which we live, when social progress, social reform, social regeneration, are in the air all about us—are the demand of the age—young Methodists find that the Church of their fathers is the Church of all others that has most studied and developed the social element of Christian life. That is a privilege which I press upon the youth of Methodism. Ours is as truly and distinctively social Christianity as it is "Christianity in earnest." In addition to this, we have material advantages, intellectual resources, civil and religious liberties; with here and there a measure of wealth and of culture which God has given in response to the faithfulness in little of those who have gone before us, and which God never meant to be drags upon our chariot wheels, but additional levers in our hands for the better lifting of the world.

Such, sir, as briefly as I can put them, are a few of the many privileges of young Methodism to-day.

What, then, are our responsibilities? Clearly, to perpetuate and to extend these glorious blessings to those who come after us; freely having received, freely to give; to work and labour, and, by God's blessing, to succeed— not only as those who have gone before us, but in the ratio of our greater means, greater intellectual advantages and wider open doors which are ours to-day. A mighty responsibility verily! And how shall we young men of Methodism set about it?

First, under God, by standing fast and firm by the Church

of our fathers. Granted that some here and there may conscientiously and intelligently discern their spiritual home—their mode of worship, their sphere of labour—else-where. We argue not with them. God's blessing go with them. But to those, if they were represented here to-night, who show a tendency to outgrow that which, under God, has made their fathers great, to those who seem drawn hither or thither by vague and visionary ideas of some advantage other than spiritual, to those I could talk—if they were here. I would say, first, see at least what your Church has done and is ; mark well her bulwarks ; read her history, and mark the results of her life. Truly those Old Testament saints were rightly inspired to set up memorials in the Ebenezers which marked the path of the children of Israel, and put it on record that their children were to be taught these lessons after them. And if any considerable numbers of our youth secede from us, it will largely be from our neglect of these glorious mnemonics of the past. Our history, up to date, not only of last century but of last week—it is more than an inspiration, it is an argument, it is the argument for our position. I know, lads and maidens, you will be challenged on that point, as to the position of your Church, and our right to that name. Our theologians, our Church historians, will answer that challenge for you, conclusively and satisfactorily. But I am not even "a poor local preacher" (as one speaker described himself this week). I am only a poor Sunday school teacher, neither theologian, philosopher, nor historian. I have only one simple answer as to my Church—as I call her, and ever will—the manifest working of the Holy Spirit in the labours of our fathers, the presence of God the Holy Ghost here and now. In my simplicity I have no other answer; I want no other defence. That, young men and maidens of Methodism, is the answer for the satisfaction of your own souls, and your answer to others. It is an old challenge, sir,—" By what name or by what authority have ye done this?" And I find that those early irregular preachers, Peter and John, had no occasion to rush into controversy over it; for "seeing the man that was healed standing with them they could say nothing against it." And, Mr. President, while healed souls are the product of our Methodist chapels, there is proof of ordination, there is consecration, there is our justification in the face of the whole world. And I appeal, as I said, not only to the history of the past century, but of the past week, to the few days ago when you, sir, saw these things in the county from whence I come—

> "The lame they are walking and running their race,
> The dumb they are talking of Jesus's grace."

I am further intensely anxious that young Methodism should recognise its responsibilities in upholding the old doctrines which have made not only Methodism but, as I believe, old England what she is. We rejoice to have testimony borne this week to the fact that Wesley's doctrines—that is, the teaching of St. Paul and of Luther —are now preached all around us as was not the case a century ago. But, if I can read the signs of the times aright, I am constrained to the belief that the old banner of Protestantism is to be upheld with an enormously increased responsibility resting upon evangelical Nonconformity, and especially upon our own Church. We rejoice in the spiritual activity all around us. We rejoice that revival elsewhere, notably the Oxford movement in the Church of England, may seem to relieve us of some responsibilities, but they undoubtedly increase our responsibilities in another direction, when we hear the Protestant name itself protested against, and when we hear the Reformation sought to be half explained away in the interests of an ecclesiastical historic continuity. Sir, at the proper time, we too will claim—and I see no bar to it—our share in historic continuity ; but give me

> "The living present—
> Heart within, and God o'erhead."

Give me the present. "The best of all (still) is, God is with us." God grant young Methodism to be true to its great charge in handing on to the next generation that which has been delivered to us—the Bible the only standard ; the humblest sinner's direct access to the mercy-seat ; Christ the only Priest, the one Mediator between God and man, the one Sacrifice once offered.

I referred incidentally to the peculiar claim in the present day of the social institutions of Methodism ; and by that expression I mean every social means of co-operation for the good of the souls and bodies of the people around us, and especially what we in the provinces call the social means of grace. I do recommend them to the rising race of young Methodists. I pray God that they may not outgrow the class-meeting, which in thousands of instances made their fathers what they were. I am liberal enough to admit that the class-meeting requires here and there adaptation to particular places and circumstances. I have proved that and tried to act on it. But its abolition, or its neglect, would be an anachronism and a fatal error. If we deprecate the Babel voices of exaggerated class distinctions in the world outside, let us at least strive to preserve our unity of speech and simplicity of fellowship within our walls by these weekly gatherings to help each other on.

I wish lastly to refer to the responsibilities coming to us with additional wealth, influence and culture, here and there in our midst. I stated my conviction just now that God had given these to us for a purpose. I am conscious I may be addressing a small minority, but I am addressing a minority with enormous responsibilities and with com-mensurate opportunities before them. You, sir, at least know very well of scores of Methodist youths who have advantages, material and intellectual, which their fathers had not, and as a consequence have opportunities of which their fathers and grandfathers never dreamed. And what use is the young Methodism of which we are speaking to make of these? Whitecross Street and the New Method-ist Settlement? Thank God for them. But I confess my thought was running in a different direction. I bear testimony that it is easier to witness for God in a slum than in a drawing-room. Wanted, young Methodist culture to witness for its Lord wherever it goes. This may be a harder call, but the harder call may be the direction of God's purpose for us. I know very well that our old motto was to carry the gospel, not only where it was wanted, but where it was wanted most; and I rejoice that "the poor have the gospel preached unto them." But "wanted most!" Are there not some sections of what is called society to-day that want the witness of Christianity in earnest as much as any men or women under heaven? The consecration of culture—Sir, I must not trust myself to pursue this point, the more especially as I was anticipated by Mr. Thomas Osborn on Tuesday, who so admirably and fitly dwelt on some aspects of this branch of my subject. Surely the additional intellectual advantages, the additional mental power which God has given scores of our youth to-day, should find scope in the Church of their fathers. The acquisition of knowledge, pursued in a thousand places to-day for its own sake, is not the ideal of Christianity in earnest. We have around us perplexed intellects as well as aching hearts, and Methodism has its mission to both. The furnishing of the brains of the young men under our President's charge should not be for the development of coteries of *dilettanti*, but for the benefit of man and the glory of God. It is not too much to say that Rugby under Arnold made its mark on the history of England. Why not other schools? why not one school especially present to our minds now under a servant of Christ whom all Methodism honours? Why should that not make its mark on the days to come? I want to see a stream of this young Christian influence flowing forth from us, helping to purify the press, public life, county life, municipal life, political life of the land. I do not mean that we should be all of one way of thinking on public subjects, as would become a sect; but that, as becomes a Church, whilst preserving individual independence of thought, young Methodism should bring its

Christian influence to bear on all parties and all schools of thought, and benefit our general national life.

Does some one say that this conception of wealth and culture seems to mark a departure from our old primitive simplicity, and that these things seem necessarily burdens and snares and dangers? I should like to answer that question, not by any words of my own, but by those of a celebrated townsman of mine. I had, thirty odd years ago, the pleasure of knowing something directly, and a great deal indirectly, of the prototype of *Daniel Quorm.* I think I knew the man called Daniel Quorm even better than did my other distinguished townsman who has immortalised that name. He was one of those invaluable private members of our classes, who largely help the leader with their own individual experience; and his leader was my own beloved father. One Sunday morning, which I well remember, my father came in with a more than usually radiant face from his early class-meeting, and he could not help telling us an excellent story which was then fresh from that blessed little meeting-room. There had been two young men present of relatively good position and considerable culture, as things went at that time in that part of the world. They had given their experience in somewhat, truth to tell, halting and hesitating terms, as might have been expected from those who had gifts not altogether dedicated to the service of Christ. Next the old saint, whom Christendom now calls Daniel Quorm, was called upon. Nobody ever knew what he was going to say. [That is very curious. I imagine from that laugh that in some class-meetings people do know what is going to be said.] He proceeded to tell his recent experience. He had been to see a brother in Chatham Dockyard, and had been taken to see the building of one of Her Majesty's ships. He told how he was amazed at her tremendous proportions, at her magazines, at the ports for her guns, at the quarters for officers and men, the steering gear, and all the rest. But when his brother told him that she had cost scores of thousands of pounds,

Daniel came to the conclusion that there, high and dry on
the land, he did not see value for the money; and he said,
" Brother, we've got members like that down in our class,
very expensive fittings about 'em, but no life." His
brother said, " Come again to-morrow." The next day
the vessel was to be launched. Daniel took his stand to
see it; it was a grand sight, and he described it all. I
will give the conclusion, in the vernacular, as far as you
would be able to understand it. He said—" I saw a rope
cut, I saw some wedges knocked out, and down she
slinkered through the channel, and so was right out in the
great sea. Now I can see some value in her. I can see
she can take her guns in now; now she can help to keep
the peace of the world and the honour of ould England;
now I can see value for the money; now she don't need
to be pulled about by hand, for she will hoist her sails
to the winds of heaven. And, my dear leader, I lifted
up my heart to God, and I said, ' Father, Thou know'st
those members of ours home, expensive fittings they've
got, but there's no value in them. Lord, knock out those
wedges and cut the ropes between them and the world,
slide them out into the ocean of Thy love. Then they'll
run up the old flag, then they'll use their guns 'gainst the
King's enemies. Lord, launch those members of ours.' "
I leave that parable with young Methodism to-night, and I
join in Daniel's prayer for all our youth and the consecration of all their powers to Christ Jesus.

Ten Characteristics of Young Methodism.

BY THE REV. H. PRICE HUGHES, M.A.

THERE is one advantage in coming last. You may speak
as long as you like without disturbing anyone else.

The children of the nineteenth century have a very
definite way of their own; and it will be interesting to
inquire at this stage of these historic proceedings what are

likely to be the tendencies and the actions of that young Methodism which will produce the rulers and the trustees of Methodism at the beginning of the twentieth century. I think there is no difficulty in giving an answer. We have already entered upon a new era of a very marked type. The speeches which we have heard to-night, and which we have heard on every previous night of this week, would have been simply impossible in Methodism twenty years ago.

What is this new development of which the most conspicuous manifestation is called the Forward Movement? What are the characteristics of the young Methodists of to-day?

I venture to express the strongest conviction, having a good many sources of information within my reach, that, spiritually, young Methodism is very old-fashioned indeed. Let our seniors be fully reassured. We are very intense Methodists. Let us at any rate clearly understand, on indisputable evidence within everybody's reach, that the young Methodists on whose behalf I venture to speak, are proud of their Church, and are confident of her future. It is always well that such appeals should be made as my friend Mr. George Smith has made so eloquently, but I hasten to express my strong conviction that never since I was born were they so little needed as they are to-night. There never was a time when modern Methodists hungered and thirsted after spiritual holiness as much as they do to-day. There never was a time when we loved the class-meeting and the prayer-meeting better than to-day. There never was a time when we had richer and more victorious experiences in our lovefeasts, or when we had more penitents at our services and prayer-meetings and after-meetings. You may be fully assured that we young Methodists believe, to the bottom of our souls, in revivals and conversions, and every possible agency for the deepening of the spiritual life. But many of us are disposed to agree with Principal Rainy—who has laid us under a very deep obligation by the discourse which many of us had the privilege of hearing this afternoon—that, in the immediate future, the work of God may not take the form which he described as "law work," but that we may increasingly realise that the true Christian is a Christ-like man. If there is anything that distinguishes our method of teaching Christianity it is this—the emphasis with which we assert that the essence of practical Christianity is to walk in the footsteps of Jesus Christ, and to do what He would have done had He been in our place.

The next special feature of young Methodists is that we believe Methodism is a Church. When our American brethren were in this country, during the last Œcumenical Conference, they told me that nothing astonished them so much as the excessive deference which some among us exhibited towards the Church of England. I believe that young Methodists sincerely pray for the welfare of that Church, but if the American brethren come ten years hence to an Œcumenical Conference in England, they will not notice that peculiarity. Never again will we consent to play the *rôle* of a poor relation of the Established Church. Young Methodists believe that the President of the Wesleyan Conference is as truly and eminently a minister of Christ as the Archbishop of Canterbury. As for the doctrine of Apostolical Succession, we hold, with John Wesley, that it is a fable, although accepted by many sincere and godly men; that it is as absolutely a fiction as the forged decretals upon which popes have built up their pretensions. We claim for our ministers everything that is conceded to any minister in this country. For that reason we are now insisting that the civil registrar shall not be present at marriages in our churches. We desire to be very friendly with the priests of the Anglican communion, but always on this condition, that they meet us on terms of absolute equality.

Further, we have developed a new friendliness for the ancient Dissenting Churches of this country. Dr. Dale told us very truly that the Dissenters of Wesley's days regarded our fathers with some concern, because Arminianism had unhappily been associated in this country with Socinianism. That has passed away. There is no doubt, on the other hand, that some of our fathers had a strange dislike for the Dissenters, because they were political. We regard that as all nonsense. They were not more political than other people, and they have rendered an imperishable service to the human race by teaching us that Christian men ought to discharge their civic duties. I may say, on behalf of the London Mission, that in every part of this country which we visit, our platforms are crowded by Baptist and Congregational and Presbyterian ministers. I have received an unprecedented mark of friendliness from the Congregational communion. When I was in despair, after my search for a suitable locality for the West London Mission, they placed one of their venerable sanctuaries at my disposal without charging one penny for rent.

We believe, further, that Methodism is a national Church, that it is not an obscure sect or a class religion ; and we freely admit that this involves from us two concessions.

The first is publicity. We do not wish to be any longer in a back street. We prefer the corner site, previously given to a public-house. Methodism is coming out of its shell. Our fathers preferred to do things secretly—not because they ever did anything wrong ; the affairs of Methodism have always been honestly administered. But secrecy was their policy. It is not our policy. We like to see these reporters here. Mr. Watkinson said on Tuesday that there were two Methodist papers, which did not do more harm than any other papers. I presume he referred to the *Methodist Recorder* and *Joyful News.* I fully agree with him that they are very harmless organs of opinion, but I say they are also very useful organs of opinion. We believe so much in publicity that we are delighted the representative session of the Conference has decided to admit professional reporters. That is our policy. Again we believe in freedom of speech in the

Conference and out of it. Some of our brethren do not like being criticised ; they will get used to it, as I have. It will do them no harm. It will prevent a tendency to parochialism, and living in one groove. The first time my grandfather went to the Conference, a young man, not less than forty-five years of age, rose to address the Conference. Dr. Bunting looked at him with astonishment, and then said, in a decisive tone, " Young man, sit down." And the young man did sit down. If your successor at the next Conference, sir, said that to me, I should sit down, because I am one of the most docile of mankind—but there would be a great deal of hubbub.

Once more, young Methodists have very strongly thought there was too much truth in the charge brought against us and other Evangelical Churches, that we were guilty of other-worldliness. We believe that the vision which John Wesley had was a vision not of heaven, but of earth changed and purified and blessed by the power of Jesus Christ ; and that was the vision which St. John had in the Apocalypse. He saw the City of God coming down out of heaven. For my own part, I know very little about heaven. It is down here on earth that our sympathy ought to go forth, down here where there is a public-house at the corner of every street, where the pavements are crowded with scoundrels and their victims, and where it is so difficult to do right. We believe that love to our neighbour requires that we should vote at the election of Poor Law Guardians, and of School Boards, and of Town and County Councils. We believe, also, that we are bound, when qualified, as part of our religious duties, to stand as candidates for civic offices. For example, the servants of the devil will make a tremendous fight at the coming elections for the London County Council. I call upon young Methodists to come forward as candidates, and when a Methodist like Mr. M'Dougall attacks obscenity, you ought to support him. Why is Cardiff, as you, Mr. President, have said, so largely Methodist ? Because Mr. Williams and other influential Methodists there have discharged their civic duties, and acquired the influence which good men will always acquire when they do so. We recognise our social duties, and fully appreciate the incalculable and imperishable services rendered to Christianity by the pioneer of our social work, Dr. Stephenson.

I am greatly indebted to the President for reminding me that next month the election of the Board of Guardians takes place, and it is of the greatest importance that not only young men but young women should present themselves for election. It is a striking sign of the times that the President of the Conference should have instructed me to say that. We believe that our social Christianity must exhibit itself in the form of all sorts of individual charities and social reforms. We believe that it is a part of our duty to feed and clothe and care for and entertain the disinherited and the friendless. We also believe there are seven gigantic social evils, not one of which is necessary.

The first is the gigantic evil of Drunkenness. We rejoice in the fact that we have a total abstainer in the chair of the Conference. But that, thank God, is no novelty ; we have had several. I am happy to add, however, that for the first time in Methodist history we have a total abstainer in the chair and a total abstainer as the Secretary of the Conference. My friend, Dr. Waller, has been hiding his light under a bushel for eighteen months ; I will take the bushel away.

There is another gigantic evil with which we are dealing more directly than our fathers—that is the gigantic evil of Lust. We glory in the credit that has come to us as a Church because such men as Dr. Osborn and others were amongst the very first to protest against those iniquitous laws which were introduced into the statute book at dead of night, but which, after a struggle of twenty years' duration, were blotted out for ever. We learnt during that struggle that the only true principle of chastity is one which asserts equal claims on men and women. I rejoice that the President of the Conference signed a public protest last night against the return of Sir Charles Dilke to the House of Commons until he succeeds in clearing his character. We who have defeated Mr. Parnell are to defeat him.

The third evil is that of Gambling.

With respect to Pauperism I need not dwell upon that; we have heard much from the impassioned lips of my friend Mr. Thompson and others. I will only add that we must remember that we who are not producers but consumers must be prepared to fight against the craze for unnatural cheapness.

The fifth social evil is the African Slave Trade.

The sixth is the diabolic Opium Trade with China.

We must also deal with Crime and Prison Discipline, and we must introduce a revolution into our law which will make offences against the person as serious as offences against property.

I am struck and distressed by the fact that not one single word has been said during this week against the crowning iniquity of War. My friend Mr. Smart pleaded with us that we should intervene in the terrible strife between labour and capital. Much more should we intervene to prevent war. During the last few years we have spent £2,700,000,000 on war in civilised Europe, and 2,500,000 honest lives have been sacrificed. Lord John Russell said that on looking back on all the wars which had been carried on during the last century, and looking into the causes of them, he did not know one which might not have been avoided if there had been proper temper between the parties. I trust we Methodists at any rate will not leave the Society of Friends any longer to bear almost unassisted the burden of this agitation.

The sixth feature of young Methodism, as it presents itself to me, is that it recognises not only our social but also our political duties. I entirely agree that any Church which committed itself to one political party would be a sect. But I absolutely refuse to allow any man to close my mouth in relation to any political question by saying that it belongs to party politics. It belongs to me as a prophet of Almighty God before it belongs to any party. We believe the State is as sacred as the Church. We believe with Lord Shaftesbury that a religious man must carry his religion with him into political life. When he brought forward the Factory Acts he told Parliament that he did so as a religious duty. If any man says his religion has nothing to do with his politics I can only say that both his religion and his politics are contemptible. The result of such delusions is that, as Mr. Herbert Spencer has said, we have two religions in this country—one which we profess on Sunday, and the other which we practise during the week. A distinguished Scotchman has said, "When you Christians practise on the six days of the week the religion you profess on the seventh, the millennium will come at once." Assuredly if Christian men would only stand shoulder to shoulder on all great moral questions, the millennium would soon come.

We, young Methodists, are very democratic ; we go to the masses. I entirely agree with Principal Rainy that the innovations of one age are very often the fetters of the next. We refuse to be tied and bound by red tape. At this moment the majority of the English people are outside.

The eighth feature of young Methodism is one upon which Mr. Percy Bunting touched the other night, and to which Mr. George Smith has properly referred—a new sense of trusteeship with privilege. Never before have our privileged young men and young women been so thoroughly alive to their responsibilities. The great school over which the President presides teaches that culture is not given them for their own aggrandisement.

Next, we glory in the elasticity and many-sidedness of Methodism. We all believe that Mr. Tom Osborn and Professor Davison are doing the work of the Forward Movement quite as much as Charles Garrett or Thomas Champness.

Lastly, I am deeply persuaded that young Methodism

is in favour of Methodist union. Mr. Richard Green at the last Fernley Lecture expressed our fervent aspiration that the scattered sections of Methodism may some day come together. We cannot but feel deeply the loving sentiments which were uttered by the Presidents of all the minor Methodist Churches last Monday. As a young Wesleyan Methodist, I wish to take this opportunity to reciprocate those aspirations from the bottom of my soul. We believe more and more that the overlapping and the waste in the country districts are scandalous. We shall never be able to remedy this until we have enough common sense and self-suppression to bury our differences. The representative of the Irish Conference told us of the happy results of Methodist union in that country. If a representative from Canada had been here, he would have told us that all the Methodist Churches in Canada are now happily united, and that there is only one Methodist Church from the Atlantic to the Pacific. Our brethren there have had an increase of 10,000 members every year since their blessed union. I wish to add one other fact that has not yet been mentioned. If by the grace of God we could overcome our differences at home, that consummation would be followed by Methodist union all the world over. In a few years we should have one Methodist Church in France, in Germany, in Italy, in India, in China, in Japan, in Australia. The one unanswerable taunt I have heard this week is that already, though so young, we are divided. There is no theological difference among us, there is no ecclesiastical difference that is not capable of adjustment. The day will dawn when all the bees will come back to the old hive, and we shall then have plenty of honey. Standing here to-night, close to John Wesley's tomb, on a great historic occasion, I deliberately prophesy that the devil will not be able to keep the Methodists of England apart much longer. I am fully convinced that, in the face of an aggressive sacerdotalism on the one hand and a perilous secularism on the other, we shall never be able to fulfil the mission of

Methodism until we have achieved Methodist union. We cannot protect our village Churches adequately, we cannot mission our towns thoroughly, we cannot evangelise the heathen universally, until we unite our scattered forces. But the day is coming when, in every quarter of the globe, the mechanical and oppressive unity of Rome will be confronted and mastered by the spontaneous and joyful union of the people called Methodists. When the prophet Elijah took twelve stones, to represent the twelve tribes, and built them up into one united altar of devotion to God, then the fire fell and the rain came, and the drought vanished away. And when a successor of yours, Mr. President, gathers together on this spot the scattered sections of Methodism to be united in the service of God and man, then the Pentecostal fire will fall, then there will be showers of blessing, and then the latter-day glory of which John Wesley was the herald will burst upon the whole world.

Methodism and the Sister Churches.

—— o ——

By the PRESIDENT OF THE CONFERENCE.

I AM very grateful to you, my dear friends, for this unexpected but most welcome expression of your kindness.[1] No thanks do I need. The enjoyment to me has been intense, and the stimulating power of encouragement and hope beyond all words.

I shall not detain you with many words this evening. The subject speaks for itself, "Methodism and its Sister Churches." I wish a much larger number of sister Churches could have been represented on this occasion; but in different parts of this week we have had additional representation, as you will have fully recognised. Methodism loves her sister Churches. Methodism is the friend of all, but she is united in the closest possible union with those sister Churches who can sing with her the grand Reformation hymn.[2] Methodism must sorrowfully stand aloof from those who detest the word "Reformation," but to all those who love the thought of the Reformation, and are faithful to the principles of the Reformation, although they may differ from her in many respects, Methodism desires to

---

[1] For the expression of gratitude referred to, and for Dr. Cairns' letter, see Appendix.

[2] " A safe stronghold our God is still."—the hymn with which the service opened.

come nearer and nearer still—acknowledging the glorious services rendered by each of those Churches, and wishing that all the Churches may stand together in the great battle of the Lord.

Various Churches are represented here to-night. But we have really a double motive for the meeting of this evening. Not only have we represented here that blessed union of sister Churches, but we also have elements which connect this meeting directly with the history of the great man whose name and whose life are in the thoughts of all of us this week. Who can read the Life of Wesley without recognising with deepest thankfulness the influence for good which the Moravians had upon this people? We have here with us the Bishop of the Moravian Church. We have also a representative of the Countess of Huntingdon's Connexion. And who can forget that the Society of Friends—whose glorious philanthropic work is the glory of our land—has stood side by side with us from the first in maintaining the great doctrine of the influence of God's Holy Spirit, bearing testimony before the world that nothing is great, nothing is strong, except through the Spirit of God. I am sure that to the representative of that Society you will accord a hearty welcome. One thing I must not forget: we have an ecclesiastical historian here who has done more than most men—very much more than most ecclesiastical historians—to bring out the great features of the history of the last century, and to do justice to the work of John Wesley. I will first call upon the Rev. W. Taylor, Bishop of the Church of the United Brethren to address you.

The Moravian Church.

By the Rev. W. TAYLOR.

Mr. President, Christian Friends,—

I esteem it an unspeakably great honour to be privileged to be with you this evening, and to join in your celebration of the memory of that great man, Englishman and true Christian, the Rev. John Wesley. And I beg in the first place to offer my congratulations as a humble individual, and to express the good wishes and prayers of the Church with which I am connected on your behalf.

It has just been said that the representatives of some sister Churches stand around the Methodist Church. The Church which I am privileged to represent is perhaps the oldest of those Churches. We celebrated her 434th birthday on Sunday last. She has been a persecuted Church, a Church of martyrs, a Church despised in some quarters to-day but greatly honoured for her work's sake in others. At least, we always think so when kind brethren speak of us in too flattering a strain in regard to our missionary work. But we remember that it is by the grace of God that we are what we are. I beg, therefore, dear Christian friends of the Methodist Churches here assembled, to express the good wishes of our community on your behalf in the words of the text which I find in the Moravian Text Book for to-day's date. Our Church issues an authorised Text Book every year. This custom has been maintained through a long course of years, and it strikes me that the text for to-day is a very appropriate one—viz., "Grace be to you, and peace from God our Father and the Lord Jesus Christ."

Although these words were selected nearly two years ago, they are exceedingly appropriate to our gathering this evening. When we think of these words we think of John Huss and Martin Luther and John Wesley, and others who have gone before us; and we magnify the grace of God as displayed in them and through them. I am very sure that if any of those sainted heroes knew now—as perhaps they do know—what is transpiring here, John Wesley would say with Paul, "By the grace of God I was what I have been." And therefore though, as has been stated, the Moravians had the privilege of teaching John Wesley some important spiritual truths, yet we do not say that we lighted the lamp of John Wesley, or John Wesley's candlestick, but we do say that we were used to *trim* that lamp, and to trim it so that it burned more brightly.

But we must go back to the beginning. It is very interesting to trace how, step by step, God leads on His children. You know the great Architect of the Christian Church not only prepares His plan in general and in detail, but He prepares every workman and instrument whereby that work is carried on. "We are God's workmanship."

Now, I think we may trace the grace of God in the circumstances of John Wesley's birth. He was born in the parsonage of a clergyman of the Church of England. There he saw the practice of spare living and high thinking. We should not, I think, forget the merit of the father of John Wesley. It was no small thing for a clergyman, whose income never exceeded £200 a-year, to feed and clothe and educate a large family of children as he did. He sent three of his sons to the University, and thus by self-denial he, under God, prepared the way for that vast sphere of activity into which his son afterwards entered. The grace of God placed him in that parsonage, and the grace of God gave him a mother wonderfully fitted to influence him in his after career. Her Spartan training seems to have prepared her son for those Spartan labours which he kept up for eighty-eight years ; a training, mind you, which never removed her out of his affections, and which, therefore, although severe, according to our notions, was upon the whole a good and Christian training.

Well, then, I would further say that the grace of God may be traced very clearly in His permitting John Wesley to be educated at Oxford, where he had the advantages of a liberal education—a theological training and grounding in the original languages of the Sacred Scriptures—so that when afterwards he came into contact with the Brethren, they could examine the Scriptures together in the original. When they showed him that his views in many respects needed clearing, they were careful to trace everything to the original text, and not until he was convinced in that way would he consent to their views. In Oxford he had the great advantage also of coming in contact with various classes of mind. It was there that he learnt to resist temptation—to exercise over powerful intellects his great gifts for administration ; and then God prepared the way for that larger exercise of his talents, which was afterwards entrusted to him in connection with the Methodist Church.

I may proceed to claim also that the grace of God brought him into connection with some Moravians ; and I would have you note that those Moravians were a few humble people who were going to colonise Georgia, and to work actively among the heathen there as missionaries. It was their patience—not their theological discussions in any way, but their character, their patience, that struck his mind and showed him that Christianity must be a reality ; that it must have the confirmation of the Divine promise—that joy and peace in the Holy Ghost should be given to those who were in union with God through Christ, to uphold and support them in the midst of difficulties. And this is an important thing for us to remember ; for the world looks upon us individually, and it judges Christianity, alas ! not by its own evidence, but by the character of those who profess it ; and it is surely very important for us all this week—and especially for you who are here assembled—to remember this, that it is the evidence exhibited in a godly Christian life that will tell far more for Christ and the Word of God than any amount of learning, or any number of sermons preached from this pulpit. Let us be "living epistles, known and read of all men."

Well, I would briefly say that in regard to those doctrines in which the Brethren with whom he came in contact were privileged to enlighten his mind, there were two of special moment.

(1) The great doctrine of salvation through humble

trust in Jesus. That doctrine lies on the face of Scripture, and it is contained in the Creed of the Church of England. Yet it is very remarkable how sometimes men's minds are holden — they cannot see what lies plainly before them ; and so, though Mr. Wesley had known this doctrine, he had not appreciated it. He had placed works—dead works—before simple faith in the blood of " Christ who, through the Eternal Spirit, offered Himself unto God." The great lesson that sacramental religion avails not to give peace, but rather a humble trust in the blood of Jesus, is the foundation stone upon which alone the edifice of the Church can be safely built. It is my prayer for you this evening that you may ever be preserved on this foundation—that you may never be led to put your trust in forms and ceremonies—but that you may rest alone for forgiveness of sins on the blood of sprinkling.

(2) And then there is the other blessed truth—viz., the truth of the inward witness of the Spirit. I wonder how anyone can dispute that that is a Scripture doctrine. It is the promise of our blessed Saviour, " If any man love me he will keep my words, and my Father will love him, and we will make our abode with him." St. Paul said, " If any man have not the Spirit of Christ he is none of His." Again he says, " The kingdom of God is not meat and drink, but righteousness and peace and joy in the Holy Ghost." I will not detain you long. but I must say one word. There is one danger in this doctrine—viz., that of treating it as a resting-place. It is a test doctrine —a doctrine by which we are to test our condition Godward. But our only rest is in the finished work of Jesus Christ. There is a danger also of too great introspection ; but the other danger—viz., that of insufficient self-examination, is a far worse danger. If I examine my consciousness, and feel that I have not the peace of God, what must I do? I must examine myself to see if I have been acting contrary to the dictates of the Holy Spirit, who is my inward Teacher. If I find that I have

been transgressing, then I must first of all come to the Cross of Jesus and ask the forgiveness of that known sin, and then there will be a renewal of peace, a renewal of joy, a foretaste of that blessedness which remains for us hereafter, when this life is done—a heaven of endless joy, of perfect knowledge, and eternal glory.

I conclude, as I commenced, by saying, "Grace be to you, and peace from God our Father and the Lord Jesus Christ"—our common Lord and Master.

An Ecclesiastical Historian.

By the Rev. JOHN STOUGHTON, D.D.

Mr. President, my Christian Friends,

I regard it as being rather a presumptuous thing on my part and at my age to rise here to address such an audience as is now before me. Why, I am not many years behind the age of John Wesley! I think I am only about five years younger than he was at the time of his death—what do you think of that? My voice is not what it used to be, and about two years ago I had a severe illness which laid me aside, and since then I have very rarely addressed a large audience, and if it had not been that my dear friend Dr. Allon was unable to fulfil his engagement, I do not think I could have been persuaded to take any part in the proceedings of to-night. But I am here as a stop-gap.

I have very vivid recollections of Methodism in my early days. My father and mother, my grandfather and grandmother, were all Methodists. I might be said to have been brought up in the lap of Methodism. Some of my earliest impressions of a religious kind were received while I was thus connected with Methodist associations, and to the early religious impressions which I received I will refer presently. But, having spoken of my mother, I must tell you this much about her—that she used to relate anecdotes of John Wesley, whom she knew very well, and always loved him as a man, because he was exceedingly kind and gracious to the young. He was in the habit of taking up children in his arms and pronouncing upon them his blessing, and giving them a kiss. My mother used to be amazing proud of saying that John Wesley had kissed her. There are not many who can say what I can say. She used to speak of him as being a perfect gentleman: at the same time so dignified and yet so urbane and courteous. Though he was born to rule, he always swayed the sceptre with the hand of love.

I have recollections of some early Methodists. I do not think I could have been much more than four years old when I saw Dr. Coke, and he made an impression upon my mind which I have never lost. My grandfather was a steward in the Norwich Circuit—and at the opening of a chapel there Dr. Coke preached. In the afternoon there was a large gathering of people in the house of my grandfather. I remember how Dr. Coke stood upon a table (for he was a very diminutive man), and there was a large number of Methodists surrounding him. There he stood and spoke to them, and though I have entirely forgotten what he said, yet I have a very vivid impression of his having greatly interested them and delighted them.

Next to Dr. Coke, let me speak of another man, Dr. Adam Clarke. When I was about seventeen I was exceedingly anxious to hear him preach. Being in London I came to this chapel, and there was an audience, I dare say, as large as we see here to-night. I don't know whether that (pointing behind) is the same pulpit. ("Yes, yes!") Then he preached a sermon from that pulpit in support of the Royal Humane Society—in the course of which he gave a description of his own experience. When he was very young he was drowned—really drowned—and lost consciousness; and he gave a most vivid description of what his sensations were at first, and how they passed away. But, through the goodness of God, he was extricated from his peril, and he might be said to have been restored to life. I think I can now see him and hear him.

The memories of these men have always dwelt in my mind, and I have been delighted when I have been reading of the early history of Methodism that I could supply from my own recollection many anecdotes of the good and great men who then carried on the work of God amongst you. I remember a great number of names, some of which would be recognised by you, and others not. But let me say that, while I have so many personal reminiscences, there is one recollection which, above all others, impresses my mind at this moment, and that is, that you Methodists might say to me, as Paul said when he was writing to Philemon, "Thou owest me thy own self besides." How great are my obligations to Methodism for the good received in my early days! I was not, in the first instance, brought to a knowledge of the truth under the ministry of a Wesleyan minister; but very soon after I received my first impressions, I recollect hearing a very good man (not highly gifted), who preached with simple earnestness from those beautiful words, "God so loved the world, that He gave His only begotten Son, that whosoever believeth on Him should not perish, but have everlasting life." That text let in light upon my mind, and I passed through a state of thought and feeling which was very common amongst Methodists in those days. I passed through a season of great spiritual depression, seeking salvation; and at last I found it, to the joy of my heart. Well now, that gives a date in my memory which, as long as I live—aye, and in eternity too—I believe I shall often call to mind! I owe much to Methodist influences, and I do not believe that I should have done all the good that I may have been honoured to do in connection with my own denomination if I had not had first something of a Methodist baptism.

It used to be said in former days that those who had

been first Methodists and then went over to Congregationalism turned out to be some of the most effective men in their adopted Church. I might mention the very great impression that was made upon my mind by your hymnology. That still has a hold upon me. No other hymns please me as well as Wesley's hymns. Often on a Sunday night, when the day's work was over, I used to take Wesley's Hymns and read them with great feeling and enjoyment. There is a peculiarity about these hymns that I do not find elsewhere. They do not deal in illustrations of abstract truths, but they bring out what may be called the personality of religion. They bring it out most vividly before us. There we have hymns for " Believers Rejoicing," " Believers Fighting," " Believers Praying," " Believers Watching," " Believers Working," etc., etc. When I think of them it always appears to me something like reading Bunyan's *Pilgrim's Progress.* As I read these hymns, sometimes I get into " The Valley of the Shadow of Death," sometimes into " The Palace Beautiful," sometimes upon the " Delectable Mountains,"— all the phases of spiritual experience seem to come out, and one can find a share in each according to the experiences of one's own heart. I never can cease to feel the amount of obligation under which I have been laid by Wesley's hymns, and I do hope that you will always stick to those hymns. There are many modern hymns ; but I must say that the earlier ones are those which lay hold of my heart most firmly—they are the hymns that go down, as it were, into the very depths of my being ; by them I seem to be helped in my warfare and comforted in my troubles, and by them I receive fresh inspirations of hope. Oh, yes. And as I think of those hymns, and look forward to the world of light and love, I feel that it will be amongst the great joys of that future stage of existence to meet with some of the honoured men of whom I have been speaking, and to stand with them before the throne.

There comes to my recollection a saying that has been attributed to different persons, to this effect, " I am afraid

I shall not see Mr. So-and-so in heaven, because he will be so near the throne, and I at such a distance from it that I shall not get a sight of him." But all these feelings will be lost when we get there. We shall, I have no doubt, recognise one another; but all mutual affections will be swallowed up in the adoring love of Him that sits upon the throne!

Now, let me say with regard to the hymns to which I have alluded that, while there is so much of what we may call the element of personality in them, so much of spiritual experience, I can imagine some persons saying, "Yes, and there is the concentrated essence of selfishness, for the Christian is there led to think of himself, to be absorbed in himself—in his own fightings, and in his own victories!" Aye, but what is the end of all that personal and joyous experience? It comes out in "Hymns of Intercession"— intercession for the world, intercession for all classes and conditions of men. When those hymns were written people did not care much about the heathen, or about the Jews, about the perplexed, the tempted, or the sorrowing; but Wesley wrote hymns specially for all these.

This brings to my recollection a story of George III. He felt that a great deal of good had been done by the Wesleys; and when some objection was raised against Charles Wesley, jun., being appointed organist, the king said, "I believe John and Charles Wesley have done more for the advancement of religion in this country than any other names that can be named."

There are one or two other things I will mention. It may be asked, How came it to pass, if you have such a great love for the Methodists, that you ever left them? I became a Congregationalist because upon some points of doctrine, and some points of ecclesiastical order, I differed from the Methodists, and therefore on the whole I thought it was my duty to be what I am. But in becoming an Independent I did not cease to be a Methodist. All my life long Methodism has had a strong hold upon my sympathies. Wherever I have met a Methodist I have felt that I was in society with a brother. And the feeling I have towards Methodism has been responded to by a great many Methodists. Once, in Cornwall, I was engaged to preach an anniversary sermon at an Independent chapel. But when I arrived in the town I saw the walls placarded with announcements that I was to preach at the Methodist chapel. I asked what it meant. The Congregationalist pastor explained, " The fact is, sir, that when the super-intendent minister of the circuit heard of my coming, he said, ' Now, you know that Mr. Stoughton belongs just as much to us as to you, and if he preaches for us he will have a very much larger congregation than if he preaches for you, and you will have the benefit of a much larger collection.'" And so it came to pass. Instead of preaching to 500 people I preached to 1,200, and instead of a collection of about £5 the result was about £20. I always loved to be in union with Methodists.

I sympathise with all who are here present. Especially do I sympathise with you in the emphasis you lay upon *conversion.* I have a theory of this kind (I think I got it from Richard Baxter) that if Christian education and training were just what they ought to be, and children were brought up in the fear of the Lord, so that they received the Holy Spirit and were made new creatures in Christ Jesus in their early days, there would be no need for their being converted afterwards. But we know that the great majority of those who are around us have not been so trained, and are living now in the spirit of the world, heedless with regard to their souls, indifferent to eternal things; and when that is the case there must be, according to the teaching of Jesus Christ, a great change wrought in them. " That which is born of the flesh is flesh, and that which is born of the Spirit is spirit." And until a man is born of the Spirit of God, he remains in the flesh. He needs, therefore, to be converted — changed. " Marvel not that I say unto you, ye must be born again." Now, all the way through, Methodists have been accustomed to preach that doctrine. We do; but perhaps not in that emphatic way that old-fashioned Methodists used to do. I do not know exactly what is the tone of your preaching now—although I very often worship at the Methodist Church at Ealing, and, indeed, have my name occasionally on the circuit plan.

The older we grow, I think, the more are our hearts drawn towards each other. I have, of course, my own preferences, but they are all lost when I come to think of that beautiful union which exists between souls renewed by the Spirit of God, and that are putting their trust in Christ, feeling that He is to them "All and in all." We are all of one mind here, so far—we are all looking to Christ as our Saviour—all looking to heaven as our home. The things that separate us now cannot last longer than our mortal lives. I often think of our peculiarities as being earthly garments which, as John Bunyan says, we shall leave in the river. Yes! we shall leave our differences there, and then when we get to the other side, and when the chariot takes us up to the gates of the golden city—when we get amongst the sanctified ones—we shall have no more controversy, we shall have no more disputes, we shall be of one mind and heart; therefore, let us strive to maintain the spirit of union whilst we are upon earth.

May God be with you, and "may the peace that passeth all understanding keep your hearts and minds in the knowledge and the love of God."

Countess of Huntingdon's Connexion.

By the Rev. J. B. FIGGIS, M.A.

Mr. President,—

I think, with the silvery cadences of "the old man eloquent" running in our ears, it would be almost best for us to rise and go home. Next to coming here, if it were possible, to hear the Rev. John Wesley speak to us, I think to hear the Rev. John Stoughton speak to us as he has done, ought to be—and that, sir, is what I have come here to catch—an inspiration.

"What mean ye by this service?" What mean these gatherings day by day? If I understand your meaning rightly, it is just that—to catch an inspiration. As I thought with some trembling of my appearing before you, there came to my mind the 21st verse of the 13th chapter of the Second Book of Kings—where you read of a funeral —a strange and hasty funeral—more hastened and more strange than the funeral of John Wesley in that early morn a hundred years ago. It was a time when war was in the gates. They were burying a man—as when our country-men, burying Sir John Moore,

> " Heard the distant and random gun
> Which the foe were sullenly firing ; "—

So these men heard the tramp of armed troops, and they threw down the body, and the corpse fell into a grave. It was the grave of Elisha. "And it came to pass that when it touched the bones of Elisha, he revived and stood upon his feet." God grant that, by this our contact with the illustrious dead, we may revive!

We are come here to-night for nothing less than this. Outside this venerable, this honoured sanctuary, you have erected a statue. I could not keep the tears from my eyes as I looked upon that statue ; and yet I can fancy that the bronze and the marble will not satisfy the spirit of John Wesley in heaven, if he is like the John Wesley that he was on earth. I can fancy that unless his preachers are preaching Christ, and his teachers are teaching Christ, and his workers are winning souls for Christ, he will say, " My children ask for bread, and you give them a stone." The only bread that will be as food to him at the heavenly table, and will satisfy the heart-hunger of that great longing soul, with its passion for saving men, will be to hear that the work of saving men goes on, and goes on faster and on a more extended scale than was possible in his day.

When I read about your multiplication of pastors and teachers—your extended organisation and machinery—and think of the millions who are looking towards this spot, I almost tremble for your greatness. You are a great people. See to it that you are what you were when you were a smaller people. See to it that your love of souls remains, that you work for souls, and weep for souls, and pray for souls, and preach for souls. And that you may do so, take care that you "ask for the good old paths." There is a little pamphlet that I have often quoted, and often given away—a little pamphlet to put into the hand of the anxious soul wherever he may be found — it is as fitting for him now as on the day when it first came from the pen of John Wesley. It is called *First Believe*. It says :—"Whoever thou art that desirest to be forgiven and reconciled to God, do not say in thy heart, 'I must first do this, I must conquer every sin, break off every evil word and work, and do good to all men ;' or, 'I must first go to Church, receive the Lord's Supper, hear more sermons, and say more prayers.' Alas, my brother, thou art clean gone out of the way ! thou art still ignorant of the righteousness of God, and art seeking to establish thine own righteousness as the ground of thy reconciliation. Knowest thou not that thou canst do nothing but sin till thou art reconciled to God? Wherefore, then, dost thou say, 'I must do this first and that first, and then I must believe ?' No! thou must first believe on the Lord Jesus Christ, who is the Propitiation for thy sin. Let this good foundation first be laid, and then thou shalt do all things well."

Wesley and Whitefield (with whose band I am somewhat associated) were as one in the preaching of this truth ; and, if I mistake not, as you have been hearing about some debt that you owe to other Churches—you owe this little debt to ours — viz., that it was George Whitefield who thrust forth John Wesley to preach the gospel in the highways and hedges. And if I am not mistaken, too, those words that you have just heard quoted by Dr. Stoughton, as falling from the lips of

Wesley, had reference to Whitefield. It was when White-field died that some one, wishing to flatter Wesley, expressed a little doubt whether he would ever see him in heaven. Wesley responded in words that must have frightened his interlocutor: "I very much fear we shall not. I think he will be so near the throne, and we may be so far away, that it is doubtful whether we shall see him at all."

Oh, my brethren, let us be true to the preaching of Christ—Christ in all His attributes, in all His efficacy, in all His sufficiency; let us go throughout the length and breadth of the land knowing nothing but Jesus Christ and Him crucified.

When I think of your multitude of adherents I ask, "Who are these that fly as a cloud, and as doves to their window?" And the answer comes, "These are they that, in response to the preaching of Christ by learned men, and by illiterate men too, are coming to trust in the living God." To use an old illustration. As upon some day when you look upon the clouds sailing aloft, you ask, "What are these, and where do they come from?" And the answer is, "They come from many a muddy pond, from many a stagnant pool; but they have left the filth and the mire and defilement down here, and up there they are white and bright and beautiful." Even so, as we look round the great amphitheatre of heaven, we shall ask, "Who are these arrayed in white robes, and whence came they?" And the answer will be, "These came from many a great assembly, and from many a tiny chapel, from many a great family, and from many a poor, despised flock; but they have left all that was of the earth and of sin down below, and up here they shine for ever in the light of God through the salvation that is in Christ Jesus."

Besides that truth of the Cross, or of Justification, are we not come here to gain fresh inspiration about other truths —it may be as weighty and dear to the heart of your Founder? Do you know what was the subject of John Wesley's first published sermon? Do you know what was the subject of John Wesley's first printed tract? The subject of each was Sanctification. I am not prepared to endorse every word that may be found in those publications, or in other utterances of his or others upon the subject. He did not endorse them all himself. In later years he wrote at the bottom of the page of more than one of them, "Too strong," "Much too strong." But I am here to ask, in the name of my brethren and fathers around me, and in the name of the holy men who have joined the general assembly above, Are there many among you who at this day are lifting up your voices for the truth of sanctification? Are there many among your people and ours who at this time are being "convicted for holiness?"

John Wesley went up and down the country interested deeply in this doctrine, and inquiring how many were affected by it. First of all, a score or two of persons; then, by the year 1762, something like 650 members of your Society in London were spoken to by him upon this subject. "Their testimony," he says, "I have no reason to doubt." He gives examples of it. "I felt it," says one, "not only outwardly but inwardly." Another says, "It seemed to press upon my whole being, and to diffuse all through a holy sin - consuming energy." Another, "For a few minutes the deep of God's love swallowed me up. All its waves and its billows went over me." May I venture to read you another Christian experience of a hundred years ago, a little more in detail? "My whole heart," says the writer, "has not one single grain this moment of thirst for approbation. I feel alone with God. He fills the whole void. I have not one wish, one will, one desire, but in Him. He hath set my feet in a large room. All but God's children seem as so many machines appointed for uses with which I have nothing to do. I have wondered and stood amazed that God should make a conquest of all within me by love. Others may be conquered by less gifts and graces, but what must that evil heart be that nothing but the love of God can conquer? I am brought to less than nothing—broken to pieces like a potter's vessel. Oh, may you thus be sub-jected! May these tears be your meat night and day. I long to leap into the flames — to get rid of my sinful frame, and that every atom of these ashes should be separate—that neither time, place, nor person should stay God's Spirit?" That, sir, is the experience of Selina, Countess of Huntingdon. I venture to think it may be placed side by side with the experience of Hester Ann Rogers, or John Fletcher of Madeley, or any of your sainted dead. And I venture to think therefore, that, in spite of all that in the old days divided hearts and lives, they were really one. My only fear is that either amongst you or amongst ourselves there may be a waning of such light or life, and we may have fallen upon days in which it would be hard to parallel such experiences.

God grant that the touch of Elisha may revive all our hearts, that our flagging love may kindle into a flame, that our faith may glow, and that we may know what it is to say, "For to me to live is Christ, and to die is gain." The one hiding-place both for the sinner and the believer is Jesus Christ.

> "I've tried in vain a thousand ways
> My fears to quell, my hopes to raise :
> But all I need, the Bible says,
> > Is Jesus.

> "My soul is night, my heart is steel,
> I cannot see, I cannot feel ;
> For light, for heat I must appeal
> > To Jesus.

> "He died, He lives, He reigns, He pleads,
> There's love in all His acts and deeds,—
> All, all a guilty sinner needs
> > In Jesus.

> "What tho' the world despise or blame,
> I'll go in spite of fear and shame,
> I'll go to Him because His name
> > Is Jesus."

Go, unsaved one; go and be the best monument on Wesley's grave, and we will go with you. We will go and renew our oath of fealty unto God, and ask Him to "save us from" our "sins;" and so shall men "know that there hath been a prophet among you."

The Society of Friends.

By J. BEVAN BRAITHWAITE.

Dr. Moulton, my Christian Friends,—

I need not say how greatly I feel the privilege of addressing such a body as this on such an occasion. I look upon this gathering as a little foretaste of the General Assembly and Church of the Firstborn who are written in heaven; in which we are permitted, in a united act of faith and love, to drink of the same cup of salvation; and, resting in the love of the same ever blessed Saviour, to join in the anthem of the redeemed before the throne, "Thou wast slain, and hast redeemed us unto God by Thy blood."

Respected members of the Church of England have expressed their regret that the attitude which was assumed towards John Wesley in the course of the last century was such as ultimately to lead, very much against his own original expectations and desires, to the founding of a distinct religious community, which in England and America now numbers its millions. In reading Archdeacon Farrar's address in this house a few days ago I did not quite understand whether he shared this regret— I know that it has been shared by many. I was privileged to be present when my relative, the late Bishop of Lincoln, in company with the present Archbishop of Canterbury, then his chancellor, and his son, the present Bishop of Salisbury, met a few distinguished members of your body at my house, some eighteen years ago. He desired, I fully believe with true honesty of purpose, to prove how he rose superior to the prejudices which had actuated so many during Wesley's life, by asking whether free access to the pulpits of the Churches throughout his diocese to every Wesleyan minister in full connection would be accepted ; adding that he would himself offer no obstruction. The answer of Dr. Osborn to this appeal deeply impressed me. " Your Lordship is eighty years too late." That of William Arthur was even more significant—" I should have no more objection to preach in Lincoln Cathedral than I should from a wheelbarrow, nor from a wheelbarrow than from the pulpit in Lincoln Cathedral."

I confess that, whilst deploring the often gross breaches of Christian conduct and courtesy towards so eminent a servant of the Lord Jesus Christ, as the instrument chosen by Him for the gathering in of your Societies, I can only rejoice that they were thus gathered into a separate organisation—free from so many of the trammels which would have obstructed their growth and usefulness in connection with our Church Establishment. To suppose that the unity of the universal Church is broken by accidents of separate organisation is to overlook the great truth that that unity is dependent, not upon the manifold earthly forms of outward organisation, but upon a real spiritual union with our once crucified but now risen and eternally glorified Redeemer, the one Head of the Church in whom it has pleased the Father that all fulness should dwell. This is a unity not necessarily visible to the natural eye. It is a unity of our unseen but not unfelt minds and hearts wrought, by the unseen but not unfelt and most real presence of that one and self-same Spirit, dividing to every man severally as He wills.

We are here this evening, my Christian friends, to bear witness to the mighty fact that Christian brethren—I was about to add sisters—when I remember such labourers as the devoted Mary Fletcher—may be true ministers of the Lord Jesus Christ, in the true apostolical succession through the outpouring of the blessed Spirit, without the laying on of any episcopal hands.

You have permitted me to stand among you with my friend here, the Clerk of our yearly meeting, as living witnesses of the reality and sufficiency of the baptism of the Holy Ghost ; and that it is this baptism, and not the mere application of outward water, that must from age to age make men new creatures—children of God, and inheritors of the kingdom of heaven. What a testimony is all this against the pretensions of Ritualism in all its forms ! Dear Christian brethren, let us hold fast this profession of our faith without wavering.

It is not possible for me on an occasion like this to express all that I have felt, as I have once more recurred with deep instruction to the published Journals of John Wesley. You are all familiar with his unrivalled hymns, his incessant labours, his habits of early rising and of constant self-denial, and all the details of his life-long devotedness to his Lord. Shall I take too much upon me in uttering the heart-felt prayer—that, in dwelling upon that life of holy consecration, you may ever more and more drink into the spirit of his Divine Master. It is true that, as the work went on, differences were developed on points more or less important between him and some of his earlier fellow-workers. But what a joy to think of him and his brother Charles, the sweet singer of your Israel ; John Fletcher, and their coadjutors too numerous to mention ; with Whitefield, Augustus Toplady, Rowland Hill, and others associated with them ; now, after all their labours and conflicts, rejoicing together in that glorious rest where the redeemed see eye to eye, and all their aspirations after a union of holiness and perfected love are satisfied for ever.

May I venture before I conclude to note one or two points that have struck me.

In the preface to his Sermons, John Wesley, speaking of the Holy Scriptures, says, " God Himself hath condescended to teach us the way to heaven. For this very end He came from heaven ; He hath written it down in a book ! O give me that book ; at any price give me the Book of God ! I have it : here is knowledge enough for me. Let me be, *homo unius libri.*" Amidst all the conflicts of opinion in the present day, let the Churches be faithful to this great trust—let them not desire to be wise above that which is written in the Holy Scriptures, or to know more of the things of God than Christ and His Apostles. Rather let them determine with the Apostle of old to confront all the attacks of a covert scepticism, or of a false philosophy and vain deceit, with the simple, experimental knowledge of Jesus Christ and Him crucified, applied with power, to the transforming of man's inner nature, by the living Spirit of the living God.

And may the Christian Societies called by the name of Wesley never falter in their testimony to the cardinal truth involved in the words of the apostle, " Being justified by faith, we have peace with God, through our Lord Jesus Christ." The whole of Wesley's preaching was a continued testimony to the glorious reality of such an experience, through the living presence and work of the Spirit of God. If we may combine the two readings familiar to your President in Romans v. 1, with a slight variation of the rendering of the word εχωμεν warranted by other places in the New Testament, the exhortation would run— " Being justified by this precious faith we have, and so having, let us hold fast, peace with God, through our Lord Jesus Christ."

May this great Celebration prove a fresh and a wholesome stimulus to all the Churches under your name ! It is not possible, either for the individual believer or for gathered Churches, to live upon past experiences. We cannot look upon the Churches of the East, or of North Africa, where once flourished Ignatius and Polycarp, Basil and Chrysostom, and the great names of Tertullian, Cyprian, and Augustine, without realising the awful warning which their present desolation is designed to give to the Churches in these favoured islands and across the Atlantic.

Dear brethren, I need not remind you that the experience of even John Wesley will not save you. It must be repeated from age to age. And such a celebration as this will serve a blessed purpose if it serves afresh to ground us all in the impressive and never-to-be-forgotten words of our Holy Redeemer : " Abide in Me, and I in you : for without Me ye can do nothing."

The President is aware that I have been lately interested in a little tribute to the memory of George Fox, on the occasion of the bi-centenary of his decease in the early part of the present year. I will conclude with two short extracts from two of his last epistles, which might have been written to you by your own Wesley, and which are a precious evidence of the unity of experience which is begotten by the Spirit of God in the hearts of true believers. " All of you,"—these are the words of his last epistle, written three days before his death,—" live and walk in Christ Jesus, so that nothing may be between you and God but Christ, in whom ye have salvation, life, rest, and peace with God."   And again in an epistle left, to be opened after his death, " Let no man live to self," are his emphatic words, " but to the Lord, as they will die in Him, and seek the peace of the Church of Christ and the peace of all men in Him, for blessed are the peacemakers ; and dwell in the pure, peaceable, heavenly wisdom of God, that is gentle and easy to be intreated, that is full of mercy—all striving to be of one mind, heart, soul, and judgment in Christ ; having His mind and Spirit dwelling in you ; building up one another in the love of God which doth edify the Body of Christ, His Church, who is the Holy Head thereof! So, glory to God through Christ in this age and all other ages, who is the Rock and Foundation, the Emmanuel, God with us, the Amen, the Beginning and the Ending. In Him live and walk, in whom you have life eternal."

The Wesley Centenary.

—————

PART III.

A Centenary Diary, other Addresses, &c.

FROM A CENTENARY DIARY.

CENTENARY STATEMENT.

ALLAN LIBRARY: Statement by Rev. M. C. Osborn.

UNITARIAN ADDRESS.

LETTER FROM REV. THOMAS CHAMPNESS.

AN ADDRESS FROM ITALY.

LETTER FROM REV. DR. CAIRNS, Principal of the United Presbyterian College, Edinburgh.

ADDRESS BY REV. DR. CAIRNS, Principal of the United Presbyterian College, Edinburgh.

386

Centenary Diary, other Addresses, &c.

—o—

From a Centenary Diary.[1]

SUNDAY, March 1.

MORNING.

THE morning is fair and genial. By eleven o'clock City Road Chapel is nearly full. A few seats near the ceiling, in the far gallery corners, await late comers. Elsewhere it is difficult to discover an empty place. There are chairs down the aisles, and about the doors people stand. The Ex-President conducts the whole service. John Wesley's abridgment of the Liturgy is used. The psalms read are cxxii. and cxxiii.; the lessons, 1 Sam. iii. and Luke iv.; the hymns, James Montgomery's fine Centenary hymn,

"One song of praise, one voice of prayer:"

and after the sermon,

"Arise, my soul, arise."

The congregation is most interesting. In the body of the chapel, especially, there is a preponderance of men, both young and elderly—perhaps as six to one. The President occupies a new chair, constructed of very old,

[1] Very much of this Diary was actually written during the Services therein described.

357

solid Spanish mahogany, carved, and upholstered in morocco. The Revs. Charles Garrett, William Wilson, Jabez Palmer, and others, are with the President. Many country visitors are present on the platform. Accidentally I am able to name a few of the circuits or districts represented on Saturday and Sunday : — Cardiff, Tredegar, Leominster, Leicester, Dorking, the Potteries, Liverpool, Dereham, Lynn, Mildenhall, and Yorkshire. The oldest member of Society present is a lady who has been a member sixty-four years, and for five-and-forty years in London. Mr. Kelly preaches a Centenary sermon. Its first sentences seize the congregation, and the interest grows more and more intense as for forty minutes the preacher gives thanks to God for the man, his teaching, and his work. The close deals with the present and future of Methodism.

MONDAY, March 2.

MORNING.

The tram-travellers look down upon the chapel-yard wonderingly. It is full. Above the crowd towers the draped statue, under a temporary canopy. You can see the outstretched hands and the Bible. Curiosity as to face and figure is a little checked by the knowledge of the fact that the bronze statue itself is not on the pedestal, but only the plaster cast. This everybody can see.

The crowd surges to and fro, divided in opinion as to the wiser course to take. Everybody wishes to see the lifting of the veil, and also to secure a seat inside the chapel. In the President's reception room (into which the upper room in Benson's buildings has been transformed) all the notabilities gather. In the Morning Chapel a procession is formed, headed by the President. With some difficulty a narrow lane is opened through the crowded yard. At the end of the lane is a small square. The statue fronts the square, and boys and girls of the

Children's Home, in black and white, front the statue. Archdeacon Farrar, Ex-Presidents, distinguished laymen, and Members of the Committee are grouped around the statue. A hymn, in which the people join; a prayer, offered by Dr. Greeves; an unloosing of strings; a touch from the President's gentle hand, and the statue is unveiled. A photographer on a platform in Mr. Murrell's little garden takes pictures, and the artist of the *Daily Graphic*, at a corner of the square, swiftly sketches the scene and faces in the crowd.

The President's speech is brief, and exactly what the occasion demands. How we who are outside reach the inside of the chapel it would be difficult to explain. From floor to ceiling City Road Chapel is full. In the far corners heads of standing men cast shadows on the overhead mouldings. Window-sills full; gallery and aisles full; boys with white collars in the front gallery pew; girls in black and white behind; a backing of Richmond students for bass and tenor; a row of West End Sisters in silver grey hold the left front gallery pews. Below, the aisles to the back of the lobbies, with all their side avenues and the space behind the platform, and the communion itself, are densely packed by standing Methodists. The windows of the Morning Chapel are swung open. A little maiden sits in one, and through the other nothing can be seen save human heads and feminine bonnets. Such a suffocating pack no one of my acquaintance has ever seen in City Road Chapel. There is not an inch of standing room wasted. Old Sir George Elliot comes to the platform, anxious to see and hear. Efforts are made to make a space for him, but eventually he retreats in despair.

Look at the platform. This is how they sit:—

On the right of the President:— Revs. C. H. Kelly, Ven. Archdeacon Farrar, Dr. Rigg, Oliver M'Cutcheon, Dr. Greeves, Dr. Young, H. Douthwaite, Hugh Price Hughes, G. Kenyon, N. Curnock, G. Green.

On the stairs Mr. Ralph Smith, the oldest trustee, and in the pulpit—the Rev. Robert Foster.

On the left of the President:—Dr. Gregory, Dr. Stephenson, Dr. Waller, Right Hon. H. H. Fowler, M.P., A. M‘Arthur, M.P., T. Morgan Harvey, Revs. R. Roberts, W. Wilson, Walford Green, John Walton, M.A., W. Higman, F. C. Bourne, Mr. Munt, Revs. T. E. Westerdale, F. J. Murrell, R. Spears.

The reception given to Archdeacon Farrar is a visible and vocal enthusiasm. His address is frank, brotherly, electric. Every point catches, and at every sign of halting the cry rises "Go on." Mr. Fowler, though following one of the most eloquent and popular men in England, is equal to the occasion. Not for a moment is the hallowed feeling allowed to cool or flag. It grows, indeed, more and more intense and solemn, till

> " Heaven comes down our souls to greet
> And glory crowns the mercy-seat."

At five minutes to one the meeting is too exhausted to listen to more speaking. Mr. Alexander M‘Arthur should have spoken earlier. Wisely, he abridged his speech; but it will not be lost.

A pretty thing occurred at the unveiling. Mr. Murrell laid two wreaths on the pedestal of the statue, on behalf of the children of Methodism from the Sunday school children of St. Austell. The wreaths were woven snow-drops, gathered by the children last Saturday in the Cornish fields. And a little girl who, from the beginning, has gleaned among the reapers for the Children's Memorial, brought lilies which lay on the pedestal by the side of the snowdrops.

MONDAY, March 2.

AFTERNOON.

The chapel is again crowded to its uttermost. The Secretary of the Conference, according to custom, reads the liturgy, which, appropriately, is Wesley's abridgment.

The psalms appointed are the 56th, 122nd, and 135th ; the lessons Isaiah xii. and Rev. i.; the anthem finely sung by the choir of the Children's Home, strengthened by select voices from Richmond College, " Be thou faithful unto death," from Mendelssohn's " St. Paul ; " and the hymns are " Glory be to God on high," " Give me the faith which can remove," and " I'll praise my Maker."

The President's sermon must be read to be fully appreciated. Its earlier expository portion is too finely wrought to be followed by so vast and inconveniently placed an audience. But the after-part catches the popular ear, and the close is given amid profound stillness. The sermon will be read with delight.

The question is always asked when friends return to the country from great services, " How did the President acquit himself ? " There can be no doubt that the success of the Centenary is largely due to Dr. Moulton. Of course he has not had the incessant labour and anxiety which Dr. Stephenson and his colleagues, Mr. Westerdale and Mr. Murrell, have had. But he has never lost an opportunity before or during the services of helping the work and relieving the anxiety. In difficult and perplexing questions his counsel has been invaluable, and always, whether in Committee or at public meetings, he has presided firmly, wisely, and with perfect regard for everybody rather than for himself. It will be of interest to many to know that Dr. and Mrs. Moulton have taken up their abode for the week in the lodging which is always ready for the President at the Book-Room. Every afternoon friends drink tea with the President in the extemporised reception - room adjoining the Morning Chapel, and both before and after each service there are pleasant little gatherings in the ministers' vestry or behind the platform. The example of friendly intercourse set by the President is imitated on all sides. The Centenary has become a kind of feast of tabernacles. The tribes have come up to Zion in force. Country Methodism from far and near crowds the chapel yard every day. The talk is serious, as befits the occasion. But with all the solemnity there is great gladness. You never meet a minister or a layman or a woman—"eminent" or otherwise—whose face is not radiant with hope, and whose talk does not reflect the universal thankfulness. The President's uppermost anxiety before the services began was that the Centenary might be a victory of faith, a revival of spirituality, a time of refreshing from God for all Methodism. The wish has already been abundantly fulfilled.

MONDAY, *March* 2.

EVENING.

For the third time there is a pack. How worn, dingy, low-ceiled the dear old chapel looks! Those who have pleaded hard for roof-raising point to the galleries. Scores of people must at this moment be in course of conversion to the same view through the pains of asphyxia. Men standing on the backmost seats, by a tiptoe movement, might have battered in the plasters with their skulls. The President opens with brief and cheery words, cleverly playing on the reunion which is already an accomplished spiritual fact. Dr. Stephenson wisely talks his statement, and does it with wit and force. Like all the earlier speakers—the President excepted—he is drawn out by the enthusiasm of the meeting and probably says more than he set out to say. What can an enthusiast do when at almost every other sentence the people cheer him on? Mr. M'Cutcheon, of whom Ireland may be proud, tells his story in a manly, sensible, interesting fashion. But he, too, is drawn out and forgets all time and toil and care. The most polished and thoughtful speech of the evening is Mr. Le Huray's; the most powerful and telling Mr. Myers. But they are all good. There is a splendid ring about them, nor is there from beginning to end a single jarring note. When Mr. Hallam says that the Primitive Methodists had nothing to forgive, the cheering is very fine. So, also, when he follows with " lines of demarcation, but no impassable gulf." Mr. Higman (Bible Christian President) looks for all the world like an old *Magazine* portrait come to life again. And he talks as he looks. It is a bit of early Methodism. Mr. Green, representing the smallest though not the youngest Church, lets the people rest and breathe while he talks modestly and with good sense. It is a glorious meeting —not perhaps so perfect as might have been, because over - weighted — the influence of which will be incalculable and undying.

TUESDAY, March 3.

AFTERNOON.

Under ordinary circumstances it would not be necessary, or perhaps fitting, that any report or description of a sacramental service should be given. In one respect, however, this occasion is exceptional. Dr. Rigg's address, which devotionally is worthy of prayerful study, as a contribution to the Sacramentarian Controversy, especially as related to John Wesley, is of the utmost importance. It is sad that at such a time it should be necessary to stand for the defence of the truth against bigotry and misrepresentation. Deliberate attempts, however, are being made to persuade members of the Methodist Church that John Wesley, at Oxford and to the end of his life, held views practically identical with the views of modern Ritualists. Dr. Rigg's address pricks this bubble, and does it effectually. Not even at Oxford was John Wesley in line with modern Ritualists upon the question of the Sacrament of the Lord's Supper.

TUESDAY, *March* 3.

EVENING.

From whatever cause, this meeting is even more densely packed than any that has yet been held. The Chapel itself cannot contain more than it contained thrice yesterday. But the Morning Chapel also is filled to-night. The windows are peopled, and to the end of the open lobbies nothing can be seen but heads. Mr. Thompson fills Mr. Clapham's place, and speaks with immense energy and power. Mr. Champness, whose illness creates profound sympathy, has no substitute, which is fortunate. The most extraordinary feature of this meeting is the grip Mr. T. G. Osborn and Mr. Watkinson win with addresses on such unlikely subjects as " Education and Literature in relation to Methodism." The quality of the meeting may be judged from the fact that these two addresses are listened to, not only with profound attention, but with an enthusiasm such as was scarcely exceeded even on Monday morning. It is no Philistine mob to which Mr. Osborn speaks and Mr. Watkinson reads. Mr. Olver, who, at short notice, supplies Dr. Jenkins' unavoidable lack of service, performs the extremely difficult task of holding and rousing an exhausted and dissolving meeting. He is himself at white heat, and, as Dr. Dale said yesterday morning, scatters sparks around, and sets the meeting on a blaze of missionary enthusiasm.

WEDNESDAY, *March* 4.

MORNING.

[My diary for this morning is a blank. To Dr. Dale I could only sit and listen.]

WEDNESDAY, March 4.

AFTERNOON.

Opening of the Allan Library.

This afternoon is given to the Allan Library. The public meeting is held in the Chapel, the body of which is filled and the gallery partially. Mr. Alexander M'Arthur presides. Mr. M. C. Osborn reads a Statement respecting the Library. Dr. Rigg, through whom the late Mr. Allan presented the Library, gives an interesting account of Mr. Allan and of the circumstances under which he built up his costly Library and gave it to the Connexion.

The President of the Conference shows the catalogue, and tells us that the Library contains 20,000 volumes and 8000 pamphlets. Mr. Kenyon, the Hon. Librarian, states the present financial position of the Library, and presents a silver key to the President.

Mr. Atkinson, in an amusing and practical speech, offers a copy of Shakespeare and a selection from his store of rare Bibles.

The ceremony of opening is quite simple. The President, ex-President, Mr. Kenyon, Mr. Alexander M'Arthur, and others gather at the closed glass door. The silver key is used, and the stream of people passes slowly between protecting cords, viewing the shelves, until they come to the balcony, where the President pronounces the Library open. Above the Library is a large, empty room, which quickly fills. The ex-President recites, without book, the hymn :

"Jesu, Lover of my soul."

The President, with powerful voice, leads the singing; and the people, all standing, sing "as in the ancient days." The enthusiasm of this informal meeting is extraordinary. The people sing and shout until one doubts whether it is not a revival prayer-meeting. The Allan Library begins its career with the Divine blessing, and the hearty good-

will of the children of the author of "The Christian
Library."

—

Everybody must know by this time that to be a Centenary Secretary means some capacity for labour. But
until to-day no one knew that the office involved peril.
The little, dark, wiry man, sitting near the President, had
a narrow escape last night. Not long ago he caught two
cadgers, one of whom has been preying on Methodists for
years. Last night, having a quantity of Centenary letters
to post at a late hour, he disturbed a gang of thieves who
were robbing a gentleman outside the Allan Library.
After a long chase he secured the capture of one member
of the gang.

The " Social Work of Methodism," under these circumstances, is a fitting subject for to-night's meeting. The
crowd shows no signs of exhaustion. There must be
2000 men and women in City Road Chapel. After the
President's brief introduction, the Rev. H. T Smart comes
to the front. His work for artisans is well known. The
congregation settles down to listen to a practical man's
exposition of the part Methodism can to-day play in a
sphere to which John Wesley was no stranger. Mr.
Smart is a cool, plain, straightforward speaker. He
attempts no oratory, and deals in no rhapsodies or wild
socialistic flights. His handling of the difficulties and
complexities which beset the great labour question is
firm, judicious, sympathetic.

The name of " Bunting" brings a great cheer. The
editor of the *Contemporary Review*, and treasurer of the
West Branch of the London Mission, is not what is called
a popular speaker, nor is he unpopular. Like all the
Buntings of a bygone time he is gifted with word-power.
His sentences are crisp, yet graceful and musical. Those

who think while they listen are charmed by his cultured
and entirely natural talk. It is thinking—aloud. The
tongue of Dr. Bunting's grandson is like the pen of a
ready writer—a pleasant, earnest, most sincere pen. His
doctrine is essentially socialistic, though of a high order
and suffused by Christian light and feeling. All schools
of thought, whether agreeing with Mr. Bunting or dis-
agreeing, must be thankful that the philosophy he
expounds is presented. It would be a precursor of
stagnant indifference if only one side of many-sided truth
were put.

Mr. Lewis Williams of Cardiff is another thinker, but
on a very different plane. He stands on the President's
left—a Celtic man, small, dark, compact, with a keen,
lively, kindly face. He is intensely practical, a Justice of
the Peace, Chairman of a great School Board, municipal
but not "parochial," bent on doing his duty with all
righteousness and with a tender regard for mercy—a
God-fearing man whose religion never sleeps and is
always shining. There is given to him a wide subject—
"Methods of Rescue Work." It is a congenial subject.
It drives him to talk experimentally, and this the people
like. He modestly apologises for an inevitable appearance
of egotism. But the people are delighted—and rightly so.
He warms to his subject, tells facts, and tells them well.
At times he is eloquent. The crowd catches fire. "God
is with us," and joy, and hallowed feeling.

Mr. Morgan Harvey tells us that his "double" is with
him on the platform. The two men are distinctly different ;
and yet in height, age, style of thought and speech, are
sufficiently alike to be mistaken the one for the other.
Lewis Williams and Morgan Harvey will go down to
posterity in Methodist history as doubles. Mr. Harvey,
in spite of a hoarseness which comes of Centenary singing
and excitement, speaks effectively—never more so. He,
too, has a congenial subject—"Temperance." He has carefully prepared, and he thoroughly understands what he
means to do. His audience is in full sympathy with him,

and he is drawn on and on until his voice is all but gone. But the people hold on in spite of the clock which glares down on Dr. Stephenson, who should speak next, ominously.

At last the senior Centenary Secretary rises and looks round doubtfully on the few who are compelled to make a rush for their trains. He offers to return his notes to his pocket, lest he should weary a splendid meeting into dulness. The meeting laughs his suggestion to scorn. It is a very Shylock of a meeting. Forgive an advertised speaker! "Go on! go on!" it shouts. "But it means twenty minutes." "Never mind; go on!" and on he goes like a racehorse, and never spoke better.

THURSDAY, March 5.

Afternoon.

Even the most sanguine are wondering whether it will be possible to sustain the interest much longer. Principal Rainy is not so well known south of the Tweed as Dr. Dale and Dr. Clifford. Will the congregation be comparatively small? May we not now look for signs of weariness? These not unnatural doubts are dissipated as the invited guests fill the platform. The Chapel is full, and from beginning to end the service takes rank with similar services of the days that are past. Standing in John Wesley's pulpit—massive, white, masterful—the preacher is a striking figure. The sermon which, like all the sermons of the Centenary, is read, takes hold of the congregation. Its strong points wake the laugh or devout murmurs, which tell of intelligent and sympathetic hearing. The appeals towards the close are particularly impressive. Everybody is thankful that the Free Church of Scotland should be so nobly and so usefully represented in these Centenary services.

THURSDAY, March 5.

EVENING.

There is no falling away either in numbers or enthusiasm. There is the same dense, raised, broad line of
heads down each aisle ; the same human lining of side
walls ; the same block in remote corners; the same
occupancy of stairways and window-sills, pulpit and apse.
It is a sea of faces—two seas, one like rings of wave-
crests threatening to pour down upon the other. The
repetition, without abatement, of such phenomena, night
after night, is one of the most impressive features of the
Centenary. The spirit of hearing is upon the people.
They are more eager to-night than at the beginning.
Nothing like it has been seen within the memory of
man.

It is an intensely religious crowd. Every allusion to
the most spiritual and practical side of religion is caught
and flung heavenwards in cheering that is more praise
and prayer than applause. Is City Road Chapel this
week the pulse of Methodism? If so, the beat is full,
strong, regular. It may quicken under the stimulus of
strong or witty words, but when it settles down again to
its normal rhythmical beat, there is no reaction into fitful
feebleness.

The President presides as Costa used to conduct. He
has energy, sympathy, tact, and an incapacity for weariness. He makes no long speeches, and the little inter-
ludes in which he tells the origin of a hymn, or announces
the collection, or rectifies any little misunderstanding, or
emphasises the interest of a new phase in the programme,
or suggests the piano singing of a particular hymn, are
quiet and yet inspiring. It is only bare justice to say
that he does not appear to have made a single mistake ;
error in point of taste or devoutness he probably could not
commit even if he tried.

And the Secretaries—Dr. Stephenson, Mr. Westerdale,

and Mr. Murrell, with their many helpers, both ministers
and laymen—have rendered excellent service. Only those
who have been behind the scenes can form any idea of
the amount of downright hard work which their duties
have involved. If they had yielded to weariness, or had
allowed themselves to be hustled into irritability, every
reasonable man would have been swift to forget and
forgive. But they seem to be superior even to excusable
weakness, and sit "calm on tumult's wheel"—always considerate, courteous, and anxious to do the best thing
possible for everybody. Their reward—the only reward
for which they care—is in the success of the services.

The platform changes slightly with every service. To-
night there are several new features. Principal Rainy sits
in Mr. Wesley's chair by the President's side. Near to
him is a stalwart Presbyterian supporter well-known in
North London Methodist circles, and also in Canada—
Mr. Thornton, minister of Camden Town Presbyterian
Church. The younger Methodist Churches are well
represented by the Revs. J. Kirsop and A. Crombie, who
sit by Mr. George Smith's side in the front row. Dr.
Watts and Mr. J. S. Simon, who have often crossed
quarter-staves in controversy, sit lovingly side by side.
Mr. T. Allen—tall, iron-grey—is speaking as I write.
He is blowing up the smithy fire. With a steady, powerful swing he drives heaven's pure oxygen into the embers.
All the forge is in a glow. And now the "heat"—how
white it is—is on the anvil. The sparks are flying, and
there is the ringing music dear to Methodist ears. Yet,
with all the resonance and sparkle and swing, there is
quite enough of balanced hitting to remind us that it is a
man of discretion who is manipulating the "heat," while
the huge audience wields the sledge-hammer with all its
hands and a thundering roar.

The children's anthem comes as a pleasant relief. By
the time that the last bar is sung, the last vacant place in
the chapel is filled. The windows down the right side
are swung open. You look through "over the heads of

window - seatholders," and you can see nothing except more heads and the wall of the Morning Chapel above them. It was so on Monday and Tuesday nights—more so on Tuesday than Monday—more so, I fancy, to-night than on Tuesday.

Mr. Scott Lidgett is speaking. There is a touch of the old *Magazine* portrait about his head. He is neat, compact, resolute, refined. He plunges into a vehement speech. Every sentence is perfect. Doubtless he has carefully prepared, as indeed has every speaker. Yet there is no stilted formality. He is bringing the power of a living past to bear upon the needs of to-day. Conversion he believes in, pleads for, centralises on his radiant field of vision. "The Church of the Future," as sketched by the leader of the coming University Settlement, is not such as Mr. Stead, borrowing Mr. Whistler's brush (or palette knife), has sketched, but a Church instinct with spiritual life. Leaders he calls for, and rouses a storm by satirical side-thrusts at men who are content to do "a tidy, decent little bit of business"—a style of Christianity from which Mr. Scott Lidgett evidently thinks the world needs to be purged.

How the collection gets through the dense masses it would be difficult to say. The only hope for it that I can see is in launching boxes at one end of the chapel, on the faith that they will come out full and safe at the other end.

Mr. Clough is up, as are the people. For, whatever may be the practice of individual Methodists, their collective creed—their opinion when massed in public meeting —is wholly in favour of the local preacher. It is a clever stroke to hand over Susanna Wesley's advice respecting the first local preacher—"Go and hear him for yourself" —to the rich men of Methodism. Mr. Clough's six circuits and his strings of figures are handled with consummate address. There is a rotund and rubicund completeness about this vigorous Yorkshireman. The people take all he says, silently, but with intent attention, until there comes a smart saying, and then away go hands and throats. He pleads for the training of local preachers, for a centre in every circuit, which may raise the intellectual life of his brethren. His enthusiasm rushes the meeting so utterly that one forgets note-taking. And when the end comes, we wake up to the fact that a capital speech has been made.

Mr. Westerdale looks over-wrought, as well he may, after months of incessant toil. The strong point in his speech is the defence of Methodism against the charge of decay. As is so often the case, he is most effective when he lowers his voice and speaks calmly and slowly.

Mr. George Smith, son of the late Dr. Smith of Camborne, gives a speech which can only be ranked with Mr. Fowler's, Mr. Osborn's, and Mr. Bunting's. And the people listen. How can they help listening to such manly, glowing, reasonable words! But, even if the earlier portion had been less eloquent than it was, the end would have won every eye and ear. A new story about the real flesh-and-blood *Daniel Quorm*, with snatches of Cornish dialect, was enough to drive the people delirious with delight. For if there is one thing more than another that the children of John Wesley love, it is a story.

There are very few speakers living who can compare with Mr. Hughes as a platform man. Even with the disadvantages of notes and a late hour and an exhausted atmosphere, he holds the people as by spells, and makes his points tell. To have developed fully a speech, the scheme of which had ten heads and a vast complication of appurtenances and burning questions, would have required two hours. Mr. Hughes really attempted to condense into half-an-hour all imaginable phases of Methodist Churchmanship and Christian Socialism. I cannot deny myself the pleasure of emphasising the section on "Methodism—a Church, and not a poor relation of the Church of England." Apostolical succession! John Wesley declared it to be a fable—as great a fable as the forged decretals on which the Popes built the Church of Rome.

FRIDAY, March 6.

MORNING.

Dr. Clifford's service I was only able to hear in part. This, as I expected, was a serious loss. The sermon, I am told, was the most popular of the series. It cannot be compared with Dr. Dale's, or with Dr. Rainy's, being wholly different in style. But of its kind, and for its purpose, it was a masterpiece. Judging from the little I heard, it came nearest to the sort of sermon which one needed to complete the cycle of characteristic discourses. If I may venture a word of criticism, where everything was so fit and intrinsically excellent, what we lacked was a sermon — not in place of any one of those actually preached, but additional — a sermon such as Spurgeon, John M'Neill, or "Wee Macgregor" would have preached —a great, popular, heart - searching, soul - saving sermon. This, however, must be remembered. In all probability the "wondrous gatherings day by day" were almost, if not exclusively, gatherings of converted persons, devout believers, earnest workers. For such, all the sermons and addresses were exactly appropriate—Dr. Clifford's not less than either of its companions.

FRIDAY, March 6.

EVENING.

The President's reception-room was crowded for after-noon tea. Mrs. Moulton, who has been present at every service, did the honours. Miss Stephenson helped her, and girls from the Children's Home waited. New faces were present—Bishop Hawkins and his wife, Dr. Dallinger, who had just completed his service as Gilchrist Lecturer in Scotland, and several distinguished representatives of sister churches. An hour later the minister's vestry presented a scene which no one who saw it will ever forget. Indeed, day by day I have regretted the impossibility of preserving pictorial records of the vestry-groups. They have been historic.

The crowd in the chapel is, if that were possible, greater than ever. The absence of Dr. Cairns is a disappointment. Dr. Allon also is missed, but his inability to attend was already known, and Dr. Stoughton is sure to be an excellent substitute. To each of these honoured men a telegram was sent during the evening.

Very appropriately Bishop Taylor, representing the Moravians, is the first speaker. He receives a warm welcome, and strikes precisely the note which all desire to be dominant at this last public meeting. There is an old-world look about the good man. One can fancy him in the pulpit at Fetter Lane, surrounded by memories of the past. We forget dead controversies as the Bishop speaks, and think only of the springs among the hills. Even now there is much that Methodism might learn from the United Brethren. Like a shower of summer rain falls the benediction of the representative of Count Zinzendorf and Peter Böhler. It is the text for to-day in the Moravian Text-book, "Grace be to you, and peace from God our Father, and the Lord Jesus Christ."

Dr. Stoughton is quite the old man. But he speaks as freshly as if he were in his prime. As we left the vestry he told me that he was going to "talk." And talk he does, to some purpose. His mother was one of the children, about whom we have so often heard, who were kissed by the dear old John Wesley. His own memory goes far into the past. His "own self also" he owes to Methodism. The Wesley hymns have soothed and cheered him on Sunday nights after the work of the day was done. And now he stands on the border, waiting to join the great company. "Why has he left the Methodists? He has never left them." Very impressive is the emphasis he lays on the old-fashioned Methodist doctrine of conversion, and very beautiful the glimpse we catch of the City beyond the river, where we shall have no more controversy or disputes. And so the old man ends—with the benediction of peace.

From the gallery rises a clear sweet voice, "How beautiful upon the Mountains," and presently all the children and young students join the chorus.

Mr. Figgis, of the Countess of Huntingdon's Connexion, raises the tone still higher. His address is too beautiful and loftily spiritual for description. The people, by this time wrought into an intensely devout and thoughtful frame, are losing their applausiveness. Prayer, praise, communion with God, alone seem to befit the hour. The old story of the frightened bird, which suggested Charles Wesley's hymn, "Jesu, Lover of my soul," is turned to a new and mystic use. Christ is the bird, and we make a nest, it may be of bits of straw and hair; and Christ comes and dwells in us. This parable pictures the experience of the congregation whilst these good men are speaking. Friday evening is pre-eminently a means of grace.

Mr. Braithwaite, of the Society of Friends, completed the roll of sister Churches. The old gentleman, tall and dignified, quaintly dressed in a Quaker coat, with a broad white cravat, might have come back from the last century. His address is read tremblingly and with an occasional stammer. It is intensely spiritual, and contains several points of exceptional interest. Although unadorned by rhetoric or eloquence, it commands an intelligent hearing. It will be read, I am sure, with great delight.

Here the meeting should have closed. But Bishop Hawkins was present, and the people were anxious to hear him. An African, eighty years old, who knew the bitterness of slavery, who for sixty years had held what he called a "through ticket for Heaven," and who now appeared in John Wesley's Chapel as the minister of a Canadian Methodist Church,—such a man was sure of an enthusiastic welcome.

SATURDAY, *March* 7.

EVENING.

The chapel once more is crowded. Stewards in charge of baskets and old-fashioned lovefeast mugs look doubtfully at the aisles, wondering how they can possibly make their way from pew to pew. James Calvert, without whom a great City Road lovefeast would not be complete, is in John Wesley's chair, with his wife by his side. Sisters from Mewburn House, Katharine House, and the Children's Home are near, as are many laymen—leaders in all manner of good work. The Rev. J. Idrisyn Jones sits on the Chairman's right. With the exception of the secretaries, who are all three in their places, there are not many ministers present. After a week of services, and Sunday so near, it is not possible for ministers to come. Mr. Murrell is obliged to leave early, for eight hundred people are waiting for him in New North Road Chapel.

Dr. Stephenson, with his Mustel organ and no choir, leads the singing. The first hymn is—

"O for a thousand tongues to sing."

Mr. W. Allen, who tells me that he distinctly remembers hearing Mr. Charles Wesley, junior, play the organ in Marylebone Church, offers prayer, after which comes the simple meal—a small queen cake and a draught of pure water, with a collection to follow.

Thanks have scarcely been offered when the superintendent of the circuit rises, and in few words tells how he found Christ, and how in early life he used to sit in City Road Chapel.

Without the loss of a moment the "presiding elder" tells his story.

The "chief singer" testifies to the fulness of God's love, gives thanks for the success of the Centenary, pleads that City Road might be made a great centre of fellowship and work, and suggests two watch-nights and two such lovefeasts in the year.

A minister from Ireland has a joyful experience, and a store of Wesley reminiscences.

A Methodist of the third generation, converted twenty years ago, springs to his feet on the platform, and ascribes his conversion to a godly father and the Sabbath school. He is a local preacher now, and the superintendent of one of the largest suburban Sunday schools.

A brother in the aisle, with an auburn beard and a loving face, tells us that his grandfather and father were Methodists, and that he, long ago, was converted, and that his wife and children were all members—one family in heaven or on the way to heaven.

Away in the far end of the left gallery a working man, strong and sturdy, says he was brought up as a Roman Catholic, but is now a member of the Methodist Society, and happy in the love of God.

A railway man in full dress, from a pew to the left, tells how his foster-mother taught him to tell the truth; how, in a mission-room worked by the Queen's Road Society, he was impressed; how, at a covenant service, to which he went out of curiosity, the impression was deepened; how, under a student from Richmond, he was smitten down in penitence; and how a brother's hand was laid on his shoulder in the prayer-meeting. "I feel the touch of that hand now. They go to college to get a degree— Bachelor of Arts, I think they call it. But *I* went to Jesus to be Born Again." He, and his ten children and their mother, are travelling the same road.

In the front of the gallery a sister in mourning, the widow of a local preacher, says she is a sinner saved by grace, converted under the preaching of Mr. Neville Andrews.

In the same front row, nearer the platform, an iron-grey man testifies that for fifty years he has been following the Master. In St. Sidwell's, Exeter, Joseph Wood brought him to decision with the text, "My son, give Me thine heart." Five-and-twenty years he spent in Exeter, first as a prayer-leader and then as a local preacher. There came a call to London, which he feared to obey. " I thought I should never see the sun in London. But God said, ' Go, and I will go with thee.' And I went and gave my note of removal to the Rev. George Perks, in City Road. And I took him the first-fruits of my increase— seven-and-sixpence—the first money I made. I've worked with brother Beauchamp here, and with brother Munro; and they've gone home, and now I can't *do* much." With the great hearing-trumpet to his ear, he looked like the old man in the picture of John Wesley's death.

A Welshman in the body of the chapel, pursued after he came to London by a mother's letter, was converted in an East-end mission-room over a stable, and telegraphed the news to his mother.

From South Petherton, originally, comes the next—a working man, who thanks God that ever he came to London, and declares that the sceptical working men are really, many of them, searching for truth.

The meeting is at white heat. All over the Chapel brothers and sisters, young and old, are up. Dr. Stephenson, with his hands on the keys, is waiting for a chance to sound the notes of a hymn. James Calvert rules splendidly and, notwithstanding the intense excitement, there is no disorder.

The leader of the Leysian Mission speaks from the aisle at the right corner of the platform. His, too, is a story of mother's love and prayers. "Our mouth is filled with laughter and our tongue with singing."

"My God, I am Thine" sounds from the Mustel. Verse after verse, each with its hallelujah chorus, is sung—how sung let red-hot Methodists imagine.

Number fourteen is an old man with a grey beard, who for forty-nine years has enjoyed religion, and finds it better than ever. It was the hymn, "My God, I am Thine," sung in a packed school-room, that set his heart " beating pit-a-pat." He found his wife in that same school-room, and she found Christ.

The old man's son in the corner under the platform

greets his father across the crowd—for himself and his
wife, and I know not how many relatives. A teacher
boxed his ears by mistake. With his silk pocket-hanker-
chief the repentant teacher wiped away the lad's tears,
until they flowed as tears of penitence. And now he is a
teacher himself, and a class-leader.

Under the platform rises a Southwark brother. His
witness, too, is full of "mother" and the Sunday school
(John Street).

Far away in the gallery an old St. John's Square soldier
of the Cross quotes Dr. Dale's sermon, and declares that
"the fire from over the wall" has this week re-kindled
him. They have all had a fresh baptism of fire and love
and power.

Whereupon down go the hands on the organ keys, and
the people are singing with all their might—to "Falcon
Street"—

> "The men of grace have found
> Glory begun below."

Dr. Stephenson wishes to sing the whole verse of eight
lines ; but the popular tune and the outbursting emotion
sweep the lovefeast into the chorus :—

> "Praise ye the Lord ! Hallelujah !"

The Doctor laughs, lifts his hands from the keys, and joins
the chorus.

An African from Lagos—a class-leader, and one of the
first circuit stewards—speaks from under the left gallery
and is transplanted to the platform.

From the same side, but nearer the door, a young man
catches the chairman's eye. His father was a parish
clerk. Mr. Webb-Peploe and Great Queen Street appear
to have worked together for the speaker's good. He is
not a Methodist, but is made to feel very much at home
in the lovefeast.

A man in the reporters' pew has been night after night
to the services. His wife said, "What, are you going
again?" "Yes," he replied, "I shall not have a chance

to attend the Bicentenary, and I mean to get all I can now." At Abingdon he heard a minister from Fiji preach on "Brethren, pray for us"—not *at*, or *with*, but *for* us. The word was blessed to him. He did not know when or where he was converted. But he *did* know that, whereas once he was blind, now he saw. "I've learnt this week more about Wesley and Methodism than I ever knew before. I mean to have the Journals, and other books will follow in time."

An old man tells the story of a lovefeast in 1839, and of the great Conference lovefeast in Toronto after the fusion of all the Methodist Churches into one. He frankly unveils the cause which led to his loss of wealth, and thanks God for the discipline which brought him back to his first love. As he speaks I remember how, as a boy, I rode in his carriage and spent holidays in his beautiful house.

A Scotchman, having suffered many things from Calvinism of a type nearly if not quite extinct, desires to enlarge on his escape into the freer faith of Methodism, but falls a victim to the Chairman's inexorable command, "To the point, brother." But no one can be offended under James Calvert's rule, and the lovefeast rushes on to the music of shouts of praise.

Far away under the ceiling, indistinguishable in the dense crowd, one of the Leysian Mission trophies lifts his voice in thanksgiving. He is not now in the prize-ring, or, as he was this time last year, on his way to a hall for boxing.

A Welsh collier, converted through his father's prayers, is now, after five years on the Rhondda plan, on his way to a new sphere as a lay evangelist.

We sing with tremendous energy,—

"O happy day that fixed my choice!"

and Mr. Alger leads in prayer.

Again and again a young man on the extreme edge of the left gallery has essayed to speak. "Come to the front, brother." He looks in despair at the crush in front, and

mounts the seat instead. What a testimony he bears!
Years ago in City Road Chapel he heard the late Mr.
Kirtland give out, "so quietly,"—

> " Terrible thought, shall I alone."

That was the beginning. There followed a meeting for
young people with the text, " Be of good cheer;" then
two years in China, where he met C. T. Studd, the
University student and first cricketer in England, who
gave up all for Christ; then a covenant service in
Plymouth immediately after his return; then the Bible
opening on the words, "Sin shall not have dominion;"
then Levi Waterhouse giving out the hymn beginning

> " Come, Holy Ghost, all quickening fire,
>   Come and in me delight to rest; "

" I can see him now," said the speaker.

But I can give no idea of the sweet, simple force of
testimonies like this.

From the platform the Rev. Idrisyn Jones speaks as a
Methodist Congregationalist, who owes much to Methodism, who reads the *Recorder* every week, whose father
translated John Wesley's *Primitive Physic* and Adam
Clarke's *Commentary* into Welsh, and who, himself,
preaches Wesley's doctrines—"Jesus died for all" and
" Perfect Love."

A brother near the organ was converted under a sermon
on the " Prodigal Son " by the late Nehemiah Curnock, in
the Mint Chapel, Exeter.

After a brother from Barrow-in-Furness, a man by one
of the pillars tells an interesting story of William Booth
who, years ago, when he was a New Connexion minister,
walked with him through the Thames Tunnel, and
casting his arm round his neck implored him to "Go in
for souls."

There follows a Richmond student, who tells how Mr.
Vinter, of Woodhouse Grove, took him into his study and
besought him to give himself to Christ.

Then a Methodist Free Church man ; then a West
Central sister, who never knew the time when she was not
under religious impressions, and who was led to full
consecration by a sentence from Dr. Arnold on the greatness and happiness of entire Christlikeness ; then a
marvellous story by the contractor for the Liverpool
Exhibition, and a touching testimony from one of the
Mewburn House sisters.   A New Connexion preacher
from Reading crowns the roll of thirty-five witnesses.

On their knees, in death - like silence, two thousand
Methodists (they are all Methodists for the time) consecrate themselves afresh to God, and sing twice over—

> " Lord, in the strength of grace."

Mr. Idrisyn Jones prays, James Calvert gives his
blessing, and we spring to our feet singing—

> " Come, let us anew our journey pursue."

But, as the vast family dissolves, once more the joy
breaks forth—

> " Above the rest this note shall swell,
> My Jesus hath done all things well."

SUNDAY, *March* 8.

The rain fell, and it was cold and cheerless.   Neverthe
less, the Chapel was nearly full on Sunday morning.   Mr.
Macdonald preached a sermon that all preachers, students,
reading people, and helpers in the work of Methodism
ought to hear.   It contained features of exceptional value
and interest.   Wesley was a theologian—a teacher of
truth ; for that work he was spiritually prepared : he
spiritualised theology.   We cannot afford to undervalue
theology ; it is the only safe basis of all true and lastingly
successful work.   But theology, to be a power for good,
must be taught by men with a definite spiritual experi-

ence. The comparison between Bishop Butler and John Wesley—both, at the same time, face to face with the problem of evidences which left room for the possibility of doubt—and the contrast between their several modes of dealing with the problem, was one of the finest things I ever heard.

Mr. Murrell's children's service in the afternoon was a great success. He delighted the children for half-an-hour with stories of Wesley.

In the evening the Chapel was once more crowded, and Mr. Waddy preached like one inspired. It was a happy thought to use the last service, before the closing of the dear old Chapel, for the enforcement of the great promise —the analogue of Wesley's dying and life-long cry—" Lo, I am with you alway, even unto the end of the world." The platform was filled with local preachers. Mr. Adams-Acton was in the congregation, and many other notable people. The service was an admirable finish to the best series of services that the Methodists of this generation have seen.

The rain came, and, on Monday, the snow from heaven. They will not return void. The spring is at hand. May we not accept the sign? "So shall My word be that goeth forth out of My mouth. It shall not return unto Me void."

Centenary Statement.

ON Monday evening, March 2nd, Dr. Stephenson made the following Centenary Statement :—

" I speak now as representing my colleagues in the Secretaryship, and I desire, in a single word, to express my great indebtedness to them. When the work of preparing for this Centenary celebration first began, I was under the shadow of a heavy cloud, and was not able to take my proper part in the financial appeal. But my colleagues, Messrs. Westerdale and Murrell, took the matter in hand most energetically, and carried it to a triumphant conclusion.

"Mr. President, I have to ask you to accept the chair in which you are sitting, which is a gift from Messrs. Garnett and Co., of Warrington, members of a very old Methodist family, who have desired, in connection with these Centenary services, to make a presentation. I have no doubt that when the Bicentenary of Wesley's death is celebrated this chair will have a halo of antiquity about it, and be a highly-valued relic. Whether the Conference decides to have it sent to the Conference towns year by year or not, it should be kept here as a general rule.

"Next, I have to present a most interesting communication from the British and Foreign Bible Society. At the Committee Meeting this morning, with Lord Harrowby in the chair, that Society resolved upon the following motion:—'That the Committee now sitting send a message of friendly and sympathetic greeting to the President of the Methodist bodies assembled to commemorate the Centenary of the death, on March 2, 1791, of their great Founder, John Wesley.—(Signed), HARROWBY, President.' When we think that that great Bible Society not only helps all the Churches, but belongs to them all; when we think of the enormous services it is constantly rendering to the cause of Christianity throughout the world; when we think of the high distinction of the Committee that manages its affairs, I am sure this will be one of the pleasantest incidents in connection with this Centenary gathering.

"Now, I am happy to tell the congregation that this building is perfectly safe; it has been very well tested to-day. We found some time ago that the foundations were very seriously defective. This is no reflection on John Wesley; because when he sanctioned the plan for the new Chapel—it was then in the Moor Fields—the foundations were such as to promise stability for many generations. At that time the ground was very moist, and timber was necessarily used for the foundations. But

the great main drainage system of London having subsequently drained off the water, the wood has rotted away,
and the chapel for some years has been standing upon a
sort of dry black powder. The building has gone about
four inches out of the perpendicular. Happily, these facts
were discovered in time. The foundations have been
taken down to the virgin earth in concrete, and this was
finished on Saturday night. We have every reason to
believe that a hundred years from now, the people who
will then crowd this place will find it as sound as ever.

"We really are not very proud of the interior. We value
its sacred memories. We are glad that it is a great representative of a good Methodist preaching-house—capitally
adapted for it. But I sympathise with our friends in the far
corners. John Wesley would never have consented to put
them there. In his time the pulpit was four feet or six feet
higher. At the end of the Chapel there was no lobby, but
a large open space, in which the people used to stand, and
in which, just a hundred years ago, the body of John
Wesley lay in state, passed by ten thousand people altogether. This building is hardly equal to its position as
the principal, the representative Chapel of the Methodist
Church. So we are going to restore it thoroughly. We
shall take away those pillars, which are not perfectly
sincere. They are shams—wooden pillars pretending to
be stone. The new pillars have been given by the Methodists of Ireland, Australasia, the Methodist Episcopal
Church South, the West Indies, and Canada. We hope
the South African Methodists will join their brethren in
this matter, and the seven pillars of this house will then
represent the seven great developments of the old Methodist Church in different parts of the world. The staircase
will be placed in annexes, thus giving additional room in
the main building. We are going to put in new pews of
solid oak—for Methodism is going to last. We are going
to make all the arrangements of the building suitable for
the many great gatherings which we hope will assemble
within these walls. The poorest man shall be as comfort-

able as the richest. We shall make arrangements that all strangers shall feel perfectly at home when they come into this building. We are not merely anxious in this way to leave behind an enduring monument of these services, but we hope all these arrangements will help this place to be once more a great centre of evangelistic activity. For this, the mother church of Methodism, ought to be foremost in all that is best, in the great work that God has committed to us. I hope that in years to come we shall have this place as full every Sunday as it is to-night. If we look after the young men in the city, and the young women who are employed in places of business, the working men who inhabit the great blocks of model dwellings within a stone's-throw, and Methodists coming from the country and all parts of the world, we shall see great and glorious days in connection with this Chapel."

The Origin and Organisation of the Allan Library.

At the Meeting held on Wednesday, March 4th, in connection with the opening of the Allan Library, the Rev. M. C. Osborn, secretary of the Committee, read the following statement :—

"The Allan Library, consisting of many thousands of rare and valuable books and pamphlets, was presented to the Conference of 1884, through the Rev. Dr. Rigg, by the late Mr. Thomas Robinson Allan, 'to the intent that the same be constituted a Library for the use of ministers of the people called Wesleyan Methodists, similar, so far as the said Conference may seem advisable, to the Library of Sion College, founded by the Rev. Thomas White, D.D., canon of Christchurch, Oxford, for a corporation of all the ministers, parsons, vicars, lecturers, and curates, within

London and the suburbs; or to the Library, founded by Dr. Daniel Williams, for the use of the Nonconformist denominations.'

"This gift was gratefully accepted by the Conference. A number of ministers and laymen were appointed to act as trustees, in whom the Library has since been duly vested, and a Committee of Management was appointed.

" At the same time the Conference resolved :—

"1. That, in the first place, all ministers and preachers on trial, whose names appear on the printed minutes, shall have right of access to the Library, subject to such regulations as shall hereafter be determined.

"2. That persons other than ministers shall also be admitted to the benefit of the Library, under such regulations as shall hereafter be determined.

" The Regulations suggested are :—

"1. That the Library and Reading Room shall be open to all *Wesleyan ministers and preachers on trial and local preachers*, on payment of an annual subscription of *half-a-guinea ;* and to others on payment of an annual subscription of one guinea ; but that, in the event of any books being taken out of the Library, the charge for carriage shall be defrayed by the subscribers to whom such books are sent.

"2. That all donors of ten guineas and upwards shall be life members.

"3. That all donors of books of the value of twenty guineas and upwards shall be life members.

"4. That the above subscriptions shall entitle the subscriber to two volumes at a time, to be taken from such books as may be taken from the Library.

"5. That the Library and Reading Rooms shall be open to subscribers and members on all week-days from ten to five (Saturdays ten to two), except Good Friday, Christmas Day, and bank holidays, also the first week of March.

2 D

"[The Reading Room is furnished with many reviews and magazines, maps, atlases, railway guides, and writing materials for the use of members. Writing-paper, envelopes, and stamps may also be obtained from the attendant.]

"6. That special terms be arranged for a supply of books to the members of the local preachers' meeting in any circuit, and to the readers connected with circuit libraries.

"At the Burslem Conference a subscription list was opened amongst the ministers for initial expenses, and a sum amounting to nearly £300 was promised. The Book Steward was authorised to make advances towards the necessary costs of management and maintenance, pending arrangements for the permanent accommodation and settlement of the Library.

"Diligent inquiries were made as to a site on which a suitable building for the accommodation of the Library might be erected, and the cost of such erection, and also as to the possibility of hiring premises for the purpose; but these all proved abortive, until at length it was ascertained that the trustees of the Book-Room were intending to extend their premises, and the then Book Steward, the Rev. Theophilus Woolmer, offered to the Committee to include in his extension provision for the Library on advantageous terms. This offer was gratefully accepted, the new buildings have been erected, and the Library is now suitably housed therein. The original gift of Mr. Allan has already received large additions. The library of the late Dr. Rule, that of the late Rev. W. M. Bunting, and valuable books presented by Mrs. Jobson and other friends, have largely increased the value and usefulness of this unique collection. No doubt many other books of equal value will be added year by year. The Committee contemplates the addition of modern books, £200 having already been given for that purpose by the Fernley Board of Trustees.

" Large expenses have been incurred in the maintenance
of the Library during the last seven years, and in the
fitting up and furnishing of the large and handsome rooms
in which it is now lodged. The last Conference authorised
an appeal to the Connexion to provide this cost, and for
annual subscriptions. Such appeal is now made with
all confidence as to its propriety and claim. Your help,
either as an annual subscriber or a donor to the Furnishing Fund, will be gratefully received. Some friends may
prefer to make a special gift of furniture, or of books
which shall be known as their personal contribution, as in
the case of the generous gift of the trustees of the late
Mr. John Fernley. The Committee will be glad to
respect your wishes in this matter. Every economy will
be used to secure a comparatively small annual cost in
working the Library. The Librarian gives his services
without stipend. The Sub-librarian, the Caretaker, the
moderate rent, and the incidental expenses, will not exceed
£600 (more than one-half of which is for rent, warming,
lighting, etc.). This sum, however, must be provided by
subscribers.

" At the Sheffield Conference of 1889, a number of gentlemen met to consider the claims of the Library, and a sum
of about £500 was contributed towards initial expenses,
and £30 as annual subscriptions. A sum of £5000 could
be well employed in the purchase of modern books, in the
furnishing of the rooms, and in the establishment of a fund
for the continued supply of new books for the special use
of general readers.

" It is hoped, now that the matter is placed clearly before
the Methodist people, that the necessary funds will be forthcoming, so that this great opportunity may be embraced
for the building up of a Methodist Public Library, which
shall be an educational endowment for all time."

The Rev. GEORGE KENYON stated the sum total
received and promised amounted to £1,220. The
treasurer had in hand about £120, the whole of which

would be expended in rent and taxes, payment of Caretaker and Sub-librarian, to the ensuing Conference. He
had a very modest request to make—viz.. that fifty persons
would at once constitute themselves life-members by a
donation of ten guineas each, and that 500 persons would
become guinea subscribers. The Committee would also
thankfully receive gifts of suitable books. He would ask
the President of the Conference to accept the silver key
which he had now the honour of presenting to him where-
with to open the Library. The honour of that ceremony
was due to the President, not simply because he was the
President, but because he was at the head of the great
Methodist educational establishments throughout the
country. The key had on it the following inscription :—

"The Allan Library, March 4, 1891.
"DR. MOULTON *from* GEORGE KENYON."

In reply, the PRESIDENT said,—I very gratefully accept
the honour which the Committee has put upon me, and
I heartily thank you, Mr. Kenyon, for this visible expression of it. My interest in the Allan Library is very
deep, and will be lasting.

Mr. H. J. ATKINSON, M.P.. in response to an appeal
made by the Secretary, said he would be glad to give him
a good copy of Shakespeare. He had also a rare collection of Bibles, to a selection from which the Committee
would be welcome.

The congregation accompanied the President to the new
building in City Road, where the doors of the Library were
duly opened, the President completing the ceremony thus:—

"With hearty gratitude to the munificent donor of this
Library ; in reverent memory of our great Founder, who
taught us the lesson of the right use of books ; and with
prayer to God that the use of these books may be for the
lasting advantage of our Connexion, and thus for the glory
of Almighty God, I declare this Library open."

Unitarian Address.

On Monday, March 2nd, after the unveiling of the statue, the following remarkable incident occurred :—

The Rev. Dr. STEPHENSON said that an unlooked-for honour had been put upon him. He had to introduce a gentleman, the bearer of an address from a great many distinguished persons connected with the Unitarian denomination. They did not feel themselves at liberty to assume that their friends would desire to take part in their celebration. Spontaneously and entirely of their own accord that address was forthcoming.

The Rev. ROBERT SPEARS was then introduced to the President, and read an address which testified the "profoundest reverence for the memory of John Wesley," and congratulated the Methodist Churches on their success.

The Address was signed by representatives of over two hundred Unitarian families, including the Earl of Carlisle, Dr. Martineau, Dr. Crosskey, the Rev. Stopford Brooke, several members of Parliament, many knights and magistrates; and was stated by Mr. Spears to have been suggested by Miss Sharpe, daughter of the late famous Egyptologist.

The PRESIDENT, in reply, said,—You have already practically authorised me to express to the Rev. Mr. Spears, and to those whom he represents, our very warm thanks for the kindly feeling expressed by the words he has used, and our very deep interest in discovering that admiration of John Wesley, and deep interest in John Wesley's work are found amongst those whose doctrinal convictions differ so widely from his, and differ so widely from our own. This incident illustrates how very wide-reaching is the admiration felt for him whose memory we celebrate to-day. The services that have been arranged for this week, the various meetings that have been announced, have most of them direct reference to the evangelistic work of the Rev. John Wesley—the foundation of all his work—that part of his work which is continually in our thoughts; and it is very well for us at this first meeting to remind ourselves that the interest extends far beyond our own community ; that the interest is shared by all the Churches of the land, for we believe that there are very many who cannot be personally present with us this morning who are with us in spirit ; and that this interest is carried beyond the ranks of those who would profess to belong to any religious community, but who are careful students of the history of their own country. The historian of the eighteenth century, whoever he may be, cannot pass over the social, moral, and, I may say, the political effects of the work which John Wesley carried out.

Letter from Rev. Thomas Champness.

IN a letter to the President explaining that illness had compelled him to relinquish his engagement, the Rev. Thomas Champness said, "As a man who has studied rural Christianity, studied it for years, studied it on the spot, and watched it year by year with increasing eagerness and anxiety, I have come to the conclusion that the battle between Liberty and Sacerdotalism has to be fought in the agricultural parts of the country. *I look upon every village chapel as an outpost of Protestantism,* and I say to all who care for right of conscience, liberty of speech and hearing, stand by those who preach the gospel to the men who live by the plough."

An Address from Italy.

ON Wednesday, March 4th, the following Letter of fraternal greeting from Italy was presented to the Meeting :—

"*To the Rev. Wm. F. M. Moulton, M.A., D.D., and the Ministers and Brethren of the City Road Wesleyan Chapel, London—*

"The late lamented Dr. Punshon, in a grand and

eloquent lecture on 'John Wesley and his Times,' when speaking of the character of this great and noble servant of God, used these words :—

"'Since the days of St. Paul the world has not felt the power of a man more noble or greater than he.'

"We, the brethren of the Wesleyan Methodist Church, Pozzuoli—the Puteoli recorded in the Acts of the Apostles, xviii. 11, 14—the Puteoli at which St. Paul landed on his journey to Rome, and where, finding some brethren, he was desired to tarry, remaining with them seven days,—

"With Christian affection we salute the hour in which we celebrate the first Centenary of the death of this great and noble Founder of the Methodist Church.

"'They of Italy salute you' (Hebrews xiii. 24).

"They of Pozzuoli salute you.

"FRANCESCO SCIARELLI,
"*Minister.*

"POZZUOLI, *Feb.* 25, 1891."

Letter from Rev. Dr. Cairns,

PRINCIPAL OF THE UNITED PRESBYTERIAN COLLEGE, EDINBURGH.

10 SPENCE STREET, EDINBURGH, *Feb.* 27.

" MY DEAR DR. STEPHENSON,—I have received the valued tickets so kindly sent by you ; and now, how unwelcome is the communication I have now to make, that, through a failure of strength, I feel the work which I had undertaken to be too great for me, and that I must most sorrowfully resign the hope of being at your great Centenary. . . . It is one of the greatest disappointments I have ever experienced in my public life. I had hoped in the speech I should have delivered, of some twenty or twenty-five minutes, to have had the occasion of touching on the relation of Wesley to the German Reformation, most of all in his conversion by hearing read in the Moravian Meeting-house Luther's Preface to his Epistle to the Romans, a fact of kindred magnitude to that of Bunyan by the Commentary on the Epistle to the Galatians, and proving that the Reformation, however decried, is still shaping and moulding the world. I cannot conceive that Luther would have more rejoiced over any of his spiritual children. I should have touched also on his immediate visit, after his conversion, to Germany, and the influence on him of Zinzendorf, with the missionary impulses that he must have received, the hints towards organisation, and the feeding of the Methodist hymnology from the old fountains of Germany, which he then studied and in part transposed. I should have ended by speaking of the place of Methodism in our British and American religion as recalling the Puritans, supplying the failing element in the great apologists like Butler, and originating the greatest and most pervasive of spiritual movements on the soil of Anglo-Saxon Christianity. These things, however, I can only hint at. May God bless to all of us so glorious a memory, and make the celebration a year of His own right hand.—I am, my dear Dr. Stephenson, ever most cordially, though sorrowfully, yours,

"JOHN CAIRNS.

"To the Rev. Dr. T. B. Stephenson."

The President said,—There is one point that I omitted to mention. It will be your wish that some expression of our deep regret at the absence of Dr. Cairns and Dr. Allon should be forwarded to them, and I may and also the name of the Rev. Thomas M'Cullagh, whom we expected to be present and to take part in one of the services of this week, but who has not been able to come. It has been suggested that, as Dr. Cairns carefully thought out what he was intending to say to us we may beg him to allow us to print what he would have said, and with your authorisation I will send a telegram to him this evening to beg him to do us this kindness.

Address by Rev. Dr. Cairns,[1]

PRINCIPAL OF THE UNITED PRESBYTERIAN COLLEGE, EDINBURGH.

IN taking part in this great celebration of the work of John Wesley, as we can now survey it a hundred years after his death, I am bound to begin with a personal reference, and to contribute a fact apparently not generally known in the early history of Methodism in the capital of Scotland. This has for me all the greater interest, because it is the only point of contact that I know between John Wesley and the Church of which I am a minister—the United Presbyterian Church. This Church was formed in 1847 by the union of two other Churches, the Secession and Relief, each of which had previously had a large career. The Secession originated in 1732, when Ebenezer Erskine and three other ministers seceded from the National Church, on the ground of opposition to the law of patronage, but on the deeper ground of attachment to the doctrines of grace. With them, and especially with Ralph Erskine, Whitefield had for a time friendly intercourse, though afterwards interrupted; but what I have now to mention respects the contact of John Wesley with them at a later period. The Secession from the first struck its roots deep in Edinburgh, and though divided, numbered two large congregations. The largest of these, called Bristo Street, in 1783 disagreed in the choice of a minister. The majority called a man who became most venerable, the Rev. Dr. James Peddie, whose son, Dr. William Peddie, still lives, having made up with his father over this same large congregation a ministry of one hundred and eight years. But the minority, nearly equal in numbers, called another eminent minister, Dr. James Hall, and could not be made to acquiesce. Hence a split from the original stock, and a fight with the rigid Presbytery of those days, who fought as hard against church extension as men now fight for it.

---

[1] This Address, but for the indisposition of Dr. Cairns, would have been delivered at Meeting in City Road Chapel, March 6. 1891.

The Secession Synod, that was appealed to, only granted a separation on condition that the complainers should remove to a great distance ; nor could they find a temporary place of worship within the limits ; and the only refuge in all Edinburgh was the Methodist Chapel, built twenty years before, in 1763, and lasting till 1788. Of this, Tyerman says (ii. 471), "Of the Methodist Chapel, which during the year 1763 was built in Edinburgh, we know nothing." I am happy, therefore, to add to Tyerman these facts regarding the place where the Seceders found a shelter. It was in the Low Calton, under the shadow of where the present Post Office stands, but in a humble block of buildings vulgarly called the "Saut-Backet," from its resemblance to a wooden salt-cellar, still used in some parts of Scotland. Here the Seceders were allowed by the Methodists to worship at a separate hour, paying a rent of half-a-guinea each Sabbath, and "ten pounds besides for liberty to *set* (let) the seats." This continued for one year or more, from 1785 till the end of 1786, when these Seceders went off to the new church built by them in Rose Street, where Dr. Hall came to be their minister. Now the interesting thing is, that all these arrangements, as to the use of this Methodist chapel, were made with the knowledge and concurrence of John Wesley himself, six years before his death, and when the whole Connexional property was still in his hands. How little could he have foreseen that this Presbyterian separation was to grow up into three large and flourishing congregations—Rose Street, Broughton Place, and Palmerston Place—all in Edinburgh, each with a high name in connection with Christian work at home and abroad. The whole United Presbyterian Church is thus under a debt to John Wesley ; and well may I record it, who have for more than fifty years been connected with Broughton Place congregation, the oldest representative of those exiles from Bristo, whose next minister after Dr. Hall was the Rev. Dr. John Brown, one of the greatest men we ever had, and, with Jabez Bunting, one of the founders of the

Evangelical Alliance ; and of whose present ministers, the
one—Dr. Andrew Thomson, has preached one of your missionary sermons ; and the other, the Rev. John Smith, will
do so, if spared, in due season. Let me only remark before
I leave this point of the early contact of the Seceders with
Methodism, both in the history of Whitefield and of
Wesley, that the two movements, in England and in
Scotland, agreed, more than at the time they recognised,
in being efforts to revive the Reformation, to shake off
the lethargy into which, in both countries, after the brighter
days of Puritanism, Christianity had fallen, and to bring
home to the mass of the people the great gospel of a present
salvation, and of a life superior to the world. And the
theology on each side, though different, were not so
different after all ; for the Seceder believed in an atonement which expressed the love of God to mankind sinners
as such ; and the Methodist held to a call and a witness
which only grace could give, and which thus tended from
and to eternity. This is to me the most interesting side
of Methodism, as the renewal of the Reformation to
England and to the world. In this sense it is very significant that the conversion of Wesley should have come—at
least in its final shape—through the hearing read in 1738
of Luther's Preface to the Romans. In this it recalls the
earlier influence of Luther's Epistle to the Galatians upon
Bunyan. That earlier conversion was destined to exert a
world-wide effect; and with a soul of poetry in Bunyan
which Luther would have hailed as congenial to his own.
But there was not less that was congenial in Wesley, who
seized with a giant-grasp the doctrine of Justification by
Faith, and with the kindred doctrine of the New Birth made
it the foundation of his whole theology. Nor is it without
interest to see how even pre-Reformation influences assert
themselves in the conversion, and subsequent religious
experience and work of Wesley. The Moravian Brethren
propagate in him the spirit of Huss, and so far also of
Wycliffe. However much he may have afterwards modified his impressions derived from intercourse with Peter

Böhler and Zinzendorf, and his visit in 1738 to Herrnhut, where he saw the life of Moravianism on its favourable side, it can hardly be questioned, that he gained something from what he witnessed of it in its spiritual depth, its elevation above the world, and its diffusive power. Nor must we omit to mention the more mystic element which appears in the Methodist hymns, and which connects them not only with the general German type, but so far also with the best in the Moravian. Charles Wesley is not alone the fount of this, but also John, whose translations from the German rival the originals, as in the great hymn of Rothe,—

> "Now I have found the ground wherein
>   Sure my soul's anchor may remain;"

one of the stanzas of which is an imperishable utterance of the doctrine of Justification :

> "O Love, thou bottomless abyss,
>   My sins are swallowed up in thee !
> Covered is mine unrighteousness,
>   Nor spot of guilt remains on me,
> While Jesus' blood, through earth and skies,
> Mercy, free boundless mercy cries !"

But while I dwell on these points of succession to the German Reformation, and might also have touched on its affinity to the somewhat earlier effort through Pietism in the hands of Spener and Francke to revive the German Reformation on its own soil, I now must mention some features of novelty in the great Methodist movement, which show that God never simply restores the past, but always with elements of adaptation to the existing age. These circumstances then, I think, discriminate the Methodist uprising from what went before in the German, and I may add, in the English Reformation.

1. First, *it was not so much a Reformation as an Evangelism.* No doubt it opposed Rome ; and Methodism has always been one of the strongest Anti-Romish influences. It also opposed the Church of England, where it had departed from its own formularies, and other Churches

where the essence of the gospel had slipped away. But it was still more essentially a preaching to the masses, irrespective of old theological lines and antagonisms. The Word of God and human experience became the great text-books. Its appeal was " Come and see." This was its reply to Deism and every form of unbelief, not to the rejection of Butler and the Apologists, but to the supplementing of them by a nearer argument—the present work of the Holy Spirit. This was its mission, too, over against indifference, worldliness, and sin of every kind.

> " Awake from Nature's guilty sleep, and Christ shall give you light.
> Cast all your sins into the deep, and wash the Ethiop white."

The long-drawn arguments of the Protestant confessions against Romish and other error, had less place. It was a living Christ guaranteeing a present and a self-evidencing salvation. "Come unto Me, all ye that labour and are heavy laden, and I will give you rest."

2. Wesley, in the second place, *escaped the difficulties of the Reformers in dealing with the relations of Church and State.* I am far from saying that the Reformers went out of the line of their duty in trying to settle these, though they may have settled them mistakenly. But Wesley saw from first to last that this was not his call. He had only to build up a Society; and to this, with admirable wisdom and energy, he limited himself. Hence the struggles of Luther, of Calvin, and of Knox, do not reappear in his career. He is liker Paul and the early Christians, appealing no doubt to Cæsar, when stoned and beaten, but willing to suffer till his rights, not as a Roman citizen, but a British subject, should be conceded to him and to his followers. No part of Wesley's course appears to me more noble than the stedfastness with which he adhered to this spiritual side of his commission ; so that at length toleration came, and peace, and as much just influence upon the State, as so great a body ultimately could not but acquire. Hence Methodism in all the world has looked at spiritual work as its first and greatest,

and has trusted to converted souls as the right and true materials of a Christian commonwealth.

3. As a third point of difference, the Wesleyan revival *added to the Reformation type of the organisation of the Church.* The universal priesthood of believers was indeed a watchword of Luther ; but it has failed to this day to be adequately developed in the Lutheran Churches of Germany. In those of the Presbyterian type, which, following the lead of Zwingli and Calvin, sprung up on the Rhine, in Switzerland, Holland, France, and also in Britain, the organisation went so far as to supply, in addition to the teaching body, under the name of elders, valuable spiritual help and guidance ; and the Congregationalist movement, whether Independent or Baptist, beyond anything that preceded, led, especially in England, in the Commonwealth time, to a large assertion and practice of preaching by laymen. Yet a combination was ultimately made, under Wesley and his helpers, of these elements of Christian organisation, such as hardly existed before. They did not aspire to found a Church, but only to build up a Society ; and yet that Society, even before Wesley's death, and still more after it, had a range and a flexibility, which had not in any Reformed country been seen before. It escaped the territorialism of the State Churches, being founded on spiritual birth. It had a regular ministry like all the Churches, and yet a local preaching better drilled and controlled. It had a class-meeting more warm and vital than any average Presbyterian eldership, fortified by a better system of finance ; and whereas in England, Episcopacy, nominally one for a whole kingdom, had never got over the boundary of a diocese, or Independency of a congregation, and Presbytery, after the Westminster Assembly too often saw its order with its faith become a dead letter, there sprang up in Methodism, with its annual Conference, a real unity, stamping upon the great rising body everywhere the same energy and spiritual aspiration.

4. I mention, fourthly and lastly, that Methodism went beyond the Reformation *in its direct and speedy advance to*

foreign missionary enterprise. No doubt the Reformation had only too good a defence of itself on this side, that it had to fight, both on the Continent and in Britain, for bare life, and lost the glow of its zeal for souls amidst the trials and temptations of the battlefield. There can be little doubt that, with a less terrible adversary than a militant Romanism, the Protestant fire would more quickly have spread into the rest of the world. This was the felicity of Methodism, that it came after the age of Gustavus Adolphus, and Cromwell, and William III., and also when British Colonies might be a stepping-stone to the heathen field. Wesley's early Georgian experiences had not been lost upon him ; and the restless fervour of Whitefield in crossing and re-crossing the Atlantic must have been a stimulus to all the Methodist leaders. But the deepest cause after all was the internal life of the Methodist Society itself. A great Home Mission cannot be limited any more than a zealous Foreign Mission can leave home neglected. Much of the missionary zeal, that led by the end of the century to the formation of the great Societies, was indirectly a result of the Methodist awakening ; and on the Methodist soil itself, though the special Society came later, the impulse was coeval with its origin. The missionary genius of Methodism is seen in Dr. Coke, who not only connects himself with the gigantic expansion of the work in the United States, but embraces both the East and West Indies. Other names follow, never to be forgotten, carrying the Wesleyan memories to Sierra Leone and Western Africa ; to the Cape ; to Kaffirland ; to Ceylon and China ; to every solitude of Australia and New Zealand ; and in the mighty transformations in the Fiji Islands, rivalling the greatest missionary wonders of any age or country. Happily there is not the least evidence of this tide tending to any ebb ; and by another centenary of Wesley's death, may it not, with other kindred streams, have covered the earth as the waters the sea ?

MORRISON AND GIBB, PRINTERS, EDINBURGH.

NEW AND RECENT PUBLICATIONS

OF

THE WESLEYAN METHODIST BOOK-ROOM.

Wesley and His Successors. A Centenary Memorial of the Death of John Wesley. Consisting of Portraits and Biographical Sketches of the Wesley Family, and of the Presidents of the Conference from the Death of Wesley to the Present Time. The Portraits are, with a few exceptions, engraved on Steel. Crown 4to, handsomely bound, cloth, gilt edges, 30s.

The Living Wesley. New Edition. Revised throughout and much enlarged, including a chapter on the Progress of Universal Methodism since the Death of Wesley. By Rev. J. H. RIGG, D.D. Crown 8vo, with Portrait, 3s. 6d.

The Father of Methodism. A Life of the Rev. J. Wesley, A.M. Written for Children and Young Persons. By Rev. NEHEMIAH CURNOCK, Sen. New and Enlarged Edition. Forty Illustrations. Crown 4to, paper covers, 6d.; limp cloth, 9d.; cloth boards, 1s.; cloth boards, gilt edges, gilt lettered, 1s. 6d.

The Life of Bishop Matthew Simpson, of the Methodist Episcopal Church. By Rev. G. R. CROOKS, D.D. Demy 8vo, Illustrated, 512 pp., 12s. 6d.

James Bickford: An Autobiography of Christian Labour in the West Indies, Demerara, Victoria, New South Wales, and South Australia. Demy 8vo, 450 pp., with Portrait and other Illustrations. 7s. 6d.

Studies in Theology. By R. S. FOSTER, D.D., Bishop of Methodist Episcopal Church. Three Volumes. Vol. I., "Prolegomena"; Vol. II., "Theism"; Vol. III., "The Supernatural Book." Medium 8vo, 25s.

Darwinism a Fallacy. By W. W. POCOCK, B.A., F.R.I.B.A. Crown 8vo, 1s. 6d.

Our Sea-Girt Isle: English Scenes and Scenery Delineated. By Rev. J. MARRAT. Second Edition, Enlarged. 217 Illustrations. Imperial 16mo. 3s. 6d.

Marion West. By MARY E. SHEPHERD. Crown 8vo, Five Illustrations, cloth, 3s.; cloth, gilt edges, 3s. 6d.

A Modern Exodus. By FAYE HUNTINGTON, Author of "Those Boys." Crown 8vo, Frontispiece, 2s. 6d.

Black Country Methodism. By A. C. PRATT. Crown 8vo, Six Illustrations, cloth, 2s.

Mina's Burnished Gold. By EMILIE SEARCHFIELD. Crown 8vo, Frontispiece, 1s. 6d.

The Mission of Methodism. By the Rev. RICHARD GREEN. Being the Fernley Lecture for 1890. Demy 8vo, paper covers, 2s.; cloth, 3s.

London : C. H. KELLY, 2, Castle Street, City Road, E.C.;
AND 66, PATERNOSTER ROW, E.C.

NEW AND RECENT PUBLICATIONS—continued.

"A Piece of an Honeycomb:" Meditations for every day in the Year. By H. G. McKenny. Crown 8vo. Red lines round each page, extra cloth, red edges.

"An exquisite volume in every respect. It is no mere collection of commonplace reflections on various texts, but a rich store-house of beautifully short and practically helpful thoughts of just the kind intelligent and earnest Christians need for daily refreshment and guidance."—*Wesleyan Methodist Magazine*.

The Sabbath for Man: An Enquiry into the Origin and History of the Sabbath Institution. With a Consideration of its Claims upon the Christian, the Church, and the Nation. By Rev. W. Spiers, M.A., F.G.S., F.R.M.S., etc. Crown 8vo, 2s. 6d.

"We recommend this book very highly as an able exposition and successful defence of orthodox teaching on the Christian Sabbath."—*Methodist New Connexion Magazine*.

Rambles and Reveries of a Naturalist. By Rev. W. Spiers, M.A., F.G.S., F.R.M.S., etc., co-Editor of the *Journal of Microscopy and Natural Science*. Crown 8vo, with above Sixty Illustrations, 2s. 6d.

By Canoe and Dog Train among the Cree and Salteaux Indians. By Egerton Ryerson Young. Introduction by Rev. Mark Guy Pearse. *Fifth Thousand.* With Photographic Portraits of the Rev. E. R. Young and Mrs. Young, Map, and Thirty-two Illustrations, 3s. 6d.

The Credentials of the Gospel: A Statement of the Reason of the Christian Hope. The Fernley Lecture for 1889. By Rev. J. A. Beet. *Fourth Thousand.* Demy 8vo, paper covers, 1s. 6d.; cloth, gilt lettered, 2s. 6d.

"An uncommonly interesting production. The matter is digested with admirable skill, and the expression is clear as Horace's Bandusian Spring, and precise as logic itself."—*Christian World*.

Sermons, Addresses, Charges. By Rev. Joseph Bush, ex-President of the Conference. Crown 8vo, with Portrait, 3s. 6d.

"The ex-President is so well known as a preacher and a writer as to render all characterisation of his strikingly individual style and cast of thought a meritless work of supererogation. . . . It is quite enough to say that these deliverances are alike worthy of himself and of his office."—*Wesleyan Methodist Magazine*.

Prayers for Christian Families. The New Book of Family Prayers. Containing Prayers for the Morning and Evening of each day for Nine Weeks, and for Special Occasions. With an Introduction on Family Prayer, by the Editor. Crown 8vo, cloth, red edges, 3s. 6d.; half morocco, gilt edges, 7s. 6d.; Persian grained, gilt edges, 8s. 6d.

The Christian Conscience. A Contribution to Christian Ethics. By Rev. W. T. Davison, M.A. Being the Fernley Lecture of 1888. Demy 8vo, paper covers, 2s.; cloth, 3s.

The Creator, and what we may know of the Method of Creation. By Rev. W. H. Dallinger, LL.D., F.R.S. Being the Fernley Lecture of 1887. *Tenth Thousand.* Paper covers, 1s. 6d.; cloth, 2s. 6d.

Covenant Comforts. A Companion and Supplement to the Form of Covenanting with God. Extracted from the Works of Joseph Alleine, and edited by G. Osborn, D.D. Fcap. 8vo, 1s.; gilt edges, 1s. 6d.

London: C. H. KELLY, 2, Castle Street, City Road, E.C.; AND 66, Paternoster Row, E.C.

NEW AND RECENT PUBLICATIONS—continued.

John Wesley. By Rev. RICHARD GREEN. Small Crown 8vo, 1s.; gilt edges, 1s. 6d.

Helpful Hints to Young Local Preachers. By Rev. S. OLIVER. Imperial 32mo, cloth, 8d.

A Synopsis of Christian Theology. For Bible Classes and Junior Students. By Rev. SAMUEL OLIVER. Second Edition. Imperial 32mo, 1s.

A Manual of Christian Doctrine. By Rev. JOHN S. BANKS, Theological Tutor, Headingley College. Second Revised Edition. Crown 8vo, 3s. 6d.

Farrar's Biblical and Theological Dictionary. Fifteenth Edition. Revised and Enlarged by Rev. J. ROBINSON GREGORY. Crown 8vo, 700 pp., 125 Illustrations and Six Maps, 3s. 6d.

Eminent Methodist Women. By ANNIE E. KEELING. Crown 8vo, with Four Portraits, 2s. 6d.; gilt edges, 3s.

The Aggressive Character of Christianity; or, Church Life and Church Work. By Rev. W. UNSWORTH. New and Revised Edition. Crown 8vo, 3s. 6d.

The King's People; or, The Glorious Citizenship of Zion. By Rev. C. NORTH. Edited, with Preface, by Rev. W. UNSWORTH. Crown 8vo, Sixteen Illustrations, gilt edges, 3s. 6d.

The Class-Meeting: its Value to the Church, and Suggestions for increasing its Efficiency and Attractiveness. By Rev. W. H. THOMPSON, Rev. SIMPSON JOHNSON, Rev. EDWARD SMITH. With Supplement containing further Suggestions, Topics, Bible Readings, etc. Small Crown 8vo, 1s.; gilt edges, 1s. 6d.

Uncle Jonathan's Walks in and around London New and Enlarged Edition. Profusely Illustrated. Crown 4to, cloth, gilt lettered, 2s. 6d.; gilt edges, 3s. 6d.

The Shadow of Nobility. By EMMA E. HORNIBROOK, Author of " More than Kin." Crown 8vo, Frontispiece, 2s. 6d.

Aunt Hannah and Martha and John. By "PANSY" and Mrs. LIVINGSTONE. Crown 8vo, 2s. 6d.

Miss Dee Dunmore Bryant. By "PANSY." Crown 8vo, 2s. 6d.

The Two Cousins. By "FRIBA." Illustrated. Crown 8vo, 3s. 6d.

Miss Kennedy and Her Brother. By "FRIBA." With Frontispiece. Crown 8vo, 2s. 6d.

My Black Sheep. By EVELYN EVERETT-GREEN. Crown 8vo, Three full-page Illustrations, 2s.

Miss Meyrick's Niece. By EVELYN EVERETT-GREEN. Crown 8vo, Illustrated, 2s.

More than Kin. By EMMA E. HORNIBROOK, Author of " The Shadow of Nobility," etc. Crown 8vo, 2s. 6d.

London: C. H. KELLY, 2, Castle Street, City Road, E.C.;
AND 66, PATERNOSTER ROW, E.C.

NEW AND RECENT PUBLICATIONS—continued.

Mad Margrete and Little Gunnvald. A Norwegian Story. By NELLIE CORNWALL, Author of "Granny Tresawna's Story." Crown 8vo, Three whole-page Illustrations, 2s. 6d.

Eighty-seven. A Chautauqua Story. By "PANSY," Author of "Judge Burnham's Daughters," etc. Author's Copyright Edition. Crown 8vo, 2s.

Judge Burnham's Daughters. By "PANSY," Author of "Eighty-seven," etc. Crown 8vo, 2s. 6d. Copyright Edition.

Raymond Theed : A Story of Five Years. By ELSIE KENDALL, Author of "Friends and Neighbours." Crown 8vo, Frontispiece, 2s.

For the King and the Cross. By JESSIE ARMSTRONG. Crown 8vo, Frontispiece, 2s. 6d.

The Two Harvests. By ANNIE RYLANDS. Crown 8vo, Frontispiece, 1s. 6d.

Among the Pimento Groves. A Story of Negro Life in Jamaica. By Rev. HENRY BUNTING. Crown 8vo, Six page Illustrations, 2s.

The Happy Valley: Our New "Mission Garden" in Uva, Ceylon. By Rev. S. LANGDON. Crown 8vo, with Map, Portrait of Mrs. Wiseman, and numerous other Illustrations, 2s.

Brookside School, and other Stories. By MARGARET HAYCRAFT. Small crown 8vo, Frontispiece, 1s.

The Spring-tide Reciter. A Book for Band of Hope Meetings. By MARGARET HAYCRAFT. Small crown 8vo, 1s.

Severn to Tyne ; the Story of Six English Rivers. By E. M. EDWARDS. Crown 8vo, Illustrated, 2s. 6d.

Grand Gilmore. By REESE ROCKWELL. Crown 8vo, Six page Illustrations, 2s.

Psalms and Canticles.

(Pointed for Chanting.)

Words Only. Limp cloth, 4d.; stiff cloth, red edges, 6d.
With Chants (343). Staff Notation. Limp cloth, 1s.; cloth boards, 1s. 6d.
With Chants. Tonic Sol-Fa. Limp cloth, 1s.; cloth boards, 1s. 6d.
With Chants. Organ Edition. 4to, cloth, red edges, 5s.

"The book supplies a great want in a way that should make it popular in our congregations."—*London Quarterly Review.*

Psalms and Canticles *(Words Only)*, with Sacramental, Baptismal, and Covenant Services. Limp cloth, 8d.; stiff cloth, red edges, 10d.; cloth boards, 1s.

London: C. H. KELLY, 2, Castle Street, City Road, E.C.;
AND 66, PATERNOSTER ROW, E.C.

www.ingramcontent.com/pod-product-compliance
Lightning Source LLC
Chambersburg PA
CBHW031056110726
47900CB00003B/947